"An exciting series of chase ___ ___
high adventure against the b___ ___"
—*Chronicle*

"Engaging . . . Action-packed . . . this novel stands out with its intriguing spiritual explorations." —*Publishers Weekly*

"Far-future, planet-hopping adventure . . . pulse-pounding action sequences make for a fast and enjoyable read . . . full of inventive concepts and . . . a richly detailed setting. For fans of space opera and action/adventure, this one is not to be missed."
—*Kirkus Reviews*

"Dietz's honorable addition to depictions of the far future, from Wells's *Time Machine* to Asimov's *Pebble in the Sky* to more recently the works of Clarke and Baxter, is distinguished by the brisk pacing and fleshed-out action scenes that have already made him a respected name in military SF." —*Booklist*

"An exciting thriller . . . [a] strong science fiction tale."
—*Midwest Book Review*

Praise for *For Those Who Fell*

"A genuine adrenaline rush." —*Publishers Weekly*

Praise for *For More Than Glory*

"Exciting military SF fare. Series readers and *Starship Troopers* fans will want this." —*Booklist*

Praise for *EarthRise*

"An intriguing look at the psychological and sociological essences of two alien races as well as the human reaction to a first encounter . . . An insightful . . . action-packed novel."
—*Midwest Book Review*

Praise for *DeathDay*

"Breakneck pacing, good action scenes, and unexpectedly strong characterizations. Alien invasion buffs should enjoy!"
—*Booklist*

RUNNER

WILLIAM C. DIETZ

ACE BOOKS, NEW YORK

THE BERKLEY PUBLISHING GROUP
Published by the Penguin Group
Penguin Group (USA) Inc.
375 Hudson Street, New York, New York 10014, USA

Penguin Group (Canada), 90 Eglinton Avenue East, Suite 700, Toronto, Ontario M4P 2Y3, Canada
(a division of Pearson Penguin Canada Inc.)
Penguin Books Ltd., 80 Strand, London WC2R 0RL, England
Penguin Group Ireland, 25 St. Stephen's Green, Dublin 2, Ireland (a division of Penguin Books Ltd.)
Penguin Group (Australia), 250 Camberwell Road, Camberwell, Victoria 3124, Australia
(a division of Pearson Australia Group Pty. Ltd.)
Penguin Books India Pvt. Ltd., 11 Community Centre, Panchsheel Park, New Delhi—110 017, India
Penguin Group (NZ), Cnr. Airborne and Rosedale Roads, Albany, Auckland 1310, New Zealand
(a division of Pearson New Zealand Ltd.)
Penguin Books (South Africa) (Pty.) Ltd., 24 Sturdee Avenue, Rosebank, Johannesburg 2196,
South Africa

Penguin Books Ltd., Registered Offices: 80 Strand, London WC2R 0RL, England

This is a work of fiction. Names, characters, places, and incidents either are the product of the author's imagination or are used fictitiously, and any resemblance to actual persons, living or dead, business establishments, events, or locales is entirely coincidental. The publisher does not have any control over and does not assume any responsibility for author or third-party websites or their content.

RUNNER

An Ace Book / published by arrangement with author

PRINTING HISTORY
Ace hardcover edition / October 2005
Ace mass-market edition / October 2006

Copyright © 2005 by William C. Dietz.
Cover art by Craig White.
Cover design by Judith Lagerman.
Interior text design by Kristin del Rosario.

ISBN: 978-0-441-01409-5

ACE
Ace Books are published by The Berkley Publishing Group,
a division of Penguin Group (USA) Inc.,
375 Hudson Street, New York, New York 10014.
ACE and the "A" design are trademarks belonging to Penguin Group (USA) Inc.

PRINTED IN THE UNITED STATES OF AMERICA

12   11   10   9   8   7   6   5   4   3

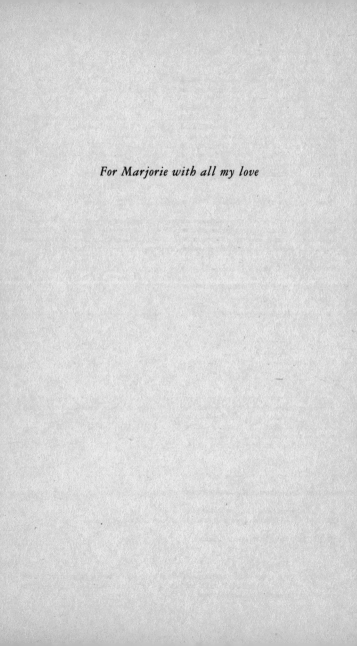

For Marjorie with all my love

ACKNOWLEDGMENTS

A special thanks to Allison E. Dietz
for her advice and counsel.

ONE

The Planet Anafa

Once accepted, a contract to deliver a message, package, or person will be honored regardless of cost.

—The Runner's Oath

The sun filtered through the charcoal-generated haze that hung over Seros, warmed the city's ancient bones, and hinted at the coming of summer. A great deal had changed during the more than ten thousand years since the first colony ship had landed on Anafa. A raw settlement had grown into a village, a town, and eventually a city. Not *one* city, but multiple cities, all stacked on top of each other like layers of ancient sediment.

As Jak Rebo made his way through the streets he could see the remains of the last technocivilization in the straight gridlike streets and the weatherworn pylons that marched down the middle of the main arterials. Each column was topped by a hoop of gleaming steel through which bullet-shaped vehicles had once flown, or so it appeared based on the huge floor mosaic in what presently served as the city's public market.

Some of the structures that rose to the left and right dated back to that same time. An era when power was plentiful, lift tubes carried people to the top of high-rise buildings that stood as thick as trees in a forest. But the skyscrapers were little more than empty cadavers now, hulks from which everything of value had been stripped, leaving rusty skeletons to point impotently at the sky.

Most of the structures that lined the streets were no more than five stories tall because that represented how many flights of stairs the average person was willing to climb. As buildings burned, or were torn down, new ones were built according to the tastes of those who could afford to do so. That activity, carried out over thousands of years, had resulted in a diversity of architecture. Some buildings had been hung with balconies, topped with domes, or provided with columns that they didn't need.

The older structures all had one thing in common, however, and that was the rectangular boxes from which street numbers had been removed in order to create a need for the hand-drawn maps that the writer's guild sold to people like Rebo. Many of the frames had been painted, or filled with tiles, but some remained as they had been: wounds over which no scab had been allowed to form.

Though understandable to some extent, the runner was annoyed by what he and his guild considered to be a desecration of the city's past *and* the destruction of a system by which written messages had once been delivered on a daily basis. An unheard-of luxury since the great purge 128 years before, when thousands of technocrats had been rounded up and slaughtered in the main square.

Rebo took a look around before stepping into the shadow

cast by an ancient arch to examine his hand-drawn schematic without attracting unwanted attention. Though useful, maps could be dangerous, since strangers were the only ones who used them.

Unlike some members of his guild, who dressed like dandies in hopes of attracting wealthy clients, the runner preferred to wear everyday clothes. A bandanna covered his jet-black hair, a gold earring dangled from one ear, and he hadn't shaved in two days. The Crosser ten-millimeter semiauto pistol hung butt down under his left arm, hidden by the runner's red leather jacket, but the single-shot Hogger with the fourteen-inch barrel was intentionally visible. It rode in a cross-draw holster along the front of his belly and was powerful enough to stop a three-hundred-pound heavy.

Rebo's trousers were black, baggy, and gathered around a pair of worn lace-up boots. All in all the sort of outfit that thousands of the planet's middle-class citizens sported every day. Because of that, and the fact that there was nothing inherently threatening about the man who stood by the arch, the locals ignored the runner as they set out for the local bakery, hawked their wares, or made their way into one of the local taverns.

Satisfied that no one was following him, or otherwise monitoring his movements, Rebo consulted the map. He was looking for Merchant Marly Telvas, a wealthy businessman, who was said to live in the reservoir district. Now, having passed the man-made lake from which the area took its name, the runner was on the lookout for landmarks that would help him identify the correct dwelling. He spotted the top of a small spire, figured it was the same fifty-foot-tall obelisk that appeared on his map, and started in that direction.

As the runner drew closer, a vine-covered twelve-foot-high wall appeared on his right, a sure sign that someone had something worth stealing. It turned out that the spire was firmly planted on an island located in the middle of the street just opposite a pair of well-varnished wooden gates. The city's police force, or guard, as it was commonly known, was notoriously understaffed, incompetent, and corrupt. That meant everyone who could afford to do so paid members of the watch keeper's guild for extra protection, be it heavily armed norms like those who lounged in front of the gates directly across from Rebo, or the cudgel-toting heavies who patrolled the better neighborhoods during the night. The runner looked both ways before crossing the street. While none of the brightly uniformed watchmen looked to be especially bright, one of them proved to be fairly assertive. His voice was gruff. "I don't know what you're selling, citizen—but it's safe to say that Merchant Telvas already has one of them."

Rebo could be charming when he chose to be. He summoned his best smile and displayed the lightning bolt that had been tattooed onto the inside surface of his left forearm when he was twelve. "I'm a runner. Is Merchant Telvas home?"

"What difference does it make?" the watchman demanded. "Give me the message, and I will deliver it for you."

Rebo shook his head, saw that the other watchmen were moving to flank him, and took three steps back. He hooked his right thumb into the gun belt only inches from the Hogger, and the effort to surround him stopped. "Thanks," the runner said evenly, "but I am required to put the message into his hands. That's what it says in the guild book—and that's what I have to do."

The head watchman wasn't surprised. Even though the

runner had already been paid by the person who sent the message, he wanted to deliver it personally in hopes of a generous tip. A perfectly understandable motivation, but one that he planned to quash. If anyone was to receive a tip, the guard believed that it should be *him*.

"Okay," the watchman growled, "but no weapons. They stay with us."

It was a ticklish moment. The request was reasonable since members of the assassin's guild had been known to impersonate runners, even going so far as to have fake guild marks tattooed onto their skins, but once Rebo surrendered his weapons he would be at the watchmen's mercy. Would they allow him to pass? Or take the box and deliver it themselves? Or worse yet, take the box, *keep* his weapons, and send him packing? He could summon the guard, but ultimately it would be his word against theirs.

Time seemed to stretch thin, and Rebo was about to back away, when Uba, the goddess of luck, came to his rescue. There was a loud clatter as a bell rang, a small angen-drawn cart rounded a corner, and the driver shouted at a pedestrian foolish enough to cross the street in front of it. The conveyance was little more than a box on wheels but still managed to convey a sense of importance via its well-oiled leather roof, pristine paint job, and the enormous brass lanterns mounted to either side of the brightly clad driver. The genetically engineered animal that stood between the traces still bore a strong resemblance to the horses from which it was descended, except that the angen was stronger, faster, and even more graceful. A man leaned out of a window as the cart ground to a halt. He had a full face, sensual lips, and wore a bright yellow turban decorated with a white feather. "What's going on here? Open the gate!"

The man could have been a visitor, but Rebo didn't think

so, and took a chance. "Citizen Telvas? My name is Jak Rebo . . . I have a package from your brother."

The watchmen moved to intervene, but the merchant raised a pudgy hand. "From my *brother*? Surely you are mistaken."

"He said that you might doubt his identity," Rebo replied quickly, "and told me to tell you that he was the one who took your rock collection when you were six and that he's sorry."

The merchant's eyes widened as if he was surprised, and he hooked a thumb toward the back of the carriage. "Jump aboard."

Rebo took a dozen steps forward, jumped up onto the step where a footman could ride, and grabbed on to the side bars. The gate had been opened by then, and the watchmen glowered as the cart jerked into motion. Rebo offered them an insulting gesture and grinned as their faces turned purple and the gate swung closed.

Though not especially large, the grounds were well kept and lavishly decorated. As the cart made its way up a slight incline to a formal entry the runner saw all manner of statues, seats, and fountains to either side of the drive. *Too* many in his judgment, as if someone continued to purchase objects long after the need to do so had passed.

The cart came to a halt under a portico, servants rushed out to welcome their master home, and Telvas had just stepped onto a carefully placed footstool as the runner rounded the corner of the carriage. The merchant nodded. "Feva will show you to my study. I'll be along soon."

Rebo had no desire to linger but discovered that he didn't have a whole lot of choice as Telvas turned and entered his house. The structure was three stories tall, capped by domes of varying heights, and painted an eye-searing white.

Feva proved to be a young, rather comely servant girl with waist-length hair and a floral dress. Very few strangers were allowed within the walls, so she was understandably curious about the ruffian her master had brought home, and directed sidelong glances at the runner as she escorted him into the house.

It was cool inside, and thanks to a generous supply of windows, very well lit. The ceilings were high, the rooms were generously proportioned, and the same excess that could be seen outside was visible within. Not only was each room they passed through full to overflowing with furniture, but it seemed as though every surface supported a lamp, urn, or vase, many of which struck the runner as quite hideous. The smell of freshly baked bread filled the air, the tinkle of a distant bell floated through the lightly perfumed air, and Rebo wondered if Madam Telvas had just rung for her maid.

Feva led the runner around a corner, gestured toward a long, roughly hewn bench, and curtsied. "Please wait here. Master Telvas will be along soon."

Others were waiting for an audience as well. One had the sleek well-fed look of a professional, an accountant judging from the well-worn abacus that rested beside him, while the other wore work clothes and sat with his feet on a well-crafted wooden toolbox. A carpenter, perhaps, hoping to receive a commission, or having been summoned to repair something of substance. Rebo nodded to both men, took note of their somewhat grim expressions, and decided that both had been there for a while.

Time passed, shadows slipped across the opposite wall,

and the carpenter started to snore. The runner didn't own a watch, not since a well-endowed barmaid had stolen it three months earlier, but didn't need one to know that at least two hours had passed by the time the door finally opened and Telvas stepped into the hall. The turban had disappeared, along with the robes, leaving the merchant in a loose-fitting white shirt, baggy black pants, and house slippers. It was a deceptively simple outfit that probably cost a crono if not more. The accountant started to rise, clearly expecting that he would go first, but the merchant pointed to Rebo. "*You.* Come in."

Rebo rose, followed Telvas into his study, and pulled the door closed behind him.

The merchant circled an enormous wooden desk to sit in a thronelike chair positioned behind it. There were two guest chairs, and Rebo decided to appropriate one of them without benefit of an invitation. Unlike the rest of the house, the study was nearly barren, suggesting that it was someone other than Telvas who enjoyed the process of buying things just to buy them. That observation served to elevate the merchant in the runner's estimation. "So," Telvas began, "you have a message for me?"

"No," Rebo replied, as he reached inside his jacket. "Not a message, but a package."

Telvas watched the runner produce a flat box and place it on the surface of his highly polished desk. It was wrapped in blue cloth, tied with a red ribbon, and looked a bit worn. Strangely, from Rebo's point of view, the merchant made no attempt to touch it. Their eyes met. "What does the package contain?"

Rebo shrugged. "I don't know. Your brother didn't say."

"Tell me more about my brother," Telvas said, leaning back into his chair. "What does he look like?"

It was a common question, one that runners, especially interstellar runners received all the time. Communications between star systems were infrequent at best, which meant that those who were fortunate enough to receive a letter or package often requested a description of their friends or loved ones. Usually *after* opening whatever they had received however. "Your brother looks a lot like you," Rebo answered honestly, "although he has more gray in his hair. He was nicely dressed, much as you are, and wore a lot of gold jewelry."

"Was there anything else?" Telvas demanded. "Anything unusual about his body or the way that he moved?"

Rebo thought back to the meeting that had taken place more than two years before. Unlike the present encounter it had been brief. But there had been something distinctive about the other brother's movements. "Yes, your brother had a pronounced limp."

"Ah," Telvas replied thoughtfully. "So he still has the leg . . . I know this conversation must seem strange to you, but suffice it to say that my brother and I had what you might call a business disagreement, which culminated in an injury to his leg. I had assumed that the medicos would remove it.

"So, tell me, Citizen Rebo," the merchant said, forming a steeple with his fingers. "What was your impression of my brother? I haven't seen him in many years. Is he a nice man?"

Rebo summoned up a picture of a man with hard eyes, slightly overripe lips, and freshly powdered skin. A man who looked like he'd been a killer once, but currently considered himself to be above that sort of thing, and hoped to leave the previous him behind. But did it make sense to say that? *No,* the runner thought to himself, and was about to lie when Telvas produced three gold cronos and pushed them across the desk. It was a gratuity, and a generous one, which would make a nice addition to the account that Rebo maintained with the runner's guild. "Take them," the merchant ordered, "and put them in your pocket. *Then* give me your answer—and not the one you think I want to hear."

Rebo slid the coins off into a palm, felt their reassuring weight, and stashed them in one of the many pockets that lined the inside of his jacket. With that accomplished the runner looked straight into the other man's eyes. "I think your brother is an extremely dangerous man."

The merchant nodded soberly. "So, that being the case, would *you* open the box?"

Rebo looked down at the seemingly innocent box and back up again. "No, sir. I wouldn't."

"But what if it contains a peace offering?" the other man insisted. "What then? I feel bad about what happened to my brother's leg and would like to make it up to him."

The runner shrugged. "Your brother didn't strike me as a man who makes peace offerings, but the choice is yours."

"Yes, I suppose it is," Telvas replied. "Thank you for delivering the box. And thank you for the advice. Feva will see you to the gate."

Rebo stood. "Is there a rear entrance?"

Telvas nodded understandingly. "Yes, there is. Tell Feva, and she will take you there."

Rebo withdrew after that, discovered that Feva had appeared in the hall, and glanced back over his shoulder as she closed the door. The box remained on the surface of the desk, and Telvas continued to stare at it.

The runner slipped out through the back gate ten minutes later, was pleased when none of the watchmen stationed there showed the least bit of interest in him, and started down the street. Rebo had walked about a hundred feet, and was just about to cross a street, when he heard a dull *thump* and looked back in time to see a puff of smoke shoot out of a window. The study? Yes, he thought so. There were cries of alarm, followed by hysterical screams, and Rebo knew that Telvas was dead.

The runner paused to take a long slow look around. Was there *another* runner lurking in the area? A man or woman hired to confirm the merchant's death and carry a message back to his brother? There wasn't any sign of one, but that didn't mean much, so Rebo sauntered away. It was a nice day, a profitable day, but one that left him with an unfathomable question: How could such an apparently smart man be so stupid?

Even though Lanni Norr was a stranger to the city, the marketplace was easy to find. First, because at least half of the traffic flowing into Seros was headed there, and second, because once the sensitive drew close enough she could smell the rich amalgam of spices, fried food, and angen feces that scented the air around it.

Then, as she entered the market, even more senses came into play. There were racks of colorful fabrics, bins filled with vegetables, tables covered with jewelry, booths hung with amulets, racks of handmade clothing, piles of woven baskets, bags filled with white nuts, reels of hand-twisted rope, trays loaded with fragrant candles, display boards covered with wicked-looking knives and so much more that one couldn't hope to see all of it in a single day. And there were sounds, too. The rumble of a thousand haggling voices was punctuated by the squawks, snorts, and squeals of caged angens, the incessant shouts of vendors who never stopped hawking their wares, the ring of hammers on metal, the wail of a lost child, and occasional snatches of music.

But there was more, *much* more, for Norr at least, who

unlike 99 percent of the people swirling about her could see the separate energy fields that each individual emitted, catch glimpses of the discarnate spirits who flitted through the area intent on errands of their own, and was constantly buffeted by waves of projected emotion. Not because she sought to experience such things, but because her ancestors had been genetically engineered to pick up on other people's emotions, manipulate small objects from a distance, heal the sick, and communicate with the dead.

As Norr made her way through the market, she was exposed to continual bursts of love, hate, greed, fear, lust, and happiness as those about her wrestled with what fellow sensitives referred to as the holy trinity: money, sex, and power—the basic drives behind most human activity, including hers. Because it took money to survive, which was why the sensitive had been forced to emerge from hiding and make the long, uncomfortable trek into Seros.

So, unpleasant though the task was, Norr wandered the long, tight aisles until she spotted the sign she'd been looking for. Most of the city's population were functionally illiterate, so a large replica of a quill had been hung over the booth, and therefore over the scribe who sat on a stool beneath it.

Like most of his ilk, the bespectacled clerk was a member of the so called A-strain, meaning the 80 percent of humans also referred to as norms. Most had black hair, olive-colored skin, and long, slender bodies. There were exceptions, of course, genetic throwbacks to the days hundreds of thousands of years before, when people came in a rainbow of colors. Such individuals were rare however.

This specimen sported a bowl cut, a pair of thick hand-ground lenses that were perched on the very tip of his nose, and radiated smug superiority. His aura flickered and morphed into something like apprehension as Norr approached the counter. Because even though the young woman with the pack, the long wooden staff, and the knee-high boots looked innocent enough, she had the large dark eyes, high cheekbones, and narrow face of a sensitive. A breed that the scribe, like many others, had reason to fear. Not because of a personal experience with one, but because they were said to read minds, and the wordsmith had things to hide. Like his tendency to mentally undress almost every woman he encountered. In fact he had already stripped Norr, noting that her breasts were too small for his taste, when she arrived in front of his counter. The clerk swallowed the lump that threatened to fill his throat and struggled to speak. "Yes?" he croaked. "Can I help you?"

Norr *couldn't* read minds, but she could sense the emotions that surrounded the man and was willing to take advantage of them. "You are a very naughty man," she said experimentally, and knew she had scored when the scribe's face turned bright red.

"I-I-I'm sorry," the wordsmith stuttered. "I didn't mean anything by it."

"Good," Norr replied soothingly. "Apology accepted. Perhaps you can help me."

"I'll certainly try," the clerk replied eagerly, pleased to get off the hook so easily. "What do you need? A letter perhaps?"

"No," Norr replied deliberately. "I could write that myself. What I need is some advertising."

"Ah," the scribe responded happily, "a flyer should do it! I'll write one up, send it over to the guild's workshop, and you'll have five hundred copies by noon tomorrow. The press is broken again, but the apprentices can copy it by hand. The practice will do them good."

"Thanks," Norr said cautiously. "But how much would that cost?"

"Oh, about a hundred and fifty gunars," the wordsmith replied airily, "but well worth the price."

"Perhaps," Norr said agreeably, conscious of the fact that she had only a hundred gunars in her purse. "However I'm looking for something a bit more economical."

The bright red money lust that surrounded the scribe flickered and started to fade. "Yes, well, I suppose we could use graffiti instead. For seventy-five gunars our specialists could paint one-line messages onto two hundred and fifty highly visible walls throughout the city."

Norr looked surprised. "You mean people pay for that stuff?"

"Of course," the wordsmith said matter-of-factly. "We run into freelancers from time to time, or lose messages when a citizen slaps a fresh coat of paint over our work, but it doesn't take long for them to see the error of their ways. Especially after a couple of heavies drop by to say 'hello.'"

"Okay," Norr agreed reluctantly. "Two hundred and fifty locations sounds good. But how many words to a line?"

"Ten," the scribe replied succinctly.

"I need more," Norr insisted, as she counted them in her head. "Seventeen to be precise."

"That's going to cost you five gunars," the clerk warned primly.

"Not necessarily," the sensitive countered as she leaned forward. "Remember that apology? What if your superiors were aware of what you've been up to?"

The clerk's supervisor happened to be a woman, and he could imagine what would happen if she knew that he had undressed her hundreds of times. There were worse assignments than the market, *much* worse, and he had no desire to receive one. Ink-stained fingers reached for a hand-sharpened quill, which the scribe dipped into a disreputable-looking bottle, and held poised above a blank sheet of paper. "Okay, seventeen. What are they?"

Norr looked off into space as she recited them. "Come see the famous sensitive Lanni Norr communicate with the dead Friday at eight, in the actor's guild."

"That's eighteen words."

"Okay," Norr said nonchalantly. "Make it eighteen then."

The scribe's pen made a scritching sound as he transferred the words to a piece of tan parchment. The sensitive noticed that each letter was formed with the perfection of an ancient printing machine and marveled at how precise the man was. It was evident that he enjoyed his work because as he wrote the color of his aura changed from red to a harmonious blue. "That will be seventy-five gunars," the wordsmith said as he blotted the paper. "Payable in advance."

"I'll give you forty up front, and the rest when the messages actually appear," Norr replied.

The scribe swore under his breath. "All right . . . But a heavy will show up Friday to collect, so you'd better be ready to pay."

"I will be," Norr replied confidently and counted gunars out onto the surface of the counter. "By the way, this will be a demonstration of psychic phenomena rather than some sort of show. I think you should come."

"Thank you," the wordsmith answered politely. "But I'm busy that night."

"Okay," Norr said as she prepared to leave. "But your wife is there by your side. She says that her death wasn't the least bit painful, she's happy on the spirit plane, and you should stop grieving for her."

No one knew about the true extent to which the scribe missed his wife, and he hadn't mentioned her death to the young woman, so how did she know? Tears welled up in the clerk's eyes, and he used a tattered sleeve to wipe them away. He opened his mouth to speak, to ask Norr what his wife looked like now, but the sensitive was gone.

Because the monastery had been built hundreds of years before, back when Seros was little more than a settlement, it occupied a piece of prime real estate atop one of the hills marking the city's eastern boundary. The complex was surrounded by high walls, which the brotherhood said had been built to keep ignorance at bay, but had practical value as well, for hardly a month passed without an attempt to break in and steal the gold that was rumored to be kept there. There wasn't any gold, of course, but the monastery did contain some precious artifacts, which was one of the reasons why the Dib Wa (iron men) patrolled the walls. The other reason, the person each of the warriors was sworn to protect with his life, threw a door open and bounded onto the surface of a large flat roof.

The guards smiled indulgently as the ten-year-old boy ran in circles, waved his arms, and sent a flock of white wings flapping into the air. It was a daily ritual and one of the few unstructured moments of the youngster's day. He wore a pillbox-shaped red hat like those favored by the adult members of his sect, a matching knee-length jacket, and black trousers. And, because Tra Lee was widely believed to be the reincarnated spirit of Nom Maa, a much-revered teacher who had entered the spirit realms a dozen years earlier, all the Dib Wa bowed. Not to the boy, but to the man they believed he would become, and the role that "the Divine Wind" was destined to play in the future.

Because, assuming that the reading of Nom Maa's death poem was correct, the time had come for a heavenly rebirth, meaning the reemergence of the Saa or "Way," which would serve as an important counterbalance against what the monks saw as a steady slide into barbarity. The only problem being that the competing black hat sect claimed that Tra Lee was an imposter, and insisted that a lad raised under their control was the *real* Nom Maa. But if such matters were of concern to Tra Lee, the little boy showed no sign of it as he ran along the top of the walls, played games of his own devising, and shouted orders to imaginary friends.

The period of freedom was all too brief, however, and it wasn't long before Lee's spiritual tutor, an avuncular monk named Suu Qwa, rang a tiny bell. Lee ignored the tinkling sound at first, hoping for one of the rare occasions on which Qwa might grant him some extra time, but the noise continued. Finally, shoulders slumped in defeat, the boy walked across the roof to the point where his tutor waited. "So, little one," the monk said softly, "where will we meet today?"

It was a game that the two of them played every day and Lee brightened at the prospect of it. Although he had to take part in the lesson, he could choose where it would be taught, and delighted in forcing Qwa to teach in all manner of unlikely locations. The only problem was that it was getting hard to come up with new venues. The youngster looked around, spotted the coop where the specially bred carrier flits were kept, and pointed a grubby finger in that direction. "Up there . . . On the roof."

Qwa bowed deeply. "The roof it will be. Would your majesty like me to boost you up there? Or will you climb?"

Lee eyed the structure but couldn't see any way to scale the walls. "It appears that I will need a boost."

"Yes," Qwa said as he accompanied the youngster to the coop. "All of us need help from time to time. Many are willing—but how to choose?"

Lee knew that the lesson was under way and responded accordingly. "The correct individual will not only have the desire to help, but motivations consistent with key goals, and possess the skills or tools required to complete the task."

"Excellent," Qwa said approvingly as he boosted the boy up onto the roof. "In spite of the abundant evidence to the contrary, it appears that you pay attention once in a while."

There was a momentary disturbance as the birds fluttered around their cage and cooed to each other. Most had settled down by the time the tutor hoisted himself up onto the gradually slanting surface. It was covered with droppings, and Lee had already claimed the cleanest spot. He grinned knowingly.

But it was difficult if not impossible to get a rise out of the monk, who squatted on his haunches and eyed his student with the same calm gaze that he always manifested. "Today I would tell you of a village and the monk who lived there. One night there was a loud disturbance outside his hut. He got up and opened the door to find that a man and the local midwife were standing on his stoop. Both individuals poured out their hearts to the monk, and it wasn't long before the situation became clear. The man's wife was pregnant, but the baby was in a poor position, and the midwife believed that while she could save one of the two, there was very little chance that both would survive. The man favored his wife, but the midwife argued for the infant, both calling upon the monk to render a decision. Which view was correct?"

Lee considered the problem for a moment. "The man was correct."

Qwa raised an eyebrow. "Why? The midwife argued that while sad, a new life must always take precedence over an old life, for such is the natural order of things."

"That is true," Lee answered, "so far as it goes. But the monk had a responsibility to look beyond natural cycles to the greater good. If the woman were to die not only would the man lose his wife, but her other children would lose their mother, and all she might have taught them."

Qwa nodded approvingly. "That was well said, Excellency. You are both an excellent student and a teacher. Please allow me to take this opportunity to thank you for all I have learned from my contact with you and to say a reluctant good-bye. There are many paths, and now ours must part."

Lee felt something heavy drop into the bottom of his stomach. The youth had only the vaguest memories of his real family and had come to regard Qwa and his other instructors as a group of uncles. Each brought something unique to his life, and if he lost one of them, it would be difficult to fill the gap. He frowned. "Why do you say that? Are you leaving?"

"No," Qwa answered, "but *you* are. The final test awaits. The time has come for you to travel to the holy city of Ca-Canth."

Lee felt fear mixed with a sense of excitement. He didn't want to part company with Qwa, or the rest of his tutors, but not a day went by that he didn't look out over the city of Seros and wish that he could walk its dusty streets. And Ca-Canth was on the planet Thara, everyone knew that, which meant he would get to ride in a spaceship! The very thought of it made his pulse pound. "You must accompany me, Master Qwa! I command it."

"It is true that you command many things," the monk

answered gently, "but this is not one of them. It will be a long, dangerous journey, and special arrangements must be made to ensure your safe arrival. My place is here."

"But what if I'm *not* Nom Maa?" the boy demanded heatedly. "I'll fail the test, the black hats will control the Saa, and your efforts will be for naught."

"Ah, but you are the Divine Wind," Qwa answered serenely, "and therefore have nothing to fear."

A cloud chose that moment to pass in front of the sun, a momentary darkness fell over the land, and Lee felt a chill run down his spine.

The tattoo parlor was a small dingy little shop with two workstations. Rebo sat in one of them, his back to the frowsy artist, as she added a new image to the map that already occupied the upper portion of his back. Most of the interstellar runners wore them, not because they had to, but because they *wanted* to, as a way of memorializing successful runs. Some even went so far as to will their skins to the guild, which typically had sections of the artwork removed, and fashioned into lampshades or other decorative objects. They were the exceptions of course, since most of the star runners died obscure deaths on remote planets, where they were stripped of their valuables before being unceremoniously dumped into a ravine, bog, or unmarked grave. Until that final moment they lived in the hope that they would make it back to whatever world they called home before making the run from which no one could return. Not in the flesh at any rate—which was what the tattoo artist was focused on.

The pain was intense, but rather than attempt to push it away, Rebo had learned to accept it. More than that to go beyond it, to a place where he was only dimly aware of the discomfort as the relentless needle pushed ink in under the surface of his skin. During moments like that the runner entered the equivalent of a reverie, reliving moments from the past, or entering a fantasy world where there was no such thing as pain. And that was why Rebo was slow to respond when a voice called his name. "Citizen Rebo? My name is Suu Qwa. Brother Qwa. The people at the runner's guild told me I could find you here."

The words served to bring the world back into focus, and the pain came with it. Rebo frowned as the needle plunged into his back yet again. The monk's head had been shaved, a simple red robe hung from his skinny shoulders, and he looked like he was thirty or so. The runner found that his throat was dry. "No offense, Brother Qwa, but I'm kind of busy at the moment. Could this wait?"

The monk shook his head. "No, I'm afraid it can't. A ship is due in four days. We hope to send a package out on it. So, assuming that the vessel actually shows up, we need to hire a runner."

Rebo understood the problem. Or part of it anyway. What little interstellar commerce there was took place via a fleet of spaceships that dated back to one of the last major technocivilizations. Because they were fully automated, the ships continued to link the far-flung star systems together long after the culture that created them had been destroyed.

Now, thousands of years later, the spaceships were dying because no one had the knowledge or the means to repair them. The result was that there were fewer ships with each passing year, it was no longer possible to reach some destinations directly, and entire solar systems had been left isolated. Just one of the reasons why people hired runners to carry their messages rather than handling the chore themselves.

The pain was even more intense now, and tiny beads of perspiration had appeared on the runner's forehead. "Look," Rebo said, "I just finished a run and I'm tired. I suggest that you return to the guild and ask for another recommendation."

The monk looked unconvinced. "You are the best. That's what your peers say. We will double your fee."

Rebo looked the monk in the eye. "*Double?* That's a lot of money. This package must be important."

"It is," Qwa confirmed. "Come to the monastery tonight. We will show you the package, and assuming that you agree to handle the consignment, pay half of what we owe you up front."

"And the other half?" the runner inquired.

"You will receive that when you deliver the package to the city of CaCanth on Thara," Qwa answered.

The name startled Rebo, his body gave an involuntary jerk, and the needle went deep. Thara! The planet on which he had been born, left at the age of twelve, and never gone back to since. Was his mother still alive? It seemed unlikely, but without knowing it, the monk had hit on the one thing that would change the runner's mind. Rebo's mother had worked twelve hours a day to obtain enough money to buy his apprenticeship, and now, if he could buy her some comfort in her old age, the journey would be worth it. "All right," the runner replied, "I'll see you tonight."

The monk left, the artist dabbed at her bloody work, and the torture continued.

The hall maintained by the actor's guild was second only to the local amphitheater in terms of the number of people that it could hold, and Lanni Norr peered through dusty red velvet curtains as the citizens of Seros filed in. Many carried cushions to soften the unpadded seats, blankets to protect them from the evening chill, and baskets of food. And, judging from the steady stream of people, it appeared that her advertising campaign had been a success. The actor's guild would get 10 percent of the gate, but assuming she could fill 80 percent of the seats, the sensitive figured she would take in enough money to defray her expenses for a year. She would come up with a disguise, fade into the countryside, and rent a cottage. Each day would be spent reading, painting, or simply doing nothing. That was Norr's dream—and the only reason she was willing to expose herself to the dangers associated with the impending performance.

Because while clairaudience was one thing, and the occasional demonstration of telekinesis was another, a full-blown trance was something else. Once the sensitive exited her body and allowed a discarnate soul to enter it, she would be helpless until the entity left. Yes, she had spent her last few gunars on a bodyguard, but what if the entire audience stormed the stage as had happened in the past? Norr had been present the night that an unruly crowd had accused her mentor of witchcraft and subsequently beaten the old woman to death. Norr had been forced to travel for more than a hundred miles before she finally located a cemetery that was willing to accept the sensitive's remains.

Someone touched Norr's shoulder and she jumped. It was the heavy named Loro and he was *huge*. The variant stood a full seven feet tall, weighted close to 350, and looked as though his muscles had muscles. Like all his kind, the bodyguard was the result of the same sort of genetic tinkering that had produced Norr, except that *his* body was designed to cope with heavy-gravity environments, where massive bones and big muscles were required to survive. Over time some of the big brutes had been absorbed into the general population, where they often wound up as laborers, watch-men, and freelance bodyguards. Loro's voice consisted of a deep rumble. "Where do you want me?"

"Between me and everyone else," Norr replied fervently. "Don't let anyone up on the stage. Especially while I'm in trance. Do you understand?"

The last was said as if the concept might be too compli-cated for a heavy to understand. Both norms *and* variants had a tendency to assume that heavies were stupid, but that was absurd since the scientists who designed the enormous humanoids had been trying to create *intelligent* workers. Loro was so used to the bias he didn't even take offense any-more. "Of course," the heavy replied. "I'll take care of it."

"Thank you," Norr replied gratefully. "Now, if you would be so kind as to take your place out on the stage, I think your very presence will help keep the rowdies under control."

Loro nodded, pulled one of the curtains aside, and stepped through the resulting gap. The sensitive saw that two-thirds of the seats were full, and sought the momentary solitude of her dressing room. It was her habit to meditate for a few minutes prior to a demonstration, and even that small amount of distance would help reduce the pressure from the multitudinous thought forms that pressed in around her.

Meanwhile, out in the audience, there was a stir as a metal man entered the hall. He wasn't real, of course, but a *replica* of a man, one of dozens that had appeared on the streets of Seros during the past couple of years. Nobody liked them. Partly because they were machines, and there was a segment of society that believed that machines were dangerous, but mostly because of their incessant preaching on behalf of a group called the Techno Society. In fact, hardly a day went by when one or more of the androids couldn't be found near the public market droning on about the benefits of technology.

And sometimes, for reasons known only to them, the metal men would appear at public events like this one. Only rather than preach they were content to sit and observe. Like the rest of his electromechanical brethren, the robot wore a hooded robe that revealed little more than the sculptured planes of his alloy face and hung all the way to the floor. The machine whirred as it brushed past people who had already taken their seats and plopped down between a teacher and a butcher. Neither was especially pleased, and both went to extremes to avoid contact with the creature.

Each attendee had been given a blank square of paper on which they had been invited to write their name, make their mark, or jot down a message to a dead loved one. There was a stir as the ushers called for the audience to pass the billets to the center aisle.

The metal man handed his note to the teacher, who took the moment required to read it, and was surprised to see some extremely neat printing. It read, "Milos Lysander."

Did that mean the machine was named Lysander? There was no way to know, and it was none of his business, so the teacher passed all the pieces of paper that had come his way down to the center aisle, where they were collected.

The lights dimmed, and the curtains opened, to reveal a young woman sitting on a tall stool with a table at her side. Lamplights, cleverly directed her way through the use of lenses, lit a pretty face. She had long dark hair, large brown eyes, and extremely fair skin. But slender though she was, the sensitive projected an aura of strength, and her eyes flashed as she looked about the room. "Good evening. My name is Lanni Norr. I have good news for you . . . There is no such thing as death. Only a transition from one plane of existence to another. I am not a witch, nor a magician, but a member of a small group of people who refer to themselves as sensitives. Just as phibs were bred to swim, and wings were born to fly, we were created to facilitate communications between this world and the next."

Norr emphasized her words by seizing control of the energy in the room, shaping it to her purpose, and reaching out to seize a black skullcap. It belonged to a man seated in the very front row, which meant that everyone could watch the object rise into the air and hang suspended over the man's head. Its owner looked up in astonishment, clapped a hand to his mostly bald pate, and said, "What the hell?"

A twitter ran through the crowd. One of the people seated directly behind the bald man stood and swept an arm back and forth *above* the cap to see if it was suspended by a thread. There was no reaction from the hat other than to rise even higher, move sideways through the air, and settle itself onto the skeptic's head. The audience member examined the cap, shook his head in amazement, and returned the object to its owner.

The crowd loved the byplay, and Norr could feel the amount of positive energy in the room increase. "So," she continued, "I hope that you will relax and open your minds to the possibility that there are forms of energy and planes of existence beyond the physical realm in which we currently dwell. Contact with those in the next world is never certain, but assuming that we are fortunate enough to construct a momentary bridge between the two planes, listen carefully to what I say. In many cases, though not all, friends and loved ones will attempt to communicate some fact or incident that only the two of you would be aware of as proof that they still exist and love you.

"During this process one or more of them may take temporary control of my physical body in order to speak directly. Should that occur, please remember that I am the channel, not the spirit entity, and have no control over what he or she may say.

"Please remain in your seats throughout the demonstration, and do not approach the stage, or my friend Loro will be forced to reseat you."

The heavy stepped out of the shadows at that point, crossed his arms over a massive chest, and eyed the audience. Everyone got the point.

"Okay," Norr said, "if someone will bring me the billets, we will begin. Please note the fact that I had no way to know who would come tonight—and the messages you submitted have been on display throughout the process."

A basket filled with scraps of paper was brought forward and placed on the table next to Norr's stool. The sensitive reached in, ran her fingers through the billets, and stopped when her hand started to tingle. She pulled a piece of paper out of the pile without looking at it, crumpled the parchment into a ball, and held it in her fist. Then, blanking her mind, she let what she thought of as "the other side" take over. Words and images began to appear, and she passed them on. "Is there a Loki in the audience? Your mother is here . . . She says that you are correct about Del. He *is* a good man, and it would be a mistake to let this one get away."

The woman named Loki looked shocked, the audience chuckled, and there was a scattering of applause. More than a dozen messages followed. Most contained at least one or two items that were evidential, and everything was going well, until Norr dipped her hand into the basket and chose the next billet. What felt like electricity ran all the way up her arm, the sensitive felt cold air embrace her, and knew that a spirit being was about to take control of her body. It soon became apparent that the invading entity wasn't used to a female form and didn't especially like it. But what he *did* approve of however was the prospect of a captive audience. He took control of her voice box and spoke in a voice so low that it hurt. "Good evening. My name is Milos Lysander. Prior to my death I was a scientist, a philosopher, and the primary force behind the Techno Society."

Most of crowd sat motionless, not quite sure of what was happening, or why. But the metal man was electrified by the announcement. The robot came to his feet, activated all of its onboard recording devices, and ignored the complaints directed at him by those seated behind him. "The mission of the Techno Society," Lysander continued, "is to literally re-shape the future of mankind. More than that, to use tech-nology as the means to reunite the pieces of a once-great empire and lift the scattered remnants of humanity back into the light of reason. How will we accomplish that? Well, I will tell you. First . . ."

As the scientist continued to speak there was a mutter of disapproval, followed by a scattering of insults, and a heart-felt chorus of boos. Norr could *feel* the sentiment in the room start to shift and struggled to reassert control over her body as pieces of food started to fly. A well-aimed piece of overripe fruit hit Norr in the chest, caused Lysander to pause momentarily, and gave the sensitive the opportunity that she'd been looking for. She clamped down, forced the scientist out, and raised her hands in an attempt to calm the crowd. It didn't work. The rowdier members of the audience *liked* throwing food at her, the rest were leaving, and the ushers had produced clubs, which they swung freely.

Loro urged Norr to retreat backstage, which she did. A heavy was waiting there to collect the money she owed to writer's guild and left the moment he was paid. Norr knew she should count the take to ensure that the actor's guild hadn't taken more money than they were entitled to but didn't want to take the time. The crowd was chanting something ugly, the entity named Lysander frightened her, and negative emotions converged from every side. With her bodyguard in attendance the sensitive slipped out through the back door. The metal man was waiting in the shadows, and when the twosome left, the machine followed along behind.

TWO

The Planet Anafa

In order to reestablish man's dominion over the stars, and save humanity from barbarity, it may be necessary to carry out barbarous acts against those who resist our efforts. The essential irony of this is not lost upon the governing council, which regrets the necessity to use violence.

—Techno Society Operations Manual,
Section One: Guiding Principles

The milky white light produced by the planet's twin moons filtered down through a thin layer of clouds to bathe Seros in a ghostly glow. There were no streetlights, but as the coach followed the winding road that led to the top of monastery hill, Rebo could look out over the city and see thousands of buttery rectangles, each representing a window. It was easy to imagine the warm homey scenes within and the runner felt a momentary sense of envy as the vehicle's steel-shod wheels bounced through a pothole, and a pack of feral dogs emerged from the thick roadside underbrush to run alongside. That made the angens nervous, and Rebo felt the carriage surge forward as the animals tried to escape their pursuers. The driver hollered, "Whoa!" and hauled back on the reins, but to no avail.

But the runner had hired two apprentices to accompany him, and the youngsters knew what to do. Both were armed with smooth-bore weapons. Twin flashes strobed the darkness as the youngsters fired, dogs yelped pitifully as the buckshot tore into them, and those that could ran for cover. The angens settled down after that, and Rebo felt confident enough to remove his hand from the Crosser.

It wasn't long before the carriage swung through a final turn, half a dozen members of the Dib Wa emerged from the surrounding gloom, and orders were shouted up to the driver. The conveyance jerked to a halt, Rebo opened the door, and jumped to the ground. The runner held his hands away from his body as a warrior approached, located his weapons in record time, and removed both from their holsters.

Then, satisfied that the visitor had been defanged, a second Dib Wa led Rebo to a man-sized gate that had been set into a larger gate. The runner stepped over the four-inch-high crosspiece at the bottom of the structure and followed the guard into the monastery's shadowy interior. Rebo *felt* rather than saw a distinct change, since it was just as dark inside the walls as it was on the outside. But there was no denying the profound sense of peace that pervaded the monastery, a feeling so strong it seemed to emanate from the structures around him the way accumulated heat radiates from a stone.

Though born on Thara, the planet on which the Way was headquartered, the runner had never been especially religious. Perhaps that was due to the fact that the fisherfolk of Lorval put their faith in a complicated hierarchy of nature spirits rather than a single god, or maybe it was because the runner had left home at the age of twelve. Whatever the reason the result was the same. Though conscious of the Way, and its importance to millions of practitioners, Rebo had never developed an interest in it.

Golden light spilled out through an open door to make a path across the gray flagstones. A man appeared and stood silhouetted in the opening. It wasn't until the runner was only a few feet away that he recognized Suu Qwa. "Welcome," the monk said, bowing deeply. "Please follow me."

In spite of the fact that he was an invited guest, the Dib Wa escort continued to tag along behind Rebo, and the runner wondered why an ostensibly peaceful monastery needed so much security. Perhaps the rumors were true—and the basement *was* packed floor to ceiling with gold ingots.

Various parts of the temple were connected by a maze of passageways, and there were frequent turns, but if the monks hoped to confuse the runner, they failed. Not only did Rebo have a memory worthy of a tax collector, he had an excellent sense of direction, and knew he could find his way out of the complex on his own should that become necessary.

Finally, after what he estimated to be a quarter-mile walk, the runner was ushered into a large room. One end was dominated by a twelve-foot-tall likeness of the ascended being Teon. He had eight arms, and eight hands, each of which held a symbol. The teacher sat as he always did, with his feet on top of his thighs, a feat the runner knew he wouldn't be able to duplicate even with a gun to his head.

The center of the space was dominated by a circle, representing the eternal cycle of birth, death, and rebirth. Seated within its embrace was an elderly man and a young boy. Both wore nearly identical outfits that consisted of red pillbox-style hats, matching robes, and leather sandals. Rebo noticed that Qwa bowed to the youngster first. "Greetings, Excellencies," Qwa said respectfully. "Please allow me to introduce Jak Rebo."

Being unsure of the correct etiquette, the runner delivered a short jerky bow, said, "It's a pleasure to meet you," and eyed the rather thin pillow that awaited him. Once on the floor Rebo sat with his legs crossed in a poor imitation of the Teon-like posture the monks adopted.

"My name is Dak Babukas," the elder monk announced, "and the young man to my left is presently referred to as Tra Lee, although we believe that he has lived many previous lives, including his recent incarnation as a teacher called Nom Maa. Now, after years of preparation, the time has come for Tra to make the journey to the city of CaCanth on the planet Thara. Once there he will undergo certain tests, and assuming that he passes them, will take his rightful place as Inwa, or leader of leaders. Your task is to get him there alive."

Rebo frowned. Though interested in a trip to Thara, there was a considerable difference between delivering a package and a person. Of course such runs were not unknown. In fact, he had handled two such assignments during his career. And, because both individuals had been difficult to get along with, the runner had sworn that he would never accept such a commission again. More than that, Rebo sensed something fishy about the proposal and looked the older monk in the eye. "You have more security than the governor does. So, why hire me? Why not send a squad of your warriors along as escorts?"

The boy remained silent as the adult monks exchanged glances and Qwa spoke. "Our religion consists of two sects, generally referred to as the red hats and the black hats, although the *real* differences are based on theology rather than fashion. Twelve years ago the sixteenth Nom Maa passed into spirit without naming a successor. That led to a power vacuum, which resulted in competition between the two sects and what amounts to an administrative stalemate. However, now that Tra Lee has completed his training, he is ready to take the throne."

"Yes," Babukas agreed, "except that the black hats claim that one of their boys is the real Nom Maa, and based on that assertion, believe that he should ascend the throne."

"That's correct," Qwa put in, "and there's more. The black hats may seek to prevent the Divine Wind from reaching Thara."

"*May?*" Rebo inquired pointedly. "Or *will?*"

"There is no way to know for sure," Qwa replied carefully, "but the odds favor some sort of assassination attempt."

"Which brings us back to where we started," the runner said. "Why me?"

"Because an escort of Dib Wa would attract a lot of attention," Babukas answered honestly. "There are thieves to consider . . . and the black hats can muster as many warriors as we can. But a father and son? No one is likely to notice such a pair."

"*If* I had a son, which I don't," the runner remarked, "he wouldn't be bald."

"A wig has been prepared," Qwa replied smoothly, "and appropriate clothes would be provided as well."

There was a moment of uncomfortable silence, which was broken when Tra Lee spoke for the first time. "I don't believe that Citizen Rebo is being entirely frank with us. He was willing to accept the assignment until he learned the true nature of the package involved. Now he has doubts. So, Citizen Rebo, what can I do or say to convince you that I will be a minimum amount of trouble?"

The runner looked into Tra Lee's eyes and saw unexpected depths there. The little boy sounded more like an adult than a nine- or ten-year-old. Were the monks correct? Did Tra Lee's body house the reincarnated body of a great teacher? Or did the little boy seem wise beyond his years solely because he had been raised to come across that way? It was impossible to tell, but something about the youngster's seemingly sincere demeanor caused the runner to soften slightly. Besides, Rebo *did* want to visit Thara, and the pay was extremely good. He cleared his throat and addressed his questions to Lee. "Would you follow my orders? And do so quickly? Without question?"

The boy gazed unblinkingly into Rebo's eyes. "So long as your instructions are consistent with moral law, I will obey."

The qualification bothered the runner, but he couldn't imagine asking the lad to do something *immoral,* so he nodded. "All right then, I'll take the commission. One thing though . . . See if you can find a boy who looks a lot like our young friend here. Dress him for the part, parade him about, and treat him like he's the real deal. Maybe, if we're lucky, the black hats will believe that he's still in Seros long after our ship breaks orbit."

"It shall be as you say," Babukas replied. "When should his majesty join you?"

"Tomorrow," Rebo replied. "Figure out a low-key way to deliver him to my guild. I'll take it from there."

"Excellent," Qwa replied. "Would you care for some tea? No? I will escort you out then. The first half of your pay is waiting in your carriage."

Rebo rose, hoped the monks couldn't tell how stiff he was, and said good-bye to both Babukas and Lee. Later that night the runner would return to Thara in his dreams, none of which were good.

It was dark along the street, very dark, which was one of the reasons why the locals retreated inside their homes and locked their doors within minutes of sunset. The Market Street Inn was no different. Lights glowed behind thick panes of glass, but the front door was securely closed, and presumably barred from within. A problem, but not an insurmountable one, assuming that this was the correct location.

Jevan Kane used a series of quick hand gestures to position his operatives, taking special care to post lookouts and ensure that the back entrance was covered. Finally, satisfied that no would be able to escape the structure without being intercepted, Kane turned to the metal man who stood at his elbow. "This is the place . . . You're sure?"

Robots didn't possess emotions, so the machine took no offense. "Yes, sir. The sensitive handed something to the heavy. He left, and she went inside."

Kane pulled a hood down over his face and pulled a semiautomatic pistol out of his waistband. The eyes that stared out through the precut holes were like chips of blue ice. "Good. Depart the area immediately. I don't want you and your kind associated with this kind of activity."

The machine backed into the darkness and was gone moments later. Kane gave a low whistle. A pair of hooded heavies appeared. They held a metal battering ram between them. On a signal from Kane they approached the front door, swung the ram back, and heaved it forward. There was a loud *crash,* followed by the splintering of wood, and shouts from within. The battering ram struck again, the beam that barred the door broke in two, and what remained of the barrier flew open. A man appeared in the opening. He was armed with a double-barreled scattergun, which he fired into the night. One of the heavies cried out in pain and brass arced away from Kane's weapon as it bucked in his hand. The reports were still dying away as the innkeeper fell over backward.

Three operatives pushed through the doorway after that and Kane heard more gunfire. The operative entered the tiny lobby to find the innkeeper's wife huddled in a bloody corner, while a guest who had the misfortune to be in the wrong place at the wrong time lay a few feet away. That left a sobbing maid. Tears ran down her acne-pitted face, and her body shook with fear, as a heavy held her in his grasp. "I'm looking for a sensitive," Kane told her. "A young female. Which room is she in?"

"R-r-room three," the maid stuttered.

"Thanks," Kane said, and shot her in the chest. Blood sprayed the heavy, who swore, and let go of her arm. The body made a soft *thump* as it hit the floor.

"Room three must be upstairs," one of the operatives said, having just returned from a quick exploration of the ground floor.

Boots thundered on worn treads as the invaders raced up the stairs to the second floor, where they examined the numbers on each door. "Here it is!" someone shouted, and Kane turned in that direction. "Open it," he said tersely, "but don't shoot. We need her alive."

The operative knew that, but nodded obediently, as a heavy shoulder hit the door. It flew open and Kane followed his team inside. But outside of a single bed, a dilapidated dresser, and a single chair the room was empty. Kane kicked the chair and sent it crashing into a wall. "Damn! Damn! Damn!"

Although the metal man had seen Norr enter, the android had been forced to leave long enough to make his report. It appeared that during that relatively short interval the sensitive had slipped away. The question was why? Did the young woman know that the Techno Society was looking for her? She was a psychic after all. Or was she simply prudent? The sensitive had every reason to be concerned about thieves—and might have left for that reason alone.

"We need to leave," one of the operatives said urgently. "The guard will arrive shortly."

Kane followed his men down into the street, heard the distant sound of a police bugle, and the entire group melted into the night. There was a clatter of hooves and loose equipment as the guard arrived, but the street was empty, and the shadows were mute.

The sun had been up for three hours, and the streets of Seros were already bustling with activity as the old angen plodded along its daily route. The flatbed wagon creaked and groaned as its steel-shod wooden wheels bumped through a seemingly endless series of potholes, the casks that contained the morning's milk rattled accordingly, and Tra Lee took his first unescorted ride through the city. Now, having looked down on Seros for so long, he was finally amongst its buildings.

The prospect filled the youngster with both excitement and fear. Because even though everyone assured Tra Lee that he was actually an adult named Nom Maa, he *felt* like a little boy, and a lonely one at that. Saying good-bye to Master Babukas, Master Qwa, and all the others had been extremely painful because they were the equivalent of family. Even so the chance to escape the endless drudgery of his lessons and explore what he thought of as the real world held a great deal of allure.

Lee's thoughts were interrupted as the wagon jolted to a stop, and the driver looked back over his shoulder. Though unaware of the youngster's identity, he believed in the Saa (Way), and had agreed to deliver the boy as a favor to a monk named Suu Qwa. "This is where you get off, son . . . That's the runner's guild on the far side of the street. Watch out for traffic as you cross the street."

Lee said, "Thank you," and jumped off the tailgate. A member of the Dib Wa, disguised to look like a street sweeper, watched the boy cross the street and start up the broad marble stairs. Once the Divine Wind entered the building the warrior's mission would be complete, and he would leave.

As Lee made his way upward he took note of the fluted columns, and above them, an entablature into which the words DEPARTMENT OF COMMUNICATIONS had been chiseled more than a thousand years before. Had the runner's guild been born there? Created by displaced civil servants? Or was the fact that the guild was headquartered in that particular building a matter of coincidence? Such were the questions that Master Qwa might well have asked him. Not with an eye to actually solving the mystery, but to encourage his student to question everything around him and try to make sense of the universe.

Lee switched his attention to the teenage guards who stood to either side of the large double doors. Beggars were a continual problem, and one of the apprentices was already moving to intercept the lad, when Lee spoke. "My name is Dor, and I'm here to see my father, Jak Rebo."

The apprentice had been warned to expect such a visitor and ran a critical eye over the boy. He had black hair that didn't look quite right somehow, the kind of clothes that the offspring of a rich merchant might wear, and didn't bear much of a resemblance to his father. But who knew? Perhaps the lad took after his mother. "All right," the guard said gruffly. "Follow me."

Lee followed the older boy into a huge lobby. The center area was filled with an eclectic collection of worn chairs, couches, and tables. About half were occupied by journeymen and masters. Most were awake, sipping their morning caf and chatting with each other, but some were asleep. Or unconscious. The entire area was strewn with empty bottles, dirty plates, and stray pieces of clothing. Youngsters no older than himself had been put to work collecting trash and mopping the floor.

The guard led Lee over to a desk and mumbled something to a man seated behind the tall marble-faced counter. The clerk peered down over the edge. He had narrow-set eyes, a nose that looked as if it had been permanently flattened by someone's fist, and cheeks that bore a two-day supply of black stubble. "Stay right there, boy . . . I'll send for your father."

Lee nodded mutely, eyed the faded mural on the wall opposite him, and wondered if the scenes depicted there were historically accurate or the product of some artist's imagination. There was what appeared to be a star map, hundreds of fine silver lines that ran back and forth between solar systems, and the motto: "We bind the empire together."

Rebo rounded a corner, saw Lee standing in front of the reception counter, and was struck by how small he was. He forced a smile. "Dor! It's good to see you, boy! How's your mother?"

It took Lee a fraction of a second to react to the new name. He turned, scampered toward Rebo the way he'd seen other boys do, and was swept off his feet. "Good job," the runner said in a voice too low for anyone else to hear. "Just stay by my side. We have some errands to run."

Lee felt his feet hit the floor and hurried to keep up as the runner escorted him back outside. It was a five-block walk to the public market, and all of the youngster's senses were engaged as he absorbed the many sights, sounds, and smells that the city had to offer. Rebo led Lee past countless tables loaded with all manner of fascinating objects, and stopped in front of a booth that specialized in children's clothing. The runner spoke to the proprietress, and it wasn't long before Lee found himself outfitted with three sets of used but extremely serviceable clothing. Rebo used *his* garments, those that Qwa had chosen for him, as trade-ins. That annoyed Lee and the moment he left the curtained off changing area he hurried to make his displeasure known. "Citizen Rebo . . ."

"Father, Dad, or sir, is acceptable," Rebo put in. "Citizen Rebo is not. Start over."

"*Father*," Lee said imperiously, "these clothes are *used*."

"Yes, they are," Rebo agreed mildly. "Which will help you blend in. Follow me. You'll need some personal items plus a pack to carry them in."

An hour later Lee found himself in possession of a nearly full pack. In addition to some new underwear, he was now the proud owner of a comb he didn't really need as yet, a new toothbrush, a washcloth, a towel, two bars of soap, a metal mirror, four candles, six boxes of waterproofed matches, a knife, fork, and spoon plus a metal mug, and two brand-new blankets. They were double-thick and gray in color.

"Why did you buy *new* blankets?" Lee inquired, as Rebo helped him strap them to the bottom of the pack frame. "There were plenty of used ones."

"True," the runner agreed, "but they were thin, not to mention filthy, and blankets are extremely important. Later, when we have time, we'll sew them together to make a sleeping bag." So saying, Rebo turned away, leaving a surprised Lee to heft his own pack and carry it down the aisle. It weighed a good twenty-five pounds, and while the youngster wanted to complain, he was determined not to.

The next stop was the booth located directly below a

large papier-mâché globe that had been painted to look like a free-floating eyeball complete with a black pupil and lots of squiggly red veins. The oculist was a friendly sort who helped Rebo sort through three baskets of handmade spectacles until the runner found some glasses that met his needs. The last pair had been broken in a fistfight, and while Rebo could read without them, objects more than a hundred feet away were blurry.

With that out of the way the runner sought out a booth hung with all manner of charms, amulets, and magical paraphernalia. All of which were useless pieces of junk insofar as Brother Qwa and the rest of the brethren were concerned, but which Tra Lee found to be fascinating, even though the boy knew that *true* strength came from within.

Rebo might have agreed with that, but liked to cover his bets, and always felt better when he had an edge. Having completed a lengthy discussion with the proprietor, the runner purchased an all-purpose amulet—which if properly cared for—was guaranteed to protect its owner from the skin pox, wild eye, stab wounds, night sweats, bad dreams, poor digestion, and a host of other maladies. Money changed hands, the runner secured the object around his neck, and the errands continued.

The next stop on their morning rounds was an armorer's shop. It occupied a long narrow storefront. Racks of weapons lined both walls and led to a counter in the back. There were three other customers, all examining firearms under the watchful gaze of a salesman, who was heavily armed himself. A wise precaution in Seros.

Rebo nodded to the grizzled old man who emerged from a back room to greet him and laid both of his weapons on the counter. "I need ammo for these . . . Say five hundred rounds for the Crosser, and fifty for the Hogger."

The armorer took the ten millimeter, released the fifteen-round magazine, and thumbed a cartridge onto the palm of his hand. Then, bringing a small lens to bear, he eyed the hand-loaded round. "Nice work, but mine is better. When do you need them?"

"By tonight," Rebo replied.

"Are you sure?" the shopkeeper inquired skeptically. "I'd have to charge you an extra 10 percent for such a short turnaround."

Rebo nodded. "I'm sure. How 'bout the Hogger?"

The armorer traded weapons, broke the single-shot weapon open, and withdrew a long cartridge that had a blunt nose. "A .30-30," the old man mused. "I don't see a whole lot of these. Sure, I can handle them. Come back about six o'clock."

Rebo was about to reply when he heard a *swish,* followed by a solid *thunk,* as steel struck wood. Both men turned in time to see Lee remove a second knife from the countertop and throw it at the circular target that hung against the opposite wall. It penetrated the bull's-eye one inch from the first blade and continued to vibrate. The old man raised an eyebrow. "Your son is pretty good with a knife."

"Yes," Rebo said mildly, "he is. The little devil has been practicing. I'll take both of those knives. Let's have a belt sheath for one—and a forearm sheath for the other."

Fifteen minutes later Rebo and the newly armed boy stepped out into the sunlight. Lee knew that other boys his age carried weapons, but had never been allowed to do so himself, and was very conscious of the blades that the runner had purchased for him. He hooked his thumbs under the pack's straps and looked up at Rebo. "Thank you for the knives, Father."

The runner nodded. "You're welcome. Use the belt knife

for eating, cutting rope, and other chores. Keep the other blade hidden. Where did you learn to throw a knife like that anyway?"

"I took martial arts classes one hour a day, three days a week," Lee replied. "It was fun."

Odds were that the boy had never suffered so much as a bloody nose and had no idea what it was like to participate in a *real* fight, but Rebo kept such thoughts to himself. "Good. It's nice to know that you can handle yourself. Come on, let's take that pack back to the guild and go find some lunch. I don't know about you—but I'm hungry."

As the two of them set off, a customer emerged from the store behind them and squinted into the sun. Though dressed in everyday attire, there was something about the precision of his movements that suggested a military background. He waited for his quarry to establish a sufficient lead, stepped off the curb, and followed the pair west. The word on the street was that the black hat sect would pay five gunars for information leading to the apprehension of a boy similar to the one up ahead. But was this the correct child? Only time would tell.

Jevan Kane paused in front of a store, pretended to peer in through the window, and took the opportunity to make sure that no one had followed him. Because, while the Techno Society maintained a run-down office near the public market, the location of the organization's actual headquarters was a well-maintained secret, a secret intended not only to conceal the extent of the society's resources, but to keep the government in the dark and prevent thievery. Thanks to Milos Lysander and his followers, the group had recovered thousands of high-tech artifacts over the years, and they were valuable.

Satisfied that no one had followed him, Kane turned into a narrow passageway and paused in front of a nine-foot-tall barrier. It was made out of ornamental iron and could withstand the impact of a battering ram if necessary. There was a distinct *click* as the operative pressed his thumb against a print-sensitive pad, and the gate swung open. Kane stepped through, heard a *clanging* sound as it closed behind him, and continued on his way.

A security camera mounted over Kane's head whirred gently as it followed the operative down the passageway to the point where a heavy metal door barred further progress. There was a pause as a guard eyed the operative through a peephole, followed by a momentary spill of artificial light as the door opened and Kane was admitted. A small man with nervous hands waited to greet him. He was dressed in a nondescript gray tunic and matching trousers. "You're late," Ron Olvos said accusingly. "The rest of the council is waiting."

"It couldn't be helped," Kane replied, as the two men made their way through a brightly lit corridor. "We tossed the second inn, but the sensitive wasn't there. Either she's very good at what she does, or very lucky, not that it makes much difference."

"Why *her* of all people?" Olvos wondered out loud. "There are thousands of spooks, many of whom are quite amenable. Why couldn't the founder channel himself through one of them?"

"I don't know," Kane answered honestly, "except to say that Lysander was often difficult to communicate with on *this* plane of existence, so why would he be any different on the next? Anyway, given the fact that the better part of a year has gone by since his death, and this is the first time the founder has seen fit to come through, it seems safe to assume that there's something about this particular sensitive that he likes. And we need to talk to him! The old bastard knows where the artificial intelligence named Logos is hiding, Logos knows how to reactivate the star gates, and the portals are the centerpiece of our plan. Like it or not, Norr is the key."

Olvos winced at the use of the word "bastard," wondered if Lysander could listen in from beyond the grave, and hoped that he couldn't. Servos whined and double doors swung open to allow the men to enter what had been a huge vat but now served as a circular conference room. In spite of the slightly astringent tang of vinegar that still hung in the air, the rest of the enclosure was focused on the future and equipped accordingly. Soft white light flooded the tank, a holo projector hung above the round table, at which six of the seven council members were seated, data scrolled across the curvilinear computer screens that lined the walls, and video supplied by a reactivated satellite showed that a storm was brewing off to the east.

Olvos took his seat while Kane stepped into the keyhole-shaped slot that had been cut into the table. Despite the fact that countless generations of interbreeding had erased most of the physical characteristics that once served to divide the human race into ethnic groupings, there were occasional throwbacks, and Kane was one of them. Whereas everyone else in the room had black hair, brown eyes, and olive-colored skin, the operative had longish blond hair, blue eyes, and white skin. They were looks that had turned him into something of an outcast as a child, but were later transformed into a blessing when they brought him to Lysander's attention. Because unlike the society around him, which placed a high value on conformity, the scientist had a preference for that which was unusual.

"Please excuse my tardiness," Kane said evenly, "but the last twenty-six hours have been rather hectic to say the least. As all of you know by now the founder has returned, and judging from the comments he made to the crowd gathered in the actor's hall, he continues to have a keen interest in our affairs."

"There is no excuse for tardiness, or any other form of failure," Omar Tepho said disparagingly as he turned to face the operative. Like Kane's, the chairman's body fell well outside the bounds of what could be considered normal. His skull was lumpy rather than smooth, one eye was higher than the other, and his ears stuck out from the sides of his head. And, as if that weren't enough, Tepho had been born with a spinal deformity. All of which explained why he had literally moved into the city's only library at the age of ten, taught himself to read, and eventually become so knowledgeable that Milos Lysander had taken the young man in. It also explained Tepho's burning desire to reestablish science, especially *medical* science, which had once been capable of preventing conditions such as his. And because of his passion, plus the lingering effects of an extremely cruel childhood, Tepho was absolutely pitiless where subordinates were concerned.

That alone was sufficient to send something cold trickling into Kane's veins, but when the wall behind the chairman appeared to shimmer, the operative knew there was something more to fear as well. No one knew how the bond between the rare combat variant and the malformed intellectual had been established—only that it had. Which meant that anyone who wanted to kill Tepho, would have to kill the being named Shaz first, something no one had been able to do. Partly because the variant could blend with whatever background he stood in front of, partly because of his superfast reflexes, and partly because he was very well armed. All of which made Tepho even *more* intimidating—something that Kane struggled to ignore. "I understand that."

"Good," Tepho said coldly. "You may proceed."

Kane swallowed. "After a long period of relative inactivity it now appears that we have a unique opportunity to reestablish communications with the founder, and have benefit of his counsel. No one that I know of fully understands how sensitives do what they do, or why some discarnate beings choose one channel over another, but such is the case. And, as I was saying to Council Member Olvos moments ago, I believe that every effort must be made to locate and secure the sensitive called Lanni Norr."

"So, what's the plan?" council member three demanded. "It's a big planet, and while significant, our resources are limited."

"The first thing to do is watch the spaceport," Kane answered confidently. "Norr knows someone is chasing her, and a ship is due, so she could attempt to leave the planet."

"And if she doesn't?" council member five inquired mildly. "What then?"

"Then she'll be trapped," Kane replied, "and we'll have time to track her down."

"Good," Tepho put in smoothly. "I'm sure I speak for the entire council when I say that we have complete confidence in you."

Kane knew the statement amounted to both an endorsement and the first step in placing the blame squarely on his shoulders should something go wrong. The operative nodded humbly. "Thank you. Your faith gives me strength. I will do everything in my power to find the sensitive and bring her in."

The operative felt a hand caress his shoulder, turned to see the air shimmer, and heard Tepho laugh.

The once vast spaceport had shrunk over the years as newly constructed warehouses crept in to claim increasingly large sections of its blast-scarred surface, and the elements continued to eat away at what remained. At least one square mile of surface remained, however, most of which was currently hidden beneath rows of brightly colored tents, open-air booths, and a swirling crowd. They were present to celebrate Ship Down, a biannual holiday with religious, cultural, and commercial significance.

The cessationists were there, praying that the shuttle *wouldn't* appear, thereby cutting Anafa off from external sources of cultural contamination, as were the metal men, who worked to convince the crowd that technology was good.

Of course most people were there to buy the goods that had been brought in from distant provinces, to eat the food available from countless booths, and to bear witness to whatever did or didn't happen. Would the shuttle appear? As it had for countless generations? Or would this be the year when Anafa was finally cut off for good? That day was coming, everyone knew it, but no one seemed to care enough to do anything about it. Not the elderly woman who ruled the planet, not the provincial governor, and not the people themselves. So the shuttle, or the possibility of it, drew a crowd plus the pickpockets, con men, and fortune-tellers who had come to depend on it.

One such woman, an elderly crone with gray-streaked hair, a backpack, and a walking stick, limped through the crowd hawking her services. "See into the future! Cast spells on your enemies! Speak with dead! Five minutes for one thin gunar."

But there were plenty of such services available, most of which were fake, so the heavily disguised Lanni Norr didn't find many takers. Not that she required them since the gold coins strapped around her middle were more than sufficient to her immediate needs. No, the disguise was intended to fool whoever had invaded the Market Street Inn, and if rumors could be believed, not only murdered four people but broken into her room. Or what *would* have been her room had the sensitive not checked into another hostelry an hour before.

Now she was killing time, waiting for the shuttle to arrive, with every intention of being aboard the ship when it lifted off. She still planned to find a refuge in the country, but on some other planet, a long ways from Anafa. Norr gave an involuntary jerk as someone touched her arm—and whirled to confront a liveried footman rather than the assassin she had imagined. His distaste for her was apparent in both the frown he wore and an air of stiff formality. "My mistress would like to engage your services. Please follow me."

Norr swore silently, but knew she should accept the commission, if only to protect her disguise. She reached out to take possession of the footman's arm. "Why, thank you, deary," the sensitive cackled suggestively. "I'd be happy to follow a strapping young man such as yourself!"

The footman shuddered as the crone's grubby fingers made contact with his immaculate sleeve, allowed the fortune-teller to transfer some of her weight to his arm, and escorted Norr through the crowd. It was a relatively short journey to the point where a fabric-draped litter rested on fold-down legs. Incense wafted out of small braziers mounted at either end of the conveyance, thereby making the air fit to smell for the individual closeted within. Four litter bearers, each armed with identical wooden cudgels, kept onlookers at a distance. Norr couldn't see through the gauzy material that guarded the occupant's privacy, but there was no denying the femininity of the voice that came from inside. It was light, musical, and a little girlish. "Good afternoon . . . Thank you for coming."

Norr felt a moment of envy, a fleeting desire to live the girl's life rather than her own, but that was quickly superseded by a sense of deep sorrow. "You are welcome, deary," the sensitive replied soothingly. "Why do I feel such a deep sense of sadness around you? Like an emptiness that cannot be filled. A lover's spat perhaps?"

There was a pause followed by the sudden rustle of fabric as curtains parted. The face that appeared in the gap between them was perfectly symmetrical, but too pale to be entirely healthy and framed by a fall of luxuriant black hair. Norr found herself looking into two almond-shaped eyes, both of which were protected by long lashes, and shiny with pent-up tears. *"No,"* the young woman replied emphatically. "There is no lover. Nor is there likely to be, not since the accident." So saying the girl pulled a coverlet aside to reveal that most of her right leg was missing. The stump was neatly bandaged and wrapped with a lavender ribbon. "Can one such as myself ever find happiness?" the woman inquired desperately. "Or should I forsake all hope?"

Norr felt that the answer was, "Yes," that there was very little possibility of the sort of idealized romance the girl had long dreamed of, but "saw" another possibility for her client. One that could generate even greater happiness in the long run. "There is a young man, who though not as comely as some, loves you deeply. He's not the stuff of dreams, deary, but your disability has in no way reduced his ardor, and he needs that which you would bring into his life. For while you are comfortable with people, he is not, and while the arts are second nature to you, he struggles to master them."

The girl frowned, registered a look of utter surprise, and said, "Lars? Do you mean *Lars?*"

"I know not his name," Norr answered, "but only that which lies in his heart."

"Thank you!" the girl whispered gratefully. "Thank you very much," and pressed five gunars into the sensitive's hand. The curtain closed, orders were given, and the litter was hoisted off the ground. Norr was left to watch as the brightly clad footman forced a hole in the crowd, and her client was borne away.

The sensitive had just pocketed her fee, and was about to move on, when an all-too-familiar feeling descended upon her. Not at her behest, but because an extremely powerful entity wanted to manifest through her and was determined to do so. Normally such an invasion was impossible unless Norr opened herself to it, but the process of giving the young woman a reading had opened the door, and someone was determined to force his way through.

The sensitive said, "No!" out loud, but discovered that it was too late, as Milos Lysander brushed her identity aside and took control of her body. In fact there was nothing Norr could do other than go along for the ride as her disembodied guest guided her physical body over to a platform established by a mime, shoved the unfortunate performer off his perch, and mounted the riser. Words started to flow from his, no *her* mouth, and the deep booming voice soon drew a crowd.

The mime attempted to reclaim his platform, received a backhanded blow for his trouble, and fell onto his back. That elicited laughter from the still-growing crowd. Inspired by the attention denied him in the past, the mime decided to incorporate the old crone into his act by imitating her, striking all sorts of silly postures, and generally making a fool of himself. Lysander was apparently oblivious to the performer's antics and continued to speak as if to a convention of his peers.

"And so," the scientist continued, "while the spaceships that continue to link the remnants of the old empires together do us a service, their very presence serves to sap our leaders of ambition. Soon that will end, however, as the last of the great vessels die, and mankind is trapped on a thousand islands. It doesn't have to be that way however. Rather than mourn the starships we should strive to replace them! Not with new hulls, but with the very technology that rendered them obsolete once before. Will such an effort require sacrifice? Of course it will . . . But nothing worth having comes without effort. The first step is rise up against your do-nothing government and overthrow it! Then, once the regressionists have been deposed, it will be possible to . . ."

The crowd never got to hear what it would be possible to do, because while passive in many respects, the empress took an active interest where her power was concerned. That's why her so-called monitors attended every event of any size and took steps to intervene when would-be dissidents stepped out of line. Ten of her operatives had pushed their way into the crowd and were intent on reaching the platform, when they were intercepted by three heavily robed metal men. Wood clanged on metal as the government agents brought their nightsticks into play, and both contingents were attacked by the rowdier members of the crowd.

Seeing an opportunity not only to wreak revenge, but to reclaim his personal property, the mime jumped Lysander from behind. The unexpected attack was sufficient to loosen the invading spirit's grip on Norr's body, thereby giving the sensitive the opportunity she'd been hoping for. Norr pushed Lysander out of her body, slammed the door behind him, and fell onto the mime. The impact knocked the breath out of the unfortunate performer. Norr took advantage of the opportunity to regain her feet, gather her belongings, and fade into the crowd. Had anyone sought to follow they would have come across a wig, a gob of wax that had been shaped into a bulbous nose, and a dusty black robe. Search as they might, the crone had ceased to exist.

Out beyond the edge of Anafa's atmosphere the fabric of space parted just long enough for an object to leave the dimension called hyperspace and enter the system. Though large by human standards, the ship was tiny when compared with the planet's moons, or the world itself, a fact not lost upon the artificial intelligence who thought of herself as *Shewhoswimsamongthestars.* Because as time passed, and she grew gradually weaker, everything seemed more threatening than it had been thousands of years before. So much so that the AI had even considered dropping into orbit around a stable planet and placing her systems on standby as other members of the brother-sisterhood had done. But to retire, to truly retire, would be to exist without purpose. Something the starship couldn't countenance.

So, ignoring the painlike feedback that trickled into her brain from hundreds of ailing components *Shewhoswims* slid past a half-slagged weapons platform, a space station that had gone off-line more than six hundred years before, and a mothballed in-system liner before dropping into a stable orbit. A quick scan of the standard communications frequencies was sufficient to confirm what the AI already knew: The planet Anafa and the people who lived on it were still on the long sad slide back into technological barbarity—the only kind of barbarity that mattered to the spaceship, since there was only one thing that could save *Shewhoswims* and her sisters from eventual dissolution, and that was for the humans to rediscover the wonders of science.

The AI allowed herself the electronic equivalent of a sigh, sent the usual messages to passengers waiting in her belly, and prepared the only shuttle she had left. There had been four originally, but the others had been taken out of service over the years and been cannibalized for parts.

Once the shuttle was loaded *Shewhoswims* shifted a portion of her intelligence to the smaller ship, took command, and broke away. While most of Anafa's surface was tan, it was broken here and there by the occasional patch of blue, with white frosting at both poles. Armadas of clouds swept across the planet's surface and rose to envelop the shuttle as it bumped down through the atmosphere and sent a sonic boom rolling across the city of Seros.

People shaded their eyes, pointed toward the sky, and tracked the speck as it circled the spaceport. The ship was back! The news raced through the streets. And while of interest to everyone, the shuttle's reappearance had a galvanizing effect on those gathered at the spaceport, as the cessationists began to wail and the metal men took advantage of the opportunity to reemphasize the virtues of technology.

Then, once the spaceship put down, and its passengers began to disembark, the crowd swirled as everyone sought to catch a glimpse of the daring, or possibly desperate people, who had gambled their lives and won. The group made its way down the battered ramp and squinted into the bright sunlight, before passing through the corridor that opened before them, was disparate to say the least. Some carried boxes between them, rare merchandise most likely, acquired on some distant world and soon to grace wealthy homes on Anafa. But most arrived with little more than the packs on their backs, eyes darting this way and that, still marveling at the fact that they were alive. A few faces lit up with joy as family members rushed forward to greet them, but most of the travelers went unrecognized and were soon lost in the crowd.

Then, once the last person had disembarked, an equally interesting procession began. Although there was no charge for boarding the ship, and hadn't been for hundreds of years, people were admitted through the main hatch on a first-come, first-served basis. That meant those who wanted to take their chances on the ship were motivated to arrive early. Because while some shuttles lifted half-empty, others were unable to accommodate all the people who wanted to leave, and many decades had passed since a ship had returned for a second or third load.

So, eager to secure their places in the ship's belly, a steady stream of travelers boarded the shuttle. All were heavily burdened because it had been a long, long time since anyone had been served a meal aboard a starship, and those who failed adequately to provide for themselves could starve or be forced into virtual slavery by the more provident.

Most of the onlookers were simply curious and stared at the departing passengers with the same morbid fascination normally reserved for condemned criminals. There were others, however, like the father on the lookout for his runaway daughter, a merchant who wanted to ensure that an employee boarded safely, and the monk assigned to watch for a very special little boy. An assignment that he believed to be a complete waste of time since black hat spies had spotted the so-called Divine Wind taking his daily lessons on the roof of the red hat monastery that very morning, a fact that suggested that the would-be imposter and his corrupt supporters were too frightened to board the ship and make the long, dangerous journey to the city of CaCanth. A trip that the *real* Nom Maa had begun—some six months earlier.

With that in mind, Brother Wama leaned on his staff, enjoyed the warmth of the sun, and eyed the departing passengers. A merchant's second son passed, complete with an entourage and enough supplies to sustain a small army. The merchant and his retinue were followed by a couple whose possessions hung under the pole that was stretched between them, a young man bent nearly double under the weight of his pack, and a sad looking fellow followed by an expensive coffin and four pallbearers, laborers from the look of them, who would exit the shuttle as soon as they had been paid.

The monk's thoughts were interrupted as one of his superiors appeared at his elbow, a rather nasty sort who aped humility but clearly aspired to higher office. "How's it going?" Brother Fiva inquired, eyeing the steady stream of passengers. "Have you seen any sign of the imposter?"

"No," the monk replied cautiously. "Not so far. In fact, come to think of it, I haven't seen any children at all."

"Not that you know of anyway," Fiva said critically. "For example, who, or what is hidden in the bundle that those people are carrying on that litter? You can't tell from here."

"That's true," Wama admitted. "But I don't see . . ."

"No," Fiva interrupted. "I'm sure you don't. But there will be plenty of time to meditate on your shortcomings during the trip to Pooz. Someone must make the journey, and you were chosen. It's unlikely, but if the imposter's supporters managed to smuggle the little rascal aboard, the boy will be forced to reveal himself during the journey. If that occurs, it will be your task to kill him. Do you understand?"

"Yes," the monk replied doubtfully. "But the trip will take weeks, I have no supplies, and . . ."

"On the contrary, your supplies are ready and waiting," the older man replied, and toed a pack Wama hadn't noticed before. "Good luck with your pilgrimage," Fiva added sanctimoniously. "Our prayers will be with you."

That was when Wama realized that Fiva was taking advantage of the situation not only to place an agent on the ship but to open a slot for one of his toadies. The monk opened his mouth to object, saw that two members of the Dib Wa had materialized behind Fiva's back, and bowed. "Can I have a weapon?"

"You'll find a weapon in your pack," Fiva replied gravely. "Make good use of it should you have the chance. Otherwise, report to the brothers on Pooz. They will find appropriate work for you to do."

Mas Wama considered making a run for it, knew the Dib Wa would catch him, and was forced to accept his fate. His family would wonder what had happened to him, but he would attempt to send a message back. He bent over, lifted the pack, and hoisted it up onto his back. Then, without so much as a backward glance, the monk boarded the ship.

Brother Fiva smiled thinly, waited for another five minutes, and had the pleasure of watching *another* member of the black hat sect follow Wama into the waiting shuttle. The young woman was extremely well trained, and if she noticed his presence, gave no sign of it. A single long black braid hung down the nun's back, she was dressed in inexpensive clothes, and carried a fat satchel in each hand. They were heavy and scraped the ground occasionally. In the unlikely event that the imposter *had* been smuggled onto the ship, it was safe to assume that the boy would be accompanied by at least a couple of Dib Wa bodyguards. They would almost certainly identify Wama as belonging to the black hat sect—and could be counted on to reveal their true identities by killing the unfortunate monk.

If the young woman could neutralize both the bodyguards and the boy by herself, then she would. If not, she would keep the party under surveillance and request assistance from the black hat monastery on Pooz. It was a good plan, which was to say a convoluted plan, and Brother Fiva was satisfied that it would work.

A final announcement was made, and just as the shuttle's hatch started to close, a man with blond hair pushed his way out of the crowd. He said something to the metal men that accompanied him and pointed toward the shuttle. Metal clanged on metal as the robots ran up the ramp and slipped aboard just seconds before the hatch closed.

Then, having used her external loudspeakers to warn the crowd, *Shewhoswims* fired her repellers and pushed the planet away. With that accomplished, it was a simple matter to engage her drives, gain the necessary altitude, and return to the blackness of space. That was her purpose—and it felt good to be alive.

THREE

The Planet Anafa

*Even third-class passengers will enjoy comfortable quarters,
fine food, and a wide variety of entertainment. Please join us
as we celebrate the addition of a new ship to the company's
fleet, establish a new link to the civilized planets, and place a
new star in the heavens.*

—Excerpt from the promotional holo distributed to the Interplanetary
News Association (INA) on the day that the sentient vessel
Shewhoswimsamongthestars officially went into service

Shewhoswimsamongthestars *guided the shuttle into its*
docking bay with the ease of a beggar pocketing a coin.
Rebo, Lee, and all the rest of the passengers felt a distinct
thump as the smaller vessel's skids made contact. That was
followed by the muffled whine of unseen machinery. Different people reacted in different ways. Those who had never
been on a ship before, and Rebo sensed that was the majority of them, were round-eyed with fear, while the runner
and a few like him focused on the next step in the process.
Lee, who had only recently been allowed to exit the coffin in
which he had been brought aboard, listened as the runner
spoke into his ear. "You'll notice we're positioned next to
the hatch. There's a reason for that. Right now the ship is
pumping air into the compartment where the shuttle is

stored. Once that process is complete the hatch will open, and we will be allowed to enter a decontamination chamber. A thick mist will be pumped into the compartment, but it won't hurt you. A second hatch will open a few minutes later. That's the good news. The bad news is that we'll have to tow the coffin, plus the supplies stored inside it clear into the hold. Got it?"

"Yes," Lee replied sotto voce. "But why should I concern myself with such details? That's what I pay *you* to do."

Rebo's eyes narrowed slightly, but his voice remained level. "You should remember such things for *two* reasons. First, because it's what my son would do, and the best way to *play* a part is actually to live it. And second, if someone manages to kill me, you'll be on your own. Or perhaps that thought hadn't occurred to your supreme highness."

In all truth the thought *hadn't* occurred to Lee, and now that it had, the boy wondered if Brothers Babukas and Qwa should have sent a force of Dib Wa warriors to protect him as well. Still, true or not, that didn't give Rebo the right to be sarcastic. The youngster was about to say as much when the hatch opened, and everyone shuffled into a sterile-looking compartment. There were cries of alarm as jets of greenish mist were pumped into the chamber. It penetrated their clothing, found its way into even the most tightly wrapped packages, and made everything damp. However, thanks to the calm, nonchalant manner in which the more experienced travelers reacted, the rest were reassured and began to relax.

Then, once the decontamination process was complete, a final hatch opened to admit a wave of fetid air. The runner said, "Come on!" and pulled on the heavily loaded coffin. Lee had no choice but to do likewise. Two small wheels, both set into the foot of the box, allowed it to be towed so long as the surface beneath the coffin remained relatively flat. Two or three individuals dashed out of the shuttle ahead of them, but Rebo and his youthful charge were still able to establish a lead on the majority of the passengers, all of whom were burdened with supplies. Some of the ship's lights were functional, but not half as many as Rebo would have preferred, leaving the passengers with no choice but to make their way down a gloomy corridor, through widely spaced pools of blue-green light, and into a huge hold where thousands of cargo modules had once been stored. If one looked carefully it was still possible to see yellow grid lines under the filth that covered the deck, along with reference numbers on the bulkheads that were practically invisible beneath layers of head-high graffiti.

The runner paused to get his bearings, spied what he was looking for, and pointed to the far side of the hold. "Over there, son. Where that big beam hits the deck. That's where we want to go."

Though determined to help, Lee found it difficult to keep up, and quickly discovered that if he wanted to pull, rather than be pulled, it was necessary to jog rather than walk. Added to their difficulties was the fact that the cleverly concealed wheels were too small to pass over obstacles more than a couple of inches high. That meant the pair had to weave their way between cook fires that had only recently been extinguished, piles of trash that the ship's overworked maintenance bots had yet to remove, and the makeshift shelters left by the last group of passengers. All of which added a considerable amount of distance to the trip.

Even worse was the necessity to stop and lift the heavy container over a series of man-made barriers that looked as though they had been erected as a way to define someone's territory. Rebo swore mightily as he jerked the wooden box over the last waist-high wall and dragged the object toward the darkly shadowed corner ahead. The runner glanced back over his shoulder, saw that one of the merchants had dispatched a uniformed employee to secure the same spot, and realized that the other man was coming on strong. Rebo turned to Lee. "Run, boy! Put yourself in that corner and pull your knife! I'll be there as soon as I can."

Lee looked back, spotted the threat, and took off. He was a good runner, a *very* good runner, and flew across the intervening space. It wasn't until he had arrived and turned to face his pursuer, that the boy remembered to pull the belt knife. He felt scared as the full-grown man skidded to a halt not six feet away and laughed. He raised a cudgel over his head. "Skedaddle, runt . . . Or shall I drive your head down through your ass?"

The youngster was busy trying to summon some brave words when there was a loud report, the man pitched forward onto his face, and slid six inches across the deck. The boy looked up and saw Rebo lower the long gun that he carried across his belly. The runner turned to scan the immediate area. Then, satisfied that no one else was inclined to attack, the runner broke the Hogger open. A spent shell casing popped out. It took less than three seconds to insert a new cartridge and return the weapon to its holster. A wheel started to squeak as he took the coffin under tow.

It was the first time Lee had been exposed to a violent death, and he was still staring at the dead body when the runner arrived. "You k-k-killed him," Lee stuttered accusingly as the tears rolled down his cheeks.

"Yes," Rebo agreed. "Just like he would have killed *you*. Or me for that matter. That's how things are."

"But you shot him in the back!" Lee objected hotly. "That was why you told me to pull the knife, wasn't it? Not because you thought it would stop him, but so he would look at *me* rather than you!"

"So, what are you saying?" the runner inquired patiently. "That there's something inherently virtuous about shooting people from the front? I don't think so. Dead is dead. Speaking of which, search the body. Take anything of value."

Lee shook his head. "*No.* I won't."

"Yes," Rebo insisted. "You *will.* You promised to obey me. Remember?"

"Only if what you told me to do was moral," the boy replied stubbornly. "And stealing isn't moral."

"Oh really? Well, I suggest that you give the matter some additional thought . . . Let's say this guy has five gunars in his pocket. There isn't any way for you to convey the money to his family, and if we don't take them, then another passenger will. Plus, four months from now, while staying in some flea-bitten inn, we might need five gunars to buy food. Now, do as I told you."

As with all prime campsites the corner had been occupied recently and as Rebo went to work clearing the accumulated rubbish away, Lee stood over the corpse thinking about what the runner had said while trying to work up the courage required to touch the body. The way Rebo spoke to him was strikingly similar to the way Qwa lectured him, and distasteful though the situation was, the boy could see the logic involved.

Finally, after about five minutes had passed, he knelt next to the quickly cooling cadaver and apologized as he rifled through the dead man's pockets. "I'm sorry," the little boy said, "and I hope that was your last incarnation. But if enlightenment lays ahead rather than behind you, then I pray that you will find the experience that your soul needs most, and I apologize for my role in your death."

The search yielded two gunars rather than five, and the coins felt heavier than they should have. The journey had barely begun—but Lee felt as if he had traveled a long way.

In addition to the physical sensations associated with docking, Lanni Norr felt a confusing mixture of emotions wash around her. Anticipation, dread, hope, fear, joy, and sorrow all battered her senses and made it difficult to think. The sensitive did the best she could to block the input and focused her attention on those passengers who seemed to know what they were doing. She had never been off-planet before, but there were bound to be strategies that could be employed to gain small advantages, and the sensitive was determined to identify them.

But, as the shuttle touched down, Norr had other things to worry about. Primary among them was the fact that two metal men had boarded the shuttle and appeared to be looking for someone. And, given the fanatical way the machines had reacted to Lysander's speech, the sensitive had a pretty good idea of who that someone might be. The new disguise had fooled the robots up to that point—but how long before they saw through it? Based on the conversations taking place around her, it sounded as if the voyage would last for weeks, if not months. A long time in which to pose as a man.

The sensitive's thoughts were interrupted as the hatch opened, her fellow travelers poured into the larger ship, and Norr joined the stampede. Based on conversations she had overheard, and the speed with which the more experienced travelers exited the shuttle, it was clear that they hoped to claim the best spots for themselves.

But Norr's pack was extremely heavy, which meant that a lot of people arrived in the hold before she did and were already settling into their chosen nooks and crannies by the time she paused to look around. The sensitive noticed that while corridors led off into other parts of the ship, no one seemed interested in following them, and figured that there was a reason for that.

So what to do? That was when the sensitive noticed the maze of interlocking girders that crisscrossed the area above her head and spotted a black rectangle that might have been some sort of platform. And not just a platform, but the equivalent of a nest, which would be difficult for intruders to access.

Eager to find a way up, before someone else spotted the aerie, Norr followed a filthy bulkhead to one of the supporting members. Holes had been cut into the beam to make it lighter, and judging from the way they were spaced, would serve as a fairly efficient ladder.

Knowing the pack was too heavy to climb with, the sensitive dumped it onto the floor and fumbled for the fifty-foot length of cord that was included among her supplies. Then, having tied one end to the pack and slung her staff across her back, the young woman swarmed up the beam. A few moments later she was crouched on a beam thirty feet above the deck below.

One of the other passengers, a scruffy-looking male of indeterminate age, had just spotted the seemingly unguarded pack, and was in the process of making his way over to inspect it, when the object in question suddenly rose three feet into the air, and started to twirl. The would-be thief realized what was about to take place, produced a large folding knife, and flicked it open as he ran. In the meantime, someone fired a gun, and the resulting *boom* reverberated back and forth between the steel bulkheads as another property dispute was settled.

Norr saw the movement, hauled on the cord, and managed to heave the pack up over the ruffian's head. He jumped, attempted to slash the cord, and missed. The sensitive pulled again, had the satisfaction of seeing her belongings surge upward, and soon had them beside her. The thief offered a rude gesture and wandered away.

The twelve-inch beam led Norr out toward the middle of the hold, where a makeshift platform had been established. Four sheets of metal had been removed from some other part of the vessel, hoisted into place, and secured to the girders. The surface was surprisingly clean, which Norr took as a good omen, and helped finalize her decision. The sensitive knew she would have to find a place to hide her valuables while she went to fetch water, but that was a problem that could no doubt be solved, especially if she made some friends.

Of more concern were the metal men, who, unburdened by supplies or a need for territory, could be seen roaming the deck below. Norr knew that the machines would eventually focus their attention on her. That left the sensitive with two choices: She could cede the initiative to the robots and wait for the automatons to find her, or she could go after them. The second alternative was clearly the more appealing of the two—and the hunt was on.

The shuttle had landed aboard the ship, and passengers were streaming off, when a man and a boy towed a coffin past Brother Mas Wama. It didn't take a genius to figure out that the boy had been transported in the coffin, but why? Because he was the imposter? Or for a more mundane reason? A custody dispute perhaps—or something of that sort.

The second theory seemed more likely, especially since the boy lacked a retinue of bodyguards and boasted a full head of black hair. Still, members of the red hat sect's Dib Wa could be hidden among the other passengers, and there was the possibility of a wig. Wama resolved to investigate the matter once things settled down.

Gregarious by nature, Wama offered to help a young couple with their baggage, and the newlyweds were happy to have some help. All of the best spots had been taken by the time the odd threesome arrived in the hold, which left them with little choice but to take over one of the campsites out in the middle of the deck. They invited the monk to stay, and Wama, who saw no reason to strike out on his own, was quick to agree.

So, as the young couple went to work erecting a shelter that would provide them with a modicum of privacy, Wama opened his pack. It contained a generous quantity of simple but nutritious food, a pot, a bowl, some eating utensils, and a medical kit. But there was no sign of the weapon that he'd been promised, not until Wama hit the very last layer of supplies and discovered the red hat and robe.

That was when he understood what Fiva intended. If the boy and the imposter were one and the same, he and his retainers would be much more likely to trust a member of their own sect. So much so that it might be possible for Wama to approach the boy, wrap his fingers around the little rascal's throat, and throttle the villain to death before anyone could interfere. Such an assassination would mean certain death, of course, but the wheel of incarnation would inevitably turn and deliver him back to the physical world. Strangely, in spite of the comfort that the knowledge should have produced, the monk felt slightly sick to his stomach.

* * *

One of the things that Norr liked about the platform on which she had taken up residence was the ease with which she could monitor movements below. Especially those of the metal men, who continued to watch their fellow passengers like predators inspecting their prey.

Not too surprisingly, many of the people the machines continually peered at became annoyed and weren't hesitant to make their displeasure known. The sensitive had seen the robots subjected to verbal assaults, doused with slops, and struck with a wide variety of clubs. None of those actions served to discourage them.

Days had passed since the ship had broken orbit, or that's what Norr assumed, although she had no way to keep track. Now, having spied on most of the passengers without success, it appeared that the mechanical men were in the process of exploring the rest of the ship in case their quarry had taken up residence somewhere else. That's the way it appeared anyway, since one of the robots left at what seemed like regular intervals and was gone for what had to be hours. A logical move, all things considered, and one that Norr planned to take advantage of.

Having equipped herself with food, candles, and matches, the sensitive hid her pack high among the girders and took a long circuitous route down to the deck below. Hopefully, if luck was with her, the rest of the passengers would believe that she was still up on the platform.

Rather than call the metal men A and B, or 1 and 2, Norr had named them Fric and Frac. And it was easy to tell the two of them apart because even though their features were identical, the robots wore slightly different clothing. Fric's robe hung loose and was tattered at the bottom, while Frac used a length of rope to cinch his garment at the waist.

That's how the sensitive knew that Fric was the one she followed out of the hold and into the ship's darkened corridors. At first the young woman was concerned about stumbling into the robot, or falling into some unseen hole, but the metal man hadn't walked for more than a few yards when two beams of light splashed the hallway ahead and wobbled across the grimy bulkheads.

Surprised, but pleased regarding her ability to see, Norr followed along behind. Her staff, which was the only weapon the sensitive had, was slung across her back. At one point the brass-shod tip made contact with a bulkhead and made a distinct *click*. Two white eyes swiveled toward the rear as Fric turned, and Norr sidestepped into an open hatch. Five extremely long seconds passed while the robot listened for the sound to repeat itself and, not having heard it again, continued on his way.

Norr discovered that she had been holding her breath and gradually let it go. Then, moving carefully so as not to make the same mistake twice, the sensitive pulled the staff around so it was in front of her.

Then, hurrying forward in an attempt to make up for lost time, Norr continued to follow the machine down the corridor. Now, as the lights projected by the robot's "eyes" caressed the walls, the young woman began to understand why passengers preferred to travel in the ship's hold. One stretch of the passageway had been blackened, as if by a raging fire, and Norr caught a glimpse of a tracked maintenance bot as a small hatch opened to admit it.

Farther down the hall the sensitive passed the remains of what looked like a crumpled barricade, bullet-dimpled walls, and strange burn marks. Three minutes later Fric was forced to stop in front of a closed hatch. White spray paint had been used to scrawl the words, "This section contaminated—stay out!" over a poorly rendered skull and crossbones. The lights projected by the robot's "eyes" swung back and forth as Fric paused to look around, accepted the fact that he couldn't proceed any farther, and turned to retrace his steps.

Satisfied that Frac was too far away to be of assistance, and convinced that she would never get a better chance than the one at hand, Norr twisted both halves of her staff in opposite directions. There was a barely heard *click,* followed by the gentle whisper of steel, as the three-foot-long blade left its wooden scabbard. Fric heard the sounds, paused, and spoke. "Hello? Who's there?"

"*I'm* here," Norr replied as she stepped out of the shadows and into the glare provided by the robot's lights. "You know, the person that you and your friend have been looking for."

"Really?" the machine inquired skeptically. "How do I know you are telling the truth?"

"You don't," Norr said, thumbing the vibro blade's power switch. "But ask yourself this . . . Who else would want to remove your head?"

The blade hummed as it passed through the air and made a metallic *ka-chink* as it sliced through Fric's alloy skin. Electricity crackled, and the harsh smell of ozone scented the air as the weapon emerged from the other side. The robot's body collapsed into a heap even as his head bounced and rolled to an uneven stop.

Never having done battle with a robot before the sensitive half expected the severed head to speak, but Fric remained mute as she toed his metal skull and bent to pick it up. Twin beams still shot out of the metal man's "eyes" and

Norr made use of them to examine the metal cadaver. A quick search turned up a purse heavy with coins but nothing else. The sensitive tucked the find away and used the head to light the passageway ahead. Frac wouldn't allow himself to be taken so easily, Norr knew that, but progress had been made.

Lee opened the spigot and water rattled into the bottom of the badly dented bucket that Rebo had salvaged from a scrap heap. Everyone had to fetch their water, and in spite of the boy's protestations, the runner had assigned the task to him. And not just *that* task, but other chores as well, so that the first part of each artificial "day" was spent cooking, cleaning, and running errands. And what was Rebo doing during that time? Nothing other than sitting around guarding their supplies. A task that required little if any effort.

It wasn't fair, not by a long shot, and Lee could feel the resentment bubbling up from deep inside as he made use of both hands to lift the now-brimming bucket. "Resentment is like acid," Qwa maintained, "and if left unattended, it will consume your spirit." Skillful understanding should have been sufficient to ease Lee's discomfort, but it didn't. Just one more indication that the elder brothers were mistaken and the entire voyage was a waste of time.

"Can I help you with that?" The words arrived along with a hand that took up the slack and lightened the burden by half. The response was automatic, and it wasn't until Lee had already said, "Thank you," in the same tongue, that he remembered that he wasn't supposed to know Tilisi, the language that the monks and parishioners alike spoke among themselves. It was a terrible mistake, and Lee felt the blood rush to his face as he looked upward. And there, much to the boy's surprise, stood a man in a red hat and matching robe.

"Good morning," the monk said, as he switched back to standard. "My name is Brother Wama."

"It's a pleasure to meet you," Lee answered politely. "My name is Dor Rebo."

Wama nodded solemnly, and because the introduction had been made using standard, Lee wondered if he'd been mistaken regarding the Tilisi. *Besides,* the youngster reasoned, *it's the black hats that I should fear, not one of my own.*

That logic was so obviously correct that once the water had been delivered, and Wama departed the campsite, Lee saw no reason to mention the momentary lapse to Rebo.

In the meantime, Wama was not only stunned by the extent to which the trick had been successful but alarmed by what it meant. Because, there, against all odds, was the very imposter that the entire sect was searching for! There might be some alternative explanation for what the monk felt sure was a wig, but not for the boy's facility with Tilisi, which was virtually unknown beyond the realm of the church. His duty was clear. Like it or not, Wama would have to lure the lad away form the man with the guns and kill him. The knowledge was like acid and ate at the holy man's gut as he returned to the shared campsite and began to brew some tea.

In the meantime, from her vantage point about fifty yards away, the black hat assassin kept watch. Contact had been made, and while she couldn't be sure of the exact nature of what had transpired between monk and boy, Wama's body language had been quite expressive. The long face, slumped shoulders, and lethargic manner all hinted at the same thing. Be he right or wrong, Wama was convinced that he had found the imposter. But were bodyguards other than the man in red leather jacket present? And if so, would they move to block Wama? Only time would tell. Patience is a virtue where assassins are concerned—and the woman was content to wait.

The metal men didn't maintain a campsite, not the way the other passengers did, but when not out making their rounds they had a tendency to loiter in the vicinity of the jack panel from which power could be bled from the ship.

So, when Unit A-78214 returned to that point having just completed a tour of the hold, he expected to find 218 there to engage in the usual two-way exchange of data. However, rather than his companion, 214 was confronted by the other robot's lifeless head, which had been left resting on a cross member located directly above the power panel.

A human might have experienced a sense of horror, quickly followed by deep sorrow, but 214 wasn't equipped for that. He simply noted that 218 was off-line and that the perpetrator or perpetrators wanted him to be aware of it. But why? A poorly conceived attempt to intimidate him seemed like the most likely possibility.

The metal man tapped his temple, "heard" the hatch whir open, and felt for the lead that was stored there. A steady pull was sufficient to produce a four-foot length of thin cable. The jack made a *click* as it mated with the receptacle at the base of 218's metal skull and a "thought" was sufficient to stimulate the data flow. A few seconds later 214 had relived 218's journey, had "seen" the man with the vibro blade, and immediately recognized him as passenger "M" for male 146. A seldom-glimpsed individual who made his home on a platform suspended above the hold.

Now, having heard the human admit who he/she was,

214 superimposed him/her over an image of the crone at the spaceport and a picture of the woman who had appeared in the actor's hall. The video morphed only slightly as all of the images melted into one and the truth was revealed. The sensitive called Lanni Norr and passenger M-146 were one and the same.

The metal man processed something akin to a sense of completion, broke the connection with 218's CPU, and placed the skull back where he had found it. There was work to do, and like machines everywhere, 214 was determined to accomplish it.

The message arrived wrapped around a bolt. It missed Rebo's head by a matter of inches, *clanged* off the bulkhead beyond, and fell to the deck with a soft *thud*. The strange half-light that pervaded the hold made it impossible to see who had thrown the object, but the crude block letters on the parchment were evidence enough. "Hol died . . . and so will you!"

It didn't take a genius to figure out that Hol was the man Rebo had killed shortly after boarding the ship and that the message had been delivered by one of his friends. In fact the only real surprise lay in the fact that it had taken the merchant and his minions so long to get around to it. The runner sighed, took a seat on an empty crate, and fed another piece of the coffin into the tiny fire. The ship did a pretty good job of recycling the air, but its systems hadn't been designed to cope with dozens of open fires, and a permanent haze polluted the hold.

A good fifteen minutes or so passed before Lee returned from wherever he'd been. The last couple of weeks had been good for him, or so it seemed to Rebo, and the evidence was clear to see. The previously round-faced youngster looked a little leaner and was a lot more confident. He plopped down next to the runner and held out his hand. "Look, Father! I won them!"

Rebo looked, saw three coins, and raised an eyebrow. "You were gambling?"

"I was playing a game," Lee extemporized. "And I won!"

"You won *this* time," the runner countered. "But I predict next time will be different. Once they hook you your luck will start to fade."

Lee didn't want to believe it, but deep down he knew that Rebo was probably correct and sought to change the subject. "So what's the plan for today? Wait! Don't tell me, let me guess. You're going to sit around and watch the paint fade."

"No," Rebo replied as he poked the fire. "I have something a little more challenging in mind for today. Here, read this."

The runner handed the piece of parchment to Lee and saw the boy's eyes widen as he read the message. "They plan to kill you! I know who they are . . . They watch me all the time."

"Which is why you're going to stick around camp for a while," Rebo put in. "Now that they're committed to a fight, they may try to take you hostage."

"So, what should we do?" the boy inquired eagerly. "Build some defenses?"

"No, I have something else in mind," the runner responded. "And I need your help."

Lee felt something expand inside his chest. "Of course!" he said enthusiastically. "Tell me what I should do."

The conversation continued for about five minutes before the boy fumbled around in one of their packs, slipped a package into a pocket, and grabbed hold of the water bucket. None of which struck Tal, Hol's brother, as especially noteworthy. He had been watching the man called Rebo ever since one of his cronies had thrown the bolt. The whole idea was to scare the runner, prevent him from getting enough sleep, and attack when he was weak. Everybody agreed that the equivalent of two or three days without rest would be sufficient to wear him down. That's when Hol would be avenged.

Tal took pleasure in the thought and was still lingering over it, when a series of what he thought were gunshots went off behind him. The would-be killer dived for the deck, rolled onto his back, and looked for the source of the noise. "They were firecrackers!" one of his fellow employees said from a hiding place nearby. "The boy set them off!"

The boy? Tal scrambled to his feet, peered toward the distant fire, and felt something cold trickle into his veins. The runner was gone!

The quick series of explosions brought Norr up out of a sound sleep only to discover that she was in deep trouble. The metal man loomed above her. What looked like a silver snake launched itself from a commodious sleeve, landed on her chest, and sought her throat. The sensitive grabbed the object and tried to fend it off, but the device was too strong. Within a matter of seconds the synthetic serpent had wrapped itself around Norr's throat and swallowed its own tail.

As the metallic noose tightened, it became difficult to breathe, and the sensitive's lips and fingernails had already started to turn blue when the robot said something in the universal mech language, and the steel loop loosened slightly.

"Why are you doing this?" Norr demanded, still tugging at the collar. "Remove this thing!"

Frac's eyes lit up just as they had while exploring the ship, only the beams of light converged this time, and a picture formed in midair. The image was that of a man with blond hair, fair skin, and cold blue eyes. They seemed to stare straight through her. When he spoke the sound originated from the robot. "Greetings, Citizen Norr. My name is Jevan Kane. Please allow me to apologize for curtailing your freedom, but for reasons known only to him, the founder of the organization I represent has chosen to make himself heard through you alone. Once you and my representative arrive on Pooz you will be taken to our local headquarters, where you will allow Milos Lysander to manifest through you. You can participate in this process voluntarily, and be paid for your time, or do so under duress. The choice is yours."

"Really?" Norr inquired hopefully. "Then tell this freak to remove the thing that's wrapped around my neck. Once we reach Pooz I'll be glad to bring what's his name through—especially if you pay me." The last part was a lie, because if the man with the blond hair was stupid enough to let her go, the sensitive planned to destroy Frac and run like hell.

But the effort to deceive Kane was a waste of time because the holo had been prerecorded, the operative couldn't hear her, and there was nothing left to look at beyond a few motes of twirling light.

"I don't like it up here," Frac said flatly, as his head swiveled back and forth. "Collect your belongings. We leave in five minutes."

Norr tried to think of a way out of it, but she had been transformed into a slave, and slaves have no choice but to do as they are told.

* * *

Though not the best place in the hold, the blue-and-white- striped tent had been erected on one of the better sites and was quite comfortable on the inside. So much so that the merchant named Dom Fermo rarely left it, preferring to loll within, nibble on tidbits from his well-stocked larder, and enjoy the attentions of his teenaged clerk. A winsome boy, who though not especially skilled at the arts of love, more than made up for that shortcoming with a wealth of enthusiasm.

The two of them were resting, and communicating with each other in whispers, when the point of a knife penetrated the back wall of the tent, and there was a gentle ripping sound as the razor-sharp blade sliced down through the water-resistant fabric. Fermo had turned toward the sound, and was still in the process of preparing to shout, when Rebo stepped through the four-foot-long slit. The runner pointed the Crosser at the merchant, held a finger to his lips, and made his way across the cushion-strewn floor to the point where a striped curtain blocked the entrance. "Call your employees," Rebo demanded. "*All* of them. Or maybe you'd like to take a bullet. You decide."

Fermo had full, somewhat sensuous lips. They suddenly felt dry. He ran the tip of his tongue over them. "You won't hurt me? You promise?"

"I won't hurt you," Rebo agreed. "Now call them in."

The merchant lifted a bell. It rang once, twice, and three times, thereby signaling all of his employees to enter. And, as luck would have it, they were only twenty feet from the tent still discussing the firecracker incident when the summons was heard. They entered the tent one after another and stood with their backs to Rebo. The one called Tal noticed that his employer looked especially pale, and was about to ask about his health, when the runner fired his handgun. There were three consecutive reports and each bullet found its mark. Tal felt something knock his left leg out from under him, discovered he was on the floor, and grabbed his thigh. The others were rolling around right next to him. The sound of the gunshots was still fading away when the teenager started to cry and Fermo raised a pair of pudgy hands. "You promised you wouldn't hurt me!"

"And I didn't," Rebo replied. "Now here's the deal . . . I think you'll find that all three slugs went through flesh without touching bone. Assuming that you and the boy slap dressings on those wounds quickly enough, and apply some pressure, the bleeding will stop. Then, so long as you keep their wounds clean, these lads should be up and around by the time the ship enters orbit around Pooz."

"But *why?*" Fermo wanted to know. "Why did you attack us?"

Up until that point the runner had assumed that the merchant had been behind the threatening note, but it appeared that he'd been wrong. The employees had been acting on their own. Not that it made much difference. "Because of this," Rebo replied, tossing the parchment-wrapped bolt into the merchant's lap. "I have to sleep once in a while, and I figured a few bullet holes would slow your servants down. Now, remember what I said about those dressings, or they'll bleed to death right here."

Rebo brushed the curtain aside, backed through the resulting opening, and disappeared. Fermo sat there for a moment with his mouth hanging open, before turning to the boy and subjecting him to a frown. "You heard the man! Make some dressings. The worthless fools are bleeding on my carpet!"

All of his fellow passengers had heard the rapid-fire series of gunshots but none would meet Rebo's eyes as he wound his way back to the point where Lee was supposed to be guarding their campsite. Only the boy wasn't there.

The runner frowned and took a long slow look around. Lee knew he was supposed to stay close, especially now. That suggested that someone had seen an opportunity to grab the boy and taken it. But there were no signs of foul play, and everything looked as it should have, so maybe not.

But assumptions could be dangerous, and the runner decided to consult his neighbors. Perhaps they had seen something, or if not, would agree to keep an eye on his belongings while he was absent. Especially in return for a gunar or two. Rebo paused to slide a fresh clip into the Crosser, put a bullet in the chamber, and slid the other magazine into a pocket. Then, trying to look as nonchalant as possible, the runner went a-calling.

*Ancient machinery whirred as the lift carried them up*ward, and numbers flickered on the readout high above Lee's head. "How much farther?" the boy inquired. "You said ten minutes. My father will be worried."

"We're almost there," Wama replied soothingly. "Wait until you see it! The compartment contains hundreds of plants all grown together. It's a jungle! You can bring your father. Think how impressed he will be! Don't tell anyone else, though, or they'll come and ruin it."

Lee listened to the happy babble, but wasn't satisfied by it, and still felt uneasy as the lift jerked to a stop and the monk took his hand. "Come on!" Wama said cheerfully. "We'll take a quick look and go right back."

The air was different from thick acrid fug that filled the hold. It was warmer for one thing—and so heavy with moisture that Lee wondered if it might rain. And Lee had to admit that it *was* a wondrous place. Huge branches bore even larger leaves that arched out to touch each other. And the thick undergrowth pushed in from all sides to caress Lee's shoulders. "You were correct, Brother Wama. There *is* a jungle on the ship. But I'm supposed to be guarding the campsite, and my father will be angry."

"No problem," Wama assured Lee as he took hold of the boy's arm. "See that bright red flower? Hand me your knife and I'll cut it off for you. It will make a nice present for your father."

Rebo didn't strike Lee as a person who spent much time looking at flowers, but it would have been rude to say "No," so he removed the knife from its sheath and gave it to the monk handle first.

Wama accepted the blade, smiled a crooked smile, and spoke in Tilisi. "This brings me no pleasure, little brother. But the *real* Nom Maa is already on his way to the city of CaCanth—and there is no room for an imposter. Rest assured that I will free you from your body quickly, thereby sparing you unnecessary pain, and speeding you on your way."

Suddenly Lee understood the full extent of the errors he had made and felt a deep sense of shame. He answered in the same language. *"No!"*

Wama heard the word and felt the boy stomp on his largely unprotected foot at the same time. The monk let go of the imposter's arm, realized his mistake, and saw the youngster dash into the jungle. Wama swore, slashed at an intervening vine, and plunged in after him. A relay clicked somewhere—and it started to rain.

Rebo felt an empty gnawing sensation in the pit of his stomach. He figured that the better part of half an hour had passed, and what had originally been a sense of mild concern had been transformed into out-and-out fear. Someone had taken the boy, he felt sure of it, but the question was who? His initial inquiries had come up negative, and now, as the runner approached a neighboring campsite, the young couple who occupied it looked worried. The male said something to his wife, who picked up a homemade spear. Her husband was armed with a double-barreled flintlock pistol that he wore thrust through his wide leather belt. In spite of the fact that the design was hundreds of thousands of years old, the weapon itself was of recent manufacture and potentially dangerous. Conscious of that Rebo held his hands palms out and chest high. "Sorry to bother you . . . I'm looking for my son. He's been gone for quite a while now, and I'm worried about him."

The woman's expression seemed to soften somewhat. She knew the boy, everyone did, and liked him. "Yes, as a matter of fact I did. He and Brother Wama left quite a while ago. I don't know where they were going, but I'm sure he's safe."

Rebo had seen the monk around, noticed that he belonged to the red hat sect, and therefore assumed that he was okay. That assumption looked stupid now, and the runner silently cursed himself for his own stupidity as he thanked the couple for their help and turned away. All he could do was keep asking, and keep looking, in hopes that a miracle would occur. And a miracle *did* occur, although it didn't look like a miracle at first, and the runner didn't recognize it as such.

*Frac gave Norr a shove, and the sensitive, who was bur-*dened by her supplies, nearly fell. The snakelike collar was tight, *very* tight, and squeezed her neck from time to time as if to remind her of its presence.

Then, having regained her balance, Norr looked up to see a man coming her way. He was big and wore an expression that could only be described as grim. The sensitive had seen him before, from the platform above, living with a boy she assumed to be his son. Now, as if the memories were a trigger, she "saw" a man in scarlet robes lead the youngster away. The words seemed to speak themselves. "I know where your son is."

The collar tightened, Norr clawed at her throat, and fell to her knees. "You will remain silent!" the metal man commanded sternly. "Now get up."

Rebo paused as the woman struggled to rise under the weight of her pack. For reasons that were anything but clear, the robot had a female prisoner. The runner had never seen or heard of such a thing before but didn't consider it to be any of his business. Or wouldn't have, except for the words she had spoken, which were very interesting indeed. He moved to help her. "What was that? What did you say?"

"The female is not allowed to speak," the metal man said coldly. "Nor are you allowed to touch her. I suggest that you . . ."

"And I suggest that you shut the hell up," the runner said, drawing the Hogger and aiming the weapon at the robot's head. "Now, loosen the thing around her throat, or I'll blow whatever passes for your brains all over the deck."

Lacking weapons other than its hands, the machine had no choice but to comply. Norr felt the collar loosen slightly and reached up to massage her throat. "Thanks," she croaked.

"My son," Rebo insisted. "Where is he?"

Much to her joy the sensitive discovered that she had some unexpected leverage. "Free me, and I'll take you there," she replied.

Rebo turned to look into a pair of opaque sensors. "Free her. Do it now."

"No," number 214 replied. "That is forbidden. I must take her to . . ."

The runner squeezed the trigger, the Hogger bucked in his hand, and the resulting *boom* echoed back and forth between the steel bulkheads. The metal man's head snapped back, he collapsed onto the deck, and Norr felt the metal band fall away.

"All right," Rebo said. "You're free. Let's go."

"But my pack," Norr complained. "It's heavy."

"That's too bad," the runner replied unsympathetically. "Leave it if you want to. Now, where is my son?"

Norr "saw" thick green foliage part to let her pass, felt her heart start to pound, and knew that danger followed only steps behind. "Come on!" the sensitive exclaimed. "He's in trouble!"

The woman tried to run, but the pack was too heavy for that, and slowed her progress. Rebo swore, ordered the sensitive to dump her burden, and shouldered it himself. Then, following what she sensed to be the right path, Norr led the runner to what looked like a sealed hatch and pressed her palm against the cold, damp metal. There was a loud *hiss* as the door opened, and the sensitive stepped into the dimly lit interior. Rebo was hesitant, but she waved him in. "Come on! Hurry!"

The woman seemed so positive, so certain, that the runner obeyed. The hatch closed behind him, the lift jerked into motion, and the platform started to rise. "How do you know where my son is?" Rebo demanded suspiciously. "Are you friends with the monk?"

"No," Norr answered truthfully. "I'm a sensitive. I don't understand why I can see where your son is . . . But I can."

"And he's alive?"

Norr felt herself trip on a root, scramble to her feet, and start to run. But the monk was closer now, crashing through the bushes just behind her, yelling words in a language she had never heard before. "Yes," she said softly, "for the moment at least. We'll be there shortly."

The rain fell in sheets as Lee forced his body through a thicket of woody reeds only to confront solid durasteel. Brother Wama had intentionally herded him into a corner! Lee turned, ready to use his small size and greater agility to escape, but the monk was there with knife extended. Rivulets of rain streamed down across Wama's face, his robe was ripped and plastered to his body. Red dye ran down his skinny calves to pool around his sandals. "There's no point in making that which is already hard even more difficult," the monk said kindly. "I am truly sorry that it is I who must free you from your body, but your elders seek to deceive all of those who follow the way, and it is my duty to stop them."

Lee licked rainwater off his lips, noticed how sweet the liquid tasted, and stuck his right hand into his left sleeve. The second knife was there, hidden against just such an emergency, and his fingers closed around the hilt. But should he use it? According to the precepts he had been taught, Lee had an obligation to resist evil and to protect others, but was not required to defend himself. Yet he wanted to live, and more than that, to complete his life purpose. Assuming that the elders were correct regarding his spiritual identity. But there was no time for debate or meditation so the boy stepped forward. "It seems that there is one thing we agree upon," the boy said, "and that is the importance of duty."

Wama mistook the boy's movement for an act of surrender, and was caught completely unprepared as the youngster drew the second blade and brought it upward. The underhanded blow, plus the difference in their heights, meant that the knife entered the monk's unprotected abdomen. He felt tissues part followed by a dull pain. Wama released the belt knife in order to reach down and fondle the weapon that protruded from his belly. Blood mingled with the red dye and trickled down his bony legs. "Oh no," the monk said reproachfully. "Look what you've done!"

"I'm sorry! I really am," Lee said, as he backed away. And he was. The horror of what he had done was still sinking in as the tears started to flow.

Wama felt dizzy. He staggered but managed to keep his feet. "So tell me," he said in Tilisi. "Was I wrong? Is *that* why I am about to die? Are you the Divine Wind?"

Rain pattered on the leaves around them, causing each to bob and sway as Lee struggled to come up with an answer. Finally, after what seemed like an eternity but was only a matter of seconds, he spoke. "I honestly don't know."

Wama's eyes registered disappointment, rolled back in his head, and remained open as he fell. There was a splash and water flew in every direction as the body hit, and Rebo forced his way into the clearing. Norr followed so closely that she almost ran into the runner as he came to a sudden stop. The adults took in the body, the scared little boy, and could see what had occurred.

Norr went over to wrap an arm around Lee's shoulders. She could feel what he felt, and the weight of the boy's sorrow was almost too much for either to bear. His body shook, he started to sob, and tears ran down his cheeks. "It wasn't your fault," the sensitive assured him. "You had no choice. Come on . . . Let's get you into some dry clothes."

Rebo watched the two of them head back toward the lift and returned the Crosser to its holster. The woman seemed to know how to handle the boy, and for that he was grateful. The runner turned his attention to the body. It seemed safe to assume that the monk was a black hat assassin—but was he operating alone?

A careful search of the monk's robes turned up nothing more than a few coins. Just what one would expect of a professional. Disappointed, but not surprised, Rebo removed the blade from Wama's abdomen and wiped it on the dead man's clothing. Then, having retrieved the belt knife, Rebo left.

The *real* black hat assassin waited a full five minutes before emerging from a thick tangle of vegetation to kneel next to the body. She had arrived too late to save the monk *or* kill the boy. Wama's death had been useful however. It now appeared that *two* bodyguards had been sent to protect the imposter. The nun wondered how many more carefully disguised warriors were lurking among the passengers. Time would tell.

The assassin took a moment to close Wama's staring eyes and recited the prayer for the dead. The rain stopped, a mist rose and wrapped the nun in a steamy embrace. All of the blood had been washed away by then—and there was peace in the garden.

FOUR

The Planet Anafa

*Just as electronic media enabled homogeneous societies on in-
dividual planets, the advent of star gates laid the groundwork
for a multisystem government having a common language,
laws, and customs.*

—Heva Manos, Advisor to Emperor Hios,
in his biography, *A Web of Stars*

Though secret now, the subsurface facility had once been
regarded as little more than a utility portal, through which
low-ranking technical personnel could travel to distant
planets to perform maintenance on the then-pervasive system of star gates that held the far-flung empire together.
But time had passed, a terrible war had been fought, and the
computer that controlled the network had been destroyed.
Or that's what most historians believed. But not Milos
Lysander, who insisted that the artificial intelligence called
Logos had been lost rather than destroyed, which meant
that the days of nearly instantaneous star travel could be restored if the AI were located. It was the very thing the
Techno Society had been founded to bring about.

Now, as Jevan Kane made his way down into the catacombs lying below the Society's headquarters on Anafa, the operative knew that the system he was about to use had been created to operate in parallel with the more important public network. The maintenance system worked then, and it still did, largely because it was extremely simple compared to the network that it had been created to support. A fact that enabled members of the Techno Society to move around with a degree of freedom unimaginable to most people.

The stairs twisted down through a pool of light, descended twenty feet or so, and turned yet again. Steel clanged under Kane's boots, and the operative's stomach began to feel queasy as the radiation produced by the nearby power core invaded his body. The medicos weren't sure what sort of long-term health problems might result from prolonged exposure to the core, and Kane had no desire to find out. The key was to get in, pass through, and put the potential danger behind him as quickly as possible.

The stairs ended, Kane palmed a door, and was admitted to a clearly marked decontamination lock. Even though a great deal of knowledge had been lost over the years, the Techno Society's scientists had studied the ancient texts and were aware of the problems that could occur were the organisms from one planet allowed to successfully colonize another. That's why the operative was nude with the exception of his boots, which he removed as he entered the chamber. They would get wet the moment the shower came on—but that was preferable to the hassle of obtaining off-the-shelf footwear on a planet like Pooz. Clothes, weapons, and all the rest would be waiting for him.

There was a *hiss,* which quickly transformed itself into a roar as jets of hot water mixed with a broad-spectrum antibacterial agent hit Kane from all directions. The wash-down lasted three minutes and was followed by blasts of prewarmed air. A door slid open, which allowed Kane to enter a circular room. He left wet footprints on the cement floor. The curvilinear walls were covered with hundreds of video tiles. Each displayed a still photo of a distant world with the appropriate name printed below. Roughly half of the images were darkened, indicating that the gate that once provided access to that location was no longer available. But the rest were lit, meaning that the operative could travel there if he chose.

The square labeled POOZ showed a desert, a craggy-looking mountain range in the distance, and a scattering of high clouds beyond that. Having spent the better part of a month searching for Norr in and around Seros, Kane had concluded that the sensitive had boarded the ship and was in transit to the planet he was presently looking at.

The operative double-checked to make sure that he had read the destination correctly, touched the mountain, and felt the tile give. The room lights flashed on and off as the voice of a woman long dead issued through overhead speakers. "The transfer sequence is about to begin. Please take your place on the service platform. Once in place check to ensure that no portion of your anatomy extends beyond the yellow line. Failure to do so will cause serious injury and could result in death."

Although Kane had never seen, much less used gates large enough to transport hundreds of people and tons of cargo from place to place, he imagined that flesh-and-blood attendants had been present to ensure that customers kept their extremities inside the transfer zone. Boots in hand Kane stepped up onto a raised dais, checked to ensure that he was standing at the exact center of the safety circle, and uttered a silent prayer. There were no recorded incidents of a gate's failing during a transmission, but an unprecedented death was not what Kane wanted to be remembered for.

There was a brilliant flash of light as all the atoms in the operative's body were disassembled, transmitted through hyperspace, and systematically reassembled within an identical containment on the surface of Pooz. Kane felt the usual moment of disorientation, followed by a few seconds of dizziness and a bout of nausea. Then, eager to escape the room and the nearly palpable radiation present there, the operative stumbled into the local decontamination chamber, where he was disinfected all over again.

Finally, having donned his soaking-wet boots, Kane exited into a stairwell and climbed four flights of stairs to a platform where Mar Von stood waiting. Containers of mail were sent through the star gates on a regular basis, and the station on Pooz had been told to expect the operative. Von was nearly six feet tall, a few years younger than Kane, and wore a two-piece outfit that revealed a well-toned midriff. She was an admirer of men, especially *strong* men, and was confident enough to let that show. Von took an unapologetic look at the Kane's well-muscled body before wrapping it in a thick locally made robe and handing him both ends of the tie. "Greetings, Operative Kane. Clothes, weapons, and food are waiting."

Kane could feel the sexual energy that emanated from the woman but gave no sign of it. He would have her, assuming there was time, but only if his primary purpose on the planet had been served. "Thank you. Has the ship arrived from Anafa yet?"

"No," Von replied as she led the operative through a door and into an artificially lit hallway. "Assuming that the vessel is running on time—it should arrive in about two days."

Kane nodded. There was usually some dilatation involved in a transfer from one planet to another. Those who constructed the system had presumably calculated such differences and been able to forewarn travelers about what to expect, but such niceties were a thing of the past. He had departed Anafa a week early, or believed that he had, only to lose five days in transit. Still, the situation could have been worse, so he felt fortunate. "Good. Please call a staff meeting. I'm convinced that a woman of great interest to the society is traveling aboard that ship. Our metal friends may have taken her into custody by now. If not, it's imperative that we intercept and capture this individual the moment she lands."

"Of course," Von replied obligingly. "Welcome to Pooz."

The Planet Pooz

Although the shuttle's arrival wasn't surrounded by the same level of excitement as it had been in the city of Seros on Anafa, quite a few of the citizens of Gos still turned out to greet both the ship and its passengers.

However, because of the impact of climatic changes that had swept across the surface of Pooz during the past five thousand years, large areas of what had once been fertile land had been converted to desert. Then, as an army of sand dunes marched up from the south, walls had been constructed to protect Gos and its spaceport. Over time both the sand and the walls had risen until onlookers could gather around the rim of the circular retaining wall and look down on the shuttle as it discharged its passengers, a process that was a good deal more formal on Pooz than it had been on Anafa. Having stumbled down the ramp into the blistering heat of a spring day, the bleary-eyed travelers were funneled through a double cordon of brightly uniformed lancers and into the shade cast by a gently flapping awning.

Then, each having waited his or her turn, the recently arrived passengers were shown into the presence of a man whose only qualification for his job was the fact that he was related to the Shah by an accident of birth. He was elderly, but still handsome, and dressed in immaculate white robes. Though never trained for the task, the official still took his duties very seriously and subjected each person to a long list of questions meant to establish his or her identity, reasons for traveling to Pooz, and their future plans. Information that was recorded by two serious-looking scribes.

Then, having assured himself that none of the travelers had come to Pooz for the express purpose of overthrowing the Shah or joining the ranks of the unemployed, the official concluded each interview by demanding a hefty landing fee. Those who couldn't pay, and there were six of them, were arrested and led away. Later, having served three months at hard labor, they would be freed.

No one was allowed to approach the immigrants until they had been interviewed, which meant that there was nothing for Kane to do except scan the passengers through a small pair of binoculars and wait for the process to end. The sensitive had proven herself to be something of an expert where disguises were concerned, so the operative examined each face with care. But that turned out to be unnecessary, because it wasn't long before Kane spotted a female sensitive standing next to a metal man, and knew his search was over. *But what happened to the second robot?* the operative wondered to himself. He didn't really care however, not so long as Lanni Norr was in custody.

Some terse orders sent Von and two of her functionaries scuttling along the circumference of the retaining wall to the point where two brightly uniformed heavies blocked access to the long, curving ramp that led down to the blast-scarred surface below. Once there, all Von and her men could do was elbow their way to the front of the waiting crowd and prepare for the moment when the last passenger cleared customs.

It was midafternoon by the time the last person had been processed, a whistle blew, and the heavies stepped out of the way. Von and her functionaries ran down the ramp, plowed through the crowd below, and closed in on the couple that they had been looking for. Von was still ten feet away when she realized that something was amiss. Though mostly hidden by a tattered, ankle-length robe, the metal man's face appeared to have slipped slightly, revealing a patch of olive-colored skin. And, now that she was closer, the operative could see that while made up to look like a sensitive, the woman who stood next to the machine was clearly a norm! She pointed a finger at the couple and yelled, "Grab them! Remove that mask! Wipe the makeup off her face!"

Her subordinates obeyed, but rather the tussle that Von half expected to ensue, the couple made no attempt to resist. Instead the young couple laughed, as if expecting to be intercepted and not the least bit concerned.

Von examined the metal mask, saw that the faceplate had been removed from a *real* robot, and held it up for Kane to see. The operative lowered his binoculars, swore bitterly, and brought the device back up. Faces blurred as Kane panned the crowd, but the sensitive was nowhere to be seen. Somehow Norr had managed to neutralize both of the metal men and make her escape. The woman was maddening.

Von arrived a few minutes later. Her breathing was normal in spite of the fact that she had run all the way up the ramp. "We missed them, but the imposters provided what could be some useful information. About halfway through the voyage the sensitive was taken into custody by one of the metal men—but another passenger freed her. Subsequent to that she spent most of her time with the man and his son. It seems the disguises were his idea."

Kane nodded thoughtfully. "Good work, Citizen Von. Put out the word. The city of Gos is a lot smaller than Seros. Given any luck at all we'll find them."

In addition to the ramp that curved up along the side of the retaining wall to access the planet's surface, there were three spaceport-level tunnels that provided access to the largely subterranean city and allowed the threesome to enter without going up onto the surface. It was a good deal cooler underground, and the runner noticed that new shops had moved in to replace some of the businesses he had frequented on a previous visit and that the efforts to reinforce the city's once-sagging support columns had been completed during his absence. The basic layout was the same, however, and Rebo had no difficulty finding his way around.

Hundreds of carefully maintained skylights, some of which were equipped with mirrors to direct the sunlight downward, served to illuminate the main thoroughfares, plazas, and squares. Smaller streets, and the labyrinth of narrow passageways that wound through the tightly packed residential neighborhoods, were lit with lamps fueled by natural gas. The system had been in place for more than a thousand years and drew upon a field located twenty miles away. It was an important resource and one that helped make the city of Gos possible.

But what *really* kept the city alive was the Dimba River. It flowed through the middle of town and formed the community's east–west axis. Not only did the Dimba provide the citizens of Gos with drinking water—it was the watery highway that brought raw materials in from the east. Finished goods were packed up and sent downstream to those who lived in the cities, towns, and villages located along the edge of the Great Sea.

So, knowing how central the river was to life in Gos, and not averse to showing off a little, Rebo led Lee and Norr out of a side street and onto the river walk that ran along the river's north bank. Having consumed nearly all of their supplies aboard ship, the group was only lightly burdened. Lee barely felt the weight of his pack, or so it seemed, as he peered through shop windows, jumped up onto the waist-high wall that kept people from falling into the Dimba, and was immediately ordered to get down.

The first thing the newcomers noticed about the river as they looked down into its blue-green depths was that it seemed to be in a hurry to join with the great sea. The water was very clear. That meant they could actually see incoming cargo modules as they whipped past. Though more industrialized than the west end of the city, Mountainside as the locals called the neighborhood they were in, was a lot more interesting. Rebo pointed to rows of hand-operated cranes and the nets that were stretched between them. "They lower the nets into the river, catch the cargoes sent down from the highlands, and pull them out. It's a fast, inexpensive way to bring raw materials down from the mountains."

"But how do they keep track of who gets what?" Lee wanted to know. "And how do they keep everything dry?"

"Well," the runner answered, "each merchant maintains an agent up in the highlands. They buy the materials and load them into special watertight containers. Weights are attached to achieve neutral buoyancy. Then they mark each barrel with a code and toss it in. The river does the rest. Clever, huh?"

"Very," Norr put in as she watched a wooden crane lift a net loaded with dripping containers up out of the river. "But what's to stop thieves from deploying their own nets upriver?"

"The river comes to the surface only a few times between the headwaters and Gos," Rebo responded. "And those locations are well guarded. Come on, we'd better find a place to stay, before the other passengers grab all the rooms."

The other two nodded in agreement, and as they turned to leave, a poisoned dart flew past Lee's neck and lost itself in the river. The youngster remained blissfully unaware of his narrow brush with death as Rebo led them toward the west.

Still concealed by shadow, the black hat assassin lowered the hollow tube that doubled as her staff and marveled at the boy's good fortune. Or, had his survival been predestined? And, if so, what would that imply?

Norr felt a sudden need to turn and check on Lee. He looked up at her, smiled uncertainly, and took the sensitive's hand. In spite of her efforts to counsel him, the youngster continued to have nightmares about the battle with the monk and was no longer willing to carry his knives.

Part of the problem stemmed from the trauma involved in having to kill a man, but this boy bore a larger burden as well. Lee had been raised to believe that he was the Divine Wind, a great teacher sent to the physical plane to usher in an era of spiritual enlightenment, which would benefit millions if not billions of people. But now, having been confronted by an obviously sincere individual who was willing to sacrifice his life in order to stop what he saw as an imposter from ascending the throne, Lee wasn't sure what to believe. "If I were truly an avatar, I would think nothing but important thoughts," Lee had told her in confidence, "and I would know who I had been in previous lives. What if the black hats are correct? What if the boy they sent to CaCanth is the *real* Nom Maa? Perhaps it would be better if I were dead."

Norr had worked long and hard to convince Lee that murder was wrong, no matter what the supposed justification, and that he had been correct to defend himself. But while he smiled, and seemed to agree, the sensitive knew that doubts remained.

A series of turnings brought the newly arrived travelers to a narrow street lit only by lamps. The Starman's Rest was reputed to be so old that it dated back to the time when starships landed on a weekly basis, and the little hotel had been a favorite among professional spacers. Now, no longer able to rely on off-worlders for a substantial portion of its revenue, the inn had become a home away from home for coastal purchasing agents, many of whom lived in Gos for months at a time.

Rebo took the usual look around prior to approaching the inn and wondered what to do. It had been clearly advantageous to form an alliance with Norr in the aftermath of Lee's fight with the black hat monk. First, because two pairs of adult eyes were better than one, and second because the sensitive had been able to help the boy deal with the trauma he had experienced, something the runner knew he wouldn't be much good at.

Now, with the first leg of the journey behind them, Rebo wasn't so sure that the alliance made sense anymore. First, because there was no particular reason for the threesome to stay together, and second because while he had disclosed the true nature of Lee's identity to the sensitive, she had never seen fit to explain why the metal men were pursuing her and remained somewhat secretive. With those facts in mind, the act of checking into the Starman's Rest together might send the wrong signal. But how to gracefully disengage?

The front door swung open, providing entry to a comfortable lobby, which was filled with staid but well-cared-for furnishings. The man behind the front desk had put on some weight since Rebo had last seen him last, but there was no mistaking the shaved head, gimletlike eyes, and bushy black beard. It was Mo Jahn all right and Rebo smiled. "Who's in charge of this worthless dump anyway?" the runner demanded loudly. "I've seen better pigsties."

Jahn's brows came together in one uninterrupted line, and the proprietor was reaching for the black-market blast stick that was racked under the counter, when something about the stranger's voice triggered a memory. "Jak Rebo? Is that you? Why you worthless piece of crap! Look at you! You're all grown-up!"

Lee looked up at Norr, who shrugged. "I know it's hard to believe, but I get the idea that they like each other. It's a man thing . . . Once you grow up maybe you can explain it to me."

Jahn came out from behind the counter, the two men exchanged hugs, and Rebo heard himself tell an unrehearsed lie. "Mo, this is my wife Lanni, and our son Dor."

"You're married?" the proprietor exclaimed. "My wife will never believe it."

Norr was still in the process of evaluating the falsehood and wondering why the innkeeper found Rebo's marriage so hard to believe, when Jahn wrapped her in a bear hug. "Welcome to the Starman's Rest," the businessman said. "I will personally take you to your room."

Because of the ovenlike conditions up on the surface, anyone who had a desire to acquire additional square footage was forced to expand *downward*. That meant the newer hotel rooms were those located at the very bottom of the structure. Jahn showed the threesome into the boxy twelve-foot-by-fifteen-foot room as if ushering them into a palace. Which, based on Rebo's previous experience, wasn't that far from the truth. Space was at a premium in Gos, and judging from the number of beds that had been crammed into the gaslit room, it sometimes serviced as many as six guests.

Jahn had just completed a review of the room's amenities, and was about to depart, when the runner took his arm. "One last thing, Mo . . . Please put some other name on your register. And, if someone comes looking for us, please let me know."

The proprietor's eyebrows inched higher. "Oh, so it's like that, is it? I should have known. Some things never change. Of course . . . I'll speak to my staff."

Norr waited until the door had closed before dumping her pack onto a bed. "Well, sweetie, how long have we been married anyway? About ten years?"

Rebo grinned sheepishly. "Sorry about that . . . You can bail out anytime you want to. I assume you intend to make for the coast. That's the most pleasant place to live on this planet."

"Yeah, sure," Norr replied, eager to cover up the fact that she had no plan other than to escape Anafa. "Don't get me wrong . . . I appreciate your hospitality. Jahn seems like a nice man. How did you come to know him?"

"It was one of my first runs," Rebo explained. "I brought him a letter from his long-lost father. I had to wait four months before I could board a ship and spent most of that time living here."

"Is that how long we'll have to wait?" Lee inquired, speaking for the first time.

"I'm not sure," Rebo answered honestly as he lowered his pack to the floor. "I was bound for Anafa back then—and we're headed for Ning. The ship will leave from Tra. That means a cross-country trip in order to get there. That much is for sure . . . The question is when will the next vessel depart from Tra? Assuming it's still running, that is."

Although Rebo had disclosed Lee's true identity, the sensitive had been unaware of where they planned to go next and felt a sudden sense of loss. It had been a long time since she had lived with—or been close to another human being. Still, she had no reason to accompany them, so a refuge along the coast made sense. "Yeah, well, I'm sure you'll figure that out. So, given the fact that this is our first night on Pooz, how 'bout a celebratory dinner? I'm buying."

Rebo grinned. "Sounds good! I know just the place. Assuming it's still there."

The illumination provided by the skylights had started to fade, and an army of lamplighters had just started to make their evening rounds, when the threesome left the hotel. Night came early below ground, but Rebo liked the warm buttery glow that the gas lamps generated, as well as the way that shadows slid across the city's ancient walls. Not only that, but the runner knew that most of the shops wouldn't close for hours yet, and all manner of pedestrians were out strolling the streets.

But, appealing though the city was, Rebo knew that dangers lurked in the less-traveled passageways, and kept to the main thoroughfares. He also left the Hogger where would-be cutpurses could get a good look at it, kept Lee close by his side, and looked back over his shoulder from time to time.

The black hat assassin was extremely skilled, however, as were the Dib Wa provided to her by the local monastery, all of whom were dressed in ordinary attire. The runner saw them, but had no way to know who they were, or what they intended.

The Falls restaurant was an open-air affair that consisted of twenty linen-covered tables, each of which had its own candle, and were grouped around the storefront that contained the kitchen. The falls, for which the eatery had been named, could be seen on the opposite side of the river walk, and roared gently as the Dimba tumbled down a series of man-made ledges before entering a calm stretch, where outgoing cargo modules were being dumped into the water.

It was early yet, which meant that the threesome were soon seated at one of the centermost tables, a location that Rebo deemed to be safest because newcomers would form a protective wall around his ten-year-old charge. The runner felt reasonably secure as the three of them settled into their chairs, but would have felt less so had he known that a black hat assassin was in the process of being seated at a nearby table, and that one of the waiters had already dispatched a message to the Techno Society.

Having placed their orders, and talked for a while, Rebo and his companions were still at work on their appetizers when the street urchin arrived with Kane, Von, and two of her functionaries in tow. Unable to intervene in such a public setting, and with the centermost tables having already been taken, the newcomers were forced to sit at the very edge of the river walk.

It wasn't until the main course arrived, and Norr had consumed her first forkful of baked river fish, when fingers of inky blackness started to find their way in among the otherwise benign thought forms that hung all around her. The sensitive frowned, swallowed, and dropped her fork. It clattered on her plate. "Jak, I don't like the feel of this place. We need to leave."

Rebo's hand slid in under his jacket, and his eyes scanned the diners seated around them. Though not acquainted with the exact nature of the sensitive's powers, he knew they were real. On the other hand he had barely touched his dinner and had no desire to leave on what might amount to a whim. "Can you tell me why you feel that way? Or who to look out for?"

"No," Norr said stolidly, "just that someone . . ." The sensitive's voice faltered, her eyes widened, and her hands came up as if to push someone away. "Oh, no! Not now! Go away!"

But it was too late, as Milos Lysander took control of Norr's body, rose from the chair, and yelled at the top of her voice. "My name is Lysander! This body is my channel! If members of the Techno Society are present, then come to my aid!"

Kane had no choice but to respond. He stood, drew his handgun, and yelled, "Take her alive!"

The black hat assassin had no idea who Kane was, or what he was shouting about, but saw what she deemed to be the perfect opportunity. She stood, produced an ugly machine pistol, and yelled in Tilisi. "Kill him!"

The nun meant the boy, but one of the Dib Wa assumed that she meant Kane, and fired a shot at him. The technologist felt something burn the upper part of his left biceps, heard a meaty *thud* as the slug struck Von's chest, and fired in return. A Techno Society functionary shot one of the Dib Wa, and Rebo pulled the Crosser. Food sprayed the air, and the table rattled madly as the assassin's bullets punched holes in its surface, and barely missed Lee. The runner's first bullet took the black hat assassin in the throat, the second passed through her open mouth, and the third drilled a hole between her eyes.

Meanwhile, Lysander continued to shout all sorts of non-sense as Lee threw himself at the sensitive's legs and took the woman down. That was when Rebo bent to grab the boy by the arm. "Come on! Let's go!"

"No!" Lee objected. "Not without Lanni . . . She's in trouble!"

The runner swore as a bullet pinged off a metal chair, reversed the Crosser, and made use of it to pistol-whip the sensitive. He transferred the semiautomatic over to his left hand as her body went limp. "Stay low! Grab a wrist! We'll tow her into the kitchen!"

Lee obeyed and together they were able to drag Norr's unconscious body into the storefront even as the gun battle continued to rage. By that time, Kane had identified the single surviving Dib Wa and shot him. A woman sobbed, a man called for help, and those who could scuttled away. There were shouts as a contingent of the Shah's lancers appeared a thousand yards away and ran along the river walk.

Kane turned to see a man and a boy pull Norr into the restaurant, swore for the second time that day, and backed into the embrace of some welcoming shadows. By the time the lancers arrived, and ordered everyone to remain where they were, the technologist was gone.

Having dragged the unconscious sensitive into the restaurant's steamy kitchen, Rebo and Lee soon found themselves in danger from the cooks. But even a meat cleaver is no match for a semiautomatic pistol, and the kitchen staff were forced to back off as two of their patrons towed a third through a screen door and out into the garbage-strewn passageway beyond.

"All right," Rebo said grimly as he hoisted Norr into a fireman's carry. "Let's get out of here. These passageways are home to all sorts of vermin, so your job is to watch our back trail and let me know if anyone tries to follow."

Lee nodded solemnly and soon found himself walking backward most of the time as the runner carried the sensitive down the narrow alleyway. The widely spaced gas lamps created pools of uncertain light, each separated by a hundred feet of gloom, which made for excellent places to hide.

Lee heard what might have been claws scratching against pavers, followed by the *rattle* of a garbage can, and reached for his belt knife. That was when he remembered that he had refused to wear it and why. But nothing pursued them, and the boy felt a sense of relief as they passed under a light before plunging back into relative darkness.

A rectangular glow appeared up ahead, quickly followed by a burst of laughter and the slamming of a door as the light was extinguished. Then, after what seemed like an eternity, a well-illuminated intersection appeared. A promising development insofar as the runner was concerned. Norr didn't weigh all that much, but seemed to be getting heavier, and Rebo knew he wouldn't be able to carry her all the way to the hotel. Not to mention the fact that an attempt to do so would inevitably attract the wrong sort of attention. The answer was to hire some sort of public transportation and move the sensitive in a less-visible manner.

The runner's breath was coming in short gasps by the time he emerged from the passageway into one of the city's lesser squares. A well-illuminated fountain marked the center of an area that was surrounded by shops. Locals strolled, stood in small groups, or sat on benches that faced the fountain. "Wait here," Rebo commanded. "I'll be back in a minute." The runner placed Norr with her back propped up against a wall, paused to check her pulse, and was gone moments later.

Lee didn't want to wait there, not all by himself, and wondered if it had been a mistake to rescue Norr. It was a small thought, a poor thought, and one the youngster regretted. The sensitive groaned and reached up to touch the swelling on the side of her head. "What happened? Where am I?"

"You began to shout, people shot at us, and Jak hit you," the boy answered earnestly. "As for where we are, I don't know."

"Damn," Norr said, examining her hand to see if there was blood on it. "That hurts."

The sound of footsteps combined with the monotonous squeal of an unoiled wheel caused both to turn as Rebo returned accompanied by a three-wheeled pedicab. "Here she is," the runner announced loudly. "I told her to lay off the booze, but she wouldn't listen, and passed out. Hold it right there . . . I'll put her in the back."

"I'll have to charge *three* gunars if all of you ride," the whipcord-thin pedicab operator observed as he eyed Norr. "Plus another gunar if she throws up on the seat."

"No problem," the runner grunted, as he lifted Norr up into the back of the vehicle. "Take us to the Starman's Rest—and if there's a back way, then use it." Norr felt the flimsy conveyance sway as Rebo took a seat next to her followed by a less-noticeable movement as Lee hopped aboard.

The pedicab operator had to literally stand on his pedals in order to get his rickety vehicle under way, but once the conveyance was in motion, the going was easier. The fact that there were very few inclines helped, too.

Norr closed her eyes, tried to ignore the pain that each bump of the wheels caused her, and felt a sense of hopelessness. Rather than leave the Milos Lysander entity back on Anafa, as the sensitive had assumed she would, the discarnate had followed her to Pooz, a trip that was probably a great deal easier to make on the spirit planes than it was on the physical.

Not only that, but it seemed that Lysander's followers were tracking her, too, because even as the scientist harangued the restaurant's customers, a flesh-and-blood version of the blond-haired man had gotten up from one of the tables, produced a gun, and opened fire. And, had it not been for the runner and his youthful charge, there was little doubt that Kane and his associates would have been able to spirit her away.

Norr's thoughts were interrupted as the pedal-powered vehicle coasted to a stop and light spilled onto the surrounding pavement. There was a jumble of subdued conversation as Rebo provided Mo Jahn with a sanitized version of what had occurred, paid the pedicab operator, and lifted the sensitive out of the vehicle. Norr said, "I can walk," but the runner chose to carry the young woman into the hotel instead.

Ten minutes later the sensitive was propped up in bed, with a cold compress bound to the side of her head, and her fingers wrapped around a mug of hot tea. Once the hotel's staff had exited the room, Rebo checked the door to ensure that it was locked and pulled a chair up next to Norr's bed. "All right . . . There was a time when I figured that whatever you were running from was your business. That changed earlier this evening. Who is this Milos Lysander guy? And why were those people trying to shoot you?"

Norr opened her mouth to reply, but Lee spoke first. "No offense, Father—but at least three of those people were trying to kill *me*."

Rebo frowned and swiveled around. "*Really?* What makes you think so?"

"I saw one of them, the woman, aboard the ship. She kept to herself, but she was there, I'm sure of it. Not only that, but she gave orders in Tilisi, a language that no one outside of my religion knows how to speak. Finally," the boy said gravely, "she ordered her men to 'kill *him*.' Not *her*, but *him*."

Rebo nodded approvingly. "Not bad, son. Not bad at all . . . You paid attention in spite of everything that was going on around you. I'm impressed."

Lee felt his chest swell with pride. He couldn't remember his *real* father, or mother for that matter, both of whom had been prevailed upon by the order to give him up at the age of two. Now, having been forced to pretend that Rebo was his father, the boy found that he wanted to please the runner in much the same way that he might have sought to please his real parents.

"So," Rebo said thoughtfully, as he turned back to Norr, "It appears that we were attacked by *two* different groups. Three of them were after Dor here . . . but what about the rest?"

Norr sipped her tea. She was a loner, and for good reason, since it seemed as though once identified by the surrounding society sensitives were nearly always used, abused, and persecuted. As a result she was understandably reluctant to share information that could be used against her. But her present situation was more than she could handle alone, so Norr told Rebo about the first time that Lysander had co-opted her body, about the incident at the spaceport, and the message from Jevan Kane. "He was the one with the blond hair," she added. "The one who yelled, 'Take her alive!'"

"Well, at least they aren't trying to kill you," Rebo responded grimly. "Now, please don't take this the wrong way, but why not go along with them? You took money in return for demonstrating your abilities back on Seros . . . These people are willing to pay, so where's the problem?"

It was a good question, an excellent question, and one that Norr had struggled with on numerous occasions. But how to answer without seeming hypocritical? It was Lee who came to her rescue. "The ascended master Teon once said that 'the freedom to choose' was the first gift that God presented to humanity."

Norr nodded gratefully. "Yes! That's it. I want the freedom to choose. And there's something more as well . . . Something that might be difficult for a normal to understand. When I surrender my body to another person it's like having sex with them, except *more* intimate, if you can imagine that. When Lysander takes over without my permission it's like being raped."

"Then why allow him to do so?" Rebo wanted to know.

"I *don't* allow him to do so," the sensitive insisted hotly. "And the fact that he can do it anyway terrifies me. Most sensitives can block most discarnate entities most of the time. But there are exceptions, and this is one of them. No one knows why."

There was a long period of silence as each person thought the situation over. "Okay," the runner said finally, "so here's how I see it. Both the black hats and the techno people know that we're on Pooz. Mo Jahn tells me that the ship to Ning is scheduled to arrive off-planet eighteen days from now. We can hole up here and wait for the *next* vessel, or make for Tra and take our chances. Personally, I figure it's only a matter of time before a member of the hotel staff sells us out, and someone comes in after us. So I favor making a run for it."

Norr looked quizzical. "Was I mistaken? Or, did I hear an invitation buried in that last statement?"

The runner shrugged. For reasons he wasn't sure of, or wouldn't admit, the idea of sending the young woman off on her own bothered him. "Yeah, I guess you did."

"I appreciate it," the sensitive replied, "I really do. But

I'm not sure it's such a good idea. You two have enough trouble on your hands without sharing mine."

"Odds are that we'll do better together," Rebo said pragmatically. "Besides, I've got a feeling that both groups view us as a single unit at this point, which means that they aren't going to be all that discriminating."

"That's right!" Lee added enthusiastically. "Jak's my father—and you can be my mother!"

Norr smiled. "Yes, I suppose I could."

Back before human civilization had stalled, and the long gentle slide back into barbarity had begun, there had been a time when no task was considered too great for the ruling technocrats and the scientists that they employed. Those were the days in which the city of Gos lived on the surface of the planet, and was, ironically enough, known as "The City of the Sun."

Back then, before the Dimba River had been "rationalized," it followed through a series of long, gentle, east-to-west curves before running into a ridge of upthrusting rock just short of Gos. There were holes in the barrier, but when the river split up in order to take advantage of them, barge traffic was forced to stop well short of the metroplex.

In order to remedy that situation and open the Dimba all the way to Gos, the engineers blasted a hole through the ridge, thereby allowing the water to form a single stream. That left a labyrinth of water-cut channels in the subsurface rock. The passageways, caverns, and galleries were little more than a curiosity at first, but eventually, once the dunes began their irresistible march, a group of monks took possession of them rather than dwell within the city itself. And, given the fact that the underground maze was not all that pleasant to live in, no one objected.

Later, after surface conditions grew worse, the subsurface habitat started to look a lot more attractive, and various groups tried to dislodge the monks. But the Dib Wa were a potent force—and kept the would-be invaders at bay.

Since that time the religion had split into two feuding groups, and the schism had led to occasional violence. Now, as torches flared and threw dark shadows onto rocky walls, the latest in what had been hundreds of casualties were borne toward the traditional funeral pyres. The first litter bore the tightly wrapped body of the nun from Anafa. A trained assassin, who along with two local Dib Wa, had sacrificed her current life while trying to prevent the imposter from making his way to the holy city of CaCanth. A very noble thing to do, which was why Lar Thota had insisted on funeral rites commensurate with the high rank of Ona, or truth giver. Happily, from Thota's point of view, no red hats were present to desecrate the solemn ceremony, since the last of the misguided souls had been murdered in their sleep some nine months before.

The passageway took a sharp turn, passed a pool inhabited by blind fish, and went up over a rise. Thota followed the procession into a vast chamber. Thousands of crystals were embedded in the rocky ceiling. They twinkled like distant stars.

Below them, his back still connected to the rock from which his massive body had been hewed, sat a likeness of Teon. If the great master was saddened by the deaths of his servants, there was no sign of it on his impassive face. *Nor should there be,* the monk thought to himself, *for he sees that which we seek.*

One by one the bodies were placed on a rocky platform, a sonorous chant echoed between rough-hewn walls, and Thota gave the necessary signal. Wood was a precious commodity in Gos, so natural gas had been piped into the caverns, and was lit with a torch. There was a dramatic *pop!* as blue flames rippled out to embrace the bodies, and what little smoke there was wafted upward.

Finally, once the ceremony was complete, Thota bowed to the image of Teon before retracing his footsteps and entering the medium-sized chamber that doubled as both his living quarters and office. The bioengineered beings who awaited him there were so different from members of the A-strain that they might as well have been aliens. The precise rationale for creating an offshoot of humanity that could fly had been lost to the sect's historians but the monk suspected that the so-called wings had been created in order to exploit certain habitats for commercial purposes.

Whether their creators had Pooz in mind back then, or the winged humanoids simply found the planet to their liking was unknown, but the result was the same. Just as the phibs made themselves at home in the Great Sea, their airborne cousins laid claim to the mountains, where they lived in terraced villages, farmed hardscrabble plots, and preyed on commerce below.

Two of the exotic creatures stood waiting. Both were scantily dressed, about six and a half feet tall, and very thin. Thota knew that their bones were hollow, certain portions of their skeletons had been fused to make them stronger, and the variants had muscles that norms didn't. Their leathery wings were folded vertically along their backs, both carried projectile weapons, and eyed him with what could only be described as a look of fierce independence.

"Welcome to our humble monastery," the monk said, bowing formally. "My name is Thota. I would invite you to take a seat, but I fear I don't have any suitable furniture."

"There is no need," one of the wings replied stiffly. "My name is Karth. This is Zota. What do you want of us?"

Thota perched on the edge of a handmade desk that had once been the property of the senior member of the local red hat sect. "You come right to the point. I like that. Well, here's the situation . . ."

The ensuing conversation lasted for the better part of an hour. Finally, once both sides were satisfied with the terms of the agreement, and the first of two payments had changed hands, Thota escorted the bandits up to the surface. The top of a sand dune made a good launching pad, and their long, powerful wings made a gentle *whuf! whuf! whuf!* sound as the variants beat their way upward, found a thermal, and let it loft them even higher into the sky.

The monk watched his new allies for a while, marveled at the freedom the wings enjoyed, but wondered about the price they had paid. Had the technology used to create them been a good thing? Or simply a distraction from humanity's *real* goal, which was to supersede the physical? There was no way to be sure, but one thing was for certain, the sun was extremely hot.

Thota turned, waited for a lesser monk to lift the metal lid that prevented sand from spilling into the vertical access stack, and made his way down the spiral stairway. Cool air rushed up to embrace him, a cup of hot tea awaited, and Thota was content.

FIVE

The Planet Pooz

There is only one race that can fly, that can ride the wind, that can touch the clouds. Others may walk the sands, or swim in the sea, but we own the sky.

—Author unknown,
A wing proverb

The sun had just broken contact with the horizon, which meant that the air was still relatively cool, as the team of twenty specially bred angens hauled the custom-built flat cars along the single track. Once, back before the rising tide of sand had submerged all but the tops of the pylons, the monorail had been elevated fifty feet off the ground, and sleek bullet-shaped trains completed the trip between Gos and Tra in hours rather than the fourteen days currently required.

But once the sand had risen, and off-world parts were no longer available, the bullet trains had given way to the current low-tech version. Extensions had been added along both sides of the rail so that the huge draft animals had a surface to walk on, and a system of walled "inns" had been established so that passengers had a safe place to stay during the worst heat of the day. Each fort was approximately fifteen miles from the next, built around a hand-dug well and protected by a contingent of lancers.

The trip was still rather dangerous, however, since bandit raids were not only common, but to be expected as the angens pulled the rather optimistically named *Desert Zephyr* up through the southern foothills and through Hyber Pass. An area that the wings patrolled and considered to be their own in spite of the Shah's claims to the contrary.

Which was why each sixty-foot flatcar was equipped with a venerable but still-serviceable machine gun. Each weapon squatted in a metal tub, where it could sweep the sky above, and was served by a two-man crew. A corpulent noncom was in charge of the detachment but spent most of his time dozing in the sun. There had been talk of increasing the number of guards, but because the addition of five soldiers would force the government to cut an equal number of passengers, nothing had come of such discussions. It seemed that the Shah felt the train was losing too much money already. In fact, according to what one passenger said, the only reason the *Zephyr* remained in service was the need to move official mail from one city to the other, a function the government refused to let the local runners take care of.

However, most of the other fifty or so passengers were armed. That added to the total firepower the train could muster and served as an additional deterrent. Of course there was no telling how effective the ragtag mix of merchants, civil servants, and other citizens would be if confronted by bandits. That was why Rebo maintained his own watch on the second car. A tattered awning provided the runner with a scrap of shade augmented by an oft-patched sail. It flapped uselessly on those rare occasions when a breeze found it and only rarely functioned as intended. Both the runner and his companions kept their packs at hand and were prepared to abandon the train should an overwhelming threat appear, even if that meant continuing on foot.

Rebo saw Norr appear at the back end of the first car and pause in front of the three-foot gap. It was as if the moment was frozen in time as the sun hit the sensitive's face just so, the woman bit her lower lip as she contemplated the jump, and a momentary breeze tugged at her loose-fitting robe. She was attractive, but Rebo had spent time with far prettier women, so why stare at her?

Then the moment was over as Norr completed the jump, exchanged greetings with the machine gunner, and made her way back to Rebo's scrap of shade. "Here," she said, handing the runner a small bundle. "Have some dates. One of the women gave them to me in return for reading her palm."

"And what did you see?" Rebo inquired as he untied the cloth and selected a likely-looking piece of fruit.

"She's going to die," Norr said matter-of-factly, as she stared off into the distance. "And soon. Which is too bad because she's no more than thirty-five years old."

Rebo spit the pit into the palm of his hand and threw it out into the desert. "Really? That's tough. What did she say when you told her?"

"I didn't tell her," the sensitive replied evenly. "Not the truth. I told her that everything would go well, that she would be happy in Tra, and live a long productive life there."

Rebo frowned. "But why? If she knew she was going to die, she might make different decisions."

"Exactly," Norr replied, as she chose a date for herself.

"Which is why most sensitives won't disclose death dates. First, because we're fallible, but mostly because people who believe they're going to die stop living and focus on death. She's happy. That's what's important."

"So, what about *me?*" Rebo inquired, extending his hand.

"Hmmm," Norr said, as she made use of a long slender finger to trace the curve of his lifeline. "It looks like you will travel to the stars, have many adventures, and fall into the company of a beautiful woman."

She was joking, Rebo knew that, but when he looked up into Norr's face the runner thought he saw a look of concern cloud her brown eyes, and was about to question her when Lee dropped in on them from above. "I climbed all the way to the top of the mast!" the boy announced proudly. "You can see the next fort from up there. Well, not the fort, but the tops of the palm trees around it. They're Pooz palms. That means they're variants of trees that grew on ancient Earth and were brought here by ancient colonists."

Lee had been a full-time student until very recently and had a tendency to absorb information like a sponge. The only problem was that some of it tended to be wrong. "The trees could be variants," Rebo allowed, "but they didn't originate on Earth. It's a legend—nothing more."

"Maybe," the boy said carefully, "but the ancient texts refer to it, and humanity had to come from somewhere."

Somehow, without intending to, Norr had become the peacemaker in such disputes. "Look!" she said, pointing to the east. "What is that? Some sort of bird?"

The runner removed a small but powerful pair of binoculars from a pocket and brought them up to his eyes. He panned a section of sky, acquired the object in question, and pressed a button that rolled the image into focus. The range was printed along the bottom edge of the frame. They would wear out eventually—and no one would be able to repair them. "It's a wing," Rebo reported. "And that isn't good. A scout probably, watching our progress, so he can report back."

"Can I see?" Lee inquired eagerly, and was thrilled when Rebo handed him the glasses. Other passengers were pointing by then, chattering among themselves or calling to the soldiers for reassurance. The gunner on the first car even went so far as to fire a three-round burst toward the distant target, but the airborne variant was well out of range and continued to circle as if inviting the soldier to waste even more of his precious ammunition.

Half an hour passed like that, until the train neared the next fort, and the wing banked toward the south. The foothills could be seen down there, shimmering in the steadily increasing heat, with the vague shape of a mountain looming beyond. *That's where the variant is headed,* Rebo thought to himself, and lowered his glasses. At some point during the next day, or the day after that, the bandits would attack. Would the machine guns be sufficient to hold them off? The runner certainly hoped so—but felt an emptiness at the pit of his stomach. The train jerked forward as the normally listless angens spotted the fort, realized that they were about to be fed, and broke into a clumsy trot.

Inside the fort a whip cracked, and a capstan started to turn, as a pair of elderly angens walked an endless circle. Ropes grew taut, pulleys squealed, and a pair of bullet-pocked iron doors parted to let the *Zephyr* pass between them. The sun reached its zenith not long thereafter. Those lifeforms that could scurried for cover. The rest started to die.

Clouds slid in over the desert. They concealed the moon one moment only to reveal it the next. During the brief interludes when the satellite was visible it threw light down onto the monorail, which gleamed like platinum and seemed to streak through the night. Most of the passengers had fallen asleep by then, not because they were especially tired, but because there was nothing else for them to do. There were exceptions, however, including the angens, which continued to plod along both sides of the track, the driver who sought to keep them moving, and the soldiers who sat slumped in their gun tubs.

Farther toward the rear, with his back supported by a crate, Rebo floated in the nowhere land that lies between full awareness and sleep. The gentle sway of the flatcar, the creak of wood, and an occasional *click* as the *Zephyr* passed over an expansion joint combined to take the runner back to his boyhood on Thara. He could feel the subtle roll of his father's fishing boat as it surged forward, hear the gurgle of water as it slid along the hull, and smell the sharp tang of the sea.

He would have been about ten then, back when life was good, before the storm took half the local fishing fleet, the family boat, his father, and both of his brothers. His mother had never been the same after that, working as a maid during the day and crying herself to sleep at night. The other villagers assumed little Jak would become a fisherman when he grew up and serve on someone else's boat, but his mother had other ideas. She saved every gunar she could to buy Jak a different future. Anything but the profession that had claimed her husband and two oldest sons.

There weren't many opportunities in the village of Lorval, and as time passed, Jak's mother began to feel a sense of hopelessness. But that changed one day when a stranger appeared at the inn where she worked. The stranger was a runner with a letter for those who lived in the big house up on the bluff, and he was a sight to see. Thomas Crowley stood six-six, had long gray hair and piercing green eyes. His skin had a strange pallor, as if it was rarely exposed to the sun, but the man seemed to radiate an inner strength. Rather than carouse with the regulars while he waited for his wealthy clients to compose a response to the letter he had brought, the runner preferred to read books via a small machine that he held cradled in his hands.

From the first moment that she saw him Torley Rebo knew Crowley was the man who could save her son from what she saw as certain death, and immediately went to work on him. For the next three days the runner received every attention that the maid could lavish on him, and could easily have taken her to bed, had that been his desire.

But unknown to Torley Rebo, or to anyone else for that matter, it had been many months since the runner had been interested in sex. He was ill, and not only had the nature of his disease robbed the off-worlder of his sex drive, it resulted in persistent abdominal pain and a dry, hacking cough.

Rebo remembered the morning when his mother had given him an unscheduled bath, dressed him in his very best clothes, and taken him to work with her. Then, having entered the inn via the hot steamy kitchen, Torley Rebo led her son up through a tight, winding staircase to the second floor. The runner occupied the best room the inn had to offer, and their shoes made a *clacking* sound as the two of them walked the length of the hall and paused in front of a heavily varnished door. That was when Torley patted her hair, checked to make sure that her son's jacket was straight, and rapped on the worn wood.

Rebo heard a muffled cough, followed by a hoarse "Come in!" and wondered what his mother was up to. The door swung open, he was nudged inside, and soon found himself standing in front of a man with a long, serious face. A handgun, a glass of wine, and a small machine lay on the table next to him.

The boy hadn't understood much of the ensuing conversation, only that it involved him in some important way, but remembered how profusely his mother thanked the tall man even as she handed him a purse full of coins. Then, turning to him, she had smiled. Strange really, considering the tears that ran down her cheeks, and the emotion in her voice. "This is Citizen Crowley, son. He's a runner—and you are to be his apprentice! Isn't that wonderful?"

The younger Rebo nodded dutifully, wondered what runners did, and felt a hard lump form in the pit of his stomach. Two days later he said good-bye to his mother, boarded a coach, and began his new life. He hadn't been back to Thara since.

Now, as the train murmured along the track, the runner was going home. Or hoped that he was. Was his mother alive? Had the village changed? Only time would tell. Memories morphed into dreams, and Rebo slept.

Enormous wings made a gentle whuf! whuf! whuf! *sound as* the two variants closed with the train. Although the darkness offered concealment, the cool night air forced the wings to exert themselves in order to maintain their altitude, and chilled their thin, nearly unprotected bodies. That, plus the fact that the two-car train was in motion, meant that the snatch would be difficult. But even as the air around him acted to slow Karth down, it also provided his wings with lift, a paradox he had once captured in a poem.

But this was no time to consider the gentler arts as the bandit closed the gap with the second flatcar and searched the blackness below for the beacon that was supposed to mark his target. The variant didn't see it at first, and was just about to conclude that the black hats had been unable to tag the boy, when he saw a patch of green luminescence. The substance that produced the telltale glow had been sprayed onto the youth's pack as he boarded the train. It was invisible to anyone not equipped with goggles like those the variants wore.

A quick glance to the variant's right, and a gesture from Zota, was sufficient to confirm that his companion had seen the beacon as well. Their wings beat faster, and the bandits picked up speed as they dived through the darkness. Then, just as their leathery arm flaps flared, all hell broke loose.

Norr "sensed" that something bad was about to happen, shouted Rebo's name, and came to her feet just as the variants took hold of Lee's arms. The boy had been asleep. He yelled and struggled wildly as enormous wings beat the air and lifted his body clear of the car. Although the bandits had been able avoid the sail on the way down, the boom that it was attached to chose that particular moment to swing across the flatcar and struck Zota. The wing began to lose his grip, Lee started to fall, and saw Norr reach up to grab him. But Karth was strong enough to support the youngster long enough for the other bandit to reestablish his grip.

Then, wings beating to the same rhythm, the variants bore their kicking-screaming burden toward the south. They didn't plan to fly far, just a mile or so, to the point where other members of their tribe waited with a group of desert-bred angens. But they were barely clear of the *Zephyr* when one of the machine guns opened up, and Rebo yelled at the gunner. "Cease fire, damn you! They have the boy!"

The noncom shouted an order, the machine gun fell silent, and chaos reigned as the newly aroused passengers waved weapons and peppered each other with questions.

Not knowing what might lie up ahead, and fearful of an ambush, the driver pulled back on his reins. The angens came to a confused halt, squalled loudly, and nipped at each other. Rebo jumped from car two to car one, and from there to the platform that ran parallel to the rail. Norr followed behind him. The runner figured that maybe, just maybe, something would break his way.

The fingers that dug into the flesh of Lee's upper arms were like iron, and in spite of all his struggles the boy had been unable to break their relentless grip. However, by turning his head just so, the youngster found that he could see exposed flesh. He sank his teeth into a leathery hand, heard one of the variants swear, and felt the wing let go. Zota tried to support the boy's weight, couldn't, and lost his grip as well.

It wasn't until Lee began to fall that he realized how stupid he'd been. How high was he? Ten feet? A hundred? There was barely enough time to wonder before the youngster hit the top of a dune, had the breath knocked out of his lungs, and tumbled down the side of a sandy slope.

Karth was angry by then and hopeful that the boy would die as a result of the fall. Then all they would have to carry was the little beggar's head. A lighter burden by far, and given the way his hand hurt, a task that he would relish. But how to locate the little bastard in inky blackness below? No sooner had the variant posed the question to himself than the moon emerged from behind a bank of clouds, and Zota pointed toward the ground. "There! Do you see the glow? We've got him!"

Karth circled, spotted the target, and began his descent.

Rebo welcomed the additional light as the moon emerged from behind the clouds and paused to scan the night sky.

"Look!" Norr shouted. "Can you see them? They're silhou-etted against the stars."

The runner *could* see them, two variants, circling an area ahead. But where was Lee? There was no sign of the youth dangling between variants, which seemed to suggest that the bandits had dropped him. Rebo felt a surge of anger, brought the long-barreled Hogger up, and fired in one smooth motion.

Karth heard Zota grunt, followed by the flat report of a large-caliber weapon. There was nothing the wing could do as his companion lost motor control, rolled over onto his back, and spiraled into the ground.

The second bullet, which arrived a few moments later, passed through the bandit's left wing but didn't hit any of his delicate bones. One of the *Zephyr*'s machine guns opened up at that point, filling the air with projectiles, making it impossible to land near Zota.

That meant the variant was forced to dive down into the protection of the dunes and follow a zigzag course out of the area. There would be no second payment, only the screams of Zota's bereaved mate and a symbolic death pyre high on a mountain crag. But the train? That was a different story. The train went where the track went, and like it or not, the *Zephyr* would have to go over Hyber Pass. And that was where it would be destroyed.

After Rebo and Norr had recovered Lee from where he had fallen, the next few days passed slowly for those on the train. Although the passengers were aware of the dangers inherent in the trip between Gos and Tra, the attack made their worst fears real and put everyone on edge. Laughter was sel-dom heard, people hugged their weapons like lovers, and the desert gradually surrendered to hardpan as mountains loomed ahead.

Strangely, from Norr's perspective at least, some of her fellow passengers seemed to blame Lee for the impending battle. Some had even gone so far as to suggest that, had the first variants been permitted to escape with their prize, the train might have been allowed to transit Hyber Pass untouched, a theory that was patently absurd.

Still, that was the situation that forced one of the two adults to remain awake at all times lest one of their traveling companions grab the boy and pitch him off the train in a misguided attempt to placate the wings.

As for their part, two or three of the airborne variants were always visible during daylight hours, riding the thermals well beyond rifle range, waiting for the angens to drag the *Zephyr* up into the heights. Rebo kept an eye on the airborne bandits for a while before turning his binoculars to the south and scanning the pass itself. Thanks to the long, gradual approach that led up to the crossing, it had been used for thousands of years *before* the monorail had been constructed and continued to be important millennia later.

The remains of an ancient fortress guarded the left side of the shining rail. Only one section of its crenellated walls remained standing, while what appeared to be a newer structure sat to the right, its once brightly painted dome having faded to a powder blue. A dark zigzag crack cut down across the gently curved surface to meet the boxy walls on which the roof rested. The barriers built to protect the structure had crumbled, or been blown apart, and lay in weathered heaps. None of which was especially remarkable, except for a momentary flash of bright green, which disappeared as the flatcar jumped an expansion joint and the binoculars came off their target. Rebo was about to bring his glasses back and reacquire the image when he heard a shout. "Look! The wings are coming!"

The runner swiveled to his left, spotted a grouping of dark specks, and swore softly. There were at least three dozen of the airborne bandits, more than enough to overwhelm the train, especially if other variants were already hidden toward the top of the pass.

Then came the distant *pop! pop! pop!* of what sounded like black powder muskets followed by what might have been shouting. Rebo turned back toward the pass, located the patch of green that he'd noticed before, and realized that it was just one of half a dozen brightly colored flags. Puffs of smoke could seen as the people on top of the pass fired a volley down into the rocks below. Fire sleeted back upward a few moments later, but was largely ineffective, and stopped when a dozen variants emerged from hiding to take to the air. More shots were fired, one of the wings seemed to pause in midair, then spiraled toward the ground below.

"Look!" Norr said from a position next to the runner's elbow. "The wings turned back!"

Rebo turned once again and saw that the sensitive was correct. With their ambush ruined, and confronted with unexpectedly strong opposition, the variants had called it a day. The train was a scene of wild jubilation as fear gave way to joy, the passengers waved their unfired weapons, hugged each other, and shouted insults at the distant wings.

Though pleased with the recent turn of events, the runner remained cautious as the angens labored up the long slope, and entered the broad U-shaped pass. It had been his experience that when someone fires on a mutual enemy it doesn't necessarily mean that they will become a friend.

But any doubts the runner had vanished as a horn was heard, drums rattled, and hundreds of friendly-looking people came to greet them. There were men, women, and children. And all, with the exception of the Shah's lancers, were dressed in red. They waved gaily, shouted greetings to the people on the train, and were clearly in a jubilant mood. Lee, his eyes huge, tugged at Rebo's sleeve. "Do you see how the people are dressed? They belong to the red hat sect!"

The runner eyed the crowd, confirmed that nearly all of them wore red clothing, and frowned. "You're sure?"

"Yes!" Lee answered excitedly. "I'm sure!"

"But why?" Norr put in. "Why would so many people walk all the way up here?"

There was no answer as the driver shouted an order, the angens came to a stop, and a man crossed the short causeway that extended out from the ancient fortress. He was tall, thin, and wore a pair of thick glasses. "Greetings. My name is Brother Larkas. Welcome to what was once the temple of TasTas. We are about to break a five-day fast, and you are welcome to join us."

"Thank you," Norr said, stepping forward to meet the monk. "I'm sure I speak for all of my fellow passengers when I say that it's wonderful to see you. May I ask what brings you and your adherents all the way up to the top of the pass?"

"Of course," the monk answered agreeably. "We are here to celebrate the moment when the great teacher Nom Maa paused here to rest. When the Divine Wind founded the temple he promised to return on the 262nd day of the year. So, having no way to know which year the great one had in mind, we return each year to greet him. Then, once the ceremonies are complete, we return to Tra."

Rebo looked at Norr, and she looked at Lee, who spoke before either one of the adults could intervene. The words were in Tilisi. "Greetings, elder brother. I believe it was Nom Maa who said that 'life is a journey during which each traveler must seek to learn, taking knowledge where he or she may find it, even from the silence of the stones.'"

The runner didn't know what the youngster had said, only that the red hat monk looked thunderstruck, and that a vast hush had fallen over the crowd. "Who are you?" Larkas demanded, all color having drained from his face.

"What did he say?" Rebo demanded.

"He wants to know who I am," Lee replied matter-of-factly. Then, careful to speak standard rather than Tilisi, the boy answered. "They call me Dor."

The monk's eyebrows rose, as if he had expected a different answer, and he looked at Rebo. "Is this young man your son?"

The runner nodded.

"Good," the red hat replied. "Please follow me."

Rebo looked at Norr. She shrugged noncommittally and took Lee's hand. The crowd parted to let the threesome pass, and the train's passengers watched in mute astonishment as the man, woman, and little boy followed Larkas across the causeway. From there it was a short walk up a zigzag path to the base of the temple and a slab of highly polished granite. The monument was surrounded by a border made out of slightly wilted flowers, and it appeared as if the stone's surface had been cleaned and polished. "There!" the monk said triumphantly, as he pointed at the marker. "What does *that* say?"

The inscription was in standard, which meant that Rebo could read it, and proceeded to do so. "Life is a journey during which each traveler must seek to learn, taking knowledge where he or she may find it, even from the silence of the stones."

"So?" the runner inquired. "What's the big deal?"

"It's the same quote I used by way of a greeting," Lee

replied, his voice uncertain. "Nom Maa was father to many sayings. It's a coincidence—nothing more."

It seemed that Larkas thought differently however, because the monk turned to address the crowd, and his voice carried a long way in the mountain air. "It's *him!*" The holy man proclaimed. "The Divine Wind has returned!"

There was a moment of silence as the throng processed what the monk had said. That was followed by a loud *hiss* as the entire crowd drew a deep breath and let loose shrieks of joy. Rebo heard shouts of "God be praised!" and was helpless to intervene as the multitude surged forward to surround Lee. There was a moment of chaos as people attempted to touch the boy, followed by a loud report as the runner fired a shot into the air, and Larkas joined the fray. The monk could be something of a bully when he needed to be, and a series of brusk commands, along with a flurry of well-aimed blows brought the mob under control.

Neither Rebo nor Norr understood much of what ensued, but it soon became apparent that a ceremony was under way, and Lee was to be at the center of it. That bothered Rebo, who hated to see his client's cover so thoroughly blown, but Norr was more philosophical. "Maybe it's for the best, Jak. After all, once we board the ship, we can start all over again."

The runner wasn't so sure, not if Lee was carried into the city on the shoulders of his followers, but hoped that Larkas could put things right. Given the fact that the local red hats revered the boy, it seemed logical to suppose that they would protect him, even if that meant keeping their mouths shut.

Eventually, after a good deal of praying, chanting, and singing on the part of the red hats, afternoon faded into evening. The train passengers voted to stay the night rather than travel on their own, sentries were posted, and a fire was built in front of the temple. Then, as the sun dipped below the western horizon, and firelight danced across the cracked dome, the celebrants began to toot small horns and tap on tiny drums. Then, once the proper mood had been established, legends were reborn as fancifully costumed men and women took to the impromptu stage. Rebo watched for a while, but quickly became bored, and was about to turn in, when Norr materialized at his side. He was struck by the way the light played across the planes of her face and the fresh clean smell of her. But there was something different about the sensitive. Something uncharacteristically hesitant, as if she was about to share some sort of secret. Her voice was solemn. "Hello, Jak."

The runner answered in kind. "Hello, Lanni."

"I need a favor."

"I'll grant it if I can," the runner answered cautiously.

"You remember Lysander . . . The entity who seized control of my body in Gos."

"How could I forget?" Rebo inquired dryly. "What about him?"

"Well," Norr said hesitantly, "I figure it's only a matter of time before he tries the same thing again. The question is why? There must be a reason."

"Yeah?" the runner acknowledged. "So?"

"So," the sensitive continued, "I want you to speak with him."

"Me?" Rebo demanded incredulously. "Why me?"

"Because I can't do it myself, and I trust you," Norr answered honestly. "Maybe, if I understood what the miserable bastard wants, I could get rid of him."

The proposal made a certain amount of weird sense. The runner nodded slowly. "Okay, it's worth a try. What should I do?"

"Follow me," the sensitive instructed. "We'll need some privacy."

Rebo turned to look for Lee. The youngster was seated right next to Larkas, and both of the monks were surrounded by dozens of superfanatical red hats. If the lad was safe anywhere, it was there. "All right . . . Lead the way."

The sensitive led the runner across the causeway, past the carefully secured train, and toward the dark bulk of the fortress beyond. The surety with which Norr moved seemed to suggest that she had been that way before and knew where to go. That impression was confirmed a few minutes later when Norr led Rebo through a door and into the ruins beyond. A series of turnings brought them into a roofless room that had once served as the commanding officer's private quarters. A match flared as the sensitive bent over the makings of a fire, flames were born, and sparks swirled toward the starry sky. "There," Norr said, pointing toward a carefully positioned chunk of rock. "You will sit there, and I will sit here, next to the fire."

Rebo nodded, and was about to take the seat assigned to him, when Norr spoke. "Jak . . ."

The runner turned. "Yes?"

"Can I ask another favor?"

Her voice was so thin, so hollow, that Rebo found himself answering without hesitation. "Of course. What is it?"

The sensitive took two steps forward. "Hold me."

The runner opened his arms, Norr took one final step, and felt him pull her close. The embrace was firm, but gentle, just as she had known it would be. And, as Rebo's strength flooded in and around her, the sensitive felt the first stirrings of a physical need that she hadn't thought about for weeks.

Rebo felt a shiver run through the young woman, remembered her description of the last time Lysander had taken control of her body, and knew that what she proposed to do was equivalent to allowing a man she didn't know to have sex with her. His right hand found the hollow between her shoulder blades and their lips met a few moments later. Not because either one of them had planned it, but because it seemed like the natural thing to do. Norr stood on tiptoes, locked her fingers behind his neck, and returned the pressure with interest. The kiss lasted for half a minute or so and was broken as she pulled away. "That was nice, Jak. *Very* nice. But I need to do what we came here for, or I'll lose my nerve."

The runner released the sensitive and waited for her to sit on a chunk of stone before taking the seat assigned to him. "Don't touch me while I'm in trance," the sensitive cautioned, "and assuming that Lysander comes through, please try to discover what he's after."

Rebo nodded and watched silently, as Norr closed her eyes and positioned both hands palms upward. The runner had attempted to make contact with his mother once but without success. Did that mean she was alive? Perhaps, although the medium he had hired had cautioned him that some spirits don't want to return.

Later, Rebo had wondered why he hadn't sought to speak with his father, and concluded that while he respected the big fisherman, he'd always been afraid of him, too. Other than that single attempt, the runner had been focused on life rather than death, figuring that he would deal with next plane of existence once he arrived there.

Then, with no background sound other than the distant

thump! thump! thump! of the red hat drums, there was a long period of silence. So long, that Rebo had just about given up on the makeshift séance, when the sensitive opened her mouth and spoke. But, rather than *her* voice, the runner heard a deep baritone instead. "You! The fool on the rock! Where am I?"

"*You* are dead," the runner responded unsympathetically. "I, on the other hand, am located at the top of Hyber Pass, on the planet Pooz. Is your name Lysander?"

There was a moment of silence as if the spirit entity was taking a moment to consider the question. "Yes, I was once known as Milos Lysander, although I have had many other names as well. Including that of Nilo Hios, father of the star gate, and ruler of the Imperium."

"Congratulations," Rebo said evenly. "So, your eminence, what *is* a star gate? And why would anyone care?"

Though more than a little contentious, the question had the desired effect, and Milos Lysander, aka Nilo Hios, launched into a long rant. By the time it ended the runner had the impression of a once-glorious empire tied together by a network of high-tech portals that rendered spaceships obsolete and allowed travelers to move between planets as easily as they might step from one room to another. "Okay," Rebo said agreeably, "so what happened? Why aren't the gates in use now?"

"With the exception of a maintenance system, which I discovered during the course of my last incarnation, all of the portals were destroyed," Lysander responded darkly. "In spite of the gift I gave the people of the Imperium, some labeled me as a tyrant, rose up, and tore my government down. My former self was murdered, the star gates were destroyed, and a fleet of sentient spaceships were created to serve in their place."

"Wait a minute," the runner interjected. "Did I understand you to say that some of the gates remain in operation?"

"Yes, of course," Lysander said loftily. "They continue to operate under the auspices of the Techno Society, which I founded and dedicated to the full restoration of the star gates. It's the only thing that can arrest mankind's steady slide back toward the barbaric past."

"So? What's the problem?" Rebo inquired.

"New gates can be copied from those that remain operational," Lysander answered. "That lies within our power. The missing element is the artificial intelligence required to reenergize the interplanetary grid and operate the system. Unfortunately, the knowledge required to construct such an AI was lost hundreds of years ago."

"So, that's why you keep trying to communicate?" the runner demanded. "In order to find this AI thing?"

"Logos isn't a *thing,*" Lysander said reprovingly. "He is, for lack of a better description, an artificial person. I don't especially like him, but I *need* him, and he's far too intelligent to allow some mob to destroy him. That's why I continue to visit your wretched plane of existence. Because my operatives have been unable to find Logos."

"But why *this* particular channel?" the runner insisted. "She doesn't want to take part in your search, and there are thousands, perhaps millions of other sensitives. Why not annoy one of them for a change?"

"Coming back is difficult," Lysander responded. "It requires a great deal of effort. That's why a relatively small number of entities make the attempt. However, when a preexisting link exists between the spirit and the channel, that makes the task easier."

"A link?" Rebo demanded doubtfully. "What sort of link

could possibly exist between the channel and yourself? The two of you never met."

"Not during our most recent incarnations," Lysander admitted. "But, back when I was known as Nilo Hios, the channel was my daughter. She didn't like me, but a bond exists nonetheless, and that makes communication easier."

There was a moment of silence while Rebo tried to absorb all the implications of what he had just heard. The fire crackled, collapsed in on itself, and released a column of sparks. "Okay, let's say you're right, how 'bout some sort of a deal? Rather than turn Lanni over to a bunch of homicidal maniacs—why not help her find this Logos thing?"

But if Lysander heard the words, he was unable to respond to them, as the connection between the two planes of existence suddenly snapped. Norr shuddered, opened her eyes, and swallowed. Her voice was hoarse. "Is he gone?"

"Hell, I don't know," the runner answered. "You tell me."

Norr frowned, then nodded. "He's gone. So, tell me . . . What did he say?"

"You couldn't hear?"

"Some, but not all. I kept drifting in and out."

So Rebo told the sensitive what Lysander had said, starting with the star gates, and concluding with her previous relationship to him. That caused Norr to shiver and wrap her cloak around her body. "It's disgusting, but makes a strange sort of sense. The same thing can't be said for the deal you offered him, however. What led you to believe that I would knowingly cooperate with him?"

The runner's eyebrows rose. "Do you want him to leave you alone or not? And, given the situation, do you have a better idea? Besides, what if what he says is true? What if we could bring back the spaceships? The medical treatments that the ancients had . . . And all the rest of it? That would be a good thing, would it not?"

Norr knew that technology had been used for evil as well as good. Something that Lysander made no mention of. But there was little doubt that technology *had* delivered benefits to the human race in the past—and she was ready to try just about anything in order to rid herself of the insistent spirit. "Yes," she said reluctantly, "I suppose it would."

Drums beat an insistent rhythm, a breeze slipped through the pass, and the fire stirred by way of a response. Some, if not all, of her questions had been answered, but the essence of the problem remained.

Having made its way up through Hyber Pass—the rail on which the *Zephyr* rode fell toward the plain beyond. With red hats not only crowded onto the cars, but hanging off the sides as well, the driver was forced to brake constantly in an effort to prevent the train from colliding with the angens that half galloped ahead of it. Smoke issued from a wooden block as it made contact with the metal rail, a cloud of steam appeared as one of the lancers dumped a bucket of urine onto the primitive device, and the wet wood squealed in protest.

But, worrisome as the mechanics of the situation were Rebo welcomed the feel of the early-morning sun on his face, the smell of the mountain air, and the knowledge that bandit country lay behind rather than in front of him. Further bolstering the runner's spirits was the fact that Larkas had ordered his flock to treat Lee as they would any other boy. Had the black hats inserted a spy into the group? Probably, but Rebo hoped to board the next ship before the opposition could get organized. As for the blond man, and the

Techno Society, only time would tell. The runner knew it was foolish to involve himself in Norr's problems, especially when such involvement could compromise his mission; but, try as he might, Rebo couldn't bring himself to part company with her. Not yet anyway.

As the monorail wound its way down through grassy foothills, it crossed back and forth over a smoothly flowing river and swept past a multitude of well-kept farms. Then, as it emerged from the hills, the train rumbled straight toward Tra. Unlike Gos, most of which lay below ground, the towers of Tra seemed to leap up off the plain as if intent on touching the sky. And, unlike the high-rise buildings back on Anafa, which remained unoccupied because of a lack of power, *these* structures were very much in use. That was made possible by the plain that surrounded the city, the winds that blew in from the west, and rank after rank of two-hundred-foot-tall propeller-driven generators that provided Tra with electricity. There were gaps, of course, times when for one reason or another the winds refused to blow, but the local citizenry had adapted to that. When the power faded so did they, quitting whatever they were doing to take a nap, or breaking to eat a meal.

It hadn't always been like that of course, because back in the beginning, when Tra was founded, the wind-powered generators had been used as a supplemental rather than primary source of electricity. But, after the fall of the Imperium, and the destruction of the technocracy that followed, the city's power core eventually wore out. And, not having the parts to repair it, one of the Shah's ancestors had commissioned additional wind-driven generators to make up the difference. A comparatively simple technology local machine shops could support. Some even hoped to reactivate the monorail one day, but there wasn't enough surplus power for that, and the Shah was rumored to oppose it. He liked the way things were, or so the wags said, and perhaps they were right.

Now, slowed to little more than a crawl by the weight of all the extra passengers, the *Zephyr* rolled through a gleaming forest as a persistent breeze caused the gigantic propellers to turn. The enormous structures rumbled so loudly that they stole the sound of the wind—and seemed to converse with each other in a language that mere humans could never understand.

Eventually, as the train slowed to a crawl, some of the passengers got off in order to lighten the load and stretch their legs. Rebo was among them, as was Lee, who walked at the runner's side. "So," Rebo shouted to make himself heard over the wind-driven generators, "how's the Divine Wind?"

"Don't call me that," Lee said crossly. "While I doubt that I'm anyone other than myself, your sarcasm would be inappropriate if I were the Divine Wind."

"Sorry," the runner replied contritely. "Please allow me to rephrase the question. The people all around us believe that you are very special. How does that make you feel?"

"It scares me," the boy replied honestly. "They think I'm Nom Maa so they believe I'm wise. But it isn't true. Yes, I can repeat what the great masters said, but so what? That makes me fit to follow rather than lead."

"I don't know about that," Rebo said thoughtfully. "Take yesterday, for example. You certainly held your own during those ceremonies."

"Yes," Lee agreed soberly, "because I was raised to do so. Rituals can be conducted by anyone willing to take the time to memorize them. But the spiritual understanding that lies behind them? That comes from within."

The runner placed a hand on the boy's shoulder. "What about what you just said? It sounded like wisdom to me . . . So where did *that* come from?"

"I don't know," Lee said miserably. "But the fact remains, if I'm Nom Maa, then I should know it! What if we arrive at the city of CaCanth, and I fail the test? The black hats will take control."

Rebo shrugged. "All you can do is try. While I admit that the black hats seem like a rotten bunch, they've been in charge before. Or am I wrong?"

"No," Lee allowed thoughtfully. "You're correct."

"And the religion survived," the runner observed, pausing to step over a pile of manure.

"Yes, I guess it did," the boy agreed hopefully.

"So, do your best and let the chips fall where they may," Rebo advised. "That's all any of us can do."

The youngster took a moment to think about it, looked up into his bodyguard's face, and grinned broadly. "That sounds like good advice. Perhaps *you* should have been a monk."

Rebo would have replied, but Brother Larkas chose that moment to begin one of his chants, and the sound of human voices merged with the rumble of a thousand propellers to create a deep humming sound. The sun inched a bit higher, the city of Tra shimmered in the distance, and Pooz continued to turn.

The crowd that turned out to meet the Zephyr *was domi-*nated by red-clad religious adherents. They insisted on scattering flower petals all about the platform while burning incense in tiny brass pots and chanting some sort of religious nonsense as they greeted friends and relatives who had completed the pilgrimage. But there were others as well, including a brace of tax collectors, a squad of lancers, and a swarm of vendors, beggars, and pickpockets. And there, hidden among them, was an informer named Mik Stipp, a man always on the lookout for potentially valuable information that he could sell to a variety of clients.

Stipp, who often posed as a beggar, elbowed his way to what looked like a good spot and wrestled a felt hat out of his coat pocket. Once opened, the heavily creased article of clothing was instantly transformed into a serviceable beggar's bowl, which the informer held out before him. "Can ya spare a gunar for the poor? A crust of bread for the hungry? A kind word for a man who can barely see? Oh, bless you, ma'am, and your children as well."

The red hats proved to be in a generous mood, and it wasn't long before a scattering of coins lined the bottom of Stipp's hat, providing the informer with what amounted to a bonus for his labors. Then horns began to sound, shouts were heard, as the heavily laden *Zephyr* pulled into the station. There was total chaos as those standing on the platform tried to board the train while those on the flatcars sought to get off. That provided Stipp with plenty of time to scan the incoming passengers, spot the sensitive, and empty the coins into the palm of his hand. Ten minutes later, with the hat pulled down to conceal the upper part of his face, the informer followed Norr in toward the center of town.

Like any good businessman, Stipp knew what his clients wanted and what such information was worth. And while of little interest to most people, the informant knew one individual who would pay good money to hear about the sensitive's arrival, and would almost certainly want to meet her. The knowledge lifted his spirits, put a spring in Stipp's step, and brought a smile to his face. Some days were better than others—and this one looked as if it would be very good indeed.

SIX

The Planet Pooz

By encouraging communications between systems, planets, and people, the ancients sought to bind their empires together. But those who wish to rule must divide populations rather than unify them. The ancients are gone. We rule in their place.

—The Shah of Pooz,
in a letter to his sons

While even the newest of Tra's skyscrapers was hundreds of years old, and not even the Shah had the resources required to construct a new one, the citizens had been busy modifying the buildings they had. The most obvious result of their tinkering was the multiplicity of sky bridges that linked the mostly vertical structures together. The spans came in all shapes, sizes, and styles. Some were enclosed, some were open, and some incorporated aspects of both. Most were fairly substantial and capable of carrying a heavy load, but others consisted of little more than four cables and some planks to walk on. Those were used as shortcuts by the city's young people, who scampered across the chasms that separated the high-rise buildings as if they were only a few feet off the ground, and seemed to delight in the risks they took. And not just at one level, but at many, so that when Rebo looked upward it was through a maze of crisscrossing structures that split the sky into small geometric shapes.

However, diverse though they certainly were, the sky bridges all had a common purpose: to enable the local citizens to travel between the skyscrapers without taking the long, tedious journey down into the crowded thoroughfares, where open-air stalls lined both sides of the streets, piles of angen manure awaited collection, and the air was thick with the acrid odor of burning charcoal.

The combination of sky bridges above and streets below made it difficult for newcomers to find their way around. Based on the research he had carried out back on Anafa, Rebo knew that unlike Gos, the city of Tra boasted a full-fledged branch of the runner's guild. That meant a secure environment in which he and his companions could hole up. But where the hell was it? He hated to ask, since doing so would identify him as a stranger, but the alternative was to wander the streets forever.

The runner scanned the street ahead, spotted one of the many cart men sipping a cup of tea, and waved. Eager to earn a gunar or two the laborer swallowed the last of the lukewarm liquid and returned the cup to the tea vendor in exchange for a copper. Then, having retrieved his hand truck, the cart man made his way over to the spot where his perspective customers were waiting. "We just arrived from Gos," Rebo proclaimed, "and we're tired of carrying these packs."

"Where to?" the cart man wanted to know, as he loaded the packs onto his conveyance and roped them into place.

"The runner's guild."

The cart man gave a perfunctory nod and took off. Rebo, Norr, and Lee tagged along behind. Mik Stipp watched the byplay from fifty yards away and hurried to follow. The newcomers weren't going anywhere too fancy he hoped, because while his clothes were fine for the street, they wouldn't pass muster above the tenth floor of all but the most disreputable buildings.

Their guide led the threesome into a metal-sheathed building, through a crowded lobby, and into a packed elevator. The cart man got off on level six. Rebo, Norr, and Lee followed their luggage through a maze of corridors and out onto an open sky bridge. It seemed sturdy enough, but Lee could see down through the metal grating and felt his stomach go flip-flop. It seemed natural to reach out for Norr's hand, and, once he had, to think of his mother.

For her part the sensitive felt uneasy, as if someone was watching her, but try as she might Norr had been unable to spot a threat. So the sensitive took comfort from Rebo's presence, kept a good grip on the youngster's hand, and tried to ignore the prickly sensation between her shoulder blades.

It turned out that the runner's guild occupied the entire twenty-third floor of a respectable building. Each branch of the organization had its own distinct personality, and while the building on Anafa was impressive, the availability of wind-generated power meant that the one on Pooz had more amenities.

Interstellar runners didn't pass through Tra all that often, so there was a stir when Rebo identified himself, verified his identity by answering questions kept on file at every branch, and requested a suite. Such was the resulting swirl of activity that none of the newly arrived travelers noticed the small commotion as Stipp tried to talk his way past security and was turned away.

An apprentice led the runner and his party to a suite that

looked out onto the eastern part of the city. It consisted of two bedrooms, two baths, and a central sitting room.

What remained of the day was spent turning the lights on and off, taking long hot showers, and flushing toilets. Finally, after a dinner that had been brought up to their room, the travelers retired. Rebo and Lee settled into one room while Norr took the other. It took the sensitive a while to get to sleep, but eventually she did, and was soon lost in a confused jumble of dreams.

All three of them awoke feeling rested and refreshed the next morning. Rebo ordered a large breakfast, and by the time it arrived, everyone was ready to eat. Rebo had established that three days remained before the next ship was scheduled to arrive. The question was what to do with the intervening time? Lee wanted to explore the city, and Norr agreed, but the runner had something else in mind. "We'll do that later," Rebo said, pausing between bites. "First, we have some research to do."

Norr sipped her tea. "What kind of research?"

"Lysander claimed that he had an incarnation as a man named Nilo Hios and that you were his daughter."

The sensitive made a face. "I was trying to forget."

"Not to mention the artificial person that he referred to," the runner continued. "Who knows? Maybe we can find some mention of him in the history books. For example, where was Logos when the Imperium fell? If we're going to find him, we need a place to start."

Norr frowned. "I appreciate the thought. I really do. But you have responsibilities."

"Yes, he does," Lee agreed, speaking for the first time. "I don't know who this artificial person is, but our trip remains on hold until the ship arrives, so we have time. Let's do some research, *then* go out and explore the city."

"That's the spirit," Rebo said approvingly. "Now finish your breakfast. With any luck at all some of the information we need is right here in this building. Most branches employ a historian. I consulted the one back on Anafa while planning this trip. In my profession it pays to learn about the place you're headed *before* you get there."

Half an hour later the three of them had left the suite, made their way through the halls, and were standing in front of the reception desk. The runner told the clerk what he wanted and saw the other man nod agreeably. "Of course, sir. There isn't enough room to house them here, so the archives are stored down in the third subbasement. Our historian lives down there and should be up and around by now. He was a runner once. His name is Wiley."

Two different elevator trips were required to reach the third subbasement. One that transported them to street level and a second that dropped them below street level.

Rebo, Norr, and Lee had the elevator entirely to themselves by the time it stopped in the third subbasement and understandably so. Unlike levels one and two there were no cross-connections to other buildings on three, the corridors were only dimly lit, and there were occasional puddles where water dripped from overhead pipes.

Rebo approached a door with the words RUNNER'S GUILD—ARCHIVES printed on it and gave it a push. The room that lay beyond was relatively small, and he noticed that regularly spaced holes dotted the walls as if to allow for some sort of fixtures that had subsequently been removed. Strangely, from his perspective at least, three large drains had been set into the floor.

The next door seemed to sense his presence and slid out of the way on its own. That allowed the runner and his companions to enter a circular chamber before being confronted by another barrier. It was crude when compared to the first two, and judging from the damage to the tile work around it, had been added at a later date. It was locked, which forced Rebo to bang on it. "Hello? Is anybody home?"

The runner's words were still echoing back and forth as Norr wet a forefinger and used the moisture to rub the grime off one of the surrounding tiles. Her finger was soon black with dirt, but part of a picture appeared, along with the word VARGA. It sounded familiar somehow, but the sensitive couldn't quite place it, and the door opened before she could mention what she had discovered to Rebo.

The man who peered out at Rebo had long, straggly hair, slightly bulging eyes, and a pasty complexion. He was clearly annoyed. "Yes? What do you want?"

"I'm a runner," Rebo answered evenly. "I'd like to do some research."

The archivist shifted his gaze to Norr followed by Lee. "And who are they?" he inquired suspiciously.

"The woman is my wife, and the boy is my son," the runner lied smoothly. "Now, will you open the door? Or will I have to go all the way upstairs and talk to the man at the front desk?"

"That won't be necessary," the man replied grudgingly. "My name is Wiley. You and your family can come in, but be sure to close the door behind you. All sorts of riffraff find their way down into the third subbasement, and I get tired of chasing them away."

Rebo looked at Norr, raised his eyebrows as if to say, "Is this guy strange or what?" and followed the archivist into his private kingdom. The runner, who had been hoping for shelves loaded with neatly bound books à la the branch on Anafa, was in for a big disappointment. There were shelves all right, what looked like hundreds of them, but rather than the volumes Rebo had envisioned they were filled with stacks of clearly unorganized papers, piles of tightly rolled manuscripts, and boxes filled with what might have been electronic storage modules. "Sorry about the mess," Wiley said defensively, "but this is what my predecessor left me. I plan to organize all of it, but I have to read everything first, and I'm only halfway through."

"How long have you been at it?" Norr inquired, as she bent over to rescue a crumpled manuscript from the floor.

"About twelve local years," the clerk responded, as he brushed a strand of dirty hair out of his face. "But enough of my problems . . . What can I do for *you?*"

The last was delivered in such an ingratiating manner that the runner decided that he preferred the hostile Wiley. "I'm looking for some general information about the Imperium, a leader named Nilo Hios, and an artificial person called Logos. Can you help me?"

"He can't," a deep booming voice replied, "but *I* can."

All three of the visitors looked around in an effort to find the source of the voice, but it seemed to originate from everywhere at once. Wiley looked peeved. "I'm the archivist here! And you're just a machine. So shut up."

Rebo raised a hand. "Wait a minute . . . Did you say a 'machine'? I'd like to hear more."

"Of course you would," the voice said confidently. "Wiley couldn't find his ass with both hands, as you can plainly see. I am a Gate Keeper model 517B, and in so far as I know, the only one of my kind still in operation. Friends call me Fil."

"Okay, Fil," the runner said cautiously, "it's a pleasure to meet you. My name is Jak Rebo. This is my wife Lanni and my son Dor. Pardon my ignorance, but what does a Gate Keeper 517B do?"

"That's a good question," Fil answered cheerfully. "But

before I answer it, a short history lesson is in order. More than a thousand worlds belonged to the empire during the final days of Emperor Hios's rule. The starships used to find and settle the member planets were considered obsolete by then and relegated to the status of mere curiosities. Hard though it may be for you to believe, interplanetary travel was carried out via a vast network of star gates. Portals like the one that you passed through as you entered the archive."

Norr remembered the tile, the picture she'd seen, and the name Varga. Of course! The *planet* Varga, which had been mentioned in some of the texts she had read as a child and was supposedly home to a large colony of sensitives.

"And Hios?" the runner inquired. "How did he wind up as emperor? Did he invent the technology behind the star gates?"

"Yes, and no," the computer replied. "Hios was part of a *team* that created the technology, and being the most ambitious of the lot, took advantage of his position to seize power."

This was, or had been her father that Fil was talking about, and Norr was naturally curious. "So, how did he do that? Seize power I mean?"

"Hios controlled an artificial intelligence named Logos," the computer replied, "and Logos controlled more than a thousand lesser AIs such as myself. So, given the fact that interplanetary commerce depended on the star gates, anyone who controlled them controlled the flow of information, the shipment of goods, and the movement of troops.

"Many observers, including myself, believe that his original intentions were good. By tying the worlds together, Hios was creating the means by which mankind could take what he called 'the next step,' to a higher level of civilization. Or that's what he said.

"But, you're probably familiar with the old saying that 'absolute power corrupts absolutely,' and such was the case. Over a period of about ten years the emperor's decisions became so self-serving, and so capricious, that many thought him mad. A resistance movement was born, heretofore obsolete spaceships were refitted, and rebellious runners began to carry messages back and forth between the planets.

"Runners like *you!*" Lee said proudly, his hand tugging at Rebo's jacket.

"Yes," Fil agreed, as he resumed his narration. "And Hios was angered by such activity. So angered that the runner's guild was outlawed, star gates were used to deliver nuclear weapons onto rebel planets, and entire cities were leveled. The citizenry rose up, or tried to, but thanks to his ever-growing network of portals Hios could move his brutal security troops around very quickly, and the resistance fighters lost every battle. Finally, when things were so dark that it seemed that all hope was lost, it was a member of the emperor's own family who brought the madness to an end."

Norr remembered what Lysander had said, that *she* was the one who had ended the emperor's life, and felt a chill run down her spine. Rebo remembered, too—and wrapped an arm around her shoulders.

The AI had no way to know about the sensitive's relationship to Hios and continued his narration. "No one witnessed the murder, but it's said the emperor's daughter left her quarters via an open window, negotiated the ledge that ran the circumference of the building, and jumped down onto her father's private balcony."

Although Norr had entered trancelike states thousands of times during her lifetime, she had never experienced anything like what happened next. Instead of stepping halfway out of her body, as she normally did, the sensitive found herself entering *another* vehicle, one that felt different. It was smaller, but very athletic, something she gave thanks for as her feet smacked against the stone tiles of her father's balcony.

Outside of the door to his private suite, which was heavily guarded, the balcony represented the only other entrance to her father's bedroom. So far so good. But could she complete the task she had assigned herself? Her father was clearly evil, so the justification was there, as was the need to take action. Because no one except for a member of the emperor's immediate family would have the opportunity to kill him. Not with combat variants guarding him around the clock.

But to sneak into his bedroom, tiptoe up to his bed, and sink a knife into her own father? That was a lot to ask of any daughter, even one who was ashamed of what had been done in her family's name and desperately wanted the horror to end.

Still, that was the task that Princess Cara had set for herself, and that was what she was determined to accomplish no matter the price. High-quality synsilk whispered softly as the young woman made her way to the entrance, tried the handle, and felt it give. The well-lubricated hinges were silent as the door swung open and she entered the cavernous bedroom. She paused, listened for signs of alarm, but heard none. Light, such as it was, emanated from the slightly luminescent baseboard that circled the room.

Then, having removed the hunting knife from the sheath strapped to her thigh, the princess advanced on the bed. There were two forms under the covers, one of which represented her father, while the other belonged to whatever woman he had chosen to sleep with the evening before. Just the latest in a long string of lovers he had taken since his wife's death three years earlier.

A dozen steps carried Cara to her father's bedside. He was snoring gently as she raised the knife into the air; but then, just as she was about to plunge the blade into his unprotected chest, the emperor gave a sudden snort and his eyelids fluttered. He must have been able to see her in the dim light, because his eyes widened, and he spoke. "Cara? Is that you? What are you doing?"

Norr heard her previous self say, "I'm sorry," as she brought the weapon straight down. Her father produced a grunt of expelled air as the steel entered his chest, arched his back, and shuffled his feet. That was when the woman lying at his side awoke, saw Cara jerk the bloody blade out of her lover's chest, and screamed. The noise brought two combat variants into the room. They saw the assassin and opened fire.

Rebo felt Norr jerk as if something had struck her, saw her eyes pop open, and realized that while he had been listening to Fil she had been somewhere else. "Lanni? Are you all right?"

Norr, who was surprised to discover that she was still alive, nodded weakly. "What Fil said is true. I killed my father."

"*You* killed him?" Lee asked, his eyes huge. "I'm sorry."

"So am I," Norr replied sadly, patting the boy on the shoulder.

"Well, no one else was," Fil commented emotionlessly. "Once the word of Hios's death got out there was dancing in the streets—and that was the beginning of the end. The emperor's son tried to hold the Imperium together, but he wasn't up to the job, and the whole structure came apart. Mobs located and destroyed most of the star gates, not to mention the AIs who operated them, and a new government came to power. It lasted fifty-four years before it was replaced by what amounted to a technocracy, the same one that built a fleet of sentient starships to replace the star gates."

"So, what happened to Logos?" Rebo inquired pragmatically. "Lysander, that is to say Hios, told us that Logos is too smart to let himself be destroyed by a mob. Would you agree with that?"

"Logos is, or was, extremely intelligent," Fil agreed. "But that doesn't mean that he survived. After all, we Gate Keepers were pretty smart, too, and most of us were destroyed. Still, I have no hard evidence regarding a termination, so there's no way to know."

"Let's say he's alive," Norr put in. "Where would he be?"

"That's hard to say," the AI replied cautiously, "but I can tell you this . . . The last directive I received from him originated from Etu."

"That's where we're going!" Lee said brightly. "Just before Thara."

"Maybe, and maybe not," the runner responded, frowning to signal his displeasure regarding the information that Lee had unintentionally divulged. "Well, thank you very much. You have been most helpful." The threesome made their way out through what remained of the ancient star gate and into the basement beyond.

Meanwhile, back in the archive, Wiley scowled and made a note to redouble his efforts to find the AI's central processing unit as he locked the door behind them. He should spend the rest of the morning reading, the archivist knew that, but decided on a nap instead. After all, he reasoned, the manuscripts stacked all around him had been there for hundreds of years. A few additional hours wouldn't make any difference.

The lock made a gentle click *as the key turned, the door* opened, and the lights came on as four heavily armed men burst into the suite. Rebo awoke, and was in the process or reaching for his handgun, when two of the intruders entered the bedroom that he and Lee shared. "Hold it right there," one of them shouted, and pointed a double-barreled shotgun at the runner. Rebo held both hands up and away from his body.

Lee was frightened, but determined not to show it, and sat huddled on the couch where he had been sleeping. His eyes were big, but his mouth formed a straight line, and the runner felt proud of him. Especially since it seemed reasonable to assume that the men were there to kidnap the boy on behalf of the black hats.

But that assumption soon proved to be incorrect as Rebo came to realize that both intruders wore military uniforms, and a voice was heard from the next room. "All right! We have her! Time to pull out."

The soldier nearest the door backed through it, but the man with the scattergun remained where he was. Rebo wanted to go to Norr's aid, but the twin shotgun barrels looked like railway tunnels. The intruder seemed to read his mind. "There's nothing to worry about. Prince Palo would like to meet your wife. No harm will come to her and she will be compensated for her time. Once the audience is over we will bring her here. In the meantime I suggest that you go back to sleep."

Having provided what he believed to be comforting words, the soldier backed out of the room and closed the door behind him. The outer door slammed a few seconds later, and Rebo knew that the intruders were gone. The runner swore bitterly as he grabbed his weapon, swung his feet out onto the carpet, and left the bedroom to confirm what he already knew. Norr was gone.

Lee watched solemnly from across the room as Rebo returned. "Are you going after her?"

The runner was pulling his trousers on by then. He shook his head. "I can't. But I am going to go down and have a conversation with the desk clerk. Somebody gave those bastards a key to the front door. I want to know why."

Lee frowned. "Why not? Go after her I mean."

"Well, there's my responsibility to you for starters," Rebo replied. "Plus, judging from what the guy with the shotgun had to say, the Shah's son is the one who put the snatch on her. What am I supposed to do? Attack his palace?"

"Lanni wouldn't abandon *you,*" Lee objected as he pulled his clothes on. "And don't use me as an excuse! I'm going after her, so if you intend to guard me, you're coming, too."

Rebo stopped what he was doing to look at the boy. His eyes narrowed. "You promised to obey me and to do so without question. That means you're staying right here."

"No," Lee replied defiantly, "I promised to obey you so long as your instructions were consistent with moral law. This one isn't."

"The soldier said they would return her safe and sound."

"And maybe they will," Lee responded, as he laced his boots, "but anything can happen when Lanni goes into a trance. Nobody knows that better than you do. I want my knives."

There was something different about the way that the youngster spoke. He sounded like a man rather than a boy. Rebo frowned. "Your knives? You haven't worn them since the fight on the spaceship."

"That's right," Lee said determinedly, "but I'm going wear them now."

The runner thought about what that implied. Lanni

meant so much to Lee that he was not only willing to defy his bodyguard but to kill in order to protect the sensitive. Because she had become a sort of mother figure? Because he had a crush on her? It hardly mattered. Rebo nodded grudgingly. "All right, have it your way. The knives are in my pack. But don't go off half-cocked! If we're going to commit suicide, we'll do it my way. Understood?"

Suddenly the man was gone and the little boy had returned. Lee grinned. "Yes, sir."

"Good," Rebo replied gruffly. "Get a shirt on. We have work to do."

A partially clothed Norr was still kicking and struggling as she was carried out into the guild's lobby, past the worried-looking desk clerk, through security, and into an elevator. That particular car had been taken out of service by a frightened maintenance man who hurried to close the door once the sensitive and her abductors were safely aboard. He turned a key, and the ancient box-shaped container shuddered slightly as it began its descent.

Then, tired of trying to restrain the woman without striking her, the soldiers put her down. "Here," a noncom said, as he shoved a wad of the woman's clothing at her. "You're going to have an audience with the prince, so you might want to get dressed."

That was when Norr remembered that all she had on was a short-sleeved pullover shirt and a pair of panties. A fact that wasn't lost on the other soldiers, all of whom had taken the opportunity to ogle her long, slender legs.

The sensitive managed to resist the temptation to try and cover what the soldiers had already seen and sorted through the ball of clothing that had been thrust at her. Finally, after dumping most of the items onto the floor, she assembled a halfway-decent outfit. Norr was just about to get dressed when the elevator coasted to a stop. "So," the sensitive demanded, "what's it going to be? Should I finish dressing here? Or are you going to march a half-naked woman out through the lobby? That should start some interesting rumors about the prince."

The noncom looked annoyed. "Go ahead and finish. Hurry it up though . . . We haven't got all night."

Norr frowned and folded her arms across her chest. "I'll start the minute that you and your men leave the elevator."

The noncom started to object, appeared to think better of it, and gestured toward the open door. "You heard the lady . . . Wait outside."

The soldiers left, the sensitive ordered the maintenance man to close the door, and proceeded to glare at him until he turned his back. She tried the same technique on the noncom, but he'd been around for a while, and didn't trust the variant farther than he could throw a howitzer. "You haven't got anything I haven't seen before. Now get on with it."

That left Norr with little choice but to turn her back on the soldier, remove the pullover, and replace it with a bra. Then, having attempted to shake the wrinkles out of her only black dress, the sensitive stepped into it and pulled the garment up the length of her body. In the meantime her mind was racing. When she awoke to find men standing next to her bed the sensitive's first thought had been for Lee. Then, once it became obvious that they were after her rather than the boy, Norr had assumed that the intruders worked for Lysander's Techno Society. But now, as she straightened her dress, the sensitive realized that theory was wrong, too. Assuming that what the noncom said was true, and Prince Palo wanted to see her. The question was why? "Don't just stand there," Norr said pointing back over her shoulder. "Zip me up."

The noncom considered the order for a moment, decided that he could handle the spook if necessary, and took two steps forward. The zipper rose smoothly, Norr said, "Thank you," and turned to face him. "So," the sensitive said suggestively, "how do I look? Good enough for an audience with the Shah's son?"

The answer was that the variant looked a lot better than she had any right to given the circumstances, but the noncom wasn't about to say that. "It wouldn't be for me to say, ma'am. Please exit the elevator. The captain is waiting."

Having been unable to learn anything from the noncom, Norr stepped into a pair of seldom-used evening slippers, wished they were black instead of dark blue, and was herded out into the lobby. The soldiers gave her admiring glances, wondered what the noncom had seen, and hoped he would share.

It was late, so with the exception of the street people huddled outside, no one was present to witness the sensitive's departure. A ragged-looking beggar, one of only three metal men in the city, noticed that the female was a 92.5 percent match with a person he had been ordered to watch for and snapped a series of digital photos via his "eyes" as the sensitive walked past him. The photos would be downloaded to a tiny disk, which would be secured to one of the birds that constantly flew back and forth between Gos and Tra, and sent on its way the moment the sun rose.

The vehicle that waited curbside had once been equipped with an engine, but it had long since been removed to clear out a space where the coachman could sit. The conveyance was shaped like an elongated teardrop, boasted permanently darkened windows, and crouched on six tires—two in front and four in back. Running boards and handgrips had been added so that a contingent of bodyguards could cling to the vehicle's sides. The sensitive noticed that six perfectly matched angens waited to pull the carriage and that each of them sported a black, red, and silver hood, the same colors favored by the Shah and members of his immediate family.

One of the soldiers opened a gleaming metal door and motioned for Norr to enter. The sensitive looked back over her shoulder, half-expecting to see Rebo come charging out through the lobby, and realized how absurd that was. In spite of the fact that he had been kind enough to take an interest in her problems, the runner had Lee's safety to consider, not to mention needs of his own. And that was fine she assured herself. After all, she'd been on her own for a long time and was perfectly capable of solving her own problems. So why did she feel disappointed? Because she was being silly, that's why—an indulgence she couldn't afford.

Norr turned back, hiked her skirt a tiny bit higher, and slid into the coach. The interior was lit by candles concealed inside cleverly designed wall sconces. A man in fancy-looking uniform sat waiting for her. He nodded his head. "Captain Rik Tovar at your service. Please make yourself comfortable. We're late."

The candles flickered as the door closed, and the driver shouted an order to his team. The vehicle jerked into motion as the sensitive raised a well-plucked eyebrow. "Late? Late for what?"

"I thought that would be obvious," Tovar replied. "You are a sensitive. Individuals having your, ah, talents are rare hereabouts. Prince Palo would like to avail himself of your services."

Norr frowned. "Couldn't he ask? And schedule something during the day?"

"His highness has no need to *ask*," Tovar replied dryly. "And the summons was by way of an impulse. I apologize if we frightened you."

"Oh, no," the sensitive said caustically. "People barge into my room, point guns at me, and haul me off nearly every night. What exactly does he want?"

Tovar was relatively young, extremely well groomed, and possessed of a black mustache that he smoothed with a knuckle. "The prince has brothers, both of whom want more power, while his father seeks ways to keep all three of them at each other's throats. That makes for a great deal of uncertainty, which is one of the reasons why his highness tries to get an edge on his siblings by taking counsel from all manner of psychics, oracles, and fortune-tellers. So, once an informer reported that a sensitive had entered the city, the prince was eager to hear whatever nonsense you might choose to spout. I recommend that you take care however . . . The more obvious frauds end up working in the mines."

The officer was a skeptic, the kind of person who assumed that all sensitives were frauds, a breed that Norr had encountered many times before. She sat silent for a moment, cocked her head as if listening to someone, and nodded. "A woman is here to greet you . . . But she was a little girl when you last saw her. She says that she liked the name you gave her so much that she still goes by it even though there have been hundreds over the course of many incarnations."

All the blood seemed to drain out of Tovar's face. "A little girl? Are you sure?"

"Yes, I am," the sensitive replied. "Her name is Kia."

"My God," Tovar said, as tears ran down his cheeks. "It's true! My daughter is alive! Thank you."

"You're very welcome," Norr replied sincerely. "Listen,

I'm sorry to press you, especially at a moment like this. But what can you tell me about what I'm going to encounter? It could make a difference."

The officer used a crimson sleeve to dry his cheeks. His demeanor had changed. Now, in place of the cool skepticism that characterized his earlier comments, he seemed genuinely concerned for her safety. "You already know about Prince Palo and the situation within the family, so the only other counsel I can offer you has to do with his temper. Avoid it if you can."

Norr heard the driver shout a muffled order, felt the carriage start to slow, and saw lights through the darkened windows. The officer had regained his composure by then—as well as some of the smugness that went with it. He caught the sensitive's eye. "I trust that our conversation will remain confidential?"

Norr nodded. "Of course."

A servant opened the door, and Norr exited the carriage to find herself in what felt like a fantasyland. The roughly three-story-tall building clearly predated the skyscrapers around it and was bathed in artificial light. The structure's roof consisted of a dome that was very reminiscent of the temple in Hyber Pass, except that this one was in perfect condition and gleamed with fresh paint. Norr had the impression of a peaked pediment, horizontal entablature, and sturdy columns before being led around the side of the structure toward what she assumed was a service entrance.

Meanwhile, the manner in which the sparsely lit highrise buildings encircled the area, plus the gardens around the palace, conveyed the impression of a park. And that was when the sensitive realized that the structure had once been open to the public. A museum, gallery, or library created for the enjoyment of regular citizens rather than a single family.

But that line of thought was subsumed by a tidal wave of emotion as Lysander's distinctive personality flooded in around her. She hadn't felt his presence since the session in the pass, and it came as a shock. His words seemed to reverberate inside her head. "Listen to me! It's important."

The sensitive shook her head. "No! Not now! Go away!"

Tovar paused in front of an open door and turned to look at her. "What did you say?"

Norr, who had been unaware that she had spoken out loud, shook her head. "It wasn't important. Please lead the way."

The officer took the young woman at her word and led her inside. The service entrance opened into storage area and the kitchen beyond. In spite of the fact that breakfast was still many hours away, the staff was already hard at work preparing the wide assortment of fresh-baked flatbread, butter rolls, and sweet cakes that would be served to the prince and his family should they decide to make an appearance before noon.

Having exited the kitchen, Norr was led through a maze of hallways and ushered into a small but formal room. She was the only person present, but judging from the benches and chairs, up to a dozen people were required to wait there at times.

Norr had no more than sat down and heard the lock click, when Lysander took another run at her. The discarnate entity seemed very agitated, even for him, but the sensitive had no intention of allowing him through. What if the guards came for her only to discover that she was busy channeling the lunatic who had once been her father? No, that wouldn't do at all.

So Lysander pushed, Norr pushed back, and the two of them were at what amounted to a psychic impasse when the lock clicked and the door swung open. In place of Captain Tovar, who the sensitive expected to see, was a long-faced majordomo. He was dressed in a loose-fitting high-collared black tunic that fell well below his hips, trousers to match, and a pair of pointed slippers. He introduced himself as Simms and produced a bow so modest it was little more than a slight inclination of his torso. "The prince will receive you now."

A heavy weight rode the pit of Norr's stomach as she forced a smile, stood, and followed the servant out into the hall. Two members of the palace guard followed as the sensitive was led out into the formal passageway that circled the building and from there into the chamber where Prince Palo and his family preferred to receive unofficial guests.

Unlike the throne room that Norr had imagined, it was furnished with comfortable-looking furniture, and the walls were lined with thousands of leather-bound books. A large pair of double doors fronted what the sensitive imagined to be a terrace and stood slightly ajar. Her arrival went almost entirely unnoticed as the prince threw both doors open and stood between them. His voice was angry. "What's going on out there? Who's making that noise?"

Norr had been so focused on her own situation up till that point that she hadn't noticed the insistent *thump! thump! thump!* of drums interspersed with the occasional almost discordant blare of distant trumpets. It was a strange sound—yet oddly familiar at the same time. The majordomo looked unperturbed. "The red hats have entered the public gardens, sire. They are staging some sort of religious celebration—or so I am told."

"Well, they can damned well celebrate somewhere else," the prince fumed, as he closed the doors. "Inform Captain Tovar . . . Tell him to chase the beggars away."

Simms nodded gravely. "Do you want them arrested, sire? The captain will want to know."

The nobleman shook his head. "No, let them go. We can rely on the black hats to keep them in check. If only my father and brothers were so easy to deal with."

Norr felt her pulse beat a little faster. The red hats! Was that a matter of coincidence? Or, were Rebo and Lee connected to the commotion somehow? And if so, to what end? There was no way to know.

"So," Prince Palo said as he turned his back to the doors. Except for his nose, which was a little too large, he was a handsome man and well aware of it. He was dressed in a white jacket, red sash, and black pants. His back was ramrod straight, and his voice was stern. "We have a visitor . . . What's your name?"

"Norr, sire," the sensitive responded. "Lanni Norr."

"Thank you for coming," the princess said, speaking for the first time. "I know it's late."

Norr turned to look at the other woman. They were approximately the same age, or so it seemed, although Princess Sema was prettier. She wore a lime green headdress, a filmy half veil, and a dress that fell gracefully around her. She was seated on a couch. Two children, both young, played at her feet. The noblewoman's words made it sound as if Norr had merely been inconvenienced rather than snatched from her bed. Was that intentional? A device calculated to make Norr feel more like a guest than a prisoner? Or was the princess so insulated from reality that she thought it was true? The sensitive decided that it didn't make much difference. She dropped a curtsy. "You're welcome, highness."

The prince dropped into a chair. Neither he nor his wife invited Norr to sit. "We have consulted all manner of psychics," Palo observed coldly. "But none were variants. Perhaps you would be so kind as to elaborate on the nature of your paranormal abilities."

"Some sensitives can see those who have departed this plane of existence for the next," Norr responded carefully. "Others have the ability to sample past lives, or view events from a distance. Still others can hear discarnate entities speak, cause small items to fly through the air, or heal by the laying on of hands.

"As for my particular talents I am clairaudient, clairvoyant, and have the ability to leave my body for short periods of time, thereby allowing spirit entities to occupy it."

"Others have made similar claims," the nobleman responded skeptically. "How can we tell which claims are true?"

"Those who have genuine talents can provide evidence of that fact," the sensitive responded. "Information that only a real channel could produce."

"Can you give us an example?" Princess Sema inquired as she lifted her son up onto her lap.

"Yes," Norr replied as her eyes lost focus, "I think I can. Please remember that while I see images of people from time to time, they can change their appearance just as we can, which means that a picture may or may not resemble the way a particular entity looked during his or her most recent incarnation. Furthermore, some of the things that I am shown are symbolic, which means that while they have little significance for me, they may be meaningful to you.

"For example," the sensitive continued, as she stared at a point above the prince's head, "I see a three-headed snake. It's at war with itself as each head attempts to inject venom into the others. In the background I hear laughter, as if someone is watching the battle, and thinks it's funny."

"Your *father*," the princess said, spitting the second word out as if it might be poisonous.

Palo refused to take the bait but eyed the sensitive instead. "You call that *proof?*" he demanded cynically. "Everyone knows that my father takes pleasure in setting his sons against each other. You could have obtained that information on any street corner."

"Wait, sire," the sensitive cautioned, "there's more. I see the figure of a man. I can't discern his features, but I sense that he's older than you are, and a little bit taller. He stands with both hands extended palms up. A crescent moon floats above one—and a sphere hovers over the other. As I watch I see his fingers close around the sphere. I don't know what those symbols mean, but a voice tells me that you do."

There was a sharp intake of breath at the mention of the crescent moon, and Sema brought a hand up to cover her mouth. Her husband nodded as if in agreement. "Zaster, my eldest brother, was born with a red crescent on his ankle. Such a mark is said to portend evil. No one beyond the members of immediate family is aware of it."

"The sphere starts to crumble as his fingers close around it," Norr continued, "and what looks like sand falls away."

"It's the planet," the princess whispered. "He plans to control it."

"Yes," the sensitive agreed. "The voice agrees with you . . . But the scene changes again as a dagger shimmers, only to be transformed into the likeness of a man. A man who extends one hand in greeting while keeping the other hidden behind his back."

And it was then, just as Norr was about to continue, that Lysander launched a surprise attack. Suddenly, without warning, the sensitive felt the discarnate entity push her out and was forced to go along for the ride as the spirit who had once been known as Hios charged across the room. Simms saw the sensitive coming, but it was too late by then, and the majordomo collapsed as Norr-Lysander fell on top of him. "He has a gun!" Lysander yelled at the top of Norr's lungs. "Help me!"

But the prince had pulled on a cloth-covered rope by then, and Norr was little more than a distant observer as half a dozen bodyguards entered the room, and jerked her body up off the floor. Palo was on his feet by then and furious. "This is your proof? An unprovoked attack on one of my servants? Take her away."

"No!" Lysander insisted. "He has a gun! And look at his right ankle. That's where you will find the mark of his *true* master."

The prince was about to refuse when the doors to the garden were thrown open and four red-clad Dib Wa entered. They were armed with razor-sharp swords and, judging from the way they moved, knew how to use them. The royal bodyguards were just starting to turn toward the new threat when Rebo appeared. Both of his weapons were drawn, and he leveled them at the guards. "Hold it right there . . . I don't want to shoot anyone, but I will if I have to." Lee emerged from behind the runner and stood with one knife ready to throw.

Norr, who was still "standing" slightly outside of her body, felt a sudden sense of warmth suffuse her being. Rebo *had* come to her rescue, in spite of the fact that it was stupid to do so and would almost certainly result in disaster.

"That's right," Lysander declared righteously. "Hold it right there. Now, search that man and take his weapon. Once he's disarmed take a look at his right ankle."

The lead bodyguard made eye contact with the prince, saw the royal nod, and turned to his men. "All right . . . Search him."

Simms turned to flee but was brought down by a flying tackle. A struggle ensued, the now-desperate servant was brought under control, and one of the guards emerged from the melee holding a pistol. "Look! He *was* armed! Just like the seer said!"

"That's not all," a second bodyguard proclaimed. "Look at this!"

Prince Palo frowned as he made his way over to the spot where one of his most senior servants lay pinned to the floor. Though already shocked to discover that the majordomo was carrying a weapon, the nobleman was completely taken aback when he saw the man's bared ankle and the red crescent moon that was tattooed there. The same mark that his eldest brother had been born with, subsequently adopted as his personal sigil and placed on all his property. No wonder his brother always seemed to be two steps ahead of him. He knew everything in advance!

The prince could hear the blood pounding in his ears and was so angry that he felt a bit dizzy as he extended a hand. "The pistol . . . Give me the pistol."

There was a sudden flurry of activity as the princess sent her personal maid and both of her children out of the room. The previously haughty spy was sobbing by then, as the prince wrapped his fingers around the weapon and felt for the trigger. The royal had brought the handgun around, and was holding the barrel only inches from the traitor's head, when a hand touched his arm. "No," the princess said. "Don't do it." Her eyes, which were normally so soft, looked like chips of stone.

The prince spoke through gritted teeth, and Simms whimpered as he wet his trousers. "Why not? The bastard deserves to die."

"That's true," the princess responded evenly, "but what if

you turn the dog against its master? Your brother will believe everything that the misbegotten whoreson says. For a while at least . . . And that's all you need."

There was a moment of silence as the prince absorbed the meaning of her words. A smile grew as he lowered the gun. "You make an excellent point, my dear. This is an interesting opportunity indeed." The nobleman's head swiveled toward the senior guard. "Lock the scoundrel up. No one is to speak to him without my permission. And both you and your entire detail will remain on the palace grounds until further notice. Not only must we must take all the steps necessary to ensure that there was only one spy—but we must do everything necessary to prevent word of what took place from leaking out.

"Now," the royal said, turning toward Norr. "It seems that I owe *you* an apology. More than that a position within my household. Your talent is not only genuine but extremely useful. So much so that it would be unfortunate if you were to fall into the wrong hands."

Norr struggled to speak but discovered that Lysander still had control of her vocal cords. "Thank you, sire," he said huskily, "but my companions and I are already committed to an extremely important task. One that requires us to depart Pooz on the next ship."

The prince raised his eyebrows. "And if I object?"

Rebo waved the Hogger. "No offense, sire. But that wouldn't be a very good idea . . . We hold the high ground at the moment, and while you could chase us down after we withdraw, there's your new secret to consider. If you allow us to leave the planet, it will be safe, but force us to stay, and the information will go straight to your brother."

The proud nobleman felt another surge of anger and was about to respond accordingly, when the princess touched his arm. "What about the red hats?" she demanded, gesturing toward the Dib Wa. "Will they leave the planet as well?"

Rebo looked at Lee, and the boy nodded. "Yes. You have my word."

The prince started to question the assertion, especially since it had originated from a mere youth, but something about the authoritative manner in which the boy spoke caused him to hesitate. Finally, having heard no objection from his wife, the nobleman agreed. "All right. But only if two members of my staff accompany you until the ship lifts—and you will agree to join my household if the vessel fails to appear."

Lysander was about to refuse when Norr managed to wrestle control away from him. "Thank you, sire," she said. "We agree."

Rebo hadn't agreed to anything and resented the manner in which the sensitive had spoken for him, but decided that it would be best to raise the issue later. He motioned for Norr to back out through the door. "We're staying at the runner's guild. You can send your men there." Then, without so much as a by-your-leave, the intruders were gone.

SEVEN

The Planet Anafa

There have always been some who could communicate with those in the next world, but it was only when the ancients found scientific proof of an afterlife that such individuals were accepted, then studied. Later, by means of techniques no longer understood, an entire subspecies of highly specialized human beings was brought into existence. Not to comfort the bereaved or access the wisdom of those who had passed into spirit, but to make money. And so it was that our ancestors were created for commercial rather than spiritual purposes— and came to be regarded with suspicion rather than respect. A curse that follows us to this day.

—Grand Vizier Horga Entube,
The History of My People

Soft white light flooded the circular conference room and threw hard dark shadows down across the highly polished concrete floor. All of the council members were present, but Omar Tepho had yet to arrive, and Jevan Kane had little choice but to wait for him. Having failed to capture Norr on Pooz, and under pressure to get results, the operative had returned to Anafa and the city of Seros. His task, which was to establish communications with Lysander, remained the same. But rather than use Norr as the channel, the technologist planned to employ the services of a more cooperative sensitive.

His name was Arn Dyson, and he was seated within the embrace of the keyhole-shaped slot that ran in toward the center of the round table. The variant was older rather than younger, and possessed shoulder-length white hair, which he wore in a ponytail. He had a deeply lined face, hooded eyes, and a strong chin. Though not the most famous of seers, Dyson had a solid reputation and, unlike the flighty Norr, demonstrated a willingness to serve. All of which boded well. Which was good, because Chairman Tepho and certain council members had grown decidedly restive of late.

There was a stir as the scientist entered, exchanged greetings with his fellow council members, and took his seat. The chair had been specially designed to accept Tepho's spinal deformity and sighed softly. In the meantime, Shaz appeared behind the chairman. He eyed Kane, treated the operative to one of his caninelike grins, and disappeared. "All right," Tepho said, "let's get on with it."

Kane sought to swallow the lump that had formed in the back of his throat and opened the meeting. "Ladies and gentlemen, all of you know why we're here, so we might as well get this session under way. Citizen Dyson? What can we do to help?"

The sensitive smiled reassuringly as he looked from face to face. "It would be helpful if those of you who actually knew Milos Lysander during his most recent incarnation would visualize his features, summon up a positive memory of him, and focus on that. In the meantime the rest of the group can send welcoming thoughts and do their best to remain open. Please turn the lights down—and don't touch me after I go into trance."

Kane ordered that the lights be dimmed, managed to summon up an image of Lysander's face, and sorted through his memories of the man, looking for one that was positive. There were a few, but not that many, even though the two of them had been close during the years prior to the founder's premature death, something Tepho continued to resent.

Lysander was a hard man to please, and even though Kane had worked extremely hard to do so, he had rarely been successful. The operative selected one of the rare occasions on which he had been praised, focused his mind on that, and hoped that the thought would function as a beacon.

Meanwhile, Milos Lysander's ethereal body shivered, began to dissipate, and came back together again as the discarnate entity paused to revisualize it. This was something he and every other spirit had to do occasionally in order to maintain a consistent appearance. Of course there were some individuals who couldn't be bothered with that sort of thing and looked like blobs of constantly shifting light. The scientist didn't care for that, however, and liked to maintain an appearance similar to that of Emperor Hios.

Now, as Lysander forced his way down through increasingly dense layers of reality, he soon found himself among the beings who liked to wallow about in the thick, glutinous muck that surrounded the physical plane, or were there on an errand of some sort. A few, like the scientist, were responding to a specific call. Some contacts were intentional, as when a sensitive attempted to communicate with a specific entity, but most were accidental. Lysander had experienced many of those. Someone, members of the Techno Society were the most frequent offenders, would think or talk about him for an extended period of time and unknowingly pepper him with thought forms.

The scientist normally ignored such signals, but some were too strong to filter out or were associated with someone he cared for. Jevan Kane in this case, the same entity who had been his son during his incarnation as Emperor

Hios and was most likely to help him now. Which was why the discarnate decided to follow the energy back to its source. And the closer he got, the stronger the attraction became, until it became a palpable force.

Finally, Lysander found himself at the source of the energy, the place where a group of people were gathered around an individual who was focused on trying to bring him through. Looking into the physical plane was like peering through thick folds of gauze, but the scientist recognized some of those who had gathered to speak with him. Among them were Kane, Eby, and Tepho. A brilliant mind, but one so distorted by his childhood experiences that it had become as monstrous as his body and was capable of anything. Still, Tepho was determined to reestablish the star gates, and that, at least, was good.

The words seemed to come from a long ways off, but once he focused in on them, Lysander discovered that he could hear most of the conversation. A sensitive, the person seated at the very center of the group, was speaking. He was male, well past middle age, and slightly nervous. "He's here . . . I can sense his presence."

"Then what are we waiting for?" Tepho demanded imperiously. "He tried to communicate with Kane on Pooz a short time ago. Bring him through!"

"I'm trying," the sensitive responded defensively, "but it's up to *him*. Discarnate entities have free will. I can't force him to communicate with you."

Lysander circled the assemblage. What Tepho said was true. He *had* attempted to communicate with Kane, although he wasn't sure about the exact time line, since the whole concept of time was little more than an intellectual abstraction on the spirit planes. So, given the fact that he *wanted* to impart certain information to the group, and a channel was available to do so, what was holding him back?

As with so many other things the answer was complicated. Thanks to the strange bond that existed between them it was easier to communicate through Norr, but there was more to it than that. Yes, it was his goal to see the system of star gates restored, but with an important difference. Having misused the portals during his incarnation as Emperor Hios, he had returned to the physical as Milos Lysander, intent on putting things right. But without the memory of past lives to guide him, the scientist soon strayed from the path, and had it not been for his premature death would have committed the same errors all over again.

All of which brought Lysander back to the present and an extremely important decision. Should he ally himself with the organization he had created, and Tepho's twisted mind, or with the woman who had murdered him?

In the final analysis the decision was easier than Lysander thought it would be. He felt increasingly drawn to the woman he still thought of as Cara. She didn't like him, Lysander knew that, and was glad of it. Knowing where he had gone wrong in the past, and with Norr as a sort of auxiliary conscience, perhaps he could put things right.

"Lysander is here," Dyson reiterated confidently. "I can see his energy circling the room. But he shows no interest in making contact, and it looks like he's about to leave."

"Well, hold him!" Kane ordered angrily. "We need him, damn it! The whole thing was *his* idea!"

Lysander knew that Kane had been his son during his incarnation as Emperor Hios, and as the outburst echoed through the foglike substance that swirled around him, the scientist was struck by the extent to which the two of them were alike. Or had been, since Lysander was determined to correct his past mistakes and repair at least some of the damage he had done.

The discarnate was already in the process of directing his energy elsewhere when Kane rose to address Tepho and the council. His voice was hard and cold. "I apologize for wasting your time. It won't happen again! The old bastard is playing hard to get. I propose that we redouble our efforts to capture Norr; failing that, we'll kill her. At that point the old coot can either come through Dyson here or forget the whole thing. I believe that he will cooperate rather than sacrifice his dream."

All eyes gravitated to Tepho. Some of the council members approved of the proposed plan while others didn't. But none of them were willing to express their opinions until the chairman weighed in with *his*. And Tepho was silent as he stared at Kane and watched tiny beads of perspiration appear on the operative's forehead.

Tepho didn't like Kane and never had. Partly because of the other man's good looks, partly because of his close relationship with Lysander, and partly because of his latent ambition. But to surrender to such emotions would be a weakness. Because Kane, like every other person in the room, was a tool. And when a cut fails to meet its intended mark the fault lies with the carpenter not the saw. "The plan makes sense," the chairman said. "Keep me informed."

Lysander heard the interchange, shook his head sadly, and left Anafa behind.

Aboard the starship *Hewhotravelsthroughtime*

Having broken orbit around Pooz, the ship named *Hewhotravelsthroughtime* had scarcely entered hyperspace when Lee fell seriously ill. It began with a vague discomfort in the area around the boy's navel that gradually developed into an intense pain on the lower right sight of his abdomen which was accompanied by a fever, nausea, and vomiting.

Rebo responded to the crises by breaking out his medical kit and brewing up one of the ready-made poultices he had acquired back on Anafa. The herbalist who had sold the preparation to the runner had promised him that it would be effective for a broad range of medical problems ranging from gunshot wounds to certain forms of venereal disease.

But even a thick application of the noxious stuff did nothing to relieve Lee's symptoms, and by the time Norr returned from a scouting mission, Rebo was quite concerned. Having been fortunate enough to emerge from the confrontation with Prince Palo without being sent to the royal mines, his client was at risk once again, only this threat was even more difficult to counter. "As far as I can tell this ship is virtually identical to the last one," the sensitive commented, as she took a seat in front of the small fire. "I even found the lift that takes you up to the garden. This one is in better shape, though, and judging from appearances, someone or something has been working to maintain it. My guess is someone, since a robot wouldn't need to cook anything, and I came across the remains of a fire. The embers were still warm."

Rebo nodded politely, but the sensitive could see that his attention lay elsewhere. "Lee is feeling even worse than he was before. I put a poultice on his belly, but it hasn't made a noticeable difference."

Norr frowned, got up, and went over to where the boy lay. Once she was kneeling by his side, it quickly became apparent that the youth wasn't asleep as she had supposed, but very, very ill. His forehead felt warm, his knees were drawn up toward his stomach, and his eyelids fluttered when she said his name.

The poultice that Rebo had secured around the lower part of Lee's torso stank so badly that the sensitive pulled her knife, cut the pouch free, and tossed it over her shoulder. The dressing landed next to one of the Dib Wa warriors who had been forced to accompany the threesome. He swore in Tilisi and threw the offensive item out into the surrounding murk. There were other passengers—but none close enough to object.

"So," Rebo whispered, as he knelt at Lee's side. "What do you think?"

"I don't know," Norr said doubtfully, as she poured water onto a handkerchief and arranged it on the boy's hot forehead. "He needs a medico."

"We don't have one," the runner replied. "But you're a sensitive," he added hopefully. "Maybe you could heal him."

"I would if I could," Norr replied regretfully. "But I lack that particular talent. There is someone who might be able to help us however."

"Really?" the runner inquired. "Who?"

"The person who is living in the garden," Norr replied, jerking her thumb back over her shoulder.

"Why? Do you think he or she is a medico?"

"No," the sensitive responded. "But we know that the ship was originally designed to carry passengers as well cargo. So it's my guess that there is a highly automated medical facility onboard. Probably in one of the many areas that we don't have access to."

Rebo looked hopeful. "It's your 'guess'? Or did one of your invisible friends tell you that?"

Though never a true skeptic, he was far too superstitious for that, the runner's faith in Norr's psychic abilities had not only increased over the last few weeks, but reached the point where he had a somewhat exaggerated notion of what the sensitive was capable of. Something Norr intended to talk to him about at the right moment. But right then, with Lee's welfare on the line, she chose to lie. "Yes. Someone told me."

"Excellent!" Rebo replied, as he came to his feet. "We'll make a stretcher. Two of the Dib Wa can carry it. The others will remain here to protect our supplies."

It was a good plan, and Norr said as much. There was a flurry of activity as orders were given, materials were gathered, and construction got under way. The stretcher party was ready to go fifteen minutes later. Lee had slipped into a semiconscious state by then, had taken to calling Norr Momma, and was clearly in pain.

Most of the other passengers were hunkered down around tiny fires, and there wasn't a whole lot for them to do, so most turned to watch as the stretcher party zigzagged its way across the hold. The majority assumed that the boy had passed away and, as was the prevailing custom on starships, would be entombed in some distant part of the hull. Not only was such a death sad, but it reminded many of their own mortality and caused them to turn back toward the warmth of their fires.

Having made use of the lift less than an hour before, Norr had no difficulty leading the others to the graffiti-covered door, where she pressed her palm against cold steel and waited for the audible *click*. That was followed by the steady whine of servos as the rarely used hatch cycled open. "All aboard," the sensitive ordered, as she gestured toward the dimly lit interior and followed the rest of the stretcher party onto the lift.

The door closed, the elevator rose, and Rebo pulled the

Crosser out of its holster by way of a precaution. While Norr seemed to assume that the person or persons who had taken up residence in the ship's artificial garden would welcome visitors, he wasn't so sure.

The lift jerked to a halt a few seconds later. The runner motioned for the others to stay where they were, sniffed the moisture-laden air, and thought he detected a trace of smoke. Then, eyes probing ahead, Rebo stepped out into a compartment that was clearly identical to the one in which Lee had been pursued by the black hat assassin. Except that this garden was relatively orderly, and while the atmosphere was humid, the sprinklers remained off.

Rebo followed a well-trodden path away from the elevator, and had just passed between a pair of fruit-laden bushes, when someone grabbed hold of him from behind. One hand went to his collar, a second to his belt, and the runner had just started to react when his entire body was lifted off the ground. Then, similar to the way a farmhand might heave a bag of grain up onto a cart, Rebo was literally thrown through the air.

Bo Hoggles uttered a victorious roar as the norm crashed through a thicket of dead branches and hit the ground beyond. That was when the heavy realized that this intruder was different from the one who had invaded his domain earlier in the "day," and started to turn. However it was too late by then, and Norr's staff made a solid *thwack!* as it connected with the side of the other variant's head and sent the giant to his knees.

But the blow didn't render Hoggles unconscious, and if it hadn't been for the Dib Wa warriors who had piled onto his back, the heavy might have been able to rise. Fortunately, the weight of the red hats, plus that of Rebo's body was sufficient to keep him down. Norr knelt next to the variant's head. "Hello!" she said cheerfully. "I'm sorry I had to hit you . . . I suppose it's hard to believe, but we don't mean you any harm. In fact, depending on how much you know about the ship, we might even pay you for some advice."

Rebo frowned. Like Norr, he was perfectly willing to pay if that would help Lee, but resented the way she continually took him for granted. But the runner knew it wasn't a good moment to broach the subject, so he let it go.

Hoggles, who had assumed that the intruders were there to rob him of his food and take his home, blinked in surprise. His hair was ragged as if large fistfuls of it had been hacked off with a knife. He had a mostly symmetrical face, an even nose, and a massive, stubble-covered jaw. Like many of his brethren, the giant was often assumed to be stupid but nothing could have been further from the truth. "Tell your friends to get off my back, and we can talk about it."

Norr looked at Rebo. "Let's give him a chance."

The runner grimaced, traded the Crosser for the more powerful Hogger, and backed away. The Dib Wa, both of whom were careful to stay out of the line of fire, did likewise. One of them went to check on Lee.

The heavy got to his feet, touched the quickly swelling lump on the side of his head, and made a face. His clothes were a uniform gray color, had been mended countless times, and were ragged around the edges. "It's hard to keep track, but I think I've been aboard for about three years now, and I guess that makes me something of an expert."

"Three years?" the runner said incredulously. "You must have been to every planet on the ship's itinerary at least two times . . . Why stay aboard?"

"That's none of your business," the variant replied haughtily, and stared out from under craggy brows. "Suffice it to say that I have my reasons."

"Fair enough," Norr said agreeably. "Based on your knowledge of the vessel, can you tell us where the ship's medical facility is located? Our son is ill, *very* ill, and needs immediate attention."

Hoggles looked at the stretcher and the red hat who knelt next to it. "No, I can't, but that doesn't mean there isn't one. I have found ways into most areas of the ship but not all of them."

Rebo directed a look at the sensitive. "You told me that he would *know*," the runner said accusingly. "This is a waste of time! Lee is dying while you lead us all over the ship."

If the conflict bothered Hoggles, he gave no sign of it. "Of course there is someone who would know," the variant said. "*If* you can get him to talk, which will be difficult to do, since he tends to regard beings such as ourselves as little more than barbarians."

Norr knew that Rebo was frustrated, not to mention annoyed at her, and understood why. The runner was worried about Lee and knew that time was running out. "Okay," she said, "who is this individual? Let's have a talk with him."

"He calls himself *Hewhotravelsthroughtime*," Hoggles answered, "and he's all around us. In fact, you could say that we're riding him, like fleas on a dog."

In spite of the fact that he had traveled aboard at least two dozen spaceships, and knew that they were sentient, Rebo had never spoken with one of the constructs. Perhaps that was why he thought of them as machines rather than people, and had never taken the time to consider how one of them might regard his or her passengers. But one thing was for sure . . . If anyone would know where the onboard medical facility was located, the ship itself would. "So, what are we waiting for?" Rebo inquired eagerly. "Let's get going."

The heavy remained where he was. "I believe there was some mention of pay."

Some quick negotiations ensued, and Hoggles was able to secure a substantial fee. Then, with the first half of the sum safely secured in an otherwise empty purse, the ragged heavy led the stretcher party back along rows of well-tended hybrid corn, past a pair of metal tanks, to a sealed hatch. "I spent weeks punching numbers into this keypad before I finally came up with the correct combination," Hoggles commented, as his huge, sausagelike fingers mashed a series of buttons. "Fortunately the code was set locally or *Hewhotravels* would have changed it on me."

Servos whined as the hatch cycled open. That allowed the huge variant and his clients to enter a maze of dimly lit passageways. Rebo managed to give the good luck amulet that hung around his neck a surreptitious squeeze before pulling the Crosser and holding it down along his right thigh. The corridors hadn't been vandalized thanks to the fact that no more than four or five people had passed through them over the last thousand years. They were dusty, though, and hung with long, ropelike filaments of dust and festooned with lacy cobwebs. However, thanks to the heavy's size, and the fact that he had created what amounted to a tunnel during his previous explorations, those who followed along behind were able to avoid most of the accumulated material. Nonetheless, Norr felt compelled to lay a handkerchief across Lee's face to protect the boy from the stuff that fell from above.

Finally, after numerous twists and turns, Hoggles led the stretcher party through a door and out onto a suspended platform. It was nearly dark within the globular chamber, and what light there was emanated from thousands of tiny lights, all moving slowly relative to the ship. That was when Rebo realized that he was looking at a map, a *star* map, of whatever part of the galaxy the ship was traversing at the moment.

A quick glance over the edge of the platform revealed that the chart extended downward as well, a sight that caused the runner's stomach to flip-flop and left him wondering why there weren't any handrails.

The heavy, who had been there before, made straight for the bulky-looking chair that sat perched at the very edge of the black abyss. "The ship's architects had a great deal of faith in their AIs," Hoggles explained, "but made provisions for a biological pilot, too. More to reassure skittish passengers than for any other reason, or so *Hewhotravels* claims, and I tend to believe him. In any case that's what the chair is for . . . All you have to do is sit down, and you'll be in contact with his eminence, assuming he's in the mood to receive guests. So, who will it be?"

Norr turned to look at Rebo. "Go ahead, Jak. You've had more experience with machines than I have."

The runner shook his head. "Thanks," he said gruffly, "but you're more of a talker than I am. And that's what this situation calls for."

If the comment was intended as a compliment, it didn't come across as one, but the sensitive thought it best to let the issue slide. "Okay," she replied philosophically. "It's worth a try."

The others watched as Norr laid her staff on the platform, circled the chair, and put her foot on the first of three steps that led up to the thronelike position above. Then, having mounted the short flight of stairs, the sensitive turned and lowered herself into the well-padded chair. A puff of dust billowed up, hung suspended in the air, and started to settle. The seat was *huge,* as if made to accommodate even the largest member of the A-strain, and the sensitive felt lost in it.

"Slip your hands and arms into the tunnels located on both sides of the seat," Hoggles instructed. "Then, depending on what sort of mood his excellency is in, he might be willing to communicate with you."

Norr examined both sides of the seat, verified the presence of twin holes, and slowly inserted her hands into the apertures. And it wasn't long before her fingers began to tingle. Though slightly uncomfortable, like the pins-and-needles sensation caused by a lack of circulation, the feedback wasn't too bad, and Norr left her extremities where they were.

A minute, that's how long the sensitive intended to put up with the prickly feeling, unless the AI made contact. She started to count off the seconds, and had just hit fifty-six, when a basso voice thundered all around her. "You don't belong here! I don't like you! Go away."

The effect was startling, and might have been sufficient to send another person packing, but the sensitive was not so easily intimidated. "You are correct," Norr agreed. "I *don't* belong here . . . But I need your help. Provide me with the information I need, and I will leave."

Rebo bit his lower lip. Lee's forehead was so hot that damp cloths no longer had the capacity to cool it, and the boy moaned constantly. Now, with nothing to do, the runner regretted the decision to let Norr interact with the ship. What if she made a mistake? What if the aggressive approach made the AI angry? But it was too late to switch, and all he could do was stand by and hope for the best.

Norr held her breath as the silence stretched long and thin. Finally, just as the sensitive had come to the conclusion that the conversation was over, *Hewhotravels* spoke once more. "What do you want?"

The sensitive took a deep breath. "One of our party is ill," she replied. "And we think he's going to die."

"So?" The single word echoed back and forth between steel walls and was heavy with disdain.

"So, we believe there's a medical facility onboard this ship," Norr answered. "And you could tell us how to access it."

"You are correct," *Hewhotravels* responded smugly. "There *is* such a facility, but it has been closed for thousands of years, and it shall remain so."

"But *why?*" the sensitive demanded resentfully. "You were created to serve humanity, to enable them to travel among the stars, and to do so safely. So why would you deny medical care to one of your passengers?"

"For a number of reasons," the AI responded easily. "Starting with the fact that while it's true that your ancestors were responsible for creating beings such as myself, that was before the race surrendered to entropy and began the long slide back into ignorance, savagery, and barbarism. Any obligation that my brothers, sisters, and I may have are to what your kind once *were*. Not what you have become. And, were I to open those areas that are presently restricted, the vermin camped within my holds would destroy what remains of my once-magnificent body, a fate that may have befallen some if not all of the ships no longer in service."

Norr remembered the brutish audience that had torn her childhood mentor apart and knew exactly what *Hewhotravels* was referring to. It seemed that knowledge had surrendered to ignorance, and though no longer capable of building a starship, there were plenty of human beings who would be happy to destroy one.

"There is truth in what you say," Norr admitted gravely. "But I'm not asking you to open every nook and cranny of your hull to the people camped in the hold. Just to one little boy . . . A spirit who, if his followers are correct, might grow up to be a great teacher one day. The sort of man who could set humanity back on the path to greatness."

Rather than dismiss the comment, as she half expected him to, the AI seemed intrigued. "A boy you say . . . And who, pray tell, is this paragon of virtue?"

"We call him Lee," the sensitive replied. "However those who lead the red hat sect believe that he is the reincarnated spirit of a teacher named Nom Maa. The truth or falsity of that assertion will be determined in the city of CaCanth on the planet Thara. But only if he lives long enough to get there."

So realistic was the panorama of stars projected on the inner surface of the control room that Rebo was taken aback when it suddenly disappeared and was replaced by a hundred competing scenes. Each featured the same man, who in spite of the fact that he appeared to be at least fifty feet tall, still managed to look benign. Perhaps that was the result of his shaved head, open moon-shaped face, and the simple green robe that hung from his roly-poly body. Or perhaps it was an ineffable something that radiated from within. Whatever the reason the runner recognized the backgrounds as being typical of what the interior of a great starship might have looked like millennia before. There were bulkheads crowded with art, compartments filled with luxurious furnishings, and throngs of well-dressed passengers, many of whom bowed as the man with the cherubic face walked past.

"You are looking at Nom Maa," *Hewhotravels* announced dramatically, "during a voyage when I had the honor of transporting his Excellency from Pooz to Ning. Please take note of the fact that while both the red and the black hats claim to follow his teachings, he opposed such groupings as counterproductive, and always sought to promote unity. That was why he wore green robes rather than red or black."

There was a moment of silence as Rebo, Norr, and the crimson-clad Dib Wa all struggled to absorb what they had heard, and eyed the larger-than-life images that loomed around them. But interesting as all of it was, Norr was acutely aware of how important the passage of time could be and forced the AI back to the subject at hand. "So, you agree with me. There *is* hope . . . And Nom Maa was a great man."

"Yes, he was," the ship admitted. "But who is to say that the man lives in the boy? You are a sensitive . . . Can you assure me that they are one and the same?"

"No," Norr answered honestly. "Back when I first met him I requested that information and was refused. Because if I knew the answer, I might tell the boy, causing him to not only act on the knowledge but bypass certain experiences that he needs to have. But Lee *could* be Nom Maa— and his life *is* at risk."

The mosaic of moving images was replaced by the star field, and a long moment of silence ensued. Finally, as Norr prepared to pull her arms out of the control sleeves, *Hewhotravels* spoke. "Follow the arrows. Use the facility. Save him if you can."

"Thank you," the sensitive said humbly. "Thank you very much."

The strange tingling sensation stopped the moment that Norr removed her hands from the control sleeves, and while there was no outward sign to confirm it, the sensitive thought she detected a change to the surrounding atmosphere. It was as if the AI's personality had substance, and once withdrawn, left a vacuum in its wake.

"Look!" Rebo exclaimed, pointing to a previously blank bulkhead. "An arrow!" It was light blue and seemed to glow from within.

Norr's boots made a *clanging* sound as they hit the steel deck. "All right . . . Let's get going."

Hoggles took the lead as the stretcher party followed a series of blue arrows through various twists and turns before finally arriving in front of a hatch that bore a large red cross. Rebo was about to palm the lock but the barrier *hissed* out of the way before he could do so.

Norr assumed that *Hewhotravels* was monitoring their progress via sensors of some sort and looked around in a futile attempt to make eye contact with one of them. "Thank you."

A series of lights flickered on as the heavy led his companions through a dusty waiting area, past the stainless-steel desk where long-dead staff had listened to an endless list of complaints put forward by often cantankerous passengers, and into the well-equipped surgery that lay beyond. Dozens of highly specialized machines, none larger than the runner's fist, could be seen crawling across the overhead and surrounding bulkheads. Each cut a damp swath through layers of accumulated grime before turning to circle the room again. A freshly scrubbed operating table crouched under a battery of overhead lights, and Norr pointed to it. "Put him there."

Lee groaned pitifully as the Dib Wa warriors strapped him to the table before stepping back out of the way.

"Now what?" Rebo inquired of no one in particular, as the cleaning robots put the finishing touches to the room.

As if to answer the runner, a female voice issued from

what seemed like every corner of the operating theater. "All nonessential personnel must exit the surgical suite. I repeat, all nonessential personnel must . . ."

"Okay, okay," Rebo said irritably. "We get the idea. Come on . . . Let's see if we can find the way back behind that window over there. Maybe we can watch."

Norr whispered something into Lee's ear, kissed him on the forehead, and followed the runner out of the room.

As it turned out, the observation room was quite small, so Hoggles accompanied the red hat warriors out into the waiting room, leaving Rebo and Norr to monitor the situation alone. Having already seen the machines that crawled over the walls and heard the disembodied female voice, neither observer was especially surprised when the table sprouted mechanical arms. They cut the boy's clothes off, made use of a liquid disinfectant to prep his skin, and placed a self-adhesive drape over his abdomen.

Once that was accomplished a long flexible tube snaked down from the overhead to make contact with the inner surface of Lee's left arm. They boy jerked as a needle penetrated a vein, went limp as the relaxant began to take effect, and offered no visible resistance when a second tube arrived. It took a peek into his mouth, found the passageway to its liking, and dived into the youth's airway.

Meanwhile, the table on which the youth lay extruded other leads that made their various connections and fed data regarding Lee's vital signs to the computer that ran the medical facility. It sent a mix of oxygen and anesthetic into the boy's lungs, waited for the mixture to have the desired effect, and gave itself permission to operate.

Still another tube deposited a handful of machines onto Lee's abdomen. One of the robots cut a tiny hole through the patient's skin, while others strained to pull the margins of the wound apart, and the rest dashed hither and yon cauterizing bleeders. Three minutes later the youth's badly inflamed appendix had been located, isolated, and cut free.

In spite of the fact that they had been watching intently, neither Rebo nor Norr were aware that the operation had even begun when a small piece of tissue materialized on top of his skin, and the procedure was over.

Fifteen minutes later the appendix had been suctioned away, Lee's incision had been closed, and the anesthetic had started to wear off. "Keep the wound clean, and notify me if you notice any fever, drainage, or significant pain," the computer ordered, as Rebo and Norr reentered the surgical suite.

The runner said, "Sure," but doubted that *Hewhotravels* would allow any of them to reenter the facility once they left it.

The other passengers, all of whom had expected Rebo and Norr to return without their son's body, were visibly surprised when a heavy they had never seen before led the stretcher party back into the hold. However, such was the wary "mind your own business" culture that prevailed in the bowels of the ship, they turned back to their fires without voicing the questions that begged to be asked.

After consulting with Rebo, Norr invited Hoggles to stay, but the heavy refused. No reason was given, but the sensitive assumed that the big hermit was on the run from something, and looked him in the eye. "Okay, Bo, but let us know if you change your mind."

The variant nodded. "Thanks, I will."

The sensitive's eyes rolled slightly out of focus. "And Bo . . ."

"Yes?"

"Does the name 'Dak' mean anything to you?"

Hoggles looked surprised. "Yes . . . Dak was my best friend. He was killed in an accident."

Well, Dak says that, 'if you're going to beat it, you've got to face it.' Does that make any sense to you?"

The variant's eyes narrowed, and he backed away. "No, it doesn't," the heavy lied, "but thanks anyway."

Norr put out a hand as if to stop Hoggles, but the heavy had turned by then and was walking away. Rebo had seen the interchange and appeared by the sensitive's side. "What got into him?"

Norr shook her head. "I don't know."

"Ah well," the runner said philosophically. "We already have plenty of problems without adding any more."

The sensitive knew Rebo was correct, but couldn't help but wonder who the entity named Dak was and what Hoggles was running from.

Lee recovered quickly, and the next few ship days passed without incident, which had a meritorious effect on the on-again, off-again relationship between Rebo and Norr. So much so that the twosome had even gone for a walk together, and rather than discuss their current difficulties, focused on happier times instead. The runner described what it was like to grow up within the topsy-turvy world of a guild, and the sensitive reminisced about the idyllic days before the night plague turned her into an orphan.

Perhaps that was why the runner not only dreamed about Norr but wasn't all that surprised when she came to him during the period that most of their fellow passengers accepted as night within the eternally darkened hold. The runner awoke as the sensitive entered his privacy shelter on her hands and knees, saw who the intruder was, and re-moved his hand from the Crosser.

Norr crawled forward, straddled Rebo's hips, and al-lowed her hair to fall forward as she looked down on him. The runner reached up to cup her breasts, saw her lips part, and was ready for an openmouthed kiss when the sensitive spoke. Her voice was low and coarse. "Greetings, runner . . . This is Milos Lysander. We meet again."

Rebo jerked his hands off Norr's breasts, fervently wished that the sensitive wasn't seated astride him, and looked up into amused eyes. "Lysander? Get the hell off me! What the hell do you think you're doing?"

"Nothing like what you were hoping for," the discarnate entity answered dryly. "Not that I blame you . . . But enough. I came here to warn you. Because I refuse to use the channel they selected for me, the Techno Society decided to redouble their efforts to capture my daughter, or failing that, to kill her. You must stop them."

"*Me?*" Rebo objected, as he tried to buck Norr off. "Why me?"

"Because you have the necessary skills, your fate is some-how linked with hers, and you love her."

"Love?" the runner demanded. "Who said anything about 'love'? Besides, she's bossy, presumptuous, and annoying."

"Which is exactly what some people say about *you*," the spirit responded. "Now, remember what I said and be ready. They know you're on this ship, and their agents will be waiting when the shuttle lands."

Rebo felt a sense of alarm mixed with frustration as he leaned back against his elbows. "Hey, I have idea . . . If you're so worried about Norr, all you have to do is cooperate with the Techno Society! You invented the bastards."

"We want some of the same things," Lysander admitted cautiously, "but for different reasons. Take care of my daughter, and I will help when I can."

Then Lysander was gone and Norr awoke to find herself straddling Rebo. "Jak? Is that you? What's going on?"

"Lysander decided to hijack your body and came by for a visit," the runner answered disgustedly. "He says that the Techno Society will be waiting for you when we land."

The sensitive frowned. "Was that all?"

"Yeah," Rebo lied, "except for *this*, which is my idea."

Norr felt the runner's hands settle on her shoulders and allowed him to pull her down. There was plenty to worry about, but that was in the future, and this was now. Their lips met, their bodies touched, and two became one.

Lysander smiled, thought about where he wanted to be, and left the ship behind.

EIGHT

The Planet Ning

Although the gravity on Ning is not so severe as to prevent norms from living there, it acted to limit the number of A-strain colonists who wanted to settle the world, and gave the heavies something of an advantage. They flourished on the planet—but have yet to gain the political power they feel entitled to.

—Tuso the Wise,
A History of Ning

For reasons known only to the thousand-year-old com- puter that lay buried many stories beneath the city, the power came on at exactly eight each evening and remained on until exactly 3:00 A.M., when it went off. No one knew how the power was generated or how long it would continue to be available, which meant that each working day ended in a moment of suspense. Was this the day when the power would fail? Or would the ancient system continue to operate for another seven hours? There was no way to know, a fact that robbed would-be inventors of their motivation, prevented the prices charged for electroartifacts from rising, and kept the city of Zand in an eternal state of suspense.

But, when the power came on, it was truly something to see. A fact that attracted pilgrims from thousands of miles away. Just as darkness settled over the city, and thousands of lanterns were lit, there was a loud *bang!* as power flowed through underground lines, encountered a multiplicity of breaks, and followed the path of least resistance to the metal pylons that had once been part of a citywide system that broadcast power through the air. Unable to follow its proper path, man-made lightning made the jump from pylon to pylon illuminated the city with a series of strobelike flashes, and bounced thunder off the surrounding hills. Then, once the display of pyrotechnics was over, and equilibrium was restored, those who desired to do so could operate whatever electrical equipment they owned.

A cheer went up all around the city as the citizens of Zand paused to celebrate another seven hours of electricity, spent a few moments wondering if it would be their last, and returned to whatever they had been doing prior to eight o'clock. In the case of those seated all around Jevan Kane, that was eating, drinking, and talking.

The restaurant sat on a hill overlooking the city and was packed at that time of day. The technologist had a good spot, and was enjoying a glass of truly excellent white wine, when a functionary named Ros Cayo wound his way between the tables. The functionary was a short, bandy-legged man who affected a pencil-thin mustache, expensive clothes, and shoes designed to make him look two inches taller than he actually was—just one of the many individuals who worked for the Techno Society but weren't part of the core leadership group. He smiled uncertainly. "I'm sorry to bother you, sir, but I have news."

Kane raised his eyebrows. "Good news? Or bad news?"

Cayo's expression brightened. "Good news . . . Or so it seems to me."

Kane nodded agreeably. "Excellent! Please pull up a chair. What would you like to drink?"

Cayo, who had every reason to believe that Kane would pay the bill, ordered the most expensive drink he could think of and savored the moment. For once, maybe the first time in his life, he was in the right place, at the right time. Hopefully, assuming everything went well, he would receive a rather substantial raise and have the funds required to rent a three-room apartment.

"So," Kane said deliberately, "what have you got for me?"

Cayo swirled a mouthful of the expensive liquor around the inside of his mouth before letting the liquid trickle down the back of his throat. "Well, sir," the functionary began, "it's like this. There's a tomb raider, a fellow named Garth, who offered to sell me a number two."

Kane frowned. "A number two? Sorry, I don't follow you."

"The second item on the Techno Society's high-priority procurement list," Cayo responded tactfully. "A gate seed."

Kane felt his pulse start to quicken. According to research carried out by Milos Lysander prior to his death, such seeds had once been common. During the early days, before the system of star gates had been fully established, runners had been employed to carry the small spheres to distant worlds, where they were "planted." Once activated, the seed sent out a signal that the computer called Logos could use to knit the new location into the overall network. Once that was accomplished, the necessary equipment was installed, the new portal was christened by the local politicos, and a star gate was born.

So, second only to finding Logos itself, the acquisition of an intact gate seed was at the very top of the society's procurement list. Partly because such a find would provide the society's scientists with the means to make copies—but also because Lysander believed that the seed could be employed to find Logos. Assuming that the AI remained on-line somewhere. But was the opportunity real? There had been many false alarms, and Kane was determined to maintain his cool. "That's interesting. So where is it?"

"I don't have it yet," Cayo admitted. "But I have Garth, and that's just as good."

"No," Kane replied softly, "it isn't 'just as good.' There's no substitute for the actual item. This Garth person could be lying to you . . . But I take your point. Assuming this individual has a genuine gate seed, and assuming it turns out to be operational, then I shall be very happy indeed. If he doesn't, I fear that my spirits will plunge, causing me to become extremely cranky. Do I make myself clear?"

The liquid that tasted so good only a few moments earlier suddenly went sour, and Cayo struggled to get it down. "Yes, sir. You do."

"Excellent," Kane said as he finished his wine. "I assume that Citizen Garth is sequestered nearby?"

"Yes, sir!" Cayo responded eagerly. "He offered to sell the seed, but set the price too high and refused to come down. I ordered some of my, I mean *your* functionaries, to put him under lock and key, hoping that would change his mind."

"Oh, he'll change his mind all right," Kane said confidently, as he tossed a handful of coins onto the table. "Or he'll be very sorry indeed."

Kane's voice was cold, *very* cold, which caused Cayo to wonder what he had gotten himself into. Unlike the offworld operative, who appeared to believe in the techno crap that the metal men preached on street corners, Cayo was in it for the money. But now, ever since Kane had stepped through the local star gate, the little man had become increasingly uneasy. There were advantages to being a nobody, not the least of which was staying well clear of people like Kane, something he would strive to do a better job of in the future.

After the power came on, the shops, factories, and other businesses that lay dormant during the day came back to noisy life, and the narrow, twisting streets filled with people who were on their way to work. As Kane followed Cayo he was conscious of the fact that every step he took required more energy than it would have on Anafa or Pooz. Not a lot more, but enough to leave him exhausted at the end of a typical day, even though he hadn't done anything out of the ordinary. Locals, on the other hand, people like Cayo, had developed musculature that enabled them to cope with the planet's gravity. Most were a bit shorter than norms on other worlds were, had stocky physiques, and looked like weight lifters. After thousands of years, the A-strain had started to adapt.

Once the two men arrived in the commercial quarter a broad flight of well-worn stairs led them down into the maze of passageways that lay just below Zand's surface. A dangerous place where visitors were well advised to watch their step, but civilized when compared to the "deeps" that lay even farther down.

There was no need for the twosome to descend that far, because the complex of rooms that comprised the Techno Society's station were located only one level down. So, having descended four flights of stairs, and having made their way along a dimly lit corridor, Kane and Cayo neared a well-guarded door. Two metal men, both of whom were armed with carbines, stood aside so that the humans could access a print-sensitive lock. Cayo pressed his palm against the smooth surface, waited for the resulting *click,* and gave the door a push. The interior was cool, clean, and well lit. Though happy to take advantage of the public grid during the hours that it was operational, the technologists had their own source of power, which had been brought in via the local star gate.

Cayo led Kane back to what was labeled CONFERENCE ROOM but actually served a darker purpose. Once the door was unlatched, and light flooded the previously darkened room, Kane could see the sturdy-looking hooks mounted on the ceiling, eyebolts that were evenly spaced along the walls, and the butcher block table that squatted at the center of the rectangular space. It was eight feet long and equipped with a variety of hardware. In fact, judging from the way the naked prisoner was spread-eagled on the stained wood, the off-world operative assumed that each of his four limbs was attached to a pulley. An effective way to keep him under control and in a psychologically vulnerable position.

The man named Garth raised his head and turned toward the spill of light. His eyes blinked in an attempt to penetrate the glare, and his voice was little more than a croak. "Cayo? Is that *you?* I need some water."

"And you can *have* some water," Kane answered, as he paused to examine the gleaming surgical instruments laid out on a side table. "But only if you tell us what we need to know."

"I can't," the tomb raider replied plaintively, wondering who the new voice belonged to. "Not unless you pay me."

"We offered to pay you," Kane countered patiently as he selected a razor-sharp scalpel. "But you raised the price. That was a stupid thing to do."

"Yes! I know that now," Garth agreed eagerly. "Free me and I will accept the original offer."

"Sorry, but it's too late for that now," Kane replied, as he turned to survey the body in front of him. It was covered with welts, bruises, and abrasions. "Now we want the information for free."

"But if I provide it, you'll kill me!" the tomb raider wailed miserably.

"Maybe, and maybe not," Kane responded calmly as he placed the very tip of the scalpel at the point just below the prisoner's zyphoid process. Garth screamed as the off-world operative made a shallow incision that led all the way down to the base of his penis. A thin scarlet line appeared, Cayo felt nauseous, and the tomb raider screamed. A beating, that was one thing, but this was something else.

"So," Kane continued, as he put some additional pressure on the tip of the blade, "what will it be? Would you like to tell me where the artifact is? Or should I keep on cutting?"

"I'll tell you!" the prisoner answered desperately. "Whatever you want to know."

Kane was slightly disappointed, or that's the way it looked to Cayo, as the off-worlder lifted the scalpel off the tomb raider's skin. "Okay, tell us . . . Where is the gate seed hidden?"

"It's down in the catacombs," the prisoner answered. "The only place where I knew it would be safe. Release me, and I'll take you there."

"Release him," Kane instructed. "If we die, then so will he."

A large lump grew to occupy the back of Cayo's throat. He managed to swallow it but not without difficulty. What had originally seemed a coup, an accomplishment that would catapult him into the upper levels of the society's management structure, now threatened to cost him his life. Still, there was nothing that the functionary could do other than to release Garth's restraints and help the prisoner down off the table.

Thirty minutes later a heavily armed party that consisted of Kane, Cayo, Garth, and two metal men left Techno Society headquarters and made its way through a warren of passageways to the point where a slime-covered ramp sloped downward. One of the city's many graffiti artists had painted a realistic-looking mouth around the entrance to the ramp, and the odor that wafted up out of the depths was so foul that Cayo felt as if he and his companions were passing into the belly of a carnivorous beast.

There were electric lights underground, but very few, which was why Kane and Cayo carried oil-burning lamps, while the robots projected beams of light through their "eyes." Soft, buttery light swept across green-black walls, momentarily glazed the bas-relief artwork of a bygone age, and sent armies of hungry vermin chittering toward their well-hidden nests.

The ramp turned in on itself, and spiraled downward, its surface slick with runoff from the storm drains and broken sewers above. Cayo noticed that there was a lot less graffiti now that they were at least three stories below street level, and that the piles of trash were smaller, a sure sign that only the most desperate of people spent time there.

Even Kane, whom Cayo had previously assumed to be fearless, sounded strained as he used his shotgun to jab Garth in the back. "How much farther?"

"We're almost there," the prisoner assured his captors, as he shuffled forward. His body hurt all over, the shackles that linked his ankles together made it difficult to walk, and he needed to pee. Would all the noise attract the attention of the half-human creatures who roamed the lowest levels of the catacombs? They hadn't attacked him in the past, but a dozen heavily armed guards had accompanied Garth on his previous visit, and the cannibals had a healthy respect for modern firearms.

Kane jabbed the prisoner again. "We'd better be . . . Because you'll be sorry if we aren't."

The tomb raider was already sorry, but knew that his captors didn't care and felt an ever-increasing sense of dread as he led them around a corner and into what had once been a small square. A mythical beast dominated the ornate fountain that claimed the center of the open area. Its mouth was open as if to roar, but it had been a long time since water had issued forth from it and splashed into the large circular basin below. "This is the place," Garth said hopelessly. "The artifact is over there . . . Inside the beast's mouth."

A brooding silence surrounded the square, and the lamplight left most of the area in darkness. Kane didn't like the subterranean cityscape, not one little bit, and struggled to hide his fear. "Cayo . . . Go get it."

The functionary winced and wished that he had the courage to say, "No," but knew he didn't. So, with his lantern held high, Cayo approached the fountain. He climbed up onto the knee-high containment and felt the trash in the basin give under his weight. Something crackled as it broke and Cayo felt his heart leap up into his mouth.

Then, with the lantern held aloft, the operative made his way over to where the beast sat on its well-sculpted haunches. The stone was cold and felt coarse under his fingertips, as Cayo placed a foot on top of a chipped paw and pushed himself up so he was level with the statue's yawning mouth. Anything could have made itself at home inside the black hole, and it required all of the courage that the functionary could muster to reach down into the cavern and feel around.

However, much to the operative's relief, nothing bit his hand, and it soon became apparent that nothing would. Moreover, once he had pulled a fistful of debris out of the way Cayo's fingers encountered something that was round, smooth, and inexplicably warm. It was the gate seed! Momentarily jubilant, the functionary withdrew the object from its hiding place and raised the sphere for the others to see. "I have it!"

Kane's face lit up. "Good job! Toss it to me. Then we'll get out of here."

Cayo did as he was told and hoped he wouldn't come to regret it. Because now that Kane had the device in his possession, the off-world operative didn't need anyone else. That shouldn't make any difference, however, not so long as the invaders departed the catacombs quickly, which Kane had already started to do.

Cayo hurried to clear the fountain, and had just joined the tail end of the procession, when the *clacking* sound began. The noise wasn't all that loud at first, but soon grew in intensity and seemed to come from every direction at once. "What the hell *is* that?" Kane demanded, as he paused to look around.

"It's the night people," Garth replied huskily, "banging leg bones together. They use them as clubs."

"Not *human* leg bones I hope," Cayo put in, but the answer was obvious, and the rest of the party ignored him.

"We need to buy some time," Kane said coldly. "Secure the prisoner to that grating. Perhaps he will distract them for a while."

Garth turned to run, but the shackles made that difficult, and the metal men were on him within seconds. The tomb raider started to gibber as a pair of handcuffs were used to lock him in place—and darkness swallowed him up. The screams started shortly thereafter and ended so suddenly that there was very little doubt as to the prisoner's fate.

Meanwhile, the intensity of the *clacking* sound continued to increase as Cayo followed the others up the slippery ramp. Now, as they fought their way toward the surface, the functionary realized how stupid they had been. Unlike the metal men, who could generate their own beams of light, both he and Kane were burdened with unwieldy lanterns, which would make it difficult if not impossible to fire his pump-style shotgun.

But that thought was driven from the functionary's mind by the sudden impact of the body that fell on him as he passed below an old ventilation shaft. Cayo had no choice but to drop the lantern in order to reach up and grab a fistful of rags. A simple jerk was sufficient to snatch the eight-year-old attacker off his back and dump the youth onto the ramp. A single blast from the shotgun took care of the rest, but the lantern had gone out by then, and it was pitch-black.

Although the muzzle flash had obliterated Cayo's night vision, he could still back up the ramp and fire the shotgun at the same time. Each *boom,* and the subsequent flash of light, was followed by a *clacking* sound as the functionary pumped a new shell into the chamber. But the tubular magazine held only eight rounds, and as the operative prepared to fire his final shell, he knew there wouldn't be enough time to fumble in his pockets for more. "Kane!" the operative shouted. "Help me!" But the off-world operative had abandoned his own lantern by then, clipped a cell-powered flashlight to the barrel of his shotgun, and was busy following the robots up toward the dimly seen light above. Ning's gravity made it more difficult to move, and his breath came in short, desperate gasps.

Cayo knew he had been abandoned when his weapon clicked empty, then something snarled and a femur struck him across the shoulders. Mercifully the next blow connected with the side of the functionary's head, which allowed him to exit his body prior to the butchery and the subsequent feast. Eventually, after the night people had claimed what was theirs and returned to the stink of their dens, silence was restored. It settled into place like a thick blanket, which was made all the more oppressive by the insistent *drip, drip, drip* of water and the occasional rumble of ancient pipes. One secret had been recovered, but there, deep within the ancient darkness, lay many more.

Aboard the starship *Hewhotravelsthroughtime*

In spite of the fact that most of the great starships were nearly identical in terms of basic design, they did have a variety of personalities, which made themselves manifest in unexpected ways, something Norr became acutely aware of as she threw more fuel onto the fire around which the group was huddled. "It's freezing in here!" the sensitive exclaimed. "What's going on?"

Rebo, who was seated on the opposite side of the blaze, took a sip of tea. "Different ships handle the problem in different ways, but it's my guess that the trip is nearly over, and *Hewhotravels* wants his passengers to pack up and board the shuttle."

Lee had his hands under his armpits in order to keep them warm. "Really? Why couldn't he just announce that? It would be a whole lot simpler."

"Because, with the possible exception of you, he thinks the rest of us are vermin," the runner replied. "Not to mention the fact that he *likes* to jerk humans around."

Norr nodded agreeably. "That sounds like him all right . . . It looks like some of our traveling companions are starting to pack."

Rebo scanned the immediate area and saw that the sensitive was correct. "Yeah . . . Well, let's get cracking. Remember, Lysander thinks the techno creeps will be on the ground waiting for us, so keep your packs light. Leave the food, your extra clothes, and anything else that can be replaced. We need to be light on our feet."

Norr opened her mouth to object, but the runner raised a hand. "Don't bother . . . You're a pain in the ass, but my client likes you, so there's no way we're going to leave you on your own."

"Well, I'm glad to hear that your client likes me," the sensitive replied sweetly. "But what about *you?*"

"That depends," Rebo replied, "on which one of your personalities I happen to be dealing with at the moment."

"And how many clothes she has on," Lee observed impishly, a grin splitting his face.

Norr blushed, and was about to reply, when a Klaxon started to bleat. "It sounds like the old boy is serious," Rebo put in, and emptied his mug into the fire. The liquid made a *hissing* sound as it hit the coals, and a cloud of steam rose as the group went to work.

Forty-five minutes later Rebo, Norr, Lee, and his red hat escorts tagged on to the end of a ragged line as the passengers filed through an air lock and boarded the waiting shuttle. The queue advanced in a series of fits and starts, and it was during one such pause that Rebo felt a hand on his shoulder. "So, runner," a baritone voice boomed, "is there room for one more?"

Rebo turned to find that Bo Hoggles was standing right behind him. The heavy was dressed in his usual assemblage of rags, wore a small knapsack high on his broad back, and carried a war hammer in his right hand. It was a massive affair that consisted of an alloy shaft fastened to a chunk of metal, which, judging from the ports that had been machined into it, had once been part of the spaceship. The runner grinned. "Beats me, Bo, but given the size of that hammer, I'll bet people will make room for you."

Norr had spotted Hoggles by that time and rushed forward to give the variant a hug. "Bo! It's good to see you again, but we have reason to believe that some rather unpleasant people will be waiting for us on the ground, so I suggest that you steer clear of us."

The heavy frowned, and his voice rumbled like distant thunder. "I'm tired of living alone. That's why I came. Perhaps the people who are waiting for you would like to meet my friend here."

Norr eyed the hammer, imagined the kind of damage that such a weapon could inflict, and smiled grimly. "Suit yourself, Bo. But you can always change your mind."

"Of course I can," the heavy replied nonchalantly. "But it isn't very likely."

The group followed the rest of the passengers into the shuttle and positioned themselves to disembark first. The logic was simple. Even though the Techno Society had shown itself to be ruthless, Rebo didn't believe they were stupid enough to fire on a large group of innocent people, especially given the fact that Norr might be killed as well. And, by placing themselves at the front of the crowd, the sensitive and her companions could make it that much more difficult for the opposition to use firearms without running the risk of hitting the wrong people. The plan was far from foolproof, but better than nothing, and had at least some chance of success.

A warning tone sounded, hatches cycled closed, and Norr

felt her body attempt to float upward as the shuttle separated itself from the ship. But the old harness held her in place, the transport began its descent, and Ning rose to meet her.

The Planet Ning

What had once been a huge spaceport had contracted as the flow of interplanetary travel was reduced to a trickle and other enterprises crowded in around it. Now, little more than a circular pad remained, as a crowd had started to gather. However, unlike the free-spirited celebrants who came to greet new arrivals on Anafa, this mob was made up of street vendors, pickpockets, and would-be guides. One of them, a strange-looking man with blond hair, was accompanied by a retinue of heavily robed robots, the same sort of metal men that preached on street corners.

If not exactly happy, which might have been constitutionally impossible for someone of Jevan Kane's disposition, the operative was in a relatively good mood. And why not? The gate seed, which Kane was unwilling to entrust to anyone other than himself, hung round his neck and formed a large lump beneath his shirt. That alone represented a successful mission and would be sufficient to silence those who had been critical of him.

Now, assuming that he managed to capture Lanni Norr, the technologist would be able to return to Seros in triumph. The off-worlder's thoughts were interrupted by a shout and an excited buzz as a white contrail appeared, and a loud *boom* rolled across the land. It was a welcome sound, and Kane looked upward with all the rest.

*Though compelled to send part of himself down to the sur-*face of planets like Ning, *Hewhotravels* took no pleasure in it and considered the whole process of transporting barbarians between worlds to be a terrible waste of time. Unfortunately, such was not only his fundamental purpose but the way he was programmed, which meant that he was fated to perform such chores until his body disintegrated. This bleak prospect was largely responsible for his perpetually bad mood.

So, eager to complete the odious task as quickly as possible, and without regard for the comfort of the vermin who traveled in his belly, the AI turned and sped north over the outskirts of Zand. A sonic boom followed along behind him, rattled windows, and sent flocks of drab fliers into the air, where they circled aimlessly before returning to their roosts.

And for that brief moment, as the shuttle skimmed the land, the past came back to life. Because once, long before any living memory, such events had been so commonplace that not even the birds noticed them. And that, it seemed to the ship, was a great loss indeed.

Rebo felt the transport start to slow and knew what that meant. Soon, within a matter of minutes, he and his companions would exit the passenger compartment and walk into a fight. Not only that, but judging from what felt like a mantle of lead that had settled onto his shoulders, the gravity on Ning exceeded that maintained aboard the ship. A definite disadvantage.

The runner checked to ensure that none of those seated around him was looking before giving the amulet that hung around his neck a surreptitious squeeze. And not just for himself, as had once been his practice, but for his companions as well—an odd amalgamation of personalities that combined to weigh him down and lift him up at the same time. Norr was the best example since his feelings for the sensitive ran the gamut from desire to frustration. It was all very confusing, and the runner didn't like things that were confusing, because they were, well, confusing.

But as the shuttle touched down, Rebo knew it was important to put all such thoughts aside and focus on the matter before him. "All right," he said, in a voice pitched just loud enough for his allies to hear, "stick with the plan. And whatever you do, remember to keep moving, because if they surround us, it will be next to impossible to break out."

Norr nodded, Lee forced a smile, Hoggles produced a grunt of acknowledgment, and the red hat warriors sketched religious symbols into the air in front of them. Then the hatch opened, fresh air surged into the cabin, and it was time to leave. Rebo came up out of his seat, made a *clacking* sound with the three-foot-long fighting sticks that he had shaped for the occasion, and uttered a roar intended to freeze the rest of the passengers in place.

The unexpected sound had the desired effect, and that allowed the runner and his friends to exit first. Rebo had not been to Ning before, and there was no time in which to appreciate the scenery as he led the rest of the small company down a metal ramp onto heat-scorched duracrete. He had the lead, with two Dib Wa warriors to either flank, and Norr at his back. Hoggles, who still insisted on taking part, brought up the rear with Lee riding high on his shoulders. It was a sturdy formation, or so it seemed to the runner, who spotted the waiting crowd and charged straight at it. But his movements weren't as quick as they would have been aboard the ship—and it was like trying to run through deep water.

Jevan Kane had been watching for Norr and spotted the young woman right away. But while the technologist had been aware of the fact that Norr had what he assumed to be a lover, he had no reason to expect an escort that included four red hat warriors and an unkempt heavy. All of whom were not only armed but clearly ready for trouble. That took the operative by surprise. How could they know? Then he had it. Lysander had been present during the meeting on Anafa but refused to manifest through Dyson. But he could have listened in and, having done so, told Norr what to expect. The rotten bastard was switching sides!

But there was no time for further thought as the metal men rushed forward in an attempt to surround and capture Norr while bystanders screamed and ran in every direction. The robots were dressed in nearly identical black robes that flared as they ran. Each android was armed with a wooden cudgel, which judging from the nicks and cuts they bore, had clearly seen action.

Wood clanged on metal as Rebo closed with the first machine and brought both of his fighting sticks together in the attack called "clapping hands," shifted his weight to his right foot, and turned to let the robot's club brush his left shoulder. Then, having brought his left foot up and back, the runner launched a kick that struck the machine's torso. The automaton toppled over backward, hit the ground, and was struggling to rise when Norr took its head off with her vibro blade. Sparks shot from the neatly severed neck, and the machine's limbs jerked spasmodically before the metal man finally went limp.

Rebo, who had been unaware of the fact that the sensitive's staff concealed yet another weapon, barely had time to say "Thanks!" before the next robot came at him. Meanwhile, the Dib Wa were engaged as well. One of the warriors brought his sword down only to have it blocked by a wooden cudgel, and then, while working to free his blade, took a fatal blow to the head.

Metal rang on metal as another red hat sought revenge, but discovered that unlike Norr's vibro blade, ordinary steel couldn't part the android's alloy skin in a single blow. But the religious warriors were resourceful, and it wasn't long before they learned to bring the automatons down by throwing shirts over their heads and beating them to death. But the heavier gravity put them at a disadvantage, and another Dib Wa fell, tried to rise, and was slaughtered where he lay.

In the meantime Kane, who had chosen to follow the robots into battle rather than lead them, saw the opportunity that he'd been waiting for. Having conserved his strength, and with both sets of combatants fully engaged, it was a simple matter to slip between the skirmishers and make for Norr. But the blond hair was hard to miss, and the sensitive was preparing herself to fight the operative, when she came under a different kind of attack. With so much of her attention focused on the physical battle, the sensitive had inadvertently lowered her psychic defenses, opening herself to Lysander. Norr attempted to resist, but it was too late by then, and the discarnate took control of her body. He took a swing at Kane, swore as the vibro blade sizzled over the operative's head, and felt his former ally wrap his arms around Norr's torso.

Lysander felt a sudden stab of fear as he struggled to keep Kane from simply lifting the female body off its feet and carrying it away. But Norr was heavier than Kane expected her to be, and the discarnate took advantage of that fact to knee his onetime son in the groin. "You're fighting for the wrong side," Lysander lectured Kane, as he brought the vibro blade's hilt down on the back of the other man's skull. "We need to restore the gates, but for the benefit of humanity, not ourselves! That's where we went wrong last time."

Kane let go of his aching privates, felt a moment of vertigo, and struggled to keep his feet as the planet sought to pull him down. "Lysander? You old bastard . . . Is that you?"

"You bet your ass it is," the scientist replied, and was about to take another swing with the vibro blade when a metal man seized him from behind. Lysander struggled, but soon discovered that Norr's body wasn't strong enough to break the machine's steely grip, and saw Kane smile as the machine pulled him backward. "We have what we came for," the operative shouted. "Take her away!"

But Norr's capture had not gone unnoticed, and even as the metal man began to carry the sensitive away, Hoggles brought his homemade war hammer down on the android's head. Metal crumpled, circuitry failed, and sparks shot out through the metal man's eyes.

Lysander felt the robot's arms fall away, and was about to counterattack, when a wave of androids swept around him. Strong though he was, Hoggles was hard-pressed to stay upright, and thereby keep Lee safely above the fray, as three of the machines attacked simultaneously.

The last of the Dib Wa warriors had fallen by then, and as he and his remaining companions were surrounded by what seemed like an army of cudgel-wielding metal men, Rebo knew that the battle was lost. Or so it seemed until a huge shadow spilled over him, a blast of hot air washed across his shoulders, and a huge skid nicked the side of Kane's head. It was a glancing blow, but one from a large shuttle, and the Techno Society's operative fell like a rock.

Hewhotravels had never been in a fight before. And had it not been for the fact that the little boy who might be Nom Maa was involved, would have stayed clear of this one. But given humanity's steady decline, and so little reason for hope, the ship found itself unable to sit by while what might be a great teacher came under attack. And though not specifically equipped for combat, the AI discovered that he didn't need to be, as he sent combatants scattering in every direction.

Rebo got a grip on Norr's arm, and was about to drag the sensitive to safety, when Lysander jerked it loose. "Not yet, you fool! The lump under Kane's shirt . . . It's a gate seed! We need it!"

The runner wasn't so sure about the "we" part, but took the opportunity to plod over to where the operative lay and cut the thong to which the metal sphere was attached. Then, with the seed safely stashed in a pocket, Rebo led Norr, Hoggles, and Lee off the pad. The surviving metal men attempted to follow, but *Hewhotravels* wasn't about to allow that and moved to block them. So, with no way to pursue their quarry, there was very little that the surviving robots could do other than give aid to their fallen leader. Once Kane had been carried away, dozens of vendors, pickpockets, and guides returned to the pad. They neither knew nor cared what the fight had been about. All that mattered to them was the possibility of profit and the fact that the day was still young.

Zand was a complex city, which made it both hard to gov-ern and easy to hide in. First, because there were numerous distinct neighborhoods, each of which wanted to govern itself. That meant that local officials were sometimes less than cooperative where the city's police force was concerned. And making the situation even more difficult for local authorities was the fact that many of those who lived in the city made their livings from the hundreds of caravans that entered and left Zand on a daily basis. Since those caravans transported not only all manner of legitimate goods but contraband, too, the axiom ASK ME NO QUESTIONS AND I'LL TELL YOU NO LIES was inscribed over the eastern gate to the city.

All this meant that Rebo, who had quite a bit of experience where such things were concerned, had little difficulty locating a place where he and his companions could stay. The key, as his mentor Thomas Crowley had taught him, was "to find the middle." By which the sickly runner meant accommodations that weren't so posh as to be targeted by the thieves guild, nor so low as to be the focus of whatever passed for the local police force. "What you want," Crowley had advised, "is to render yourself invisible."

Easily said, but hard to do, when you're traveling with a sensitive, a heavy, and a ten-year-old religious leader. Still, after a bit of research, Rebo managed to locate a small hotel that was located on the edge of a middle-class neighborhood called Levels, because of the way it had been terraced into a hillside. The hostelry was located on a sleepy street, in a wood-frame stucco-covered building, not far from a small but serviceable market. Just the place to rest, regroup, and prepare for the cross-country trek that would take the travelers to the spaceport in Cresus—a city located more than a thousand miles away.

Ideal though the hiding place might be, Rebo knew that all sorts of people would be on the lookout for both Norr and Lee. Norr, because the Techno Society was not going to give up, and Lee, because Zand was something of a black hat stronghold, and senior members of that sect were sure to learn that four red hat bodies had been left on the landing pad. What was less certain was whether the monks would hear about the presence of a little boy and jump to the right conclusion. But *if* they did, and the runner thought it was best to assume that they would, it seemed likely that Lee would be targeted. That was why he insisted that everyone remain in their rooms and out of sight.

Norr, who was still recovering from her latest encounter with Lysander, was quick to agree. As did Hoggles, a fact that came as something of a surprise to Rebo since he would have expected some sort of objection from a man who had spent the last few years on board a spaceship. Still, it was nice to have something break his way.

That left Lee, who had been devastated by the loss of all four Dib Wa warriors and blamed himself for their deaths. He wanted to leave the hotel, not to explore the city as he normally sought to do, but to visit a temple where he could apologize to the dead warriors. Norr and Rebo had attempted to dissuade the boy but to no avail.

And, making the problem that much more difficult, was the fact that the only temple in Zand belonged to black hat monks. A fact that didn't bother Lee, who swore he could go there without being recognized, but worried Rebo no end. All those factors accounted for the tension in the room where the group was gathered. A table had been pulled out away from a wall, chairs had been brought in so that everyone could sit, and a curtain had been drawn in front of the single horizontal slit-style window that local architects favored. While that ensured their privacy, it was necessary to light candles in order to see. The hotel's owner claimed that later, when the power came on, the disk-shaped fixture mounted on the ceiling would start to glow, but Rebo had his doubts and made a mental note to request an oil lamp.

Norr, who had a tendency to become moody when surrounded by large groups of people and their emotions, was even more so immediately after one of Lysander's invasions. She sat with the newly acquired metal sphere balanced on her fingertips. The hair-thin lines that zigzagged across the object's surface seemed to suggest that it could be opened somehow, but no amount of twisting and turning had been sufficient to make it do so. The metal housing felt warm, and that suggested some sort of internal power source, as well as a purpose. The sensitive frowned. "What did Lysander call this thing?"

Rebo sighed. He had already answered that question half a dozen times. But Norr had a tendency to gnaw at things, especially when depressed, and wasn't aware of how annoying that could be. "He called it a 'gate seed.'"

Not to be left out, Lee, who had voiced the same possibility before, did so again. "We could grow a star gate!"

"Or trigger some sort of disaster," Rebo said darkly, as he fingered the amulet that hung round his neck.

Hoggles, who hadn't commented on the subject until then, broke his silence. "Maybe you should give it back. Otherwise, they're going to come after you."

Rebo looked at Norr. "Bo has a point . . . Why keep it? Kane is alive. Once the bastard recovers, he'll be after you with a vengeance."

Candlelight reflected off the ball as the sensitive continued to rotate the sphere with her fingertips. She knew that both men were correct. If she kept the seed, both Kane *and* Lysander would come after her. The latter was the worst in some ways.

But, just as she had resisted their efforts as Princess Cara, Norr found herself unwilling to give in to either one of them now. Not without a full understanding of what such a surrender would mean. "You're right, Jak. I know that . . . But, what if the seed could make a difference? There's so much suffering. I can feel it everywhere we go. A system of star gates could bring back the days when scientific knowledge flowed back and forth between the planets. Just think what that would mean to the field of medicine alone!"

"Yes," Rebo agreed somberly. "But only if the system is used for good. So, who do you trust? The man who was so tyrannical that you were forced to murder him? Or the man who wants to enslave you?"

Norr sighed. "That's the problem. The potential for good is there, but I can't trust either one of them. Not yet anyway."

"Which means?"

"Which means," Norr replied, as she stared into her own badly distorted reflection, "that the gate seed will stay with me."

NINE

The Planet Ning

The schism between black and red stems from disagreements regarding the relative merits of mind versus emotion as paths to enlightenment. Such considerations are a waste of nas (spiritual energy), and equivalent to debating which is more valuable, the left hand or the right hand. Both come together to pray, work, or play.

—The tenth Nom Maa

In spite of the fact that the overhead light had been ex-tinguished as Lee was put to bed, not even the curtain that Norr had pulled across the window could block the ghostly green glow produced by the streetlamp outside, and all manner of shadows populated the walls. Time seemed to creep by as the boy waited for Hoggles, then Rebo, to enter the room and go to bed. Finally, once the heavy had started to snore, and the runner was breathing evenly, Lee made his move.

Slowly, so as to generate as little noise as possible, the youth threw his covers back and swung his feet out onto the cold floor. He was already dressed, so it was a simple matter to pick up his boots and tiptoe over to the door. Lee knew Rebo was a light sleeper and likely to wake at the slightest

sound, which was why the boy exercised great care as he removed the chair that the runner had propped up against the
door. Not in an attempt to block the entrance, but to serve
as an alarm, should someone with a key attempt to open it.
Once that was accomplished it was a simple matter to un-
lock the door, retrieve his boots, and tiptoe into the corridor. Having gained the hall successfully, the youngster
closed the door so gently that there was no more than the
faintest *click,* as the spring-loaded bolt found its well-worn
hole and slid home.

After that it was a simple matter to pull on his boots,
lace them up, and slip out of the hotel. The power was on,
the streets were crowded with people, and it was easy for Lee
to assume the persona that he had prepared for himself. If he
were stopped, which seemed unlikely given all of the children out on the streets, the youngster would say that he was
running an errand for his father, a claim he would substan-
tiate with a shopping list prepared earlier in the day. And, if
attacked, Lee had both of his knives. Those, combined with
his speed, would get him out of trouble. Or so the youth
hoped.

But there were no signs of trouble as Lee made his way
down a street that switchbacked down the hillside. Just the
opposite, in fact, as shoppers paused to look through shop
windows, street vendors hawked their wares, and a metal
man took a moment to explain the benefits of technology to
a hungry dog.

Lee gave the robot a wide berth and continued on his
way. Rebo had taught the youth a great deal about how to
move around in a strange environment without attracting
the wrong sort of attention, so the youngster knew better
than to ask strangers for directions, and was relieved when
he saw a black hat initiate pass by. Could the nun be headed

for a place other than the local monastery? Yes, but given the fully loaded shopping bags the girl carried, Lee felt reasonably sure that the initiate had been sent to do some shopping and was on her way back to the temple.

The theory soon proved to be correct as the nun led Lee through a maze of passageways, across an open plaza, and up to the monastery beyond. Unlike the soft, often curving lines that red hat architects favored, the black-hat-inspired structure was a study in hard angles, flat planes, and geometric shapes. It was a design aesthetic intended to emphasize mind over emotion, control over chance, and man's ultimate ascendancy over nature.

Lee didn't care for it, but knew that people tend to be most comfortable with familiar forms and forced himself to consider the structure's virtues. The long, slanting roofline, for example, which pointed up toward god consciousness, as well as a line of eight triangular entrances, each representing one of the eight paths to enlightenment and full mastery of the way. All of which combined to help focus the mind.

The nun entered the building through door five, the entrance that symbolized skillful livelihood, leaving Lee to choose an entrance of his own. Given the nature of his journey, the youth decided it would be appropriate to pass through portal one, which stood for skillful understanding.

The interior was well lit, and the walls were intentionally bare, lest the faithful be distracted by gratuitous decorations. Still another element of the black hat mind-set that made logical sense but didn't appeal to Lee, who enjoyed religious art.

No matter which door an aspirant chose, he or she wound up in a single hall, or "way," which was symbolic of the manner in which each individual had to walk all eight of the major paths before achieving self-mastery. The hallway gave access to a large rectangular room and a fifteen-foot-tall likeness of Teon that sat with its back to a white wall. The ascended master had golden skin, and the symbols that he held in each of his eight hands seemed to glow as if lit from within. The boy paused to bow respectfully before turning into one of the aisles and seeking a place in which to kneel. He had never been allowed to enter a black hat temple before, and while part of him was afraid, the rest was at ease. For there, surrounded by those intent on traveling the same path that he had chosen, Lee knew he could meditate in peace.

Meanwhile, at the rear of the chamber, Abbot Hico Marth stood watching those at prayer. Having completed some of the bureaucratic chores that plagued his days, and having granted himself a bowl of sweet berries by way of a reward, the monk carried them into the temple proper. And it was there, while leaning against the back wall, that the black hat noticed the little boy. First, because the youth was alone, second, because there something special about the way that the youngster held himself, and third, because he brought his palms together as he bowed. A small thing, but just one of many small things that distinguished red hats from black hats, who always kept their hands at their sides when they bowed.

It was nothing really, and the abbot would have dismissed the boy as a convert, had it not been for the battle that had taken place just days before—a strange conflict in which a force of metal men attacked a group of newly arrived travelers. Of particular interest was the fact that four red hats had been killed—and a little boy had been seen riding high on a heavy's shoulders.

Marth surveyed the room, assured himself that it was empty of both metal men *and* variants, and turned his attention back to his berries. What did the incident at the landing pad mean? Nothing probably, except that among the papers that had arrived along with the latest ship, was a letter from a monk who identified himself as Brother Fiva, alerting all of the monasteries that lay along the route between Anafa and Thara that a ten-year-old pretender might pass their way. Could that boy, and *this* boy, be one and the same? It didn't seem likely, but there was no way to be sure.

Unaware of the extent to which he was being scrutinized, Lee visualized each of the fallen warriors, apologized for his role in cutting their incarnations short, and said prayers for them. It wasn't much, but the youth had faith his thoughts would reach the red hats, and the knowledge made him feel better.

Spiritually refreshed, and eager to make his way back to the hotel lest his absence be discovered, Lee rose and bowed. Other worshipers were both arriving and leaving. The boy fell in behind a family of four, and was just about to exit the chamber, when a heavy hand fell on his shoulder. The unexpected contact startled the boy, and he looked to his right to discover that a rather imposing monk was staring down at him. The top of the cleric's head was obscured by a round hat, but those portions of his scalp that remained visible had been shaved, leaving only a haze of black stubble. His cheeks were gaunt, his skin was pitted as if by a childhood disease, and the smile belied the look in his eyes. "And why, if I may be so bold as to ask, would a red hat deign to visit our humble temple?"

The comment, which was intended to shock, had the desired effect. Lee felt a heavy weight hit the bottom of his stomach and knew that an expression of fear had already registered on his face. He had given himself away somehow, and rather than offer denials that the black hat was unlikely to believe, Lee knew that his best chance lay in providing the monk with an opportunity to reach the wrong conclusion. For, as the great Teon once said, "Errors occur not by chance, but through choice, which was god's second gift to humanity."

"I meant no disrespect," Lee stammered in Tilisi, "but it was my desire to communicate with the being within, and I was told that yours is the only temple in Zand."

Not only had the boy offered an honest reply, but he had done so in a respectful manner, and Marth allowed his demeanor to soften. "You are a stranger to the city then?"

"Yes," Lee answered truthfully. "We arrived a few days ago. We came a long ways, the journey was difficult, and some of our companions were killed. I wanted to pray for them."

"And you felt comfortable coming here?"

"No, I was scared," Lee admitted. "But I remembered what Brother Qwa taught me."

The abbot raised a dark eyebrow. "Which was?"

"Brother Qwa said that while those who follow the way think with two heads, they have but a single heart, and that belongs to god."

Even though Marth had been fully prepared to dislike the youth, especially if he appeared to be the pretender, he felt his heart soften instead. Still, while he was inclined to accept the lad as a harmless traveler, some further questioning wouldn't hurt. Besides, the boy looked a lot like someone else, which while not important in and of itself, was a matter of some curiosity. "Brother Qwa is a wise man. Come, we shall have tea and speak from the heart."

The invitation was phrased as an order, and in spite of all the misgivings that he felt, Lee had no choice but to accept. "Thank you, Excellency," the youth responded humbly. "To do so would be an honor."

Pleased by the extent of his own perceptiveness, and having been charmed by the youngster's unassuming manner, Marth introduced himself and learned that the boy's name was Lee. A short trip through a series of sterile passageways brought the pair to a generously proportioned office. The entirety of the back wall was obscured by floor-to-ceiling cubbyholes, all filled to capacity with rolled manuscripts. The broad desk, which had been made out of the dark ebony-like wood native to Ning's southern jungles, sat no more than a foot off the reed mat that covered the floor and was ringed by red, gold, and green cushions. "Please," the abbot said, "take a seat. There's something I'd like you to see."

Lee sat cross-legged on a cushion, while Marth rang a little bell and provided instructions to an aspirant who appeared as if by magic. Though careful to maintain a calm exterior, Lee wondered if his absence had been discovered and wrestled with the hindrance called worry. It had been wrong to sneak out, *very* wrong, and while he deserved whatever punishment the law of cause and effect might mete out to him, such was not the case for those who had so mistakenly placed their trust in him.

"Here," Marth said, as he dropped a roll of paper onto the surface of the desk. "Take a look at that."

Lee had to use both hands to pull the scroll open. What he saw was a charcoal drawing rather than the religious manuscript he had expected to see. The face that stared out at him was that of a teenaged male. Outside of the adolescent's eyes, which seemed to reflect a brooding intelligence, there was nothing remarkable about the portrait, and Lee was at a loss to understand why Marth wanted him to look at it.

"Do you see the likeness?" the abbot insisted, as he sat on

one of the cushions. "Yanak is older, of course, but if it weren't for the fact that I know his family so well, I would swear that you were his younger brother."

Lee took another look and, having done so, could see what the monk meant. The overall shape of the teenager's face *was* similar to his own, even though the significance of that fact escaped him, and he wasn't sure what to say. "Yes," Lee said politely. "I see what you mean."

The tea arrived then, and even though Marth could tell that the boy had no idea who Yanak was, the abbot wasn't ready to suspend his somewhat oblique investigation quite yet. While the odds were excellent that Lee was just what he appeared to be, a somewhat precocious youngster raised within the intellectual embrace of a red hat monk off to the east, it was his duty to make sure.

Once the tea had been poured, and the aspirant had withdrawn, the subtle-yet-persistent interrogation continued. "In spite of the fact that Yanak's physical body is only sixteen years old, we have reason to believe that the spirit of the great teacher Nom Maa dwells within it," Marth said conversationally. "That's why he is on his way to the central temple at CaCanth. Once he arrives Yanak will be tested and take his place on the throne. After that, well, who knows? Perhaps he will find a way to heal the rift that separates black from red."

Even though he knew that the black hats had a candidate of their own, Lee had never been told the other boy's name or been shown a likeness of his face. Not until now that is. While the monks on Anafa insisted that *his* was the spirit of Nom Maa, and there had been moments when he believed the assertion to be true, such was the veil between him and his past lives that Lee had never been entirely sure. Did that mean the teenager with the aloof stare was the *real* Nom

Maa? And that he was little more than a pawn? Groomed by the red hats to serve their political ends? As he listened to Marth it seemed all too possible. And, rather than the disappointment that Lee might have expected to feel, the boy experienced a sense of exhilaration instead. Because if he was nobody other than himself, and wasn't expected to take the throne, he could live his life any way he chose! "That would be a good thing," Lee said, "I affirm whatever is for the highest and the best."

The abbot took a sip of tea. Had Lee been the red hat pretender, and been confronted with an image of his rival, the monk would have expected to see some sign of consternation on his face. Resentment perhaps, or even anger, but such was not the case. In fact, judging from appearances, the boy appeared to be anything but jealous. A good sign indeed. "Here," Marth said, as he passed three incense sticks to the boy. "Please convey these to your parents. They have been blessed and will help all of you battle the hindrance known as doubt."

Lee knew a dismissal when he heard one, felt a tremendous sense of relief, and was careful to bow once he got to his feet. "Thank you, sasa (wise one). I will tell them."

Marth rang the tiny bell even as the youngster withdrew. The aspirant, who had been waiting only steps away, appeared immediately. "Yes, Excellency?"

The abbot gestured toward the door. "Follow the boy. Don't let him see you. Once you know where he is staying report to me. It's my opinion that he is what he claims to be, but clouds can appear in an otherwise blue sky, and it is wise to remain vigilant."

The aspirant had no idea what Marth was talking about, but didn't need to know, and slipped out into the night. It was just past one in the morning, the lights remained on, and the boy was easy to spot. The rest was easy.

When Kane came to he was flat on his back looking up at a blurry sky. It wobbled, along with the makeshift stretcher that supported him, and someone snapped an order. "Watch where you're going, damn you!"

The operative brought a hand up to the side of his head, winced as his fingertips made contact with a large lump, and remembered the way the shuttle had attacked both him and his metal men. Such an action was unprecedented in so far as he knew, and would have been worthy of analysis, except that his head hurt so badly he couldn't think straight. A wave of dizziness rolled in from somewhere unknown, took control of Kane's consciousness, and carried it away.

A good deal of time was spent in the land of darkness, and when the light finally returned, Kane found that he was reluctant to acknowledge it. But there were voices that called his name, and beyond that a vague sense of urgency, as if something important had been left undone.

Like a bubble floating to the top of a primeval pond, Kane rose, popped open, and found himself looking up at a ceiling. Water had leaked down onto it at some point in the past and created what looked a world map after it dried. Yellow lakes, brown-rimmed continents, and white oceans all waited to be explored. But, before the operative could do so, a face interspersed itself between the ceiling and him. It belonged to Ron Olvos, the moon-faced council member who owned the impressive sounding title of "Operations Coordinator," but was actually little more than Chairman Tepho's all-purpose gofer. "Kane? Can you hear me?"

"Yes," the operative croaked. "And what's worse is that I can *see* you."

Olvos shook his head reprovingly. "Well, I can see that the blow to the head did nothing to improve your native charm."

The face disappeared as Kane pushed himself up off the bed, groaned as a dull, throbbing headache kicked in, and swung his feet out over the side of the bed. "Where the hell am I? On Anafa?"

"No," Olvos replied primly. "You're still on Ning. They were afraid to move you. The chairman sent me to check on you."

Kane cradled his head with his hands. "Don't bullshit me, Olvos. Tepho sent you to retrieve the gate seed . . . He couldn't care less about me."

"Well, that isn't entirely true," the council member said, as he pulled a chair up next to the bed. "Although I'd be lying if I said that the chairman was pleased to discover that, having recovered a gate seed, you chose to keep it on your person, rather than send it back to Anafa where the tech types could go to work on it."

"That was a mistake," Kane admitted, "and one I plan to rectify."

"The chairman will be gratified to hear that," Olvos observed mildly. "And in the meantime I have some good news for you. While you were on vacation in dreamland I put all of the local staff to work looking for Norr and the group of weirdos that she hangs out with. That included reviewing footage from every metal man in Zand. And, while we didn't get any hits where the sensitive was concerned, I'm happy to announce that the little boy walked through a shot in a neighborhood called Levels. The little shit's image wasn't clear enough to trigger the robot's spot and report programming, but we found it during the review. Once we applied some magnification, presto, there he was!"

Kane felt a surge of hope and looked up. "You located them?"

The functionary shook his head. "No, we were lucky, but not *that* lucky. The metal men are out canvassing the area where the boy was spotted, so it should be just a matter of time before we find their hidey-hole."

Kane threw his weight forward and managed to stand. The pain was intense. "Are you out of your mind? Norr and her companions will spot the robots and run! Then where will we be?"

"No worse off than we were after you allowed them to take the gate seed," Olvos replied pointedly. "Please, feel free to go out and set things right."

"That I will," Kane replied grimly. "Hand me my pants."

The hotel's kitchen was small, hot, and steamy. And, be- cause the restaurant it served was an important source of revenue, various members of the proprietress's family were bustling about preparing for lunch. The power wouldn't come on for many hours yet, so charcoal had been used to fuel the ancient cast-iron stove that dominated one greasy wall. Rebo, still furious with Lee for sneaking out the night before, was halfway down the center aisle when the hostelry's owner turned to block the way. She was a large woman, and given the bloodstained meat cleaver clutched in her right hand, would make a formidable opponent. Her hair hung down around her face in greasy ringlets, tiny beads of perspiration dotted her broad forehead, and her enormous bosom strained against the front of the filthy apron that hung down to her ankles. "Citizen Horko . . . Assuming that's your actual name. You're just the man I wanted to see."

Rebo, who had hoped to exit out the back unobserved, forced a smile. "Yes, Mrs. Pella . . . What can I do for you?"

"People are looking for you," she said accusingly. "A man came by early this morning, and another left just a few minutes ago."

"Yes, I'm aware of that," the runner replied. "Please tell your staff how much I appreciate their discretion."

"He offered us money," Pella replied artlessly. "A crono for information related to your whereabouts. And he knows what all four of you look like."

Rebo sighed. A counteroffer was clearly in order and would clearly have to be more than a crono, even though the actual reward was probably less. Another reason why he and his companions needed to escape the city. Negotiations ensued, and by the time they were over, Rebo's purse was two cronos lighter. But, if that was what it would take to keep the Techno Society operatives at bay for another planetary rotation, then the runner had no choice but to pay it.

Mrs. Pella made the coins disappear and stepped out of the way. Her smile revealed two rows of green teeth. "Have a nice day, Citizen Horko . . . I will see you later."

Rebo slipped out the back door and took the time required to survey his surroundings. Then, satisfied that it was safe to do so, the runner made his way down the alley, turned into a busy street, and set off for the eastern border of the city. Because it was there, along both banks of the Xee River, that the great caravans paused to rest before setting off again. One of them was bound to be headed south, or so Rebo assumed as he made his way through a succession of neighborhoods and paused half a block short of the city's eastern gate. The wall, which had been raised to defend the city from some forgotten threat, stood a good twenty feet tall and was every bit of six feet thick. The off-worlder was tired by then and felt as though he had been walking for days rather than hours.

Brightly uniformed guards stood to either side of the street, but the runner assumed that their role was largely ceremonial, since none of the soldiers attempted to interact with the hundreds of people who flowed back and forth through the ancient portal. That meant the only impediment to further progress was the trio of black-hatted clerics who stood with begging bowls extended and dispensed blessings to those who made donations.

Rebo knew that the monks might be there for no other reason than to collect alms, but he couldn't afford to take the risk, especially after Lee's clandestine activities the night before. With that in mind the runner took a quick look around and spotted an angen-drawn wagon that had approached from behind. The boxy conveyance had an enclosed cargo compartment, a raised driver's seat, and rode on four metal-rimmed wheels. The mouthwatering aroma of freshly baked bread traveled with the conveyance, and the runner figured that the contents were intended for the men, women, and children who were camped along the Xee River.

It was a simple matter to slip through the crowd, jump up onto the wagon, and claim a seat right next to the surprised driver. The old man held the reins with work-thickened fingers and looked as if a thousand storms had been etched into his skin. "Here, father," Rebo said, before the driver could object, and offered him a handful of coppers. "My sore feet would like to pay for the privilege of riding next to you, my stomach would like to purchase a bite of bread, and my ears would like to buy a portion of your wisdom."

Passengers weren't allowed, but the combination of humor, flattery, and the bribe was sufficient to overcome any doubts the oldster might have otherwise had. He produced a mostly toothless grin. "I can take care of your feet, and your stomach, but I fear for your ears."

Rebo laughed, and the two of them continued to chat as the wagon neared the gate. Then, just as the black hats started to turn their heads toward the movement, Rebo stuck his head into the cargo compartment as if checking on the load of crusty bread. The odor was overwhelming. The runner waited long enough for the conveyance to roll through the gate and had a loaf of bread clutched in his hand when he turned forward again. The runner tore off a chunk and bit into it. The monks were nowhere to be seen.

The wagon lurched as two of the big wooden wheels were forced to roll over a dead dog, and the angen pulled the wagon down the right-hand side of the thoroughfare everyone referred to as "the street of thieves." The name stuck because the bars, saloons, and whorehouses that lined both sides of the filthy boulevard were natural habitats for outlaws of every stripe, and because the shopkeepers who made their livings selling food, equipment, and weapons to the nomads were said to have the highest profit margins on the planet. A promising neighborhood for anyone who was interested in certain forms of entertainment, but Rebo's attention was focused on other things, such as the caravans and the routes they followed.

As Rebo questioned the old man, it soon became apparent that while Omar had very little formal education, he was a keen observer of everything that took place around him. And that included the nomads to whom he had been selling bread for more than forty years.

One of the first things the runner learned was that most of the caravans operated on a seasonal basis. During the winter they typically headed south, but it was summer at present, which meant most were traveling north. That meant travelers who wanted to go south, but lacked the knowledge required to make their own way, would be forced to sign on with one of the few caravans headed in that direction. Such pack trains were made up of hardy types who were willing to brave the southern heat to reap the high prices that luxury goods would fetch in cities that hadn't been visited by outsiders in months. So, secure in the knowledge that the bread wagon was slated to visit both southbound caravans, the runner was content to sit back and soak up the atmosphere while the old man made his rounds.

For obvious reasons the most popular camping spots were those located along both banks of the Xee River. But there were only a limited number of slots, which meant that some of the nomads were forced to pitch tents in the areas off to either side of the river and bring their thirsty angens down to drink in the evening, an activity that not only involved a lot of work, but put a serious dent in the amount of time available for equipment maintenance and the nightly carousing of which the nomads were fond.

However, regardless of location, all the encampments had certain features in common. Chief among them were the domed tents that sat clustered together, the moody beasts of burden that were penned up inside their makeshift corrals, and the stench of angen feces, human waste, and rotting garbage that hovered over each encampment.

The bread wagon made half a dozen brief stops before arriving at the first of the two southbound caravans Omar had mentioned earlier. The conveyance was greeted by the usual pack of yapping mongrels, a flood of grubby children, and a squad of burly women. While Omar sold his bread, Rebo went off in search of the headman, and soon found himself talking to a woman instead. She had short-cropped black hair, a heavily lined face, and solid-looking body. A hardy sort who radiated self-confidence and appeared to be exactly what the runner had been hoping for.

But, having listened to Rebo's business proposal, it soon became apparent that the nomad had no interest in escorting four off-worlders south through the badlands to the city beyond. Even the runner's offer of additional money fell on deaf ears. The chieftain had a perishable cargo to transport, which meant she intended to travel at night and cover at least twenty miles per day. A pace nonnomads would never be able to maintain.

That left Rebo with no choice but to seek out the second southbound caravan in hopes that the person in charge of that pack train would prove to be more accommodating. It was early afternoon by the time the nearly empty bread wagon pulled up in front of one of the most distant and undesirable camping spots. A single scroungy-looking mutt came out to meet them, and it was lame. And, rather than the rush of children the runner had come to expect, only six of them actually materialized. They stood in a small somber-looking group that remained right where it was until Omar offered the youngsters some free hard rolls. That brought them forward, but hesitantly, as if fearful that doing so might land them in trouble.

In the meantime, half a dozen heavily armed men had emerged from the scattering of dingy, ragged-looking tents. In spite of the fact that the bread wagon couldn't possibly be interpreted as a threat, the nomads continued to watch in baleful silence as a handful of scrawny women ventured out to make their purchases. In all truth the encampment was so lackluster that Rebo would have skipped the group entirely had there been another choice. So, feet dragging, the runner approached a sun-darkened warrior and asked if he could speak with the chief. The nomad had dark eyes, a single eyebrow, and a scar that ran diagonally across his face. He extended a hand palm up. "Pay me."

The runner looked the villain in the eye. "Take me to the chief, or I'll find him on my own, and tell him that you identified yourself as the headman."

Most of the blood drained out of the warrior's face. A sure sign that whatever his other attributes, the chief was jealous of his authority and completely unforgiving where would-be usurpers were concerned. "But that would be a lie!" the nomad objected.

Rebo produced what he hoped was a predatory grin. "Yes, but that won't make much difference will it? Not if you're dead . . . Now, take me to your chief, or get the hell out of the way."

Scarface started to bring his long-barreled rifle up, saw the newcomer's hand go to the enormous pistol that he wore crosswise across his belly, and knew he would lose the ensuing race. Well aware of the fact that his peers were watching, and mindful of his reputation, the warrior turned away. Rebo followed Scarface over to the largest tent, where the villainous nomad shouted something in a dialect the runner hadn't heard before, and pretended to examine one of his filthy fingernails.

A full minute passed before the leather curtain that protected the entrance was pushed aside and a man emerged. He squinted into the sun, belched loudly, and scratched a small but prominent belly. With the exception of a dirty loincloth and the black pelt that covered his bony chest, the headman was naked. "Yes?" the apparition said. "Who calls on Valpoon? And what the hell do you want?"

"My name is Taka," Rebo lied, "and my companions and

I wish to travel to Cresus. I heard that you and your caravan plan to go there. Perhaps we could come to some sort of agreement."

There was a momentary paused as the chieftain processed the runner's words, followed by a generous display of yellowed teeth. "Of course!" the nomad said enthusiastically. "Nothing would give my family and I more pleasure than the opportunity to speed you and your companions to Cresus. Where are these noble beings? Please summon them forth that I might greet each of them personally."

"They're in the city," the runner answered vaguely, "so the introductions will have to wait. In the meantime, perhaps you would be so good as to tell me when you plan to depart, what sort of supplies we would be expected to bring along, and how much such a journey would cost?"

Valpoon, who was fully aware of the fact that only two caravans were slated to head south during the next month, set his price accordingly. "We plan to leave in two days' time, my men would be happy to purchase your supplies for you, and the price is five cronos each."

Rebo frowned. If allowed to purchase the supplies, Valpoon and his men would no doubt charge a healthy commission, thereby fattening their purses even further. "The departure date is fine, but we will buy our supplies, and four cronos per person is considerably higher than the going rate. However, I will pay you a bonus of one crono per person, *if* you get us to Cresus within sixty days."

Valpoon was impressed by both the stranger's forceful manner and his knowledge of seasonal pricing. Not only that, but by ultimately agreeing to a total price of five cronos per person, his reputation as a tough negotiator remained intact. He gave a bow. It should have been ludicrous, especially given his lack of clothing, but such dignity had been invested in the gesture that it came off rather well. "How can an uneducated wretch such as myself even begin to bargain with a man such as yourself? It shall be as you say . . . Be careful when buying your angens, however. Thieves abound, and your lives will depend on which animals you chose."

That, at least, was good advice, and Rebo accepted it as such. The runner bowed in return. "Thank you. We will be very careful indeed."

Omar had sold his last loaf of bread by then and was waiting when Rebo climbed up onto the wagon. The old man's expression was grim. "You didn't give that scoundrel any money did you?"

"No," the runner answered. "Not yet."

"Good," Omar replied, as he made use of the reins to slap the angen's glistening back. "Because I don't like the look of this bunch. Not one little bit."

Rebo felt the same way—but there was no point in saying so. The wagon lurched over a loose rock as the sun continued its march across the sky, and night waited to reclaim the land.

It was dusk, and while the sun was about to drop over the edge of the western horizon, it was only a little past seven, which meant the power wouldn't come on for a while yet. But the citizens of Zand were used to that, which was why thousands of candles, lamps, and lanterns had already been lit and people had started to filter out onto the streets as they did every evening. And Jevan Kane was one of them. Not because he *wanted* to go out, but because he had to, headache be damned. After questioning hundreds of people, one of the local operatives had come up with a lead, the only one generated so far. It seemed that a street vendor had noticed a youth who matched the description of the boy Kane had seen on both Pooz, and on Ning, riding atop the ragged-looking heavy.

For some reason the youngster had been out running around the streets alone. The vendor had seen him pause in front of the black hat temple, look all around as if to make sure that no one was watching him, then enter alone. Later, after an hour or so, the boy had departed. That was intriguing enough—but there was more. The vendor was well acquainted with the black hats, having given all of the monks food at one time or another, so when the boy left and one of the aspirants followed, the woman couldn't help but notice.

Now, as Kane stood next to her flat-cake stand, the off-worlder sought to put the pieces of the puzzle together. Norr had been accompanied by four red hat warriors at the spaceport, the boy had been seen visiting a black hat temple, and a monk had been dispatched to follow him home. But *why?* There was only one way to find out.

Kane turned to Olvos. "Okay, I'm going in. If I haven't returned by eight-thirty, or sent word, then come in after me."

The council member nodded, but the gesture lacked conviction, and Kane knew he might renege. Especially if the black hats put up some resistance. Still, he had no other choice, not if he wanted to find Norr.

Head pounding, Kane made his way across the open area in front of the monastery and entered through one of eight possible doors. As luck would have it the operative passed through portal six, the entry that stood for skillful effort, the very thing the operative would have chosen had he been aware of the symbology involved. Once inside, the off-worlder looked around, spotted a likely-looking monk, and approached him. "Excuse me . . . I'm a stranger here—and would like to speak with the abbot."

The monk bowed, promised to return, and disappeared down a hallway. A full ten minutes passed, and Kane had started to wonder if he was being systematically ignored, when the black hat reappeared. He bowed respectfully. "My apologies regarding the delay. The abbot was in a meeting. He will see you now."

Kane followed the monk through a series of passageways and into a large office. Outside of a single overhead light fixture there was no sign of technology, and the whole notion of sitting on the floor struck Kane as primitive. The man who rose to greet him wore a black hat, matching robe, and a polite expression. "I am Hico Marth. Please have a seat. How can I help you?"

Kane waited for the black hat to take his seat, lowered himself onto a cushion, and dreaded the effort that would be required to stand up again. Then came the difficult part. Broaching a subject that might, or might not, have meaning for the monk, plus doing so in a way that wouldn't reveal too much. "Thank you for agreeing to see me. My name is Jevan Kane. I know you're busy so I'll try to be brief . . . I represent a group called the Techno Society."

Marth allowed his eyebrows to rise. "The organization that the metal men preach on behalf of?"

Kane nodded. "We don't think of our efforts to remind people of the benefits of technology as preaching, but yes, the metal men belong to us."

"I hope you'll forgive me for saying so," the abbot responded mildly, "but the metal men are more than a little annoying. But that aside, what brings you to our humble temple?"

"A little boy," Kane replied truthfully. "A little boy who arrived on Ning along with four red hat warriors, survived a battle at the spaceport, and was subsequently seen entering your monastery."

Marth, who still had the boy's hotel under surveillance, knew who Kane was referring to. Rather than reveal that knowledge, however, the black hat thought it best to maintain a neutral expression and draw the stranger out. "I see. But many boys enter our temple . . . What makes this one so special?"

The monk was already aware of the boy, Kane could sense it, and felt his heart beat just a little bit faster. That made his head throb, and he struggled to maintain focus. "The boy *isn't* special, not so far as we're concerned, but the woman he is traveling with is. She has something that doesn't belong to her, something she stole from me, and I want it back."

"Ah," Marth replied, "now I understand. If you find the boy—you find the thief."

"Exactly," the technologist answered. "Can you help me?"

"Yes," the abbot replied judiciously, as his fingertips came together to form a steeple. "I think I can . . . But first I would appreciate it if you would tell me everything you can about the boy. I'm not entirely sure as yet, but based on information I received a few days ago, there is a strong possibility that the boy is an imposter."

A ten-year-old imposter? It didn't make sense, but Kane didn't care, not so long as he got what he wanted. So, starting with the disastrous firefight at the riverfront restaurant in Gos and ending with the brawl at Zand's spaceport, the operative told the black hat what he wanted to know.

Marth listened intently. The fact that the boy named Lee had clearly been on the same ship that Brother Fiva had monitored and was pursuing an itinerary that could take him to Thara and the city of CaCanth certainly seemed to confirm his identity. Not with 100 percent certainty perhaps, but to an extent that justified a momentary deviation from the way, even if that meant negative Ka, and some additional incarnations prior to full enlightenment. Because, onerous though the results of his actions might be, the needs of the church must necessarily take precedence over his life and the boy's as well. Marth looked into the other man's ice-blue eyes. "Based on your description of what took place, I think there is a high degree of likelihood that the boy is the one we're looking for."

"I am gratified to hear it," Kane replied eagerly. "If you would be so kind as to tell me where the woman and the boy are staying, my personnel will take both of them into custody. Once that has been accomplished, the boy will be handed over to you."

The abbot smiled thinly. "Thank you, but no. I mean no offense, but the attempt to capture the group at the spaceport lacked finesse and could only be described as a miserable failure. No, I think a different approach is in order, one that won't attract any further attention. Assuming the boy is the person I believe he is, then I know exactly where he and his escorts will go next, which means we can intercept them. Not here, in the city, but well beyond the walls."

The suggestion went against all of Kane's instincts, but so long as the black hat withheld the boy's location, he had the advantage. All the technologist could do was smile, nod, and hope for the best.

The abbot ordered tea, which in spite of the fact that it didn't contain any sugar, still tasted sweet.

TEN

The Planet Ning

Each incarnation can be viewed as a pilgrimage in which we will encounter many obstacles. It is how we react to those obstacles, and the choices that we make in response to them, that determines the extent of our progress.

—The ascended master Teon,
The Way

The angen's hooves made a methodical clop, clop, clop sound and an axle squeaked monotonously as the bread wagon bumped and clattered its way along the misty alleyway to the point where a trio of overflowing garbage bins guarded the rear entrance of the hotel. That was where Omar said, "Whoa!" pulled the slack out of the reins, and brought the conveyance to a rattling stop.

The travelers were ready. Hoggles carried Lee out through the portal, lifted the boy into the back of the wagon, and climbed in after him. Norr went next, closely followed by Rebo, who pulled the tailgate up behind him and latched it in place. Then, having dropped the rear curtain and tied it down, the runner rapped three times. The reins made a slapping sound as they hit the angen's back, and the wagon jerked into motion. The entire process took less than a minute, and thanks to the early-morning hour, went unobserved. Or so the travelers hoped.

Though empty of bread, the cargo compartment was already half-full of supplies when the foursome had boarded the wagon, which meant that it was crowded. Especially given how much space the heavy required. But Rebo considered that to be a small price to pay if he and his companions could escape the city undetected. Something that would have been easy prior to Lee's midnight outing, but had subsequently been transformed into a major operation, a fact not lost on the boy himself.

As the wagon bounced and swayed Lee felt his stomach rumble in response to the mouthwatering odor that lingered from the previous day's load of bread, and wondered if he would ever manage to regain the runner's trust. One thing was for sure, no matter how long he lived, the boy knew he would never forget the moment when he opened the hotel room door to discover that he had been missed. Both Rebo and Hoggles had been out looking for him, while Norr remained behind to coordinate the search and solicit help from the spirit world.

The sensitive gave a cry of joy as Lee entered the room, pulled the boy into her arms, and gave him a hug. She was in the process of chewing him out when Rebo returned. A variety of emotions had registered on the runner's face beginning with relief, quickly followed by anger, and a look of profound disappointment.

And it was the last, the loss of Rebo's respect and trust, that Lee regretted the most. He said as much to Norr the following day, hoping that she might intervene on his behalf, but was disappointed when the sensitive told him something the boy already knew. "Trust is a fragile thing . . . It takes a long time to establish, and once created, can easily be destroyed. There are no shortcuts. Decision by decision, action by action, that's the way to rebuild Rebo's trust."

The words not only rang true, but resonated with the older, more mature being that dwelt deep inside him, a fact that made Lee all the more determined to restore that which had been frittered away.

It took the better part of a long, uncomfortable hour for the bread wagon to clear the eastern gate, pass through the street of thieves, and rumble out onto the dirt road that paralleled the Xee River. Thanks to Omar's encyclopedic knowledge of the caravans as well as the nomads themselves, Rebo had been able to purchase two prime angens the previous afternoon, and now it was time to claim them. It wasn't long before the wagon turned off the main track, rolled past a couple of well-armed guards, and the entered the semipermanent encampment maintained by Pithri Gorgo, the self-styled "King of L-phants." He was an entrepreneur who, though dishonest, was widely believed to be less dishonest than most of his peers, and therefore a good person to do business with.

Omar pulled on the reins, the wagon came to a halt, and Norr slid the rear curtain to one side. The sun had risen by then, the mist had been vanquished, and the encampment was coming back to life now that the hours of darkness were at an end. Cook fires sent delicate spirals of smoke up toward the sky, and a battalion of children were busy carrying buckets of water up to their mothers. Later, after that chore had been completed, they would turn their attention to the L-phants. Each animal had to be fed and checked for sores prior to being led down to the river to drink.

Rebo dropped the tailgate and jumped down to the

ground. Gorgo was famous for the quality of his hospitality, so it was only a matter of moments before a teenaged girl arrived with a load of caf and hot fry bread. "Try it," Omar suggested, as he accepted a steaming cup. "I think you'll like it."

None of them had eaten prior to departure, so Rebo took a bite, and soon discovered that the old man was correct. The fry bread had a crunchy exterior, had been liberally sprinkled with cinnamon, and went well with the black caf.

Gorgo arrived a few minutes later. His thick black hair was wet, as if he had just emerged from a dip in the river, and his white robe was spotless. "So," the merchant said, thereby offering his customers an extravagant display of white teeth, "you are on time. Please follow me . . . Your L-phants are ready."

A few steps carried the travelers over to a huge tree, where two of the mighty beasts stood waiting, their rear legs chained together to prevent them from wandering off. Although Rebo had observed L-phants from a distance, he had never stood next to one until the previous afternoon, and was still astounded by how large they were. The beasts weren't native to Ning, but were believed to be the bioengineered descendants of animals that humans had brought with them more than a million years before.

Having been specifically bred to carry heavy loads over long distances while subject to Ning's gravity, the L-phants had huge six-ton bodies supported by four massive column-like legs. But, what made these particular creatures different from all of the other angens Rebo had seen was not only their size, but the fact that they lacked heads. In an effort to lengthen their torsos and maximize their ability to carry cargo, L-phant brains had been relocated into the anterior portion of their chests. The animals' eyes were located there, too, which meant that while they had an excellent view of the trail ahead, they couldn't scan the horizon for danger. This modification assumed a symbiotic relationship with humans, who would eternally bear responsibility for spotting and protecting the angens from potential enemies.

Not that the animals were entirely helpless, since each L-phant was equipped with a long, flexible trunk that extended from the area immediately over its eyes and could be used for eating, drinking, and fighting. Other attributes, like their heat-sensitive skins, and the special subcutaneous tissues that could store up to fifty gallons of water, were a good deal less obvious, but just as important to performing their intended function. That was to carry people and goods over long distances. Never mind the fact that the animals produced enormous mounds of manure, were notoriously flatulent, and eternally cranky. "So," Gorgo said, as he patted a leathery flank, "if you would be so kind as to hand over the remainder of the purchase price, we can finalize this transaction. The sunny south awaits!"

Rebo was already in the process of reaching for his purse when Omar interrupted. "Excuse me, but a mistake has been made. Yesterday, while you were finalizing the price, I scratched my initials into each animal's skin. That angen still bears my mark . . . but this one doesn't. A mix-up perhaps?"

In spite of the fact that Omar knew there hadn't been any mix-up, he had been careful to leave Gorgo with a way out, which the merchant was quick to take advantage of. "Please accept my most sincere apologies! The children who brought animals out of the corral clearly made a mistake. I can assure you that they will be punished. In the meantime have some more caf . . . I will remove this beast and return with the correct angen."

Rebo waited until the merchant was well out of earshot

before turning to Omar. "Thank you! I missed the switch. What sort of scam was he trying to pull?"

"It's hard to know for sure," the oldster replied. "But I suspect that this particular L-phant, the one he tried to give you, is healthy but two or three years older than the one I initialed yesterday. It's a small thing, but lots of small profits can add up to a large one, which is one of the reasons why Gorgo does so well."

"Thank you," Rebo said sincerely, as he offered Omar a handful of coins. "I won't forget your kindness."

"It's nothing," the old man replied as he watched the remaining L-phant run its potentially lethal trunk over Lee's head and shoulders. It constituted a rather unusual display of affection given the fact that the huge beasts were famously bad-tempered. "Be sure to take good care of that boy . . . I don't know why, but he strikes me as special somehow."

"He's disobedient at times," the runner observed, "but so was I! He doesn't know that, however—which is just as well."

Both men laughed as Gorgo returned with a second beast. Omar verified the presence of his mark, money changed hands, and a bill of sale was executed. It took the better part of an hour to hoist the formfitting cargo boxes into place, secure them with straps that passed beneath huge bellies, and load them with supplies that had been removed from Omar's wagon.

Then, once the L-phants had been ordered to kneel, the travelers took their places on the bench-style seats that were built into each cargo box. Rebo watched with interest as Lee made use of a four-foot-long ponga rod to touch a massive shoulder before tapping on it twice. The runner quickly discovered that it was necessary to hang on as the animal lurched from one side to the other as it came to its feet.

Gorgo, along with some of the members of his extended

family, were clearly surprised by the ease with which the boy had assumed control of the angen, and there was a scattering of applause as the L-phant stood.

Meanwhile, the second beast, the one that Norr and Hoggles were supposed to ride, refused to stand. The heavy, who had assumed the role of L-phant driver, frowned. The ponga rod made a slapping sound as it hit the animal's hide, and each time it made contact, Norr "saw" lightninglike flashes of orange and red ripple through the envelope of energy that surrounded the angen, a sure sign that the beast was experiencing pain. "Here," the sensitive said, holding her hand out. "Let me try."

Hoggles didn't want to surrender the rod, not with the nomads looking on, but forced himself to do so. Rather than strike the animal as the heavy had, Norr made use of the very tip of the rod to scratch the spot where she sensed that the L-phant had a persistent itch, and was rewarded with sparks of bright blue light. The angen stirred, and the sensitive grinned as the beast came to its feet.

There was a second cheer as Rebo waved to Omar, the L-phants got under way, and an unofficial escort comprised of noisy children and their equally boisterous dogs ran alongside. Ten minutes later the last youngster had fallen away, the angens had established their normal rhythm, and the runner had begun to wonder whether his stomach would ever become accustomed to the rocking motion. He rubbed his amulet in hopes that it could counter motion sickness and soon felt better.

In spite of Rebo's considerable misgivings where Valpoon and the tribesmen were concerned, the runner was pleased to discover that the nomad and his family were not only packed but eager to leave. So much so that the chieftain ordered the travelers into the line and led the caravan out onto the main road without so much as a perfunctory inspection of their animals and gear. And, once under way, the column moved with what the runner thought was admirable speed. Within a matter of minutes they had splashed through the glittering Xee River, climbed the opposite bank, and turned toward the south.

Given that the L-phants could walk at six miles per hour and maintain that speed all day, Rebo estimated that the caravan could make the trip to the city of Cresus in about sixteen days, assuming that all went well, and twenty days even if they didn't. Such pace would still put them at the spaceport with three days to spare. Assuming the spaceship remained operable and actually appeared. They had been fortunate in that regard, but there was no way to tell when their luck might run out.

Of course, there was nothing that Rebo or anyone else could do about that, except keep on going, and hope for the best. The runner took the opportunity to look back over his shoulder, saw no signs of pursuit other than that provided by a couple of mangy-looking mutts, and turned back again. Satisfied that he and his companions had managed to slip out of Zand unnoticed, and still feeling a little woozy, the runner allowed his eyes to close. Not to sleep, but in an attempt to reduce sensory input and thereby quiet his rebellious stomach. Had Rebo's eyes been open, and had he been looking toward the west, he might have seen the glint of sunlight reflecting off a well-polished lens. But the moment passed, the caravan made its way up out of the river bottom, and the horizon beckoned. The journey to Cresus had begun.

The novelty of riding on L-phants, and the newness of the planetscape around them held the travelers' attention at first; but as time passed with only a brief stop for lunch to break the monotony, their interest soon started to wane. And later, having been seduced by both the warmth of the sun and the steady sway of animals beneath them, all of the off-worlders eventually fell asleep. Even Rebo, whose stomach had troubled him earlier, sat with his chin resting on his chest.

A fact that Valpoon took full advantage of by hoisting a faded red pennant on the end of a lance. The chieftain's sixth son, who had been shadowing the caravan from the start, saw the signal and raced in from east. Rather than riding one of the ponderous L-phants, he was mounted on a smaller, more graceful angen. The warrior arrived with a minimum of noise, listened to his father's orders, and was gone two minutes later. Valpoon had prepared a cover story, in case one of the off-worlders awoke while the messenger was present, but never had to use it.

Outside of the occasional farmhouse or pile of ancient ruins, there wasn't much to see, except for the increasingly arid land. Finally, as the shimmery sun made contact with the western horizon, the caravan wound its way up onto a low hill, circled a fire pit that had served thousands of nomads over the years, and came to a noisy stop as the humans, angens, and dogs all began to shout, grunt, and bark at the same time.

However, in spite of the apparent chaos Norr noticed that the women put up the clan's tents with remarkable efficiency even as their children took the L-phants off to a nearby spring, and the men stood guard. Or supposedly stood guard, since the hilltop provided an excellent view of the surrounding countryside, and the sensitive thought it unlikely that so much as a hopper would be able to approach the encampment without being spotted a full hour before it arrived.

But the roles were fixed, which meant that the males watched while the women worked, and the age-old process of preparing dinner began. Children collected the now-desiccated rounds of L-phant dung left by the last caravan to pass through and stacked them next to the glowing cook fire, where they would soon be used as fuel. Women put water on to boil, dumped all manner of dried ingredients into what would eventually become a communal stew, and dropped dollops of freshly prepared dough into pans half-filled with hot oil. The sensitive offered to help but was immediately rebuffed. With nothing else to do, she and her companions turned their attention to setting up their own tents and preparing their beds.

Meanwhile, as the stew started to burble, Valpoon approached his second wife. "Here," the chieftain said, as he handed her a vial made out of blue glass. "When it comes time to serve the indibi (human trash), transfer their food to a separate pot and empty this into the stew. Stir it well, because the taste is bitter, and be sure to use *all* of it. Do you understand?"

The woman, who was already looking forward to sorting through Norr's belongings, smiled coyly. "Of course . . . It shall be as you say."

Valpoon, who had a soft spot for his number two wife both because of her skill at making love *and* her utter reliability, patted her behind. "I know it will . . . Come to my tent after dinner to receive your reward."

Pleased by the fact that at least two of her peers had witnessed the interchange, and were certain to be jealous, the woman returned to work. As for the indibi, well, they were indibi, and of no concern to her.

Rebo was not looking forward to sharing a meal with Valpoon and his extended family, and was therefore pleased rather than offended when two of tribe's scrawny women arrived supporting a pot of stew between them. A pair of girls followed. One bore a platter of fry bread while the other carried a pot of green tea.

"It looks like we'll be eating by ourselves," Hoggles observed, once the females had departed.

"Which is fine by me," the runner responded, eyeing the aromatic stew. "I don't know about you, but I'm hungry! Let's dig in."

Though not entirely sure of what was in it, Norr decided that the stew was good, and surprised herself by eating an entire bowl. Her male companions, all of whom were equipped with healthy appetites, consumed two portions each. Hoggles even went so far as to use of the last piece of flatbread to clean out the inside of the pot, washed the morsel down with a mouthful of tea, and issued a mighty belch to signal his satisfaction.

It wasn't long before a flock of girls arrived to retrieve the pot, platters, and plates. Lee started to yawn shortly thereafter, went to bed uncharacteristically early, and was soon followed by Norr. Rebo developed a stomachache, which when combined with a sudden wave of fatigue, caused him to retire as well. "Be sure to keep your eyes peeled," the runner advised. "Valpoon and his family have been on their best behavior so far, but these are early times, and you never know."

"Don't worry," the heavy replied reassuringly, and patted the war hammer that lay by his side. "Anyone who tries to approach one of our tents is going to have one helluva headache in the morning."

Rebo grinned. "Good! Wake me at midnight."

Hoggles nodded, the runner disappeared into his tent, and a chorus of loud whistles and grunts signaled the fact that the children were herding the L-phants up onto the lee side of the hill, where they would spend the night. Stars glittered above, a light breeze blew in from the west, and the heavy tried to suppress a gigantic yawn.

Although Rebo had slept soundly, his rest had been riddled with unpleasant dreams, some of which were genuine nightmares. In spite of his desire to wake up, the runner was unable to do so, until some very sharp teeth nipped at his arm. That caused the off-worlder to cry out, and flail around, or *try* to flail around, since it wasn't long before Rebo discovered that try as he might he couldn't move his arms *or* legs more than half an inch or so.

But the effort had the desired effect, because as the runner opened his eyes, the pointy-nosed quadrupeds commonly referred to as Ning dogs drew back to see what would happen next. That was when the runner realized he had what felt like a hangover, his wrists and ankles hurt, and he had a pressing need to urinate.

Thoughts swirling, Rebo struggled to absorb what had occurred, and swiveled his head. The first thing he saw was that leather thongs had been used to secure his wrists to sturdy stakes. Other than the rocks that circled the hilltop like jewels in a rustic crown, and the slow drift of smoke from the abandoned fire pit, there was nothing else to see. The tents had disappeared, as had the angens, and the nomads themselves. In fact, except for Hoggles, who lay not ten feet away, the runner was alone. Rebo shouted Norr's name, followed by Lee's, but received no response.

First came a crushing sense of guilt, quickly followed by an almost overwhelming sense of grief, since there was every reason to believe that both of his missing companions had been murdered.

But those emotions were nothing compared to the anger that Rebo felt as he swore at the Ning dogs, jerked at his bonds, and attempted to free himself. The runner's struggles were to no avail, however, since Valpoon's warriors had soaked the leather strips in water prior to using them, which meant the thongs were getting tighter as they dried. The intent, or so it seemed, was to ensure that Rebo's death was as slow and painful as possible. The runner's efforts did produce one benefit, however, which was to wake Bo Hoggles from his drug-induced stupor. The heavy was understandably disoriented, but eventually came around and gave his bonds an experimental tug. Then, angered by what lesser beings had done to him, the giant sat up. Two three-foot-long tent stakes were plucked out of the ground as if they were little more than toothpicks. They flew all about as Hoggles bent down to access the thongs attached to his massive ankles. The heavy stood a few seconds later, undid the last of his bonds, and made his way over to where Rebo lay. "The stew," Hoggles said thickly. "The drug must have been in the stew."

"Yeah," Rebo agreed somberly, as the thongs were released. "The possibility that they might slip something into our food didn't occur to me, but it sure as hell should have. I'm an idiot."

"We're *both* idiots," Hoggles said darkly. "I must have fallen asleep without even realizing it. That's when they staked me out."

Rebo checked for his weapons, wasn't surprised to find that both of them were missing, and gave a sigh of relief when he found his glasses. With his spectacles firmly in place the runner chose a likely-looking rock and threw it at the nearest Ning dog. The missile hit its target, the animal uttered a startled yip, and took off running. More missiles, all thrown by Hoggles, were sufficient to send the rest of the scavengers scurrying for cover as well.

"All right," the runner said grimly, "let's take a look around. If Lee and Norr are here, we need to find them."

Hoggles didn't expect to find the other two, not alive at any rate, but decided to keep his opinion to himself. Together, the two men scoured the surface of the hill, but the effort didn't turn up anything beyond two dozen piles of L-phant dung and the heavy's massive hammer. It was lying a fair distance from the spot where the off-worlders had pitched their tents. That suggested that having appropriated the weapon, one of the nomads had quickly grown tired of its weight and decided to leave the object behind. A decision the variant clearly approved of as he brought the hammer down on top of an imaginary head and produced a guttural war cry.

Though disappointed by their failure to find either Norr or Lee, Rebo chose to take hope from the fact that they hadn't found any bodies, which meant that the twosome might be alive. But if so, why? Not for ransom, since Valpoon knew they had no families on Ning, so there must be another reason. What if he and his companions hadn't escaped Zand unseen? What if the technos had located Norr? Or the black hats had identified Lee? Either group might have paid Valpoon to kidnap the person they were interested in.

Of course that possibility raised still another possibility. Why would the nomads take *both* people? Unless they had been paid to do so—which implied some sort of pact between the Techno Society and the black hat sect! The runner felt a sudden sense of hope and swore out loud. "I think they're alive, Bo. All we have to do is follow the piles of angen dung. Then, once we know where they are, we'll figure out what to do next."

"I *know* what to do next," the heavy said, as he swung his hammer. "Let's go."

It took less than five minutes to pick up the caravan's well-marked trail and follow it toward the southeast. Jog for five minutes, then walk for five minutes. That was the pace Rebo set and the heavy followed. Ning's gravity weighted heavily on them and eroded their strength. The sun warmed their shoulders, the wind caressed the surrounding grass, and time slowed to a crawl.

When Norr awoke it was to the rhythmic sway of an L-phant on the move, the musky odor that clung to the angen's nearly hairless skin, and the realization that she had been secured facedown across the animal's broad back. All she could see was the L-phant's wrinkled skin, which had turned white in response to the heat from the sun and was broken by a thousand tiny lines. Her head hurt, a foul taste had taken up residence in her mouth, and the sensitive felt nauseous.

It took a while, but after a number of muffled requests, Valpoon finally vacated his well-cushioned seat long enough to free the sensitive. Once that was accomplished, the nomad invited his prisoner to join him, which forced wife number four to jump down from the still-moving L-phant, and walk alongside it. Norr rubbed her wrists as she sat down. "Where are my husband and son? And Citizen Hoggles?"

"He isn't your son," the chieftain answered reprovingly, "but the boy is on the animal behind us. He's been awake for some time now and is doing well."

Norr turned to look, saw Lee wave, and raised her arm by way of acknowledgment. In the meantime she took note of the fact that somehow, the means wasn't clear, Valpoon had discovered that two of them weren't related. "And the others?"

The nomad shrugged and looked up at the sky, as if the answer might appear there. His tone was matter-of-fact. "Dead I'm afraid . . . since there was no reason to keep them alive."

Norr experienced a horrible sinking feeling and bit her lower lip. "You murdered them—but allowed us to live. Why?"

"Because the Techno Society is willing to pay for you," Valpoon answered pragmatically. "And the black hats want the boy. I can see that bothers you, but after you've had time to think about it, I think you'll realize it's better than the alternative."

Norr wasn't so sure of that, not if meant being separated from the one man she might have been able to love and what amounted to slavery. But was it true? The sensitive tried to reach out, tried to make contact with Rebo's spirit, but was unable to do so. That left her with some hope . . . but an empty feeling as well. "Where are we headed?"

"To Station 46," the nomad replied curtly. "That's where your indibi friends will come to pick you up. And that's enough of your questions . . . Women are for screwing, washing clothes, and cooking. Not for asking questions."

Norr wanted to ask about the gate seed, but figured the nomads had the object and would deliver it to Kane. And, if by some miracle, they had thrown the artifact away, there was no point in bringing the device to their attention.

There was a brief stop for lunch, followed by a long, lurching ride, as the caravan continued its journey toward the southeast. There was no way to be sure, but Norr figured that the destination had been chosen by Valpoon rather than his clients and helped put him in control. But whatever the reason the journey continued until a shout was heard, one of the warriors pointed his rifle toward the horizon, and Norr saw what looked like a tiny black blob. As the caravan drew closer the black blob gradually resolved into a group of three low-lying domes. They were all of different sizes and sat clustered together next to a metal mast. It was at least fifty feet tall, and some sort of mechanism was mounted at the very top of it. Part of the device rotated in response to a sudden breeze, then stopped when the wind died away. The purpose of the installation was a mystery until the L-phant brought the sensitive close enough so she could read the faded white letters that had been painted on the metal structure hundreds of years before. The second "o" in ME-TEOR LOGICAL had been worn away, but that didn't matter. What had once been Meteorological Station 46 still stood.

Norr knew that scientists had been able to predict the weather with a high degree of accuracy at one time, and if some stories were to be believed, actually control it to some extent. That capability had been a boon to farmers and city folk alike. So, assuming that was true, it would have been necessary to gather data, which was where Weather Stations 1–46 came in. Or, had there been more? Yes, the sensitive decided, there must have been.

Shortly after the L-phants came to a halt and were ordered to kneel, Norr and Lee were reunited. Although the boy had comported himself with a dignity that would have made both Qwa and Rebo proud, he had been very frightened and was happy to take Norr's hand as the two of them were ushered into the main dome via a shattered doorway. There was no way to tell whether the damage had taken place during the civil unrest that followed the fall of the last interstellar government—or whether it was the work of the tomb raiders who still eked out a living by digging up ancient bits of technology. But it hardly mattered. The facility had been stripped, occasionally used as a barn by local herdsmen, and eventually reduced to little more than an empty, litter-strewn shell.

By remaining alert and staying to the narrow path that ran down the center of the main hallway, the prisoners were able to avoid the worst of the filth that covered the once-pristine floor. They turned left, into a corridor that circled the dome, and passed under a series of filthy skylights. Cubicles, which might have once functioned as offices, lined the outside wall. There were round windows, which though covered with accumulated grime, still managed to admit some light.

Eventually they came to a room that had been equipped with a grill instead of a window, was furnished with built-in shelving, and boasted a door. A sturdy affair made of interwoven rods. There was a loud *clang* as it closed behind them. The sensitive watched as the nomad she thought of as Scarface secured the door with a padlock normally used to protect the L-phants from thieves. Then, having placed the six-inch-long key on a ledge that ran along the far side of the walkway, the warrior turned to confront the teenager who had been assigned the role of jailer. "Keep a close eye on the prisoners," the nomad admonished, "and don't open the door without obtaining permission first. Do you understand me?"

The boy, who was nearly a man, drew himself up straight. "Yes, sir! You can count on me!"

"That remains to be seen," Scarface answered cynically, "but do your best. Dinner will be brought to you. And one other thing . . . If the indibi slut offers to have sex with you, don't accept. Not unless you would like to see me wearing your balls as a necklace."

"No, sir! I mean yes, sir!" the youth exclaimed. "I won't listen to anything she says."

"That's the spirit!" the warrior replied. "I'll see you later." And with that he left.

Norr, who hadn't even considered offering herself to the boy, made a face and looked for a reasonably clean place to sit. They were going to be in the onetime storage room for a while, or that's the way it looked, so she might as well get comfortable. Or as comfortable as she could be, knowing that two of her friends were dead and the future looked bleak. Suddenly the memory of the train trip between Gos and Tra came flooding back. The sensitive remembered holding Rebo's hand in hers and tracing the curve of his life-line. Rather than wrapping itself clear around the base of his thumb as it should have the crease ended well above his wrist. Palmistry was anything but reliable, but now it seemed as if the prediction had been borne out, ending not just his life but what could have been hers as well. A tear ran down her cheek, Lee watched miserably solemnly from his place in a corner, and the light started to fade.

Being a thief himself, Valpoon had a healthy respect for the other criminals who roamed the surface of Ning and never failed to post sentinels during the night. The purpose of the outermost ring of warriors was to spot a potential threat early enough to call for help, thereby summoning the rest of the clan's males. The problem with the strategy was that the family was too small to effectively guard the entire perimeter, which meant that if an enemy attacked two or even three points at once, they stood a good chance of success.

However, thanks to the fact that the tribe was extremely

poor and were seldom entrusted with a cargo worth stealing, they weren't targeted often. Perhaps that accounted
for the fact that Rebo and Hoggles were able to crawl with
a few yards of one of the sentries. The nomad was sitting
on a boulder and humming to himself as he picked at his
bare feet.

The waist-high grass provided excellent cover, and large
though he was, Hoggles made very little noise as he advanced to within four feet of the unsuspecting nomad's
back. And, if it hadn't been for the direction of the wind,
and a whiff of body odor that was markedly different from
his own, the warrior might never have noticed. The clansman wrinkled his nose, let go of his right foot, and made a
desperate grab for his long-barreled rifle.

But death was already falling by that time as the variant
brought the ten-pound hammer head down on the top of
the clansman's skull. There was a sickening *thud,* followed
by a sudden exhalation of breath, and little more than a
whisper as the grass parted to accept the dead body.

The off-worlders paused to see if some sort of alarm
would be raised, but the nearest lookouts were a thousand
yards away, and neither had witnessed the incident. Rebo
intercepted the nomad's rifle before it could hit the ground.
What little light there was came from the stars, which made
it difficult to examine the weapon in detail, but there was
no need to. After running his fingers over the long gun,
Rebo knew it was one of the Ning-made bolt-action rifles
that many of Valpoon's warriors carried. It had a wooden
stock, an integral box-style magazine that had a capacity of
five rounds, and open sights. Not his first choice in
armament—but a whole lot better than nothing.

It took less than a minute to release the dead man's cartridge belt, appropriate his dagger, and take a long pull from his water flask before handing it to Hoggles. It had been a long, tiring day, with nothing to eat and only two opportunities to scoop water out of streams. But neither man had faltered since both were driven by a powerful need for revenge. Now, within shouting distance of the domes, they burned with a common resolve. They would find Norr and Lee if they were alive—and woe be to anyone foolish enough to get in the way.

As Hoggles took one last swig of water, Rebo counted the cartridges on his newly acquired belt and opened the pouch attached to it. It was filled with wax-coated matches, the kind made for the caravan trade and carried by nomads everywhere. The runner was just about to close the pouch when an idea occurred to him. Hoggles listened intently as the smaller man whispered into his ear, nodded eagerly, and wrapped his sausagelike fingers around a handful of the phosphorus-tipped sticks.

Then the giant was gone, the grass flattened where he had passed, the stars twinkling above. Rebo placed the rifle across the inside surface of his arms and elbowed his way forward. Death stalked the night.

A lantern had been hung outside, but there was very little light, and it was nearly dark within the cell. Lee was sound asleep, and had been for the better part of an hour, when someone shook his shoulder. His eyes flew open, and rather than the scar-faced warrior that dominated his dreams, the youth saw Norr glaring down at him. Her voice was low, and rather husky, but the youngster had no difficulty recognizing it as belonging to Lysander rather than the sensitive herself. "Bestir yourself, boy! I will depart . . . But my daughter will continue to sleep. Wake her . . . Tell her that

Rebo is alive! He will attack soon, but the two of you could be used against him, which is why you must hide."

Lee had questions, lots of them, but never got to pose them, as the spirit entity exited Norr's body. The sensitive's face went blank, and she sat on a storage unit. The boy touched her arm. "Lanni! Wake up! Jak is alive!"

Norr blinked uncomprehendingly. "Alive? What are you talking about? Jak's dead."

"No!" Lee replied insistently. "He isn't! Not according to Lysander. He told me to tell you that Jak's coming, but we need to escape, or Valpoon will use us as hostages."

Though still groggy from sleep, as well as the trance that Lysander had imposed on her, the sensitive began to come around. She also felt renewed hope. Even the chance that Rebo was alive was well worth acting on. She took hold of Lee's hands. "That's wonderful, hon . . . But *how?*" she whispered urgently. "Did Lysander tell you *that?*"

The boy shook his head. "Yeah, that's what I figured," the sensitive said cynically. "The old bastard loves to give orders but isn't much good when it comes to actually getting the job done."

"No," Lee agreed solemnly, "but you can do it! I know you can."

Perhaps it was the boy's faith in her, or a moment of inspiration, but whatever the reason Norr had an idea. An unlikely idea, given the circumstances, but an idea nonetheless. "The key," she whispered. "Is it still on the ledge? Quietly now."

Lee tiptoed over to the door, peered through one of the four-inch squares, and returned. "Yes," he said, "it is. But it's behind the guard."

"What's he doing?"

"Cleaning his rifle."

"Okay," Norr said thoughtfully, "here's what I'm going

to do . . . I will reach out with my mind, lift the key off the ledge, and float it through one of the holes in the door. The moment it clears I want you to grab it."

Lee's eyes were huge. "Really? You can do that?"

"Sometimes I can," the sensitive temporized. "But not always. It takes a clear mind, perfect concentration, and some luck."

"Okay!" the boy responded eagerly. "I'll be ready."

"Good," Norr whispered as she closed her eyes. "Don't disturb me until you have the key in your hand." It was going to be difficult to muster the concentration necessary to transport the key across the corridor and into the cell, but public demonstrations were stressful, too, and if the sensitive could handle one, then why not the other?

Thus reassured, Norr worked to gather energy in around her, shaped it into an invisible pseudopod, and sent the carefully fashioned tool out to do her bidding. The guard felt his scalp tingle, ran an unsuspecting hand through his hair, but continued to focus on the rifle. He was proud of the single-shot breechloader and never tired of manipulating its well-machined parts. Now, as the key rose straight into the air, the teenager pushed the trigger mechanism down into the slot where it belonged.

Lee, his eyes locked on the piece of floating metal, found himself holding his breath as the all-important object glided out over the floor and floated toward his waiting fingers. Then, with only a couple of feet left to go, a door slammed. Norr lost her concentration, and the key fell, just as a girl called out to the guard. "Teo! I brought your dinner!"

One part of the teenager's hormone-soaked brain heard the tinkle of metal making contact with the floor, but the part that was hooked up to his raging libido heard the melodious sound of Sisa's voice, and that had priority. Had she been sent by her mother? Or chosen to come on her own? He hoped for the latter, but there was no way to know. The teenager stood, placed the rifle against the wall, and was waiting when the nubile Sisa arrived.

Lee stood with his fingers wrapped around two of the up-rights and stared through one of the four-inch holes. He could see the key! It was only two feet away—and gleamed with reflected light. Surely one of the nomads would see it . . . Surely they would . . . But that was when a miracle occurred. As Sisa walked toward the Teo the leading edge of her right sandal struck the key and sent it skittering across the floor under the cell door! Lee had just bent over to re-trieve the object when he heard a muffled *thud*. Teo frowned. "That sounded like a gunshot."

Then there was a second *thud*, followed by the sound of yelling, which caused the teenager to pick up his rifle. "Stay here!" he ordered. "Watch the prisoners! I'll be back as soon as I can."

Sisa had doubts as to whether the clan's elders would want Teo's help, but never got to voice her concerns, as the would-be warrior took off. That was when the little boy stuck an empty cup out through the bars and waved it from side to side. "Could I have some water please? I'm very thirsty."

It was not only a harmless request but one that didn't require the girl to open the door. She picked up the water-skin that was resting on the floor, carried it over to the cell, and was in the process of pouring when Norr wrapped an arm around the teenager's throat and Lee put the key in the lock.

Scarface was standing in front of the main dome, sipping hot tea, when the first flames appeared. He was more an-noyed than alarmed at first, since it was his assumption that one of clan's less intelligent warriors had struck a match for some reason and failed to extinguish it properly.

However, when the fire started to run from south to north, the warrior knew someone had fired a wad of grass and was towing it behind them in an attempt to set the whole area ablaze. He dropped the cup of tea, grabbed the semiautomatic carbine that had been looted from a country estate the year before, and ran toward the flames. "We're under attack! Form on me! We'll defend the main dome."

It was a brave thing to do, but not the smartest move, since as Scarface ran forward he was soon silhouetted against the now-leaping flames. And not just him, but other warriors as well, as they raced to obey his orders. Though better with a handgun, Rebo was no stranger to rifles, and was a reasonably good shot so long as he had his glasses. Now, with his spectacles perched on the end of his nose, the runner peered through the open sight. He had positioned himself behind a small cluster of boulders on top of a low rise. They were located about halfway between the line of fire that Hoggles had ignited and the inner circle of sentinels, all of whom rushed past him as they followed Scarface out to engage the thus-far-invisible enemy. The rest was a matter of judgment, practice, and cunning.

Rebo placed his sights on the rearmost warrior first, applied pressure to the unfamiliar trigger, and eventually felt it give. The wooden butt kicked his shoulder, the .303 slug slammed into the nomad's back, and the bolt made a snicking sound as the shell casing was ejected, a fresh cartridge was seated, and the sights drifted onto a second target. Five warriors went down before the runner was forced to reload, and Scarface realized that the enemy was *behind* rather than in front of him. That was when the surviving clansmen dropped into the grass and started to elbow their way back toward the domes.

But, with no one between him and the weather station, Rebo had pulled out by then. Conscious of the need for speed, and having forced the opposition to the ground, the runner took advantage of the opportunity to close with the domes. He had expected to see, or at least hear from Valpoon by then; but the chieftain had yet to make himself known. And, rather than the activity that one would have expected around the main entrance, it was dark and seemingly undefended. That suggested some sort of an ambush lay within, and the runner knew he would be badly outgunned.

The solution was more the result of an impulse than careful planning. Rebo ran straight at the main dome, jumped up onto the slanting surface, and kept right on going. It was difficult at first but soon became easier. His boots thundered on metal, Valpoon heard the sound, and shouted to his followers. "They're on the roof! Come on!"

More than a dozen nomads charged out into the night, only to be fired on by Scarface and the incoming sentries, all of whom mistook the shadowy figures for enemy raiders. Bullets pinged off the dome or slammed into flesh as men went down. "No!" Valpoon screamed. "Stop firing! You're shooting at us!"

Rebo was on top of the dome by then. Assuming Norr and Lee were still alive, the runner had no way to know where they were, which meant that one entry was just as good as the next. With that in mind, the runner took aim at the nearest skylight and fired. The plastic shattered and clattered to the floor below. Rebo kicked the remaining shards free, worked another cartridge into the chamber, and dropped feetfirst through the hole. Duracrete smacked the bottom of his feet, his knees flexed to absorb the shock, and a bullet buzzed past his head. The resulting *boom* echoed under the metal roof. "There he is!" Valpoon shouted from the other end of the hall. "Get him!"

But the runner didn't want to be gotten. He fired the rifle one-handed. The bullet missed, but gave the nomads reason to pause and Rebo the chance to run.

More shots were fired as the off-worlder skidded around a corner, called Norr's name, and heard a distant reply. Heart pounding, he raced down another passageway and took a left. It was a mistake. Teo was not only waiting there, but had the invader in his sights and quickly pulled the trigger. There was a loud *click* as the firing pin penetrated empty chamber and the teenager realized his mistake. In his hurry to join the fight, he had forgotten to reload! The knowledge filled him with shame.

Rebo shook his head sympathetically and pointed down the hall. "Run!"

Teo did as he was told, but the delay had been costly, and the runner had progressed no more than ten feet or so when he tripped over some debris and went down. The accident saved his life since the bullets that would have otherwise slammed into his back passed over Rebo's head instead. But the fall gave Valpoon and one of his sons an opportunity to catch up.

The runner felt the air being forced out of his lungs as the nomad brought a boot down on his back and saw the rifle slide away. "So," Valpoon said grimly. "Look who's here! It was a mistake to let you live. One I won't make twice."

Rebo felt the gun barrel press against the back of his skull, and was waiting for the inevitable explosion, when he heard a solid *thwack!* instead. Warm liquid splattered his back, and the runner rolled over to see the chieftain's head hit the floor, and roll away.

Norr, who had appeared out of the shadows just as Valpoon was about to pull the trigger, turned toward the surviving nomad. The sword, which she had found lying next to someone's bedroll, was smeared with blood. She brought the weapon up, and was about to take another cut, when Hoggles dropped the hammer on the nomad from behind. The heavy uttered a grunt of satisfaction as the body hit the floor. "That's all of them—not counting the women and children. We'd better get out of here though . . . There's no telling when company will arrive."

Rebo completed a push-up and came to his feet. "I'll second that motion! But let's grab some weapons and supplies first. We need L-phants, too—unless you'd like to walk all the way to Cresus."

Then, turning to Norr, the runner said, "You look good with a sword."

The sensitive gave the weapon to Lee, gently removed the runner's spectacles, and placed them in his breast pocket. Then, cupping his face between her hands, she kissed him.

Lee, who had been watching with considerable interest, felt a hand fall on his shoulder. "Come on," Hoggles said matter-of-factly. "There won't be any kisses for us! We have work to do."

ELEVEN

The Planet Ning

Although the caravan routes of Ning are marked by the graves of our forefathers, and have been watered by our tears, they care nothing for our people.

—Iznu Partha, nomad chieftain,
Letters in the Sand

The Cyclops beetle crouched within the two-inch-square scrap of shade cast by a small rock as it prepared to make the perilous journey to a similar refuge some two feet away. That was where a protein-rich grub lay hidden just below the surface of the dry soil. But, before the insect could begin its mad dash across the intervening wasteland, it felt the earth move. Not just once, as when the substrata that supported a ten-thousand-year-old rock finally surrendered to the weight and allowed the boulder to topple into a ravine but over and over again. Though not capable of conscious thought, the Cyclops beetle could rely on its instincts—and decided to remain right where it was as the huge L-phants passed within inches of its hiding place.

It had been four days since the travelers had won the bat-

tle at Weather Station 46, reclaimed most of their possessions, and resumed the journey to Cresus. Rebo carried a rifle in addition to his handguns—and Norr had reacquired
both her staff and the gate seed. The supplies that Omar had
helped them obtain, plus extras that the heavy had appropriated from the nomads, completed the loads secured to
the angens' broad backs.

Strangely, from Rebo's perspective at least, the days were
getting cooler rather than warmer as all of them had been
led to expect. The proximal cause was obvious. After following the well-established trail across a grassy plain, the party
had been forced to climb a series of steadily rising switch-
backs toward the jagged mountains beyond and what promised to be a snowy pass. That suggested that the badlands,
and the heat associated with them, lay somewhere to the
south.

All of them were accustomed to the back-and-forth side-
to-side sway of the L-phants by then and had grown genuinely fond of them. Lee handled the beasts best, but Norr
came in a close second, followed by Hoggles and Rebo. So
when they paused for lunch, the boy and the sensitive took
care of the animals, while the heavy prepared a simple meal.

Rebo, who was eternally concerned about security, took
the opportunity to backtrack. The pinnacle of wind-worn
rock had plenty of handholds and it wasn't long before the
runner had pulled himself up onto a ledge where previous
lookouts had carved their names into the soft sandstone.
The runner was out of breath by then, but felt better than
he had the week before and knew he was getting stronger.

Then, with his back pressed against the warm stone and
having brought his knees together to form a crude bipod,
Rebo removed Valpoon's four-foot-long brass telescope from
its hand-tooled leather case, and aimed it across the plain

below. The large fluffy clouds cast shadows down onto a sea of amber grass. And there, cutting across the prairie, stretches of trail could be seen. Not all of it, since there were places where the path dipped into ravines, but enough to suit the runner's purposes.

The off-worlder started in close, then tilted upward, as he scanned for what he knew would be there. More than five minutes passed before he spotted the momentary glint of reflected light as a metal man topped a rise, paused to survey the terrain ahead, and took up the chase once more. Four additional machines followed. Not the everyday androids that spent most of their time preaching on street corners, but something new and a lot more dangerous. They were shaped like animals rather than humans and ran on all fours. Tirelessly, in so far as Rebo could determine, although they were no closer than the day before.

Why? *Because they're not even trying to catch up,* the runner thought to himself. Having arrived at the Weather Station only to discover that Norr and Lee were gone, the technos and their black hat friends had dispatched the machines to ensure that the fugitives remained on the trail to Cresus. The question was why—and there was no way to know. Rebo returned the telescope to its case and reslung the instrument across his back prior to returning to the camp. Was it his imagination? Or did the two L-phants already look a little skinnier since departing the rich grasslands to the north? It was one more problem to worry about.

Lunch was ready by the time the runner returned, and Hoggles handed him a mug of tea. Norr was present, too, as was Lee, and three of them were waiting to hear Rebo's report. He blew steam off the surface of the drink, took a tentative sip, and let the soothing liquid slide down the back of his throat. "They're still on our tail."

Norr frowned. "Are they any closer?"

The runner shook his head. "No. But you've seen them run . . . They could catch up to us if they wanted to."

"Maybe we should lay an ambush for the bastards," the heavy commented darkly.

"We could," Rebo allowed, "but for what? Even if we manage to destroy them, and that would be far from certain, we'll still be headed for Cresus. The technos and the black hats know that. So, where's the gain?"

Lee had heard the entire conversation before and knew how it would come out. He smiled. "Teon had a saying . . . 'He who spends his life in future denies the present.' Let's eat!"

The adults laughed, food was served, and the journey continued.

The temperature fell as Rebo and his companions climbed higher. The trail skirted the edge of an ancient landslide. The rocks were brown, marbled with streaks of dark blue, and sharply jagged. Some were the size of a hut, but most were smaller, and the crevices between them served as a labyrinthine highway system for dozens of small furry creatures who surfaced occasionally, swiveled their heads to the right and left, and chittered at each other.

The slope was steep, and the humans could hear how labored the L-phants' breathing had become as jets of vapor shot out of their long flexible trunks. Rock clattered as it slid out from under enormous feet, leather harnesses creaked under the strain, and the lead angen grumbled as Lee urged it up the slope.

The ice revealed itself slowly at first, hiding in the shadows cast by the larger rocks, hinting at what lay ahead. Then, as the group moved even higher, the small, nearly translucent patches of ice grew steadily larger, even going so far as to venture out into the wan sunlight, as if testing to see whether it could survive.

Then, as the group passed a final cluster of trees, the *real* ice field appeared. It glistened pure white, like a shroud for the dead, which it certainly was. Because as the snow-ice mix crunched under the L-phants' combined weight, the tail end of an ancient caravan appeared. There was no way to know the exact nature of what had taken place but the general outline of the tragedy was obvious. It had been early spring or late fall when the travelers set out. But an unexpected storm had swept in and caught the group so high on the slope that a retreat was impractical. The snow blinded the nomads, layered their clothing in white, and conducted the chill deep into their bones.

Some of the travelers were weaker than the rest. They fell first, unintentionally bringing the caravan to a halt as their companions paused to gather them up. Then, even more heavily burdened than before, those who could continued their climb. But not for long. One by one, they, too fell, were covered with a thick layer of snow, and frozen into place. Now, more than a thousand years later, they were still there, ravaged by the slow-motion effects of geologic time, their leathery brown bodies blurred by the intervening ice.

Another hour of hard slogging brought the party to the pass itself, which was nearly bare of vegetation and home to a weatherworn granite obelisk. Empty bolt holes suggested that a plaque had been attached to the monument at one time, but that had been stolen, leaving the marker mute. It might have been interesting to pause and see what other curiosities the pass had to offer, but a battalion of clouds chose that moment to sweep over the summit and release a freezing mist. Lee urged the first L-phant forward, and it was eager to comply.

The balance of that day, and the first half of the next, were spent on a steep trail that switchbacked down the mountainside and into the foothills below. Thanks to the unique nature of their physiologies, the L-phants had a better view of the trail than anyone else, but still found it difficult to find their footing and were sometimes forced to skid stiff-legged while dropping their haunches onto the slope behind them. Those moments were the worst, when it seemed like the huge animals would lose control, and there was nothing the humans could do except trust them.

But the L-phants *didn't* lose control, the trail eventually leveled out, and the travelers found themselves high in the southern foothills. A fortress, or what remained of one, crowned a neighboring summit, as the increasingly gaunt animals followed the rocky path around the flank of a lightly forested hill and onto something entirely unexpected. Though partially obscured by countless rockfalls, the two-lane duracrete road was not only intact, but continued for almost two miles before disappearing into the maw of an ancient tunnel. It was the perfect place for an ambush, and Rebo had no intention of entering the passageway without scouting it first. "That's far enough," he told Lee. "Let's pull up and give the angens a rest."

The boy brought the first animal to a halt and ordered it to kneel. The runner removed a lantern from the pile of equipment behind him, slid to the ground, and made his way down the road. Hoggles, rifle at the ready, stood by to provide covering fire should that be necessary.

The runner paused long enough to light the lantern, drew the Crosser, and eased his way into the tunnel. Buttery lanternlight slid over grimy walls, illuminated the remains of a campfire, and revealed the graffiti that layered the walls. As Rebo advanced, lantern held high, he heard something squeal as it ran away, felt a few drops of cold water hit the back of his neck, and eventually saw daylight as he rounded a gentle curve and the far end of the tunnel appeared. A short walk was sufficient to confirm that the way was clear. Fifteen minutes later the L-phants emerged from the tunnel's cool interior and it wasn't long before Rebo found himself removing his jacket, knowing that the additional warmth was but a taste of the heat to come.

The night was spent on a gently rounded hilltop, which though exposed and bereft of water, was encircled by a hand-built stone wall and had clearly been used for that purpose before. Lee was none too happy about the need to carry water up from the stream below, but understood the threat that the robots posed and took advantage of the opportunity to practice mindful understanding by consciously transmuting the resentment he felt into a state of willing acceptance.

The next day followed what had become a regular routine as the foursome emerged from their tents, made breakfast, and repacked their gear. Norr looked forward to such moments as an opportunity to work side by side with Rebo. Nothing had been said, not directly at least, but the battle at the weather station had deepened the bond between them. To what extent was not apparent, since there was no way to know what the future might hold, but Norr chose to ignore that.

The group set out as they usually did, with Rebo and Lee riding the lead angen. As the L-phant topped a rise the runner caught a glimpse of the famed badlands off in the distance and was amazed by what he saw. For as far as the eye

could see, there were the steep hills and deep gullies that resulted from thousands of years worth of erosion. The mechanics of the process were clear. Rain fell in the mountains,
rushed down through a myriad of streams, and gushed
through the foothills and out into the lands beyond. That
was when the flash floods carved their way through weakly
bonded layers of rock creating a maze of interconnecting
ravines and a landscape so tortured it looked as if a gigantic
knife had been used to hack at it.

Then the vision was gone as the angen started down
again, and a final rank of foothills screened the land beyond.
Hoggles had told the other three that they would pass
through the village of Urunu prior to entering the badlands
and was soon proven correct. It wasn't long before dozens of
terraced gardens appeared. Though relatively small, the
well-tended plots were protected by walls of dry, fitted rock,
and serviced by a cleverly engineered system of miniaque-
ducts and carefully maintained irrigation ditches. Each and
every patch was protected by brightly colored prayer ribbons that did double duty by scaring foraging flyers away
while simultaneously drawing God's attention to both the
crops and the farmers who depended on them. The pennants
fluttered from poles, fences, and even ropes that had been
suspended over the road.

Lee felt his heart jump when he saw the ribbons because
they signaled the presence of people who followed the way
and believed as he did. But which sect did they hold dear?
The red hats as Hoggles claimed? Or the black hats? There
was no way to tell from the ribbons alone, and in spite of the
fact that the crops were well tended, not a single farmer
could be seen. A strange state of affairs, which the boy
brought to Rebo's attention. Thus alerted, the runner drew
the bolt-action rifle from its scabbard, checked to ensure

that a cartridge was seated in the chamber, and signaled Hoggles to do likewise.

But, ready though they were, the travelers weren't prepared for the sight that greeted them as they rounded the next bend and paused on a section of relatively flat road that overlooked the village of Urunu. It consisted of a main street lined with sturdily built stone homes that led up to a domed temple. The building had an organic appearance, as if it had been extruded from the earth, which wasn't far from the truth since it had been constructed with tailings from the mine located behind it. An ancient enterprise which, while played out, still served the villagers as both a granary and communal tomb. Farther down the hillside, unseen but not unheard, a river roared its way through a narrow canyon.

But it was the brightly attired crowd that had gathered in front of the temple that claimed Rebo's attention, not to mention the temporary gallows that had been established there and the frail little girl who stood with a noose looped around her neck. "They're wearing red hats," Rebo observed dryly. "I assume that qualifies them as friends of yours."

"Not necessarily," Lee replied, as he stepped up onto the surface of the seat in order to get a better view. "They plan to kill that girl! You must stop them! And that's an order."

Whatever else he might or might not be, Lee was a ten-year-old boy and in no position to give orders. But such was the authority in his voice that Rebo hesitated for a moment, and had just opened his mouth to put the youngster in his place, when the second L-phant drew up alongside the first. "I think you should listen to him," Norr put in. "They plan to kill a little girl! It isn't right."

Rebo's mouth closed, then opened again. "Are the two of you crazy? We could bring the entire population of the village down on us . . . Besides, how the hell would I stop them? We'd never get down there in time."

"Shoot the rope," Lee replied pragmatically. "You can do it if you wear your glasses. *Please,*" the boy implored him. "Trust me."

The runner looked into Lee's eyes and would have sworn that the personality reflected in them was different somehow. Rebo mumbled to himself as he laid the rifle across his knees and fumbled for his glasses. Then, with the spectacles firmly planted on his nose, he looked down through the open sights. A cheer went up as a red-robed monk finished exhorting the crowd, and a man with a wooden mallet prepared to knock a plank out from under the girl's slipper-clad feet.

The off-worlder needed time, a lot of it, but knew he wouldn't get any. Steadily flapping prayer pennants pointed in the direction that the wind was blowing and the runner made a tiny adjustment to compensate for it. As the executioner pulled the mallet back, and the little girl closed her eyes, Rebo fired. The hammer hit the plank, the bullet nicked the rope, and the youngster fell. Norr gave an audible gasp, but the girl's weight was sufficient to break the remaining strands of fiber, and the prisoner was still alive when she landed on the flagstones below.

The crowd flinched as the gunshot echoed back and forth between the hillsides before turning to see where the bullet had come from. The monk shouted something incomprehensible and pointed up at the L-phants. "She isn't out of danger yet," Lee said grimly, as an old man hobbled forward to help the girl up. "Take me down there."

"Sure," Rebo replied sarcastically. "Why force the villagers to climb the hill? Let's go down where they can dismember us more easily."

But the boy was determined, and truth be told, having saved the little girl once, the runner wasn't about to let the locals hang her again. So the crowd swirled as the L-phants lumbered down into the village. Weapons appeared, and Rebo began to sweat. They might be farmers, but the villagers were tough enough to keep bandits at bay, and it wasn't long before he and his companions were completely surrounded by rifle-wielding locals. The angens came to a halt, and Lee stood on the seat. His hands were on his hips and his anger was plain to see. *"You!"* he said as he pointed at the red-robed monk. "What is your name? And what is going on here?"

The words were in Tilisi, and delivered with such authority, that a stir ran through the crowd. The holy man's long, narrow face darkened, his eyes seemed to converge on each other, and his voice was stern. "My name is Fas Fadari," the local replied. "Who are *you?*"

"Switch to standard," Rebo ordered, his eyes sweeping the crowd. "We need to understand what's being said."

"My name is Nom Maa," the boy replied confidently. "I hold the rank of Prelate, and as such, expect to be treated with the respect due a person of my seniority."

Due to the fact that the L-phants stood side by side Rebo and Norr were seated only a few feet apart. They looked at each other in amazement as the boy with whom they had been traveling laid claim to both an attitude and a title they hadn't been exposed to before.

The monk appeared to be a little less sure of himself at that point but remained defiant. The contempt that was visible on his face extended to his voice. "Oh, *really?* Well, your highness, perhaps you would be so good as to prove your identity."

Lee was at a complete loss. He carried no badge of office,

no symbolic scepter, nothing beyond the testimony of his personal bodyguard, which the monk was sure to disregard. Suddenly what had previously seemed so simple, so obvious, wasn't any longer. The silence had grown long and thin by that time, and it was clear that Fadari was about to dismiss the youth as an imposter, when Norr came to Lee's rescue. "Tell him that you can see an old man with a long white beard standing at his right side," the sensitive whispered from a few feet away. "Tell him that the old man is saddened by what nearly took place."

So Lee did, and no sooner were the words out of his mouth than a loud murmur ran through the crowd, and every man, woman, and child bowed. Because the man the boy described could be none other than the hermit who once lived in the hills above and passed away the year before. Fadari looked stricken. "Ona (truth giver) Hybok is *here?* Beside me?"

Lee glanced at Norr, saw an almost imperceptible nod, and turned back again. "Yes."

"Then I apologize," the monk said, dropping to his knees in the street. "Teach me that I may learn."

Later that day Lee had an opportunity to meet with Fadari, the village elders, and the girl named Odani. Having refused the ornate chair that had been brought out for his comfort, Lee sat cross-legged on a mat laid down in front of the temple. The others arranged themselves in a circle. Hoggles kept watch over the L-phants while Norr and Rebo looked on. Though momentarily safe, the little girl was still under a sentence of death and sat with downcast eyes. Tears ran down her face as the monk made his case.

"Teon wrote that we must honor our parents," Fadari began. "He also said that we should take their counsel, see to their needs when they grow old, and protect them from harm. Odani saw her mother fall into the river, and rather than go to her rescue, allowed her own flesh and blood to be swept away. Teon taught us that to allow someone to die, when we could have saved them, is no different than murdering them ourselves. And murder is punishable by death. Therefore, like it or not, Odani must die."

Lee sat with his back perfectly straight. He was reminded of the lessons that Suu Qwa had attempted to teach him, the hypothetical situations that he had been forced to respond to every day, and discovered that he couldn't remember one that even came close to the situation he found himself in. Yet there he was, surrounded by adults who believed that they were in the presence of the great Nom Maa, even though that had been a lie, as was the title of Prelate, and his claim that he could see Fadari's discarnate mentor standing by his side. The lies were wrong, he knew that, but the intent was good. And qualified or not, he would have to find a way to convince the villagers that he was correct, or the little girl was going to die. She stared at him from the far side of the circle her eyes bright with hope.

"It may or may not be relevant," Lee said cautiously, "but if someone would be so good as to fetch a copy of the *Path,* I think they will find that what Teon actually said is that when it comes to our parents we should *consider* their counsel, which is different than being required to 'take' it." The actual text wouldn't make much difference, not really, but the boy was stalling for time.

Fadari frowned, but had little choice but to send one of the elders after the book and to read the passage once the old man returned. Having done so he bowed. "I stand corrected. The Prelate is right . . . The correct word is 'consider.'"

Everyone, including both Rebo and Norr, looked at Lee

with increased respect. Because, relevant or not, the boy's knowledge of Teon's teachings had been proven to be at least momentarily superior to Fadari's. "All right," Lee said, having used the delay to create a strategy. "I would like to hear from the accused . . . Odani, is what Brother Fadari claims true? Did you allow your mother to drown?"

Odani looked down at the ground. "Yes," she said miserably, "it is. I'm very sorry."

"You see?" Fadari exclaimed triumphantly. "The girl admits it herself! No offense to the Prelate, who was understandably distraught when he saw that a child was about to be put to death, but the situation is clear."

"But *why?*" Lee demanded desperately. "Why would you do such a thing?"

The girl remained mute and kept her eyes fixed on the ground. Norr had worked her way around behind the child by then. She could "see" the streaks of red-orange pain that darted away from the girl and bent to take double handfuls of her flimsy dress. There was a loud ripping sound as the fabric parted and Odani clutched at the front of her garment. "Here's your answer," the sensitive replied grimly as she lifted the girl to her feet and forced the child to turn a circle. "Look at her back."

There was a mutual gasp of surprise as the group looked upon more than a dozen angry red welts, and more than that, the puckered scar tissue left behind by the countless whippings that had gone before. There, right before their eyes, was the reason why Odani allowed her mother to drown.

"But *why?*" Fadari inquired softly, his words echoing Lee's. "Why didn't you tell us? We very nearly killed you."

"Because," Lee answered for her, "the teachings counsel us to honor our parents. And Odani did. It's up to us, those who have taken up the task of interpreting written text, to bring it fully and fairly to life."

And it was then, as Lee glanced up to meet Rebo's eyes, that the boy saw the very thing that had been missing for so many days: respect. It filled the youth with pride, and suddenly he felt whole again.

Brother Fadari bowed until his forehead touched the ground. "We give thanks that the Prelate chose to pass this way. I will never forget the mistake that I made and will work diligently to look beyond text to the realities of life."

Lee felt guilty about the lies he had told, but was forced to tell one more by touching the back of the monk's closely shaven skull with two fingertips and giving the traditional blessing. "May God be with you, for you are the instrument of God, and the hope of humanity."

The council was concluded after that. Odani's father had been killed by bandits two years earlier, but the elders assured Lee that a good family would take the child in, and she would never be abused again.

Word of what had taken place during the meeting spread like wildfire, and once the true nature of Lee's journey was understood, the entire village turned out to celebrate the passing of the boy who might be the next Inwa (leader of leaders). There was a feast, and fires burned long into the night, but the other three off-worlders didn't take part. They took a group of five well-armed men back up the trail, told them about the metal men, and established an ambush.

But the night passed without incident, and Rebo insisted on an early departure, lest still another day of travel be lost. Brother Fadari watched the L-phants lumber down the road, cross over the ancient duracrete bridge, and climb the opposite slope. The holy man knew that the Prelate and his party would soon enter the badlands, where they would face all manner of dangers, not the least of which would be the summer heat.

He couldn't prevent that, but there was something that he *could* do, which was why the monk ordered all of the elderly and children into the deepest recesses of the ancient mine before taking up a rifle and leading the remaining adults up to the point where they would confront the killer constructs. To take a life was wrong, the *Path* made that clear, but the machines weren't alive, and that meant he and his flock could attack the constructs with spiritual impunity. Not that it made much difference, since such was the strength of Fadari's belief in the spirit who had just passed through the village that the monk would have doomed himself to a hundred hellish incarnations had that been necessary in order to protect the Prelate. The sun warmed his back, the holy man could see his breath, and he had never felt so good before.

The yellow-orange sun hung directly over head, so there were no shadows to speak of, just the unrelenting heat. Rebo ran his tongue over cracked lips, but his mouth was so dry that it didn't make much difference. Four days had elapsed since they had departed the village of Urunu, and two days had passed since the near-disastrous attempt to travel at night. Although the trail was well-worn, and relatively easy to follow during daylight hours, the opposite was true at night. That was when the details that seemed so obvious at high noon disappeared, and, illuminated by nothing more than starlight, every branching of the trail looked equally important. And that was how the group had taken a wrong turn, and spent hours meandering through a maze of ravines, only to wind up in a box canyon just before sunrise. That left the dispirited travelers with no choice but to follow the now-modest deposits of L-phant dung back to the point where the original mistake had been made in order to get back on course.

Thus having been forced to travel during the day, both the humans and the animals were teetering on edge of exhaustion. Having consumed their reservoirs of water and fat, the angens had taken on the appearance of walking skeletons and were too tired to even complain. The humans were in somewhat better condition, thanks to the fact that they could ride, but water was in short supply, and the runner knew that it wouldn't be long before he and his companions began to suffer from dehydration. That was what made the town of Higo so important. Although Hoggles had only passed through it once, and was therefore unsure exactly how many days would pass before it appeared, the heavy insisted they would come across it before long. Once they did, the travelers would have the opportunity to rest for a couple of days, feed and water the angens, and purchase some much-needed supplies.

And Rebo believed him. The problem was that he had seen, or thought that he had seen the community a dozen times by then, only to have seen buildings morph into chalky cliffs, its streets dissolve into rock-strewn steambeds, and its crenellated ramparts turn to dusty stone.

So, having been fooled many times, the runner didn't take the clusters of what looked like trees very seriously until the distance closed, the greenery remained right where it was, and a faded sign appeared. It read, WELCOME TO HIGO. A message that would have been a good deal more convincing if it hadn't been for the bullet holes that marred it.

Still, such was the group's eagerness to enter a town, *any* town, that the humans perked up as the L-phants waved their trunks in the air, picked up the scent of water, and hurried to trumpet the news. Their calls were answered by angens located somewhere on the other side of Higo, thereby alerting residents to the fact that strangers were about.

A pack of half-starved dogs lay in the shade provided by a pod-heavy snap-snap tree, tongues lolling from their grinning mouths, as the newcomers plodded past. Had it been in the early morning, or in the late evening, the animals would have given chase but this was the middle of the day, a time when nothing moved unless it absolutely had to.

That imperative applied to humans as well, because as the travelers entered the town, it soon became apparent that the citizens of Higo were lying low, waiting for the worst of the heat to pass before emerging from their various lairs.

That didn't mean that the travelers went unobserved however. Norr could feel the sudden spikes of energy as the locals took notice of the newly arrived foursome quickly followed by feelings of curiosity, avarice, and greed.

The structures that lined both sides of the dusty main street were made of adobe and equipped with deep porches. Some were simply places to get in out of the sun, but most had a commercial function as well, as was made clear by the signs that hung above them. Rebo counted four saloons, two eateries, one hotel, and one store, all of which signaled that while the drinks would be cheap, the rooms and the supplies wouldn't be. And, in addition to the problems associated with buying supplies in a town with only one store, the runner knew it would be a challenge to keep what they already had. Because as the L-phants continued down Higo's main street, the runner saw curtains move in upstairs windows, and knew that dozens of hungry eyes were taking inventory of the group's scanty belongings.

Just as the angens neared the southern end of town, and

Rebo was about to stop and ask someone for directions, he saw what he'd been looking for. A thick grove of trees, surrounded by high stone walls, and the unmistakable odor of L-phant dung.

There was water within, or so the runner assumed from the eagerness with which his mount approached the massive wooden gate and trumpeted loudly. A boy in a long, ragged shirt and sandals watched the angens with big eyes as they entered the enclosure before turning to push the door closed. There was the squeal of unoiled metal followed by a loud *clang* as the gate hit its stops.

Hoggles, who had last seen the enclosure during his flight north from Cresus many years before, was of the opinion that it hadn't changed much. It was a little more dilapidated, if such a thing was possible, but essentially the same. Other angens were present, about two dozen of them, although the park was large enough to accommodate ten times that number. There was a cacophony of trumpeting, grunting, and farting as the animals greeted each other, and a pair of wizened men exited one of the huts and made their way forward. They were twins, but since both were named Abo, there was no need to figure out which was which, a convention Rebo approved of.

The decision of where to stay was made easy by the fact that the town had a single hotel. Having no reason to trust the Abo brothers, the runner insisted on having all of their belongings transported to the local hostelry, where they could be locked up, and would have taken the L-phants along, too, had that been possible.

Having been assured that the angens would be watered and fed, and accompanied by a dozen heavily burdened youngsters, the group trudged into town. The hotel had been named the Warfarer's Rest by the man who built it, and since none of the subsequent owners had seen any reason to incur the expense of a new sign, the name was still in force.

Though dry as a bone at present, a veritable river of water flowed down the main street during the worst days of the rainy season, which explained why all of the buildings had been raised off the ground, and stairs led up to elevated walkway that connected the storefronts. The hotel's lobby was spacious, if somewhat sparsely furnished, and open to the street. A ceiling fan turned slow circles as a girl on what had been a bicycle pedaled to make it move. Insects circled a scattering of tables, landed, and took off again. The proprietress sat behind a barricade-like counter and waited for the newcomers to approach. Her face was as expressionless as the lime green wall behind her.

Hoggles, who had been forced to sleep out on the edge of town during his previous visit, opened negotiations. Not because he truly believed that he would get the price down, but to establish that he and his friends were experienced travelers, and therefore not to be cheated any more than the regulars were.

After some hard bargaining the corpulent hotel owner dropped the outrageous price by a largely symbolic copper per room, handed the heavy two iron keys, and pointed toward a flight of stairs. "Your suites are upstairs and toward the back. It's cooler there."

Hoggles led the rest of the party upstairs and had to duck under a series of supportive crossbeams, before arriving in front of Room 203. The key turned smoothly, the door swung open, and if it was cooler inside, the heavy was unable detect it. The furnishings consisted of two mismatched beds, a rickety-looking chair, and a sooty oil lantern that sat on a beat-up table. "Well, here it is," the variant said sarcastically. "Home sweet home."

All of the gear that had been brought over from the caravan park had to be stowed and the next few minutes were spent stacking it along the walls of both 203 and 204. Unfortunately, much of it, especially the L-phant trappings, smelled like the animals themselves. That, combined with the warm air, made for a thick, rather unpleasant atmosphere. Norr opened the window in the room she was slated to share with Lee but discovered that it didn't make any difference.

Once everything had been put away, and the youngsters had been paid off, it was time to take much-needed baths and share an enormous meal in the restaurant next door. The eatery was a natural gathering place, especially around lunchtime, which meant that the place was already more than half-full when the foursome arrived. Rebo took immediate note of the fact that just about all of the other customers were armed. Some, one group in particular, seemed to be especially interested in Hoggles. That wasn't unusual, however, since the heavy stood out like a sore thumb.

Still, there was something about the way the men stared at Hoggles and continued to whisper among themselves that bothered the runner. So much so that he brought the matter to the heavy's attention. "The three men in the corner seem to be especially interested in you . . . Have you seen them before?"

Hoggles, who was not only well aware of the threesome but worried about them shook his head. "Nope . . . People stare at me all the time. You know that."

Rebo nodded but remained unconvinced. Though unwilling to discuss it, the variant was on the run from something. Why else would he live like a hermit onboard a space-ship? And now, as they made their way toward the city where Hoggles had been born, there was something increasingly furtive about his behavior. Or was the runner imagining things? Rebo wasn't sure, but made a note to keep an eye on the heavy, as well as those who seemed to be interested in him.

The food was surprisingly good, and having checked to ensure that the L-phants were receiving the best of care, the travelers retired to the hotel for much-deserved naps. The rooms were hot, and Rebo thought it would be impossible to sleep, until Norr entered the room, ripped the sheets off his bed, and dunked them in a bucket of water. Then, once they had been wrung out and replaced on his bed the runner discovered that it was miraculously if only temporarily cool.

The same brand of magic was soon applied to the heavy's bed as well, and there was something about the brisk efficiency with which the sensitive saw to the needs of her strange brood that not only warmed Rebo's heart but made him want to kiss her. But others were present so that was impossible. Still, there was an opportunity to touch her arm and look into her eyes. "Thank you, Lanni . . . For everything."

Norr felt the pressure of the runner's fingers and saw what was in his eyes. More than that she could "see" Rebo's emotions in the rich panoply of color that rippled around him. She smiled. "You're very welcome."

Lee, who had witnessed the moment, made a face. In spite of the occasions on which he seemed to be something more, the youngster was still a ten-year-old boy. That meant he not only found expressions of adult affection to be somewhat embarrassing, but sometimes felt jealous as well. Especially where Norr was concerned. He tugged at the sensitive's sleeve. "Come on, Lanni . . . Let's do *our* sheets."

Happily wrapped in the cool embrace of his sheets Rebo soon fell asleep, and such was his need for rest that the runner continued to snooze long after the fabric around him was dry and the sun had sunk into the west. And, had it not been for Norr's insistent touch, the runner might have remained in bed even longer. "Jak . . . Wake up! Where's Bo?"

The runner opened his eyes, blinked until the sensitive swam into focus, and yawned. "Bo? I don't know . . . Isn't he here?"

"*No*," Norr answered definitively, as she pointed to the now-empty bed. "He isn't. I think he's in trouble."

Rebo swung his feet over onto the floor and fumbled for his boots. His mouth was dry and home to a foul taste. "Trouble? What makes you think so?"

Though confident of her psychic abilities, they weren't perfect, and Norr had a tendency to play them down. She shrugged apologetically. "I don't have anything solid—just a feeling."

The runner nodded. He had come to believe in the sensitive's occasional premonitions and other "feelings." He continued to tie his boots. "Where's Lee?"

"Still asleep."

"Good. Lock him in. We'll go out and take a look around."

Norr left and returned five minutes later. She had changed into street clothes, armed herself with her staff, and left a note for Lee. Given the heavy's well-documented appetite, Rebo and Norr figured it would make sense to visit both of Higo's restaurants, followed by the bars, since the variant could be thirsty.

Visits to the eateries came up empty. Not only was Hoggles nowhere to be seen, none of the locals who worked in the restaurants would admit to having seen the heavy, although Rebo wasn't sure how far he could trust them.

The saloons came next, and while one bartender admitted to having seen a heavy enter, then leave, there was no way to know if the variant was Bo. Still, the odds were stacked against the likelihood of two heavies visiting Higo at the same time, which meant that Hoggles could be nearby. The next bar styled itself as the Higo Oasis, and judging from the number of customers inside, was one of the town's more popular establishments. In spite of the relatively early hour, it was already half-full. A quick scan of the long, narrow room confirmed that most of the establishment's clientele consisted of drifters on their way from somewhere to nowhere, unemployed nomads waiting for the next caravan to pass through, and others who, if not actual bandits, lived along society's margins.

Heads turned as the twosome entered the room, eyes stared, and the heretofore incessant buzz of conversation came to a halt. The blare of a hand-cranked phonograph continued for another revolution, came to a stop as the operator took the opportunity to give himself a break, and silence took over.

Norr sensed what felt like a wall of hostility. She wanted to say as much to Rebo, but quickly realized that the runner already knew and was about to handle the situation *his* way. First, rather than attempt to reduce the tension as the sensitive might have, the runner seemed intent on running it up. His eyes swept the room, and he smiled broadly. "So," Rebo said calmly, "look at what we have here. Somebody was thoughtful enough to pile all of the town's manure in one place."

Norr felt her heart start to pound, and the sensitive

twisted both halves of her staff in opposite directions so she could draw the blade more quickly. But the violence she expected failed to manifest. Perhaps it was because of the confidence that the runner projected, or the hand that already rested on the Crosser, or the fact that he hadn't insulted any person in particular, but whatever the reason, none of the people in the room chose to move against him. *"You!"* Rebo said, drawing the Hogger so fast it was little more than a blur. "What's the stuff on the floor?"

That was when Norr realized that she hadn't taken notice of the youth in the filthy apron, the long-handled mop, or the mess on the floor in front of him. Now, as he stared into the weapon's massive bore, the adolescent entered something akin to a state of shock. "N-n-nothing, Excellency. Just some blood . . . That's all."

A man stood at the rear of the room, raised a flintlock pistol, and was slammed into the wall behind him as the Crosser spoke. The dead man looked surprised, slid toward the floor, and left a trail of blood on the wall.

The youngster with the mop had wet his pants by then, and Rebo waggled the Hogger back and forth as a way to recapture the local's flagging attention. "Sorry about the interruption, son. You mentioned some blood . . . *Whose* blood?"

"Th-th-the heavy's," the swamper stuttered eagerly. "A couple of bounty hunters hit him from behind. He went down hard."

"Did they kill him?" Norr demanded, her voice hard with anger.

"N-n-no, I don't think so," the youngster added, realizing he didn't know for sure.

"Where did they take him?" Rebo asked levelly, his eyes scanning the crowd for any sign of movement.

"I-I-I don't know," the swamper replied pitifully. "I didn't have anything to do with it . . . Please don't kill me!"

Confident that he had all the information he was likely to get, and realizing that he had already pushed his luck to the max, the runner fired two rounds from the Crosser. A bottle of booze exploded, and the bartender's fez flew off. The purpose of the shots was to freeze the customers in place and create an opportunity to withdraw. "Okay," Rebo said, as he backed toward the door and motioned for Norr to do likewise. "Stay right where you are for the next five minutes. Or come out and catch a bullet between the eyes. The choice is yours."

Would the man with the guns actually wait outside? It didn't seem likely, but except for the dead man's friends, the customers didn't have any reason to test the stranger's assertion. Especially given the precision of his marksmanship.

But the runner had no interest in lurking around outside the bar and wasted little time taking hold of Norr's wrist, and pulling her down the street. But the sensitive balked and jerked free. "Wait . . . What about Bo?"

"You heard the kid," Rebo answered impatiently. "Some bounty hunters nailed him. It was obvious that he was hiding something—now we know what it was. The big guy has a price on his head."

"So we abandon him?" Norr demanded angrily. "Is that what you would do to *me*?"

"That isn't fair," Rebo replied resentfully. "Did I abandon you back at Weather Station 46?"

"No," the variant answered, "and neither did Bo."

It was a good point, and the runner might have responded, if a couple of the dead customer's friends hadn't chosen that particular moment to silhouette themselves against the light that spilled out of the bar. A single shot fired from the Hogger was sufficient to send them scurrying for cover, but it also brought other people out into the street. The odds were getting worse. "Okay," the runner agreed, "we'll try to find him. Follow me."

"Where are we going?" The sensitive inquired, running to keep up.

"The caravan park," Rebo replied. "Chances are that the bounty hunters have at least one L-phant there. Assuming that Bo is worth a lot of money, they need to get him out of Higo quickly or risk losing him to the competition."

The plan made sense, and the variant fell into step next to the runner as they entered the ocean of darkness that lay beyond the edge of town. What little bit of light there was barely touched the caravan park's walls before surrendering to the night. That was when a quick flurry of gunshots were heard, the L-phants started to trumpet, and Rebo realized that either the Abo brothers had opened fire on bounty hunters or vice versa. Which party had fired first didn't make much difference to him, although the fact that the huge wooden gate hung ajar suggested that the heavily burdened man hunters had overwhelmed the guard and forced their way in, an act suggesting that they *didn't* own an angen and were intent on stealing one instead.

There was a considerable amount of confused shouting as the twosome entered the enclosure and the ground literally shook as gigantic feet thundered from one side of the park to the other. Rebo heard the L-phants coming, but turned too late as a mountain of leathery flesh brushed the runner's shoulder and tossed him aside. The ground came up quickly, his skull made contact with a rock, and there was an explosion of light inside his head.

Norr, who had been following a few steps behind, "saw"

a red blur as the badly frightened animal rushed past, and "felt" the resulting impact. She called Rebo's name, but heard no reply, and suddenly found herself alone in the dark. Except that it *wasn't* dark, not where her psychic abilities were concerned, meaning that while the sensitive couldn't make out inanimate objects, she could track living things, and that included bounty hunters. The variant took comfort from the fact that while Rebo was down, she could "see" the light that shimmered all around him, and drew the three-foot-long sliver of steel from its wooden scabbard. The sensitive heard a reassuring hum as she thumbed the power switch, and the vibro blade came to mechanical life.

Then, holding the weapon in both hands, and running on the balls of her feet, the variant cut across the open space in front of her to close the distance with the blobs of energy that were milling about a hundred feet away. An angen objected loudly as one of the bounty hunters beat it with a ponga rod in an attempt to bring the animal down onto its knees. His partner fired a rifle, gave a cry of exultation as a member of the Abo clan fell, and hurried to work a fresh cartridge into the chamber of his bolt-action rifle. Hoggles, who was bound hand and foot, lay at his feet. The variant was conscious and trying to free himself, but to no avail.

That was when Norr came up behind the bounty hunter and took a cut at his aura. She felt the vibro blade hesitate momentarily as it passed through flesh and bone. Though not immediately fatal, the blow removed one of the man's arms and left the bounty hunter screaming as he clutched at the stump. He fainted a few moments later—and collapsed in a heap.

The remaining bounty hunter turned, heard a boot scrape on gravel, and caught a whiff of perfume as cold steel cut through the warm night air. He felt something tug at his throat and brought his hands up to investigate, only to have them drenched with his own blood. Then he was outside of his body, looking down on it, still trying to understand.

Norr "saw" the man's life essence drain away and experienced an immediate sense of regret. The emotion faded, however, as the wounded clansman cried out in pain, and she bent to cut Hoggles free. After a quick check to ensure that the heavy was okay, and shouted explanations to the quickly gathering Abo family, the sensitive went looking for Rebo.

There was a sudden commotion as a mob comprised of townspeople, transients, and assorted ruffians surged into the caravan park. Some of them were equipped with lanterns, which they held high. That was when some of the customers from the Oasis spotted Rebo and pointed him out. The crowd uttered what sounded like a hungry growl, and Norr had just started to run toward their intended victim, when geysers of dirt shot up into the air and the quick *crack! crack! crack!* of a semiautomatic weapon was heard. The citizens of Higo saw the bullets hit, heard the gunshots echo between the enclosure's mud walls, and suddenly lost their enthusiasm.

That was when the sensitive saw that Lee was crouched over the runner. He held the Crosser in the two-handed grip that Rebo had taught him, one eye closed, ready to fire again. And the would-be assailants saw the boy as well, and even though the mob possessed more than enough firepower to kill him, there was something about the tableau that served to freeze the many-headed beast in place.

But what they didn't know was that while Lee was willing to pretend, an activity that could be characterized as skillful thinking, he was no longer willing to kill. Not for himself, Rebo, or even Norr.

The result of the standoff was an opportunity, a potentially fleeting moment when exactly the right words could turn the tide and send the townspeople home. The problem was that Norr didn't have any words, not for that situation, and struggled to come up with something to say even as she interposed her body between the crowd and her friends.

Though armed with a sword, the woman looked frail, and a friend of the man who had been killed in the bar was about to urge his companions forward when the sensitive spoke in a deep baritone. *"You!"* Lysander boomed. "The man with the eye patch . . . I see three spirits standing behind you! You murdered them in their sleep, and others, too, all for a few gold trinkets.

"And *you,* the man with the crutch, your ex-partner is here . . . He's pointing at the knife sticking out of his chest, and asking 'why?'"

The discarnate was about to continue, but his first two victims had turned pale by that time and started to back away. Seeing their example, and having no wish to be reunited with their victims, the rest of the crowd withdrew as well.

Then, having accomplished his purpose, Lysander let go. Norr's body gave an involuntary jerk as the spirit departed and left her to deal with the aftermath of the abduction and rescue. Fifteen minutes later both Hoggles and Rebo were back on their feet, the Abo family was busy calming the L-phants, and the bounty hunters still lay where they had fallen. Lee returned the Crosser to Rebo, who released the nearly empty magazine and inserted a fresh clip in its place. The runner frowned. "Nice job, son. Thanks . . . Now, with that out of the way, what the hell were you doing out running around by yourself?"

Lee shrugged. "I heard shooting, found Lanni's note, and

figured there was trouble. The door was locked, so I went out the window and circled around front. You ran past, I followed, and that's the end of the story."

"No," Rebo said, as he slipped a fresh cartridge into the Hogger. "It *isn't*. But we'll discuss that later. *After* we deal with Citizen Hoggles here."

Hoggles, shoulders slumped, stood with his chin resting on his collarbone.

"So," the runner continued grimly, "I think we deserve some sort of explanation. Why did those bounty hunters come after you? And what else did you leave out?"

The explanation came in fits and starts at first, but soon turned into a flood of words, as his inhibitions fell away, and the heavy warmed to his story. While it was true that he had been born and raised in Cresus, Hoggles had previously neglected to mention the fact that he had been something of a political firebrand during his youth, even going so far as to call for the overthrow of the all-powerful Caliph, something that not only attracted the ruler's attention, but that of his eldest son, who was in charge of the city's police force. Months of hide-and-seek followed, during which Hoggles was able to elude the authorities. Finally, having spotted the rebel, government agents followed the variant to the rundown tenement where he lived and summoned their patron.

The Caliph's son was a weight lifter whose real name was Peeno Zynthias, but was commonly referred to as "the brute" behind his back, a nickname he had done nothing to discourage. And, though not quite as large as a heavy, it was said he believed he could best one. Perhaps that was why Zynthias insisted on leading the assault team personally, and once inside the mazelike building, came face-to-face with the man who had challenged his father's rule. By breaking the upstart's bones with his own hands, the heir apparent not only intended to further his reputation, but to end the resistance movement once and for all.

Hoggles chose not to go into detail where the ensuing fight was concerned, but Rebo had the impression of a hard-fought battle the heavy ultimately won, but not by much. "I killed him," the variant admitted regretfully, "but the price was high. A few weeks later, while I was hiding in the countryside, I learned that my entire family had been executed." With a price on his head, there was nothing the fugitive could do but run. He fled north to Zand, boarded a space-ship, and stayed. Now, after years of lonely introspection, the variant was determined to return home.

Once the story was over, Norr felt a great deal of sympathy for the heavy, but Rebo shook his head in disgust. "Perfect. Just what we needed. A high-visibility three-hundred-pound fugitive with a price on his head."

"It could be worse," Lee allowed philosophically. "After all, it's not like Bo is being pursued by religious fanatics or homicidal robots."

There was a brief pause while the others considered the boy's words, followed by mutual laughter. "Come on," Rebo said, touching the spot where his head had connected with the rock. "Let's bandage our wounds and get some rest. We have a long way to go."

TWELVE

The nice thing about rivers is that you know where you'll end up.

—River Captain Vog Duther

Unlike ancient cities like Seros, and Gos, Cresus was only a few hundred years old. That was because the city on the land north of the point where the Juno and Esper Rivers came together had been leveled during the last techno war, and rather than rebuild atop the ruins, the survivors founded a new community along the south shore instead. And, like most towns built on trade, Cresus was more the result of happenstance than a singular vision. So, while the original city had been laid out around the badly cratered spaceport, New Town, as it was sometimes referred to, was oriented to the river, and for good reason. Because as the high-tech transportation systems faded away, the planet's rivers carried an increasing amount of commerce and were vital to trade.

In fact both the Juno and Esper Rivers conveyed a steady flow of log rafts and heavily laden barges down to the point where the waterborne traffic was forced to pass between the three carefully sited gun batteries that the Caliph's grandmother had commissioned many years before. Not to defend Cresus against invaders, but to ensure that all who passed paid a hefty fee, a tradition that remained in force. The money the tax generated was sufficient to provide the Caliph and his extended family with the lavish lifestyles to which they were accustomed and pay the police force that kept them in power.

All of this was interesting, but of no particular importance to Kane, who had no intention of staying in Cresus one moment longer than was absolutely necessary. There were numerous reasons for his dislike of the city, including the poorly constructed timber buildings that seemed to lean in over the claustrophobic streets, the pervasive odor of urine that rose to envelop Cresus once the sun rose high enough to look down into the capillary-like passageways and footpaths that crisscrossed the city, as well as the sullen, eternally suspicious manner in which the citizens interacted with strangers.

None of it was pleasant, and having just returned from the shattered spaceport on the north side of the Juno River, the operative was looking forward to a shower as he mounted a flight of creaky stairs, made his way down a dingy hallway, and inserted the handmade brass key into its lock. That was when Kane noticed that the thread he had spit-glued across the doorjamb had disappeared and started to back away.

But it was too late by then, far too late, and as the door swung inward, the variant named Shaz stepped out into the hall. The enforcer was so fast that Kane barely had time to wrap his fingers around the gun butt before a bony fist hit the side of his head. It hurt, but by the time the pain registered on his brain, even more blows had landed. The operative was down on his knees by the time the variant kicked him in the head.

Later, when the technologist came to, he had a throbbing headache. He attempted to move but quickly discovered that he couldn't. Not while seated with his wrists secured behind him and his ankles tied to the legs of a chair.

"Ah," Shaz said. "The prince awakens. You were a prince once . . . Did you know that? No, I suppose you didn't. But I did some research. You might want to try it sometime. It could improve your thus-far-abysmal performance."

Kane continued to blink his eyes until the room eventually swam into focus. As if determined to illuminate the room, the sun continued to push its way in through the louvered shutters. Bars of horizontal light slashed the floor and the opposite wall. They rippled as Shaz passed through them. The variant circled the operative and leaned in to sniff him in the same way that a dog would. "You stink of fear . . . But that is as it should be. Those who fail Chairman Tepho have every reason to be afraid. And yours is the most significant failure of all."

Kane cleared his throat and opened his mouth to object. His head snapped to the left as a backhanded blow struck the side of his face. "I'll let you know when it's time to speak," the enforcer said coldly. "Now, where were we? Ah, yes. Your many failures. You let the sensitive slip through your fingers on Anafa, again on Pooz, and now on Ning. Then, in a misguided attempt to rectify your many errors, you entered into an unauthorized alliance with the black hat sect. And, as a result of that decision, the warriors you transported to Cresus know about the star gates."

It was risky, but the pause could be interpreted as permission to speak, and Kane was determined to defend himself. "I need the manpower . . . The resident staff isn't large enough! The black hats are at the spaceport waiting for the sensitive to show up."

Kane felt Shaz grab a fistful of blond hair and jerk his head back. The variant's long, muzzlelike nose, close-set eyes, and oversized ears gave the enforcer a canine aspect. His lips curled back to expose a double row of extremely sharp teeth. "I know *that*," Shaz said contemptuously. "They're hard to miss. Fortunately, they haven't had either the time or opportunity to communicate with their superiors. Once you kill them our security will be intact."

"Kill them?" the operative asked incredulously. "How?"

The air seemed to blur slightly as Shaz released his grip on Kane's hair. "I don't know—and I don't care. That's *your* problem. That and the sensitive. Chairman Tepho is tired of your incompetence. Finish the matter, and finish it here, or join your friend Lysander in the spirit world. The choice is yours."

The variant seemed to float toward the door. Kane struggled against his bonds. "Aren't you going to untie me?"

"No," Shaz replied evenly. "You, like the rest of humanity, must free yourself." And with that the enforcer was gone.

Because the transition took place gradually it would have been impossible for Rebo to identify the exact moment when he and his companions put the badlands behind them. But once green vegetation reappeared, and the seemingly endless maze of tortured ravines gave way to a gently rolling plain, it seemed safe to assume that the worst was over. That impression was reinforced when they had to circle around stands of virgin timber, the headwaters of the Juno River appeared, and the travelers began to pass isolated cabins. Later, as the L-phants carried them into the town of Iz, the runner knew that particular leg of the journey was over. But the clock was ticking, and with only ten days left until the shuttle was scheduled to depart from Cresus, there was no time in which to relax.

With the possible exception of Rebo, the rest of the party had come to like the L-phants, who, obnoxious though they were, had faithfully carried them all the way from Zand. But the river offered a much faster means to reach Cresus, and local loggers were willing to pay good money for angens that could be used to drag newly fallen timber down out of the surrounding hills. So, having made a profit on the animals, Norr, Lee, and Hoggles said their final good-byes to the L-phants while the runner and a bemused timber merchant looked on.

Finally, having been promised that the angens would be well cared for, the sensitive, red hat, and heavy allowed themselves to be led through the bustling town of Iz down to the banks of the river, where all manner of jetties poked their wooden fingers out into the free-flowing current. Farther out, rafts that consisted of more than a hundred logs each tugged at their anchors while nimble river folk used long pikes to push, shove, and otherwise coax the unwieldy lengths of timber into floats that would make the trip downstream.

Based on input from Hoggles, which had been reinforced by information gleaned while selling the angens, Rebo knew that a fast float could reach Cresus in just six days. If so, that would leave the group with a comfortable pad in which to rest prior to boarding the shuttle, and the spaceship. But only if the float hung together through three sets of rapids. If it didn't, and the raft came apart, they could drown. Or, if they managed to survive, find themselves stranded a long way from Cresus. That was why it was important to purchase passage with a captain who had the necessary experience, a first-class crew, and enough to money to construct a strong float. Because those who lacked sufficient funds, or attempted to improve their profit margin by minimizing the amount of cordage and chains used to bind their raft together, could pay with their lives.

But, by all accounts Captain Vog Duther was exactly the kind of man they were looking for, and a heavy to boot, one of the many variants who had left the repressive atmosphere in Cresus to find work in the timber industry up north. That's why Rebo preceded the rest of the group down a swaybacked gangplank and onto a flatboat, where he ordered the waterman to head for Captain Duther's float.

The boatman's teenaged son used a pole to free the scow from the mud, pushed the blunt bow upriver, and took control of the port sweep. Then, with a surety born of long practice, father and son muscled their craft upstream, knowing that the current would push them down to their destination.

There was a good four inches of water sloshing around the bottom of the flatboat, not to mention some live bait, and Norr elected to stand on one of the seats. From that vantage point she had a good view of the town, which judging from all the raw wood that was visible, had grown of late. Two- and three-story buildings stood shoulder to shoulder, columns of black smoke wound around each other as they rose into the sky, and geysers of white water soared high into the air as logs plunged into a pool of slack water. Once in place, they bobbed gently as a gang of tree walkers herded the timbers into a float.

Rebo said, "Hold on," and grabbed Norr's arm in order

to steady her as the flatboat nudged a log. Like most of the more promising rafts, the one that Captain Duther had assembled was built around a temporary building commonly referred to as the shack, which rested on the float, and housed the all-important galley as well as bunks for the tree walkers and a single cabin for passengers. All of which was fine, except for the fact that it would be necessary to cross twenty or thirty free-floating logs in order to access the shack.

But the floatboat's arrival had not gone unnoticed, which meant that half a dozen river folk were there to greet the party and help them cross the water-slicked logs. Fortunately, most of the so-called sticks were not only large, but supported by the logs to either side, which made the crossing easier. Rebo was resentful of the hand under his arm at first, but soon changed his mind when he noticed that the tree walkers wore spiked boots and realized that if he were to fall through a gap, the float would close over his head and make it impossible to reach the surface.

Once the visitors had been safely deposited on the spike-ripped planking that surrounded the shack, the tree walkers went back to work as Captain Duther emerged to greet them. He was even larger than Hoggles, and although his head was clean-shaven, he boasted a beard that more than made up for the loss up top. His eyes, which looked like chips of black stone, were set deep in their sockets. The river man's gaze swept past Rebo and hesitated on Norr before coming to rest on Hoggles. Duther frowned. "Have we met before?"

The second variant shifted his considerable weight from one foot to the other before shaking his head. "No, I don't think so."

One of the reasons why Rebo had insisted on booking

passage quickly was the fear that someone in Iz would recognize the fugitive and try to collect the bounty on his head. Now it appeared that the river captain knew who his perspective passenger was. The runner was wondering if a single slug from the Hogger would be sufficient to put Duther down when the float captain smiled knowingly. "Whatever you say, friend. It looks like you're headed in the wrong direction—but I suppose you know that. Come on, let's retire to the shack where we can drink some tea and dicker over the cost of your passage. It will most likely be a lot higher than you'd like, but I'll do my best to make you feel good about it."

*Careful to keep the lens away from the sun and any possi-*bility of reflection, Kane lay on a hot duracrete roof and surveyed the scene before him. A full day had passed since the beating Shaz had administered, and he still felt sore. Unlike spaceports on other planets, the cratered pavement and the remains of the blast-blackened buildings that looked out over it had *not* been converted to new uses and gave mute testimony to the power of ancient weapons. And, with the exception of some hardy weeds, and a pack of Ning dogs, the once-bustling port appeared to be deserted.

But Kane, who had escorted the black hat warriors to the facility himself, knew that appearances were deceiving. The religious warriors had gone to ground, just as he had instructed them to, and were waiting for Norr and her party to arrive. That was the one thing that the operative had on his side, the certain knowledge as to where his quarry would have to go, hence the opportunity to ambush them.

But not anymore . . . Tepho and the council were angry. So angry that they had sent Shaz to discipline him. Kane sighed, inched the carefully wrapped rifle forward, and deployed the built-in bipod. The operative felt a persistent itch between his shoulder blades, as if someone was watching *him*, but resisted the temptation to scan his surroundings. The roof from which he had chosen to fire was higher than all of the surrounding structures with the single exception of the decapitated control tower, which made it unlikely that anyone was looking down on him.

Still, the feeling that he was under surveillance persisted as Kane swung the powerful telescopic sight onto a gaping window and waited for the warrior hidden inside to reveal himself. Strangely, from the operative's perspective at least, his thoughts turned to Lysander as the seconds continued to tick by. Ever since the moment when they had first met, and for reasons he wasn't entirely sure of, the operative had experienced an inordinate desire to please the cantankerous bastard. And now, even though the scientist had switched sides, Kane was *still* trying to earn his mentor's approval. Not the namby-pamby Lysander, but the *original* version, who knew what he wanted and wasn't afraid to take it.

There was a flicker of movement as the black hat stepped into the scope's crosshairs, blinked as he sought to accommodate the bright sunlight, and turned his head to the right. That exposed his temple and Kane felt the trigger break, let his shoulder absorb the resulting recoil, and was already swinging his weapon toward the next target by the time the body fell.

Having heard the shot, and unaware of the fact that they were being stalked, the technologist felt sure the other Dib Wa would pop up for a look around. And, because he knew where to look for them, would make themselves vulnerable. The second target stepped halfway out of a doorway, was blown off his feet, and was still falling as the third slug slammed into a man foolish enough to fire at a target he couldn't see.

That was when silence fell over the spaceport, Kane elbowed his way back into the cool embrace of a shadow, and the last black hat went to ground. Or that's what the warrior intended to do, except that Shaz was standing directly behind the monk and promptly slit his throat. Then, having dragged the body out to a point where Kane would find it, the variant vanished. Not as a means to prove how elusive he could be, but because Kane was an excellent shot, and the variant had no desire to take a bullet in the back.

The Ning dogs moved in on the corpse shortly thereafter, but scattered when Kane arrived and were content to flop down in some shade and wait while the two-legged predator examined the body. Though pleased that his final target had been eliminated, the operative felt a chill run down his spine and whirled to see if Shaz was standing directly behind him. But the room was empty . . . and Kane was alone. Or was he? A sense of uneasiness followed the operative out into the sun and persisted even after the Ning dogs had begun their meal.

The Juno River sparkled with reflected sunlight as it turned toward the south and carried the float along at a steady six miles per hour. The men on the sweeps had to push hard to prevent the log raft from grounding in the shallows, while the tree walkers dashed hither and yon, shouted friendly insults at each other, and used iron-tipped poles to stab at the sometimes recalcitrant logs.

Rebo, who was seated on the bench that ran along the front side of the shack, never tired of watching the walkers dance from one bobbing, twisting, rolling log to the next.

And that was what he was doing when Duther rounded the corner and paused in front of him. The heavy nodded politely. "Good morning . . . Please inform your companions that we will be passing through the Devil's Chute in thirty minutes or so. We shouldn't have any trouble—but it's best to be prepared. I suggest that you make sure that everyone is ready for a swim—and assemble your group forward of the sweeps. If the float begins to separate, and you hear me give the order, be sure to go off the trailing edge of the raft. That way you'll be *upstream* of the logs—and a lot less likely to be crushed.

"Tell your people not to fight the river," the river captain continued, "but to ease their way out of the current, wait for an eddy, and swim into it. Oh, and one other thing . . . If you wind up ashore, watch out for wreckers. They live downstream of the chute and live off the sticks that escape from floats and the people who wash up along the riverbanks. Not only will they steal whatever you have—they'll probably hold you for ransom. Any questions?"

Rebo frowned as he came to his feet. "No, I don't think so. Why didn't you mention all of this earlier?"

Duther shrugged philosophically. "There wasn't anything you could do about it except sit around and worry . . . Besides, odds are that we'll make it through without difficulty. I'll see you at lunch." So saying, the river captain stepped off the platform and onto a glistening log. It dipped under his considerable weight, and water sloshed over the top of it as the variant started his morning rounds.

Rebo watched the heavy for a moment, shook his head in consternation, and went in search of his companions. The clock was ticking, and given the fact that there was no way to get off the float, the passengers had no choice but to prepare themselves for what lay ahead.

* * *

Meanwhile, a few miles downstream, a man named Horg Zikko settled into the carefully padded position that he had prepared for himself earlier that morning. The long-barreled .50-caliber rifle had been specially designed for him, which meant that the stock fit his shoulder perfectly, and the trigger was an exact match for the curve of his right index finger. That, plus the fact that he had spent the last two days shooting at floating targets, made the marksman confident that he could fulfill the terms of his contract. The float, which had been tracked since its departure from Iz, had *three* sweeps, therefore three sweep operators. One would be worth two gold cephors, two would be worth four cephors, and three would be worth *eight* cephors. A princely sum that would make the journey upriver from Cresus worth the effort.

Three wreckers, all members of the local council, watched Zikko make his final preparations and exchanged congratulations. Although various members of the wrecker community had attempted to kill sweeper operators before, none had succeeded. It was extremely difficult to hit a target that was not only drifting downriver but bobbing up and down and jerking from side to side at the same time.

But Zikko not only could, but had made many such shots over the last couple of days, a fact that caused the locals to feel very optimistic indeed. So much so that the rest of the villagers were waiting downstream, where they stood ready to pounce on whatever goodies emerged from the chute. Assuming that things went well, and there was no reason to believe they wouldn't, the next few hours would be profitable indeed.

Having successfully made their way back to the platform on which the sweep operators stood, the foursome could do little more than wait and try to stay out of the way. Like the others, Norr wore light clothing plus a small pack, which in addition to her necessaries, contained the gate seed that Lysander had stolen from Kane. Was the artifact water-proof? She believed that it was, but had no means to test her theory, and she hoped to keep the device dry.

The river had narrowed during the last half hour or so, which caused the current to run faster. So fast that the grad-ually rising banks seemed to zip past as the leading edge of the float bucked its way through a series of standing waves. Sheets of spray flew into the air and were transformed into a windblown mist. Most of the water fell on the first rows of logs, but some of it floated to the rear, where it wet Norr's face. The sensitive used a sleeve to wipe the water away and felt a momentary sense of exhilaration.

Then the float rocked from side to side, a sweep operator yelled, "Here we go!" and the raft entered the chute. Rocky walls rose to either side of river, the float began to undulate as it passed through a series of dips, and the deck shook as the raft's right flank scraped a boulder topped with a cap of green moss.

That was when the sensitive heard a loud *crack!* and saw movement out of the corner of her eye. Rebo had seen it too. The centermost sweep operator had disappeared. "Someone shot him!" the runner yelled. "Bo! Grab that sweep! Lanni, get down!"

Norr threw her arms around Lee, and had just pulled the boy down onto the water-slicked deck, when a second shot rang out. The starboard operator looked surprised, clutched his chest, and fell.

Rebo had his glasses on by then, and stood with legs spread, as he used both hands to aim the long-barreled handgun up at the embankment ahead. He spotted a group of three tightly clustered stick figures, fired the single-shot pistol, and returned the weapon to its holster. Then, having grabbed hold of a loose sweep, the runner pulled with all his strength. The float, which had been sliding toward the right up until that point steadied, and passed within a foot of a huge, gray-speckled rock.

*Zikko saw his second bullet strike home, and was prepar*ing to place his third, when one of the tiny figures below produced a long-barreled pistol and fired. It was a nearly impossible shot, but such was the pistoleer's skill or luck that the slug hit one of the wreckers and killed him instantly. The body fell on Zikko, which made it impossible to fire, and the third sweep operator was spared as a result.

The surviving council members were distraught to say the least, although it was difficult to say what bothered them more, their collaborator's death or the prospect of having to pay Zikko even though the float had passed through the chute intact. But it hardly mattered. The marksman demanded his pay, tucked it into his purse, and was soon on his way. Though not entirely successful, the trip had been worthwhile, and his family would eat.

Much to the disappointment of the wreckers who lined both sides of the river, the float was still intact as it surged out of the chute, and followed the main channel downstream. There was a fusillade of shots as the locals fired off their mostly muzzle-loading weapons; but none of the balls found flesh, and it wasn't long before even the trailing edge of the raft was out of range.

Rebo heaved a sigh of relief as the last shots sent geysers of water up behind his sweep—and felt even better when a tree walker came back to relieve him. Then, with the float under control, the passengers were free to return to their cabin. It felt good to get in out of the wind, but the bullet holes that let light through the walls served to remind the group of how fragile their shelter was and served to erode any sense of well-being they might have otherwise felt.

The river, which ran only inches under the decking, chuckled heartlessly. The only things it cared about were the raindrops that occasionally fell from the sky, the streams that contributed to its strength, and the sea that waited somewhere over the horizon. Those were everything—and nothing else mattered.

Dinner was over, and, while it was dark outside the cabin, soft buttery light flooded the interior. The wall that divided the passenger quarters from the galley and bunkroom was only one plank thick, which meant that the foursome could hear the clatter of pots and pans interspersed with muffled conversation as off-duty members of the crew mourned their dead crewmates and discussed the events of the day.

Bo was snoring in the bunk beneath him, and Lee was supposed to be asleep as well. By just barely opening his eyelids, the youngster could see Rebo sitting at the table, with the Crosser disassembled in front of him. Norr sat across from the runner with her chin resting on her hands. She looked beautiful in the soft lamplight, or that's what Lee thought, and he suspected that Rebo would have agreed. They hadn't had much opportunity to be alone of late, and there was tension at times. There was no sign of that, however, as the runner peered through the newly swabbed gun barrel. "I don't know, Lanni," he said doubtfully. "Are you sure that's a good idea?"

Norr shrugged. "You know Lysander . . . If I say no, he's

likely to come through anyway. We might as well get it over with."

Rebo lowered the gun barrel and made a face. "Yeah, and there's no telling when he'll decide to do it. Okay, so long as you're up for it, let him through."

Lee, his interest fully piqued, lay perfectly still. If a dead person was about to speak, then *he* wanted to listen.

Norr nodded and closed her eyes. Lysander was present, she could *feel* it, already trying to push his way in. The sensitive knew he couldn't take over her body permanently, not so far as she knew anyway, but feared that he would if he could. Not to hurt her, but without regard for her desires, consistent with the relationship that existed between them hundreds of years before. He had been ruthless then, and he was ruthless now, the only difference being that the discarnate had switched sides. Now he was ruthlessly good if such a thing was possible. That was the last thought the sensitive had before Lysander pushed in and took control.

Rebo saw Norr jerk as her onetime father stepped in and was ready when the dead man spoke. His voice was pitched a good deal lower than the sensitive's and sounded hoarse. "Oh," Lysander said as he stared across the table, "it's you."

The Crosser's barrel made a positive *click* as it mated with the weapon's receiver. "Yeah," the runner replied emotionlessly, "it's me. Who were you expecting? The Caliph?"

"No, you'll do," the dead scientist allowed. "Now listen carefully . . . A man named Kane and his operatives are watching the spaceport in Cresus. They don't care about you, the boy, or the heavy, but they want my daughter. More than that, they want the gate seed. You care about her, I can see that, so keep her safe."

Rebo frowned. "Thanks for the warning—but how am I supposed to accomplish what you ask? We need to get off this planet, and the shuttle is going to land at the spaceport."

"Go to Techno Society headquarters," the spirit instructed, "and use the star gate. They won't expect that."

"No," the runner agreed soberly, "they won't. But the office will be guarded. What about that?"

"That's *your* problem," Lysander said unsympathetically. "Now remember, it's absolutely imperative that you find Logos before they do, or those who control the Techno Society will make the same mistakes that I did. That has priority over everything else."

"Not for me it doesn't," Rebo replied, but the connection had been broken by then, and Norr was back in her body. The sensitive blinked and shook her head as if to clear it. "What did he say?"

Rebo slid the magazine into the butt of his gun and felt it lock into place. "He says they're waiting for us at the spaceport in Cresus."

"And?"

"And he says we can escape Ning by making use of the star gate located inside Techno Society headquarters."

Norr uttered a low whistle. "So, what do you think? Could we pull it off?"

Rebo thought about his responsibility to Lee and the fact that if the two of them were to divorce themselves from the sensitive, they would be a whole lot better off. The problem was that what he *should* do to take care of Lee was in direct conflict with what he *wanted* to do for Norr. A second had passed, and the runner was still struggling with the problem, when Lee sat up. His eyes were bright and determined. "The answer is, 'yes.' *We* can pull it off."

Norr laughed and looked from the boy to Rebo. He smiled. "You heard the boss . . . We'll find a way."

The Techno Society's offices were pleasant compared to the rooming house where Kane slept. So, when the operative wasn't out at the spaceport, he preferred to spend most of his time in the station chief's office. It had a large window that opened onto a narrow side street that was lined with stalls. The noise generated by squalling angens, merchants endlessly pitching their wares, and the steady *bang, bang, bang* of the local tinsmith had bothered the off-worlder at first, but now, after more than a week at his borrowed desk, he barely noticed the racket. He toyed with a double-edged letter opener and stared out the window.

There was a commotion out in the hall, followed by a loud *thump,* and a heartfelt swear word. Kane turned to see the station chief standing in the doorway. Her name was Ilia Posa. She was middle-aged, thick-waisted, and typically wore loose robelike garments that were intended to conceal her figure. She didn't like Kane, the task that had been assigned to her, or the fact that the operative had commandeered her office. Her voice was cold as ice. "Your visitor is here."

"Bring her in," Kane ordered, and stood while a blanket-draped stretcher was maneuvered into the room. The person who lay on it was so skeletal that the covers lay nearly flat. But the seer was there, and, though said to be near death, continued to occupy her body. Once the stretcher had been laid across the surface of the desk, and the generator-powered light had been extinguished in order to protect her eyes, Posa pulled the blankets down to reveal a skull-like face. Most of the old woman's hair had fallen out, her skin looked like gray parchment, and her lips had a bluish tinge. But when her eyes locked with Kane's, the operative could feel the power still residing in her body. Her voice was little more than a croak. "What do you want? Let me die in peace."

"My name is Kane," the operative replied. "They tell me that you have the ability to communicate with the dead."

The crone blinked. "I'm a sensitive. Everyone knows that."

"Yes," Kane agreed lamely. "Well, tell me this . . . Can you put me in contact with a spirit named Lysander?"

The old woman's eyes narrowed. "Why should I? And what will you do if I don't? Kill me?"

The joke was followed by wild cackling that Kane took to be laughter. He looked up at Posa. The station chief held a six-year-old girl by the hand. She let go and pushed the child forward. "No," Kane replied calmly. "I'll kill *her*. And I'll do it slowly . . . While you watch."

The little girl said, "Grandma!" and ran to the old woman's side.

The sensitive tried to rise but lacked the strength and fell back onto the stretcher. "You bastard."

Kane nodded as if in agreement. "Put me in contact with Lysander, and both of you will go free."

The seer closed her eyes. There was a long pause, and the operative was ready to conclude that his prisoner had either fallen asleep or passed into the next world, when her eyes suddenly popped open. "Lysander refuses to speak with you—but there's another spirit who will."

Kane's felt a sense of frustration mixed with curiosity. "Really? Who?"

"His name is Cayo," the sensitive said hoarsely. "He claims that you left him to die in the catacombs beneath the city of Zand."

The operative remembered the desperate flight up out of the depths, the sound of shotgun blasts echoing back and forth between the ancient walls, and the pitiful way in which Cayo had called his name. "Kane! Help me!"

But he hadn't helped, and now, rather than the spirit he wanted to communicate with, Cayo was attempting to come through. The reality of that sent a chill down Kane's spine but he still managed to keep his voice level. "Tell him that I'm sorry—but there was no way to save him. I hope his next life will end more peacefully."

"He doesn't believe you," the old woman replied, "but he has information regarding the woman you're looking for *and* the object you brought up out of the catacombs."

"Information?" Kane inquired cautiously. "Why would Cayo provide me with information?"

"In return for money," the sensitive croaked. "Take a hundred cephors to Zand and deliver them to his wife. Once she has the money, Cayo will tell you what the woman plans to do."

"I *know* what she plans to do," Kane replied. "She and her friends intend to board the shuttle and leave the planet."

"Cayo says you're wrong," the seer responded, "and he seems sincere."

There was a long pause as Kane considered the proposition. It seemed like a long shot, but it wasn't that much money, not by the society's standards, and thanks to the local star gate, he could travel to Zand in a matter of minutes. "All right," he said finally, "tell Cayo that I will do what he asks. Except that his wife will receive *half* the money up front—and the other half once he delivers on his promise. In the meantime both you and your granddaughter will remain here."

"You'd better hurry," the old woman cautioned, "or

you're going to need a sensitive in order to communicate with *me*."

Speed. That was the most important factor in Rebo's opinion, and the others were in complete agreement. The longer it took to reach Cresus and implement their plan, the more time their enemies would have to prepare a trap for them. And that could be important, because even though the group intended to stay clear of the spaceport, they might ultimately be forced to use it. Just because Lysander said that a star gate was available didn't mean it was so, and if it turned out that the discarnate was wrong, the travelers would have little choice but to try for the shuttle.

So, no sooner had the float successfully made its way through the last set of rapids and entered the stretch of calm water that river folk called the flat, than the foursome left the slow-moving raft in favor of a long, narrow mail boat. It was powered by two heavies pulling four oars. Captain Duther and his crew waved as sweeps flashed in the sunlight, water dripped off bright red blades, and their former passengers were borne downstream.

The river was flowing along at about two miles per hour. That, combined with the strength of the burly oarsmen, was sufficient to propel their craft at a steady six to seven miles per hour. Thanks to the fact that the boat was on an express run, carrying correspondence for the Caliph himself, there was no need for it to stop at each jetty along the way.

As time passed, and the distance to Cresus continued to dwindle, villages appeared with increasing regularity, as did river traffic, until the young woman who served as the coxswain was forced to steer a zigzag course between heavily laden barges, rafts of slow-moving logs, and a variety of boats. Most were drab affairs, dedicated to fishing or carrying small cargoes, but a few boasted striped awnings, bright metalwork, and uniformed crew people. Lee never failed to wave as the mail packet swept past them—but none of the wealthy boaters chose to return the gesture.

That was to be expected, from Hoggles's perspective at least, but what troubled the heavy was the other items that the current carried with it. There was trash of every description, ugly-looking white foam that poured into the Juno from what had once been freshwater streams, and the occasional corpse. Flood victims perhaps? Boatmen murdered by pirates? Casualties of the latest plague? There was no way to tell.

The half-submerged bodies caused the heavy to think, however, about the city and his reasons for returning there. Not to see his family, all of whom had been murdered, but to rediscover himself. Was he the firebrand of his youth? The hermit who lived aboard a spaceship? Or someone else entirely? And what about his friends? Was he ready to part company with them? And make a life for himself in Cresus? And how realistic was the idea given that there was a price on his head?

The flood of questions was interrupted as the mail boat rounded a bend, slid under a high-arched bridge, and passed between the whitewashed pylons that marked the city limits. Most watercraft were required to pull over to the riverbanks at that point and line up to go through customs, but the mail boat belonged to the Caliph and was exempt from his taxes. It sailed past the official barges, pennant fluttering gaily in the breeze, as water boiled at its stern.

Though not supposed to carry passengers, the mail boat frequently did, which was how the three-person crew were able to get by on their parsimonious salaries. This fact was not lost on the customs agents, who expected a gratuity at the end of the month in return for remaining silent, and who lived in large houses deep in one of the safer parts of the city.

Rebo, who had absolutely no interest in the extent to which the city's officials had been corrupted, was simply grateful for the fact that he and his companions had been allowed to enter Cresus without undergoing any scrutiny. It was a piece of good fortune he had never dared dream of.

While somewhat open about carrying passengers, there were limits as to how brazen the boat crew could be without eliciting the ire of their superiors, which is why they sought to discharge their illicit cargo *prior* to pulling up alongside the government dock. It was already host to one of the new steamboats that plied the river, and Lee thought the vapor-belching side-wheeler was fascinating.

Having paid the coxswain, the foursome climbed a much-abused ladder to the jetty above. From there it was necessary to thread their way between food vendors, fishermen, and pickpockets before emerging onto the busy thoroughfare that ran parallel to the river and terminated some five miles to the west.

Even though he had grown up in Cresus, Hoggles didn't know where the Techno Society's headquarters were. He pulled a hood up over his head. "Come on," the heavy said as he made a hole in the crowd, "let's find a wordsmith."

The others followed, and it wasn't long before Hoggles led them through a passageway and into the thriving market that lay beyond the row of stores and warehouses fronting the waterway. The odor of urine mixed with what the sewers routinely disgorged into the river produced a combination so malodorous that the runner was hesitant to breathe.

At one point Rebo saw light reflect off metal as one of the Techno Society's robots appeared up ahead. It was a dangerous moment, but the runner managed to hustle his companions into a tea shop before the machine marched past.

Not long thereafter Hoggles spotted what he was looking for and led the group into a storefront dominated by the steady *thump, thump, thump* of a hand-operated press, the harsh smell of chemicals, and the head scribe's frenetic personality. She was small, no larger than a normal teenager, and seemed to flit from place to place. Norr winced as the woman came out to greet them and sent a tidal wave of raw energy toward her potential customers. "Welcome! And what can we do for you today? Wedding invitations perhaps? No? Well, we can handle whatever the project is."

"We need an address," Hoggles said. "For an organization called the Techno Society."

"Oh," the wordsmith replied, her disappointment plain to see. "I'll look it up."

Five minutes later, and one copper poorer, the group was on its way. Many of the shops had changed during the heavy's extended absence, but the streets remained the same, so it wasn't long before the foursome found themselves across the street from the building in which the Techno Society was headquartered. What the others didn't know, because Hoggles had chosen not to tell them, was that the route had taken them across the square where his family had been slaughtered. There were tears in his eyes, but the heavy managed to surreptitiously wipe them away as he herded his friends into a deeply shadowed alcove and nodded toward the building on the far side the street. "That's the place," the variant said. "Right over there."

Rebo eyed the structure. It was solid, but far from fancy, and, judging from the signs that hung out front, the building housed a rug merchant and an apothecary in addition to the Techno Society. "All right," the runner said, as he checked to ensure that his weapons were loose in their holsters. "Surprise is everything. Once inside I'll take care of the staff. Lanni and Lee will look for the star gate. Any questions?"

Lee frowned. "What if Lanni and I don't find the gate?"

"Then tell me," Rebo answered, "and we'll run like hell. But let's hope you find it, because the spaceport would be a tough nut to crack, and I have no desire to live in Cresus for the rest of my life."

Hoggles grinned. "And neither do I."

Norr looked up at the variant. "Really? You're coming with us?"

The giant nodded gravely. "If you'll have me."

Rebo raised an eyebrow. "We don't know where we're going to end up."

Hoggles shrugged. "It can't be any worse than Cresus."

"You can stay with me if you want," Lee said, as he peered upward. "My brothers and sisters will welcome you."

The heavy wasn't sure that he was ready to adopt a monastic life, but nodded anyway and gave the boy a pat on the head. "Thank you, friend. We'll see what the future brings."

"Okay," Rebo said, eyeing his friends. "Bo will help me deal with the staff. Let's get this over with."

The runner led the others across the cobblestone street, up a short flight of stairs, and through a much-abused door. The apothecary was to the left and the rug merchant was to the right. A sign indicated that the Techno Society was located on the second floor, and Rebo was halfway up the wooden stairs when a metal man stepped out of a door and started down. The robot had been programmed to look for the very people now blocking the way, and while emotionless, paused to double-check the data provided by its sen sors. The machine had turned, and was about to give the alarm, when Rebo did it for him.

Though never quiet, the Hogger sounded like a cannon as it went off within the close confines of the stairwell. The slug struck the android between its alloy shoulder blades, severed the fiber-optic pathway that ran down through the center of its plastic spinal column, and dumped the machine onto the stairs. The metal man wasn't dead, not so long as its processor continued to function, but it was certainly out of commission.

Ilia Posa heard the gunshot and was fumbling for the pistol that she kept in her top desk drawer, when a man with a gun burst through her door. From the shouting that could be heard from out in the hall, she judged that he wasn't alone. "Hold it right there," Rebo ordered. "Raise your hands."

The station chief had little choice but to comply.

"What about *my* hands?" a voice croaked, and the runner turned to see that an old woman lay on the floor and that a little girl was crouched at her side. "Yeah, you too," Rebo responded backing up so he could he could keep track of all three of them at once. "Where's Kane?"

Posa saw no reason to lie. "He's in Zand."

"They're holding us prisoner," the seer said hoarsely. "Let my granddaughter go."

The runner eyed the little girl and jerked his head toward the door. "She can go."

The old crone whispered something to the girl, who nodded obediently and scampered out of the room. "So," Rebo said as he refocused his attention on Posa, "when will Kane return?"

The station chief shrugged. "The journey takes weeks."

The Crosser barked and the woman jerked as the bullet scored her left cheek. "Wrong answer," the runner said grimly.

"The trip takes no more than a few seconds if you have a star gate."

"He's got you there!" the seer cackled approvingly.

Posa touched her cheek and examined her hand. There was blood on it. For the first time since the invasion had begun, she was truly afraid. "What do you want?"

"The gate," Rebo said grimly. "Take me to it. And no tricks . . . I can find it without you."

Posa, her left hand on her cheek, led the runner down a dingy green hall. The station chief was forced to step over her security chief, who no longer looked like himself, and lay in a pool of steadily spreading blood. The rest of the staff waited beyond, faces to a wall, hands on their heads. A heavy, his war hammer drenched with blood, nodded politely.

The man with the gun said, "Keep moving," and Posa had just rounded a corner and stepped into the station's conference room, when she saw the sensitive and the little boy. They had already searched the space and discovered the hinged painting. "There it is," Norr said, pointing at the keypad that was set into the wall. "All we need is the code."

"You heard her," the runner said as he jabbed the gun into the station chief's back. "Enter the code."

Hand shaking Posa did as she was bid. Something went *thud*, a motor whirred, and an entire section of wall slid out of the way. "Check it out," Rebo said, "but be careful."

Norr nodded, motioned for Lee to remain where he was, and thumbed the power switch. The vibro blade hummed ominously as the sensitive stepped into the chamber beyond. The air was cool but stale. Though dim, the lighting was adequate, and Norr saw what she was looking for up ahead. More than that she *felt* it, as something made her stomach feel queasy and triggered a headache.

The symptoms were sufficient to claim some of the sensitive's attention, but not all of it, which was fortunate. Norr "felt" a source of life energy above her, and looked upward just in time to see the carefully hidden sentry drop off a ledge, a two-foot-long blade held in each hand. The sensitive fell backward, heard steel swish through the space she had just vacated, and rolled to her feet. The sentry grinned, and his short blades whirred as they etched patterns into the air.

But skilled though he was, the sentry was human, which meant that he was surrounded by a multicolored energy field. And because the sensitive had spent her entire adult life studying such things she could read her opponent's aura, and thus his intentions. That enabled Norr to swing her blade at the spot the sentry was *about* to occupy, which meant that when he stepped into that position, the vibro blade was there to meet him. The weapon sliced down through a shoulder blade and into his chest.

He looked surprised, and Norr felt sorry for him as his physical body fell, and his spirit remained standing. But there was no time to console the man, or offer him counsel, as Rebo entered the room behind her. The runner eyed the body, said, "Good work," and pointed at the door marked DECONTAMINATION LOCK. "Let's get that sucker open . . . Bo locked the staff into a storeroom, but it won't take them long to escape."

The lock opened in response to the sensitive's touch, the others followed Norr inside, and Hoggles pulled the door closed behind him. There was a *hiss,* followed by a roar, as jets of disinfectant-laden hot water hit the foursome from every possible angle. Rebo spluttered. "It's some sort of bath!"

The water turned to steam as it hit the vibro blade and Norr thumbed the weapon off. Her dark hair hung in wet strands all around her face, and her clothes were plastered to her body as she sought to protect the gate seed from the water. "It's about time that three of you took a shower!"

The humor was lost on the others as they were systematically drenched and buffeted with blasts of hot air, before being allowed to enter the circular chamber beyond. Water continued to drop from their clothes as they looked around. Norr immediately recognized the tiles that covered the walls as being similar to those she had seen under the city of Tra, except that some of these were lit, and clearly active. Lee was delighted by his surroundings and read some of the names out loud. "Look! There's Anafa! And Hemo, and Pooz, and Zand!"

"We need to find the one labeled Thara," Rebo said as he scanned the squares arrayed in front of him.

"Here it is," Hoggles said, "but it's dark."

Rebo felt a crushing sense of disappointment. Partly because of what that might mean near term—but for an additional reason as well. Thara was more than another destination, it was the planet on which he had been born and the primary reason why he had agreed to take on this particular assignment. To come so close, then be blocked, was hard to take. "Try it anyway," the runner said hopefully. "Let's see what happens."

Hoggles pushed on the tile, and felt it give, but there was no response.

"Then let's go to Etu," Norr said pragmatically as she pointed to a brightly lit tile. "That's where the ship would have taken us from here—and we can reach Thara from there."

"Maybe," Rebo replied darkly, "assuming the next ship is operational . . . But that's then—and this is now. Go ahead—punch us out of here."

The sensitive pressed against the shiny surface, felt the

square give, and gave an involuntary start as a woman's voice issued from a speaker mounted over her head. "The transfer sequence is about to begin. Please take your place on the service platform. Once in place check to ensure that no portion of your anatomy extends beyond the yellow line. Failure to do so will cause serious injury and could result in death."

"Come on!" Rebo urged as he stepped up onto a slightly raised platform. "Who knows how quickly this thing works!"

Because of the size of the heavy's body it was difficult for all four of them to squeeze inside the yellow safety circle, but they made it, and were locked in a group hug when they were blinded by a flash of light. Rebo lost his vision, felt sick to his stomach, and wondered if he was dead.

Posa had escaped from the storeroom, by then. She entered the control room, slapped the kill switch for the station's generator, and the lights went out. Dozens of tiles on dozens of planets suddenly went dark as Ning's number two star gate went off-line. "That should fix the bastards," the station chief said grimly, and went to get her pistol. The little girl had escaped—but her grandmother was going to die.

THIRTEEN

The Planet Etu

Because variants were created by man rather than God—they cannot be categorized as human.

—Archbishop Chario Immu,
The Church of Etu

Rebo screamed, but no one could hear him as his body was ripped apart, transmitted through hyperspace, and systematically reassembled many light-years away. A fraction of a second passed while the runner hung suspended in midair, followed by a sudden fall as local gravity took over, and Rebo crashed to the floor below. It was slanted, and he was still in the process of sliding downward, when Lee landed on top of him. There was a loud grunt as Hoggles crashed next to the pair, followed by a *thump* as Norr landed on her feet.

"Where the hell are we?" the runner inquired as he struggled to get up. The floor was cracked, slanted, *and* lower than it was supposed to be. The gravity was lighter than Ning's, however, which made it easier to get up.

"I assume we're on Etu," the sensitive replied, as she

scanned the mosaic of tiles that covered the walls. "Look! The control for Cresus is dark! I wonder what happened?"

"Beats me," Hoggles said ponderously, "but judging from the kind of folks we left behind, we'd better get ready for a fight."

"That sounds like excellent advice," Rebo agreed, and felt his stomach heave as he made for the door. It looked a little out of square, as if whatever caused the floor to buckle had done damage to it as well, and that gave rise to a series of questions: Would the hatch open? What would they do if it didn't? And what lay beyond?

The runner pressed his palm against the sensor plate and felt a sense of relief as a motor whined, and the barrier began to move. But that was when he heard a grinding noise, followed by a loud *click* as a relay opened, and the motor stopped. The runner stuck his right arm through the gap, but it was obvious that not even Lee would be able to squeeze through.

"What now?" Norr said weakly, as she battled the urge to vomit.

"Bo can force it open," Lee said confidently. "Can't you, Bo?"

The heavy looked down at the boy and forced a smile. "I don't know," he replied honestly, "but I'll try."

So saying, the variant handed his war hammer to Norr, made his way over to the door, and got into position. Then, having set his feet, Hoggles pushed. Muscles writhed, cords stood out from his neck, and all manner of veins appeared as the heavy exerted all of his considerable strength.

There was no reaction at first, and Norr had started to wonder if the task was hopeless, when she heard something creak. That was followed by a *groan* as metal gave way, followed by a *clang* as a locking pin broke, and a *rattle* as the door slid back into its housing. "See?" Lee demanded proudly. "I told you he could do it!"

"And you were correct," Rebo agreed as he removed the Crosser from its holster. "Now, let's see what's waiting for us outside."

Only half the water jets came on as the runner entered the decontamination chamber—and those that remained operational lacked force. The air blowers *were* working, however, and the runner had no choice but to wait them out, since it was apparent that the next door wasn't going to open until the cleansing cycle had completed itself.

Once the dryers clicked off, the door opened smoothly, and Rebo raised his weapon. But, rather than the blood-thirsty horde of metal men he half expected to see, the runner found himself looking out into a dusty room half-filled with debris. A few steps were sufficient to ascertain that no one waiting to ambush them, and, judging from the all-pervasive silence, the surrounding structure had been abandoned. Once clear of the decontamination room the nausea started to fade.

"Maybe they were hit by an earthquake," Norr speculated as she toed a chunk of broken duracrete. "That would account for all of the destruction."

Rebo nodded. He had been through a quake once, on a planet called Keno, and knew how destructive such events could be. "That would explain it," he agreed. "But it appears that whatever the techno crazies use for power is still operational. And that means they can follow us."

"I thought we were going to sabotage the place," Hoggles remarked as examined the damage.

The runner shrugged. "Yeah, that was the plan, but I don't have the foggiest idea how to go about it. Especially with all of this debris in the way."

"Then let's do what we do best," Norr put in. "Let's get the heck out of here."

"That works for me," Rebo agreed as he made his way toward an unobstructed archway. "And who knows? Maybe the next leg of the journey will be easy."

"Yeah," Hoggles replied darkly. "And maybe L-phants will fly."

The Planet Ning

The blowers stopped, Kane palmed the door, and waited for it to open. Except for the boots that the operative held in his right hand, he was nude as the barrier slid out of the way to reveal Posa and two members of her staff. Incredibly, and for reasons Kane couldn't fathom, they held weapons that were pointed at *him*. If they found his lack of clothing to be offensive, there was no sign of it. "Please let me be the first to welcome you back," the station chief said sarcastically. "There's some good news and some bad news. The good news is that you won't have to pay Cayo's wife the second half of the fee . . . The bad news is that rather than head for the spaceport, the way you assumed that she would, the sensitive and her ruffians came *here* instead. They murdered two of my staff members before making a jump to Etu. I cut the power after they entered the transfer chamber—but they were already in transit by then."

It was a lot to absorb, but the operative had a quick mind, and was able to make sense of it. It looked like Cayo had been correct about Norr's plans, but because of differences between the spirit and physical planes, had misjudged how much time things would take. The operative made a mental note to return to Zand, kill Cayo's wife, and retrieve the money. Not because the Techno Society was short of funds—but as a point of honor. "Okay," he said levelly, "so why point those weapons at *me?*"

"Because Shaz returned to Anafa six days ago," Posa explained, "and we're the only ones who know what happened here. You would kill us if you could, blame the murders on the sensitive, and continue on your way. *That's* why."

Kane hadn't had the opportunity to hatch such a plot as yet, but knew he would have and was forced to raise his estimate of the station chief's intelligence. "That's absurd," the operative lied, and held his arms straight out to emphasize his nudity. "I'm unarmed, not to mention a bit chilly, so how 'bout we continue this discussion in your office?"

"Give him his clothes," Posa said gruffly, "and let him get dressed. Once that's accomplished bring him to me. Everyone in this organization is accountable—even Mr. high-and-mighty Kane."

The man in question hoped it wasn't true, but feared that it was, and had little choice but to cooperate. Even though Shaz was back on Anafa, the variant was still only minutes away, and the knowledge made Kane's knees feel weak. The clothes hit him in the chest—and he hurried to put them on.

The Planet Etu

It was difficult to tell what the city of Epano had been like before the quake, because most of the buildings constructed during the last hundred years lay in ruins; but as the foursome picked their way through rubble-littered streets, Rebo got the impression of wide boulevards, which had been laid out grid fashion, ornate public buildings, some of which remained intact, and lush greenery, all of which was coated with dust.

Smartly uniformed troops could be seen, *lots* of them,

and seemed to have the situation well in hand. People were out and about, but there were no casualties to be seen, which suggested that they had been removed to hospitals. Further evidence of how organized the local government was could be seen in the gangs of workers already toiling to remove debris from the streets so that repairs could get under way.

In marked contrast to the other cities they'd been in recently, Rebo noticed that none of the civilians were armed. That caused him to remove the gun belt from around his waist and place the Hogger in his pack. His jacket hid the Crosser, so he left that weapon where it was.

The enormous war hammer was impossible to hide, but Hoggles managed to disguise the weapon by wrapping the business end with rags, which he tied into place with twine. Norr's vibro blade was concealed within her staff so there was no need to alter its appearance. *Her* appearance, however, as well as the heavy's, was a definite problem, which quickly became apparent as the travelers rounded a corner and happened onto a checkpoint.

They saw the group of soldiers up ahead and were about to angle away from them, when a sharp-eyed file leader spotted them. He frowned as if he had just bitten into something he didn't like the taste of. He wore leather body armor, a knee-length kilt, and sandal-style boots. He spoke standard but with the lilt typical of the local population. "Come on . . . Don't be shy . . . Let's have a look at you."

Rebo didn't like the situation, not one little bit, but had to comply. He stepped forward and the others followed. The file leader had thick brows, a hooked nose, and thin lips. "So," he said, addressing himself to Rebo, "who are you? Who do the freaks belong to? And where are their chains?"

Having suddenly been confronted with a series of questions that he wasn't prepared to answer, the runner struggled to come up with answers, and do so quickly enough to seem credible. It seemed safe to assume that the term "freaks" referred to the variants, both of whom looked like what they were, but what to make of the rest? Rebo decided to start with the obvious stuff and elaborate from there. "My name is Rebo, Jak Rebo, and this is my son Lee. As for the freaks, they belong to me."

The officer nodded. "Well, Citizen Rebo, these are difficult times, but you know the rules. Variants must wear restraints . . . And hoods, too. What if the big fellow were to turn on you? Or the witch were to channel an evil spirit? The laws were written for *your* protection."

Rebo thought about Lysander and could understand the concern. Strangely, while the variants had attracted negative attention, it seemed as if they had served to establish Rebo's status as a lawful citizen, too, since there had been no effort to confirm his identity.

Meanwhile, having been referred to as freaks, and discussed them as if they were little more than livestock, both Hoggles and Norr were understandably outraged. The heavy wrapped and rewrapped his fingers around the war hammer's handle while the sensitive bit her lower lip.

"Yes, I know that," Rebo said humbly. "Unfortunately my wife and I lost nearly everything in the quake. The house collapsed, and we were lucky to escape with our lives."

"Well, we don't have any hoods," the file leader responded sympathetically, "but we do have some spare leg irons." So saying the officer called for one of his noncoms and gave the necessary orders. Metal rattled as two sets of leg irons were removed from a wooden hand cart and the variants had little choice but to remain motionless as the heavy restraints were locked around their ankles.

"There you go," the file leader said as he handed the keys to Rebo, "get some hoods on them as soon as you can. I hear the slave market will reopen soon . . . The heavy would fetch a good price. Especially given all the rebuilding that needs to be done. Perhaps the proceeds could go toward rebuilding your home."

"That's a good idea," the runner agreed politely. "Thank you for all of your help."

"That's what we're here for," the soldier replied pompously, and gave Rebo a slip of parchment. "Here, show this to any unit that stops you, and good luck."

Rebo accepted the pass and tucked it away. Then, having taken Lee by the hand, the off-worlder assumed what he hoped was the appropriate demeanor. "All right, you two— that's enough standing around. We have work to do."

The chains that connected the ankle bracelets together weren't very long, which forced Norr and Hoggles to adopt a quick shuffle in order to keep up. It was awkward, humiliating, and ultimately painful.

The runner took the first turn that he could, gave thanks for the fact that there weren't any troops in sight, and gave the keys to the variants. "Here, hang on to these, but leave the shackles in place. We'll get stopped if you don't."

Norr made a face. "Okay, but walk more slowly, and let's put some padding in these things."

"All right," Rebo agreed lightly. "But try to look a little more subservient. I think I could get used to it."

"In your dreams," the sensitive replied. "In your dreams."

The Planet Ning

Someone pushed Kane from behind. He stumbled, and nearly fell, but managed to keep his balance. The seer had been laid out across the top of the station chief's desk the last time the operative had been in her office, but the old woman had disappeared, as had the little girl. There was a patch of what might have been blood on the floor, which suggested that Posa had put the two of them to death, not that it made any difference to Kane. He had problems of his own, not the least of which was figuring out how to escape before the station chief shipped him to Anafa, or summoned Shaz to Ning, either of which would almost certainly be fatal.

"Have a seat," Posa said, as she gestured toward the single guest chair. "You and I are going to have a nice little chat about the sensitive and the item she took from you. Who knows? Maybe *I* can recover it. If I do, perhaps that will be sufficient to get me out of this hellhole."

The very thought of Posa's recovering the gate seed and using it to gain the approval denied him was enough to make the blood pound in Kane's head. The operative looked down at his hands. They had been bound, but *in front of him,* in order to facilitate his trip to the men's room. That was a mistake and one he planned to take advantage of.

Kane stepped up to the desk as if preparing to sit down, raised both hands over his head, and brought them down as fast as he could. Clenched fists connected with the station chief's skull. The blow stunned Posa, who fell forward, and threw her hands down in order to brace herself. The operative took advantage of the opportunity to head butt her, saw his opponent fall backward, and knew she was out of it.

There was a guard, but he held his fire out of fear that a bullet might strike his boss, and rushed to grapple with the prisoner. When Kane turned it was with Posa's double-edged letter opener clutched in his right hand. The guard came to a stop, or attempted to, but the effort came too late.

The knifelike instrument went deep into his chest; he gave a little sigh, and collapsed in a heap.

Fortunately for Kane none of the battle had generated much in the way of sound, which meant that the rest of the staff weren't aware of what had just taken place, or the danger they were in. That was about to change, however, as Kane took the guard's weapon, plus Posa's, and all the ammo he could find.

Then, his pockets heavy with the gold coins that he had looted from the station chief's safe, the operative took the time necessary to garrote Posa with her own belt, prior to going room to room with a pistol in each hand. The unsuspecting staff members fell like targets on a combat range. Once the shuttle had come and gone, the people posted at the spaceport would return to find a nasty surprise waiting for them.

Satisfied that all of those who could testify against him were dead, and confident that he could blame the slaughter on Norr, Kane entered the decontamination chamber. The sensitive had gone to Etu, so he would too. Once on the planet he would find the bitch, kill her, and recover the gate seed. Then, with the device in hand, the operative could return to Anafa. Yes, there would be questions, but nothing speaks louder than success. Water soaked his clothes, and his stomach felt queasy, but Kane didn't care. He was alive, and even though his quarry remained a few steps ahead of him, he would soon catch up with her.

The Planet Etu

It was hot inside the flour-sack hood, not to mention claustrophobic and humiliating. Norr's vision was restricted to what two small slits allowed her to see. That, combined with the dust that found its way up under the hood, and the endless jerk-jerk-jerk of the leg shackles threatened to drive the sensitive insane.

The obvious solution was to hire or buy some sort of angen-drawn cart, so the entire group could ride, but the countryside was alive with displaced city folk, so transportation was in short supply. So, if the travelers wanted to reach the spaceport at Overa in time to board the next ship, they would have to walk.

Rebo thought conditions would improve once they put the city of Epano behind them, but Norr wasn't so sure. Variants were just another category of personal property on Etu, and since rural areas tend to be *more* conservative than urban centers, the sensitive figured that things weren't likely to get any better out in the country. And that raised some frightening possibilities. What if someone saw through their charade and turned all four of them in to the authorities? Or, what if something happened to Rebo? Or, the shuttle never arrived? Doubts plagued the sensitive, and time seemed to slow as she shuffled through each weary mile.

By that time the boulevard they had followed out of Epano had degenerated into a two-lane highway, which morphed into a single set of deep ruts served by occasional pull-outs. Occasional stretches of ancient duracrete and some sturdy bridges hinted at glories past, but such artifacts were rare. For the most part the road simply followed the path of least resistance as it wound its way between softly rounded hills, crossed rivers at the point where the water was shallowest, and meandered between small farms and vast estates.

It was easy going really, or would have been, had it not been for the misery that the variants were subjected to. Rebo was worried about them, *very* worried, but there wasn't much he could do about it. Not considering that it wasn't unusual to pass a pair of matched slaves laboring between the traces of a cart loaded with angen manure, or to see a variant pulling a plow in a nearby field, or to be passed by a norm mounted high on a heavy's back.

And sensitives were no better off. Most were used as household help, but the hooded figures could be seen escorting children to school and working in the fields as well. Chances were that their other talents were being put to use, but privately, and for the exclusive benefit of their owners. The fact that the variants had clearly been enslaved for a long time, yet continued to have distinguishing traits, suggested an enforced breeding program—a horrible thought and one that caused Rebo to shudder.

Unpleasant though the society around them was, the weather had been relatively mild, with only the occasional rain shower to interrupt long, mostly sunny days. The foursome made good time as a result, covering about fifteen miles per day, as the dirt road led them through a series of rural villages.

The routine was pretty much the same from day to day. Get up early, fix a light breakfast, and hit the road. Food for lunch and dinner, as well as the next breakfast, was purchased at the first village they came to. Lunch was consumed by a stream if possible, far enough off the road that passersby wouldn't be able to see that the variants had been allowed to remove their shackles and hoods, or the fact that their supposed owner was breaking bread with them.

Later, after the sun had dissolved into a red-orange smear on the western horizon, the foursome sought a safe spot to camp. But such places were sometimes hard to find, and there were nights when it wasn't safe to have a fire, forcing them to eat cold food. Lee made use of the discomfort an opportunity to exert mindful control over his physical body, but it made the rest miserable, especially Norr, who missed her hot tea.

But the days passed, and as they did, things started to change. There was more traffic on the road, the villages were closer together, and files of brightly uniformed angen-mounted cavalry passed from time to time. These were all signs that a city lay ahead, which according to Rebo's scribe-drawn map, was called Citro. And, judging from the speed at which they were walking, it was clear that it would be necessary to stay the night. A none-too-pleasant prospect, especially where the variants were concerned, since it didn't take a genius to realize that they wouldn't be allowed to occupy the same quarters that Rebo and Lee would.

There was nothing Norr could do about the situation, however, so the sensitive did the best she could to put the matter out of her mind as the foursome made their way across a wooden bridge, past a group of bored-looking soldiers, and entered the city of Citro. It showed no signs of earthquake damage—and was clearly less prosperous than Epano had been prior to the temblor. Raw sewage ran along both sides of the unpaved streets. No structures stood more than two stories tall, and with the exception of old ground cars that had been converted into farm wagons, there were no signs of ancient technology. Laundry flapped from lines strung between buildings, children carried buckets of water home from public wells, and piles of rotting garbage marked major intersections.

Rebo sought directions from a street vendor, gave the woman a copper by way of thanks, and led the group to a hostelry that claimed to be the finest hotel in Citro. The runner might have been more impressed had it not been for the pile of angen manure out front, the trail of mud that led up the wooden stairs to the entrance, or the somewhat threadbare doorman who waited to greet them. But, shabby or not, the employee wore an invisible cloak of superiority, which could be seen in the way he looked down his nose at the road-weary travelers. "Yes? How can I help you?"

"We wish to stay the night," Rebo replied evenly, trying his best to sound like the merchant that he was pretending to be. Not rich, but successful, even if the rigors of the road had left him and his party looking a bit disheveled.

"I see," the doorman said, as if doing Rebo a favor. "You and the boy may proceed to the front desk. I'll have one of the stable hands take the slaves around back."

"I want them fed and given a chance to bathe," Rebo insisted. "They're starting to smell."

"As are *you*," the doorman thought to himself, but nodded and blew a tin whistle. A ratty-looking twelve-year-old appeared a few moments later. He was armed with a whip, and judging from the look on his thin little face, was eternally on the lookout for an opportunity to use it. The runner had collected the keys for the shackles earlier that morning. He frowned as he handed them to the boy. "If I find whip marks on my property, *you're* the one who will wear the next set of stripes."

That, as it turned out, was exactly the sort of motivation that the youngster understood. He nodded sullenly and ordered the variants down into the street. Norr paused long enough to shrug her pack off, remove the cloth-wrapped object inside, and hand it to Rebo. "Here, master . . . This will be safer with you."

The runner knew what was in the package and nodded as he accepted the spherical gate seed. He wanted to take Norr in his arms but couldn't. "Thanks," he said gruffly. "I want to get an early start tomorrow—so make sure that you're ready."

Norr said, "Yes, master," and was led away. Hoggles, chains rattling, followed behind. The sensitive, her vision restricted by the hood, followed the boy through a narrow passageway and into a muddy courtyard where a cluster of children were busy washing a droopy-eared angen. Beyond them a low one-story building could be seen. It boasted two openings. The first, which was located at the south end of the structure, was large enough to accommodate animals. The second, which gave access to the north end of the building, was smaller and clearly intended for people. And it was through that entrance that the variants were led.

Light filtered into the reception area via four panes of thick glass. There was a counter, some rusty ring bolts that had been set into the mud-smeared floor, and the air was thick with the rank odor of the angens stabled next door. An armed guard sat on a tall stool in one corner, a potbellied stove squatted in another, and the woman in charge was protected by a crudely constructed counter. She wore a kerchief on her head, a long baggy dress, and a pair of wooden clogs. They made a rapping sound as she moved out into the center of the room. "The showers will open in two hours, dinner will be served an hour after than, and the lights go out at nine," she said curtly. "Behave yourselves, and everything will be fine. Cause trouble and you'll be sorry. Any questions? No? Good. It's been my experience that it's the troublemakers who like to ask questions. Males go in *there*," the norm said as she pointed at a sturdy door, "and females go in *there*."

Norr was forced to wait while the norm unlocked the door to the male barracks so that Hoggles could enter. Then, once the door had been secured, it was the sensitive's turn as the woman clumped from one side of the reception area to the other. The handmade key rattled as it was inserted into its hole, there was a loud *click-clack* as the lock turned, and the squeal of unoiled metal as the door swung open.

As Norr shuffled into the long narrow room she saw that rows of heavy-duty beds lined two of the four walls. A much-abused table ran down the center of the room. It was flanked by a dozen mismatched chairs, four of which were occupied by female sensitives. A couple of heavies sat beyond, their hands locked together, as they struggled to determine who was strongest. Both females had biceps the size of Norr's thighs—and neither broke eye contact with the other as the newcomer entered.

The door swung closed with a decisive *thud,* the key rattled in the lock, and Norr was on her own. "So," a voice said at the sensitive's elbow, "what have we here?"

Norr was about to answer when the hood was jerked up off her head and the fifth sensitive made her presence known. "Hello, my name is Riba," the variant said cheerfully. Though a good deal older than Norr, the woman had the same big eyes, high cheekbones, and narrow face.

"Hmmm," Riba said, as she circled Norr. "I sense something strange here."

That seemed to serve as an invitation for the others to examine the young woman as well. And not just examine, but *probe,* as only sensitives can. It had been a long time since the variant had been in the same room with another sensitive, much less *five* of them, and she had nearly forgotten what such an experience was like. The heavies were oblivious to the way in which auras flared, energy seethed, and unusual things began to happen. A cut on Norr's left arm was miraculously healed, her pack seemed to float off her shoulders, and strains of ethereal music could be heard float-ing through the air.

Norr was a very self-contained person, but she also missed her own kind, so the unexpected "conversation" if that was what it could be called, both frightened and thrilled her. "You are correct," the oldest sensitive observed. "She has something to hide all right."

"Yes!" another put in excitedly. "He's tall, a bit danger-ous, and uh-oh! He's a norm!"

"That's bad," a third agreed somberly. "But there's more . . . The lass has *another* man in her life as well. He lives in the spirit planes and was her father once. He's *here* and wants to speak."

"Oh, goody! Bring him through!" the fourth sensitive insisted. "We could use some entertainment."

"I'm not sure that's a good idea" Riba said doubtfully. "You know the rules . . . What if the heavies turn us in? The norms would burn us alive."

The arm-wrestling contest had ended by then and the heavies were listening. "You have nothing to fear from us," the female to Norr's left said stolidly. "Freaks side with freaks . . . that's what I say."

"Fair enough," Riba replied. "So how 'bout it, honey? The man wants to talk to you . . . Are you willing to listen?"

Lysander had been trying to break through for days by then, but it was dangerous to enter a trance on Etu, and Norr had been too tired by the time dinner was over. Now, surrounded by her own kind, she felt tempted. "Okay," she said tentatively, "but I'd like to sit down."

Riba said, "Of course, dearie," and led her to the table. "This is Pru, Kama, Tris, and Nina." Norr said hello to each, took a chair, and waited to see what would happen. It turned out that Tris was the one who had been elected to bring the spirit through. Not simply for Norr's benefit, but because Tris was known to have a very special talent, one that the others were eager to witness.

The woman named Riba eyed the heavies. "Would one of you be willing to guard the door? Thank you. Stall if someone attempts to open it."

Silence descended over the room as the sensitives came together under Riba's direction to gather the energy that a full materialization was going to require. Now, seated directly across from Tris, Norr saw that the other woman's eyes had been removed leaving her sockets horribly empty. It was a precaution that some of the more superstitious slave owners took to protect themselves from the evil eye, an imaginary threat that many believed to be real.

Even the heavies could feel the change that followed as something caused the hairs on the back of their arms to stand straight up, all of the available light was sucked into the center of the room, and the air above the table started to glow.

Then, as if attracted to an unseen form by means of spiritual magnetism, the light began to coalesce. The man's head, like the rest of his body, was slightly transparent. It turned from side to side, as if the spirit was unsure of his surroundings. And this time, rather than communicate through human vocal cords as he had in the past, Lysander spoke via an ectoplasmic voice box. "Who are these people?" the discarnate demanded hoarsely. "And what do they want of me?"

"They're friends of mine," Norr responded, "and they don't want anything of you."

"Tell them to leave," Lysander said arrogantly. "My words are for your ears only."

"Sorry," the sensitive replied, "but we're locked in . . . So, say your piece or leave me alone."

Lysander struggled to bring the physical plane into focus, but much to his frustration, the luminescent green blobs remained just as they were. Norr's words seemed to come from a long ways off. The scientist didn't like the situation but was determined to get his message through. "Logos is on Etu. Seek him among those who flock to Mount Pama. That's all I can say."

The sensitive was about to ask where Mount Pama was— when the heavy who had agreed to guard the door put her ear to the barrier. "Someone's coming!" she whispered urgently. Then, having raised her voice, she yelled, "Hey! Can anyone hear me? I feel sick."

The general effect was to cause the person outside to pause and consider what had been said before slipping the big handmade key into the lock. That gave Tris just enough time to break contact with the spirit world and exit her trance. As she did Lysander's image wavered, turned to what looked like smoke, and disappeared.

The door swung open, and the guard appeared. He held a shotgun in his hands and was clearly ready for trouble. But, with no evidence of malfeasance to be seen there was nothing he could do except frown at them. "Which one of you answers to the name Kama? You do? Then come on out . . . Your mistress is ready to leave. Now, which one of you is sick?"

The heavy who had been guarding the door raised her hand. "Go lie down," the guard instructed. "Once the vet is finished with the angens he'll take a look at you."

Attachments were discouraged, and slaves weren't allowed to display their emotions lest they intentionally or unintentionally generate sympathy for themselves, so there were no good-byes as Kama pulled the black hood down over her head and stepped out of the room. "So," Riba demanded, once the door had closed, "what did you make of your message? Who is Logos? And why would a slave make the pilgrimage to Mount Pama?"

Norr shrugged. "I have no idea . . . Let me know if you figure it out."

Riba didn't believe the newcomer, but she had some secrets of her own and couldn't blame Norr for keeping the information to herself. Etu was a dangerous place, especially for those with paranormal talents, and silence was the only defense that the slaves had.

Pala's lungs felt as though they were fire, and the wounds on her hips were bleeding from the most recent application of the norm's spurs, as the heavy trotted up the heavily rutted road and entered the village of Kaya. A trio of mangy dogs darted out and nipped at her heels until one of the men seated in front of the feed store whistled them back. Kane said, "Whoa!" and jerked on the reins. Pala felt the leather bit hit the corners of her mouth and came to a stop. She stood chest heaving as the off-worlder placed his boots against her lower back, pushed the sling-saddle away from her body, and dropped to the ground. He had purchased her in the slave market in Epano and ridden her hard. Pala had come to hate the man called Kane and, if given the chance, planned to kill him.

The operative, who was under no illusions regarding the way that his mount felt about him, took the time required to shackle the variant's feet together prior to climbing the wooden stairs that led up to the general store. The heavy could run if she chose to, but not very far, and only if she wanted a beating. His spurs jingled as Kane entered the one-story building and peered into the cluttered gloom. Like any general store this one carried a wide variety of items including food, hardware, and clothing. A single ray of sunshine slanted in through the front window. Dust motes orbited around his head as the off-worlder stepped in to claim it. "Hello? Is anyone home?"

"There's no need to shout," an irritated voice responded. "I'm right here."

Kane gave an involuntary start as a man in a long gray apron materialized in front of him. It seemed that the local had been there from the start, hidden among the things he hoped to sell. The operative forced a smile. "Sorry about that. I'm looking for a friend of mine . . . A man with dark hair, a little boy, and a couple of slaves. They would have passed through within the last few days. Have you seen them?"

The storekeeper had two days' worth of stubble on his pointy chin. It made a rasping sound as he ran his spatulate fingers across it. "Maybe, and maybe not."

Kane recognized the response for what it was and withdrew a coin from his vest pocket. It found an open palm. "Here, perhaps this will aid your memory."

The merchant weighed the coin in his hand, and ran a grimy thumbnail over the shiny metal, before finally tucking it away. "Yes," the local allowed phlegmatically, "there was such a group. They bought some food from me. That was two days ago."

"Tell me about the slaves," Kane demanded, "or return my money."

The storekeeper didn't like the implication and frowned resentfully. "There was a female sensitive and a male heavy."

"Good," the operative said approvingly. "Now, which way did they go?"

"Toward Mount Pama," the local answered. "Like all the pilgrims do."

Kane nodded. "Thank you. I need bread, meat, and tea. Enough to last me and my heavy for a day. Please hurry."

The merchant bustled about, gave the stranger what he had requested, and charged him the extra 10 percent that he levied on all strangers. Having followed the norm out into the street, where a tired-looking slave waited, the shopkeeper watched the blond man mount up and ride off. An obscene gesture sent the pilgrim on his way. The men sitting in front of the feed store laughed, their dogs lolled in the sun, and shopkeeper went back inside. A squadron of buzz bugs followed behind. The day wore on.

The sun had been up for little more than an hour, and a layer of early-morning mist still floated just above the ground, as the foursome topped a rise and paused to look at Mount Pama. Though too tall to be properly classified as a hill, the softly rounded elevation didn't make much of a mountain, not to Rebo's thinking at least. No, what made the geological feature remarkable was the manner in which it appeared to have been plopped down at the center of an otherwise barren plain. That, and the ribbon of people that already snaked their way up around the mountain's flanks, inching their way toward the summit.

"Look at that!" Hoggles exclaimed. "There must be hundreds of them! How will we find Logos in the crowd?"

"He's an *it,* and we don't even know what *it* looks like," Rebo commented sourly.

Thanks to a pair of really hideous glasses, and the skillful application of the makeup Rebo had purchased during their stay in Citro, the sensitive had been transformed into a homely norm. She no longer had to wear shackles as a result, but Hoggles did, and they rattled as he moved. "That's true," Norr agreed thoughtfully, "but I have a feeling that we'll know him when we see him."

"No offense," Rebo replied, "but I don't find much comfort in that. And remember, the *real* goal is to reach Overa, and the spaceship. One day, that's all we can afford to spend on this nonsense, so use it wisely."

Subsequent to Lysander's appearance in the female slave quarters back in Citro, the adults had spent a good deal of time discussing whether to go along with the discarnate's request or ignore it. The runner saw no reason to humor the cantankerous spirit, but Norr and Hoggles believed that the group should find Logos, for use as leverage if nothing else. Finally, having been filibustered, Rebo gave in. But Lee didn't care about the right or wrong of it. He couldn't wait to find out why thousands of people would travel for weeks to visit the top of a mountain. "Come on!" the ten-year-old urged. "Let's get going!"

The better part of an hour had passed before the foursome arrived at the bottom of the mountain and the settlement there. Hundreds of tents had been pitched in the surrounding area, which when combined with all manner of pilgrims, slaves, vendors, and hundreds of angens made for a colorful but chaotic mix.

By that time Rebo had noticed that most of the people making their way toward the foot of the trail were young couples. And it wasn't long before a man dressed in a spotless white robe moved to block their way. "That will be ten gunars," he said. "Payable in advance."

Rebo, who had started to run low on expense money by then, grumbled as he opened his purse. "Is that ten for each person? Or does that cover the four of us?"

"The oracle's readings are intended for couples," the attendant said condescendingly. "The admission charge covers both of you. The boy and the slave must remain here."

Though mystified by the process, and reluctant to part company with Lee, the runner had no choice but to acquiesce. He paid the fee and received two small tiles in return. The ceramic squares had been inscribed with mysterious symbols and dangled from leather thongs. Rebo passed one over the sensitive's head and let if fall against her chest. Each tile was clearly intended to function as both a receipt and a memento. The question was why?

In the meantime Lee had succumbed to attachment and therefore resentment. He wanted to visit the top of the mountain in the worst possible way, and try as he might, had thus far been unable to accept the fact that he wouldn't be allowed to accompany the adults. He was still sulking, and feeling guilty about it, when the twosome began the uphill climb. Hoggles made a show out of sniffing the air. "Come on, son . . . I smell food. We'll eat while they climb! What do you say?"

Lee was almost always hungry, and the smell of grilled food, plus the opportunity to eat without being required to build a fire, fetch water, or wash up afterward proved to be irresistible. He nodded, took hold of the leash that was attached to the heavy's harness, and led the variant toward the collection of huts that had been established to provide the pilgrims with food, necessaries, and useless trinkets.

Meanwhile Rebo and Norr followed the line upward— even as other couples continued to make their way down. Most were happy, their features alight with pleasure, but some were devastated. Tears trickled down their cheeks as they clung to each other for support and stumbled down the mountainside.

The line moved steadily for the most part, but it came to a stop every once in a while, and Norr took advantage of one such a moment to initiate a conversation with the couple directly behind them. Both had dark hair, light brown skin, and shiny eyes. Especially when they looked at each other—which was often. The sensitive didn't need to see the colors that swirled around them to know that the youngsters were in love. "So," Norr said encouragingly, "where are you from?"

Rebo watched in admiration as his companion led the pair through a series of seemingly innocuous questions. It seemed that the Oracle of Mount Pama had the power to foretell whether the children produced by a particular union would be healthy and free of birth defects. No small matter within a society where good medical care was a thing of the past. So, while some would-be couples chose to ignore the oracle, fearing what he might tell them, most sought his blessing. Those who received good news were thrilled, and came down off the mountain ready to marry, while those who had been warned not to procreate were not only devastated but faced with difficult choices. They could marry, and pray that the oracle would be wrong, marry and remain childless, or seek different mates.

"That's fascinating," Norr responded sincerely. "We come from a long ways off—so we hadn't heard about the oracle until very recently. How accurate are his predictions?"

"*Very* accurate," the young man replied. "So much so that when a couple who has been warned about their prospects produces a completely healthy child it is customary to assume that another man was involved."

All four of them laughed, the line jerked ahead, and the conversation ended. Rebo looked at Norr just as a clearly distraught couple passed them. "Are you thinking what I'm thinking?"

The sensitive's eyebrows rose. "That Logos and the Oracle of Pama are one and the same?"

"Exactly."

"Yes, I am. He wasn't designed for this purpose, but judging from our experiences with *Hewhotravels* and our friend Fil, old machines can learn new tricks."

"So what do we do?" the runner wanted to know. "If we grab the old geezer, and haul him down the mountain, that isn't going to be very popular with the people in the robes. Not to mention the paying customers."

"No," Norr agreed thoughtfully, "it wouldn't. I guess we'll have to wait and see."

More than three hours had passed, and the sun had sunk into the western sky by the time the twosome finally neared the summit. Each had purchased sweet cakes by then—plus ladles of water to wash the sticky stuff down. Now, as they made their way up onto the flat area atop the mountain, *more* vendors lay in wait.

Rebo waved them off so as to focus his attention on the small structure around which the important activity was centered. The domed roof had been white once but was currently in need of paint. The dome was supported by six fluted columns and hung with vines that served to screen the interior. And that, judging from appearances, was the location from which the oracle plied his mysterious trade.

Meanwhile, as a joyous couple left the shelter of the cupola and began their journey down the mountain, a pair of attendants urged the runner and the sensitive toward a table and the metal box that rested on top of it. It was getting cooler as the sun started to slip over the horizon, and Norr shivered as gravel crunched beneath her feet.

"Insert your hand in the box," one of the attendants instructed for what might have been the millionth time. "You will feel a pinprick. Once you do, please remove your hand."

There was something ominous about the gray metal box and the circular hole. Rebo frowned. "Are you sure this is necessary?" The attendant nodded wearily. "It is if you want to know whether your children will be healthy. And you do, don't you?"

"*Yes,*" Norr answered firmly. "We do."

Once the sensitive stepped forward and inserted *her* hand into the box, the runner had no choice but to do the same. It felt like shoving his hand into a warm glove. It seemed to shrink around his fingers and held them in place. Then, consistent with the warning they had been given, the machine sampled his blood.

"All right," one of the attendants intoned pompously, "the oracle will see you now. May the gods bring you the news that you desire to hear."

With those words the couple was ushered into the structure, where a woman waited to greet them. She had thick black hair, some of which was swept back over her shoulders, while the rest curved forward and down. Although her face was perfectly symmetrical, and therefore beautiful, her eyes were strangely opaque. The birth defect made her a living symbol of what every couple hoped to avoid.

But, riveting though she was, the oracle was nothing when compared to the ankle-length coat that she wore. It had long sleeves, shimmered as if lit from within, and seemed to be invested with a life of its own. But where was Logos hiding? There were no machines in sight.

The woman opened her mouth, but much to the couple's surprise, it was a male voice that greeted them. The woman's lips moved, but seemed to lag behind the voice, as if repeating what had already been said. That was when

Rebo realized the truth—and nudged Norr. "Logos was built into the coat," he said sotto voce, "the woman is nothing more than a person to hang it on." Norr's eyes grew larger, and she nodded in agreement.

"It's my pleasure to announce that the signs are propitious," the voice continued. "Although one of you has a unique genetic inheritance that won't be passed on to your children, they will be healthy nevertheless."

It wasn't what they had come for, and they weren't a couple, not in the official sense, but Norr felt a sudden rush of happiness. Rebo remained focused on the task at hand. "Is your name Logos?" the runner demanded bluntly. "Because if it is, we were sent to collect you."

There was a moment of silence as the oracle's lips moved soundlessly. Once it resumed the voice was harsh and demanding. "Who sent you? And *why?*"

"*I* sent them," Lysander replied, as his personality rolled in to claim Norr's body.

"Hios?" the voice inquired disbelievingly. "Is that *you?*"

"*Yes,*" the discarnate replied emphatically. "It is. Although I go by a different name now. The time has come for you to return to work."

"I *am* at work," the AI responded tartly. "Thanks to my efforts birth defects are practically a thing of the past on Etu."

"That's just lovely," Lysander commented sardonically, "except for the fact that other planets are not so fortunate. That's why you must return to the work for which you were originally designed. By helping me to reestablish the star gates, you can put *all* of the planets back into contact with each other once again. Knowledge will spread like wildfire, conditions will improve, and the slide toward barbarism will end."

"That's what you said last time," Logos replied cynically.

"But look what happened. You built an empire based on the star gates, used it to enslave billions of people, and became the proximal cause of all the destruction that followed."

"Yes," Lysander admitted sadly. "And *you* were part of the problem. So, work with me and put things right."

Logos processed both the words and their meanings. While satisfying to the extent that his role as a DNA Gate Keeper helped fulfill his inherent need to coordinate a large system, the AI's current function paled in comparison to the significance of the task that the biological had offered him, and that was tempting. Still, one thing bothered him. "Let's say I accepted," the AI temporized. "What assurance would I have that you won't revert to your old ways?"

"That's simple," Lysander responded. "I'm dead. The only way I can communicate with those on the physical plane is through sensitives like this one—and she's about to force me out. The plan is to reestablish the gates, run the network independently of whatever governments may arise, and let the increased interconnectivity have its predictable effects."

Logos could see potential problems, lots of them, but such were his personal priorities that he chose to put all of them aside. That was when an attendant entered. He looked annoyed and was armed with a cudgel. "Your time is up . . . Please exit through the back."

"There is nothing to be concerned about," Logos said reassuringly. "This turned out to be a rather complicated consultation."

Such occurrences were rare but not unknown. The attendant bowed respectfully and withdrew. The oracle stared sightlessly ahead as the AI's voice issued from the collar of her coat. "Camp at the foot of the mountain. I will find you there . . . That will be all."

Rebo didn't like the AI's somewhat imperious tone, or the prospect of adding even more complexity to an already difficult situation, but knew that so long as Norr continued to be tied in with Logos, Lysander, and the Techno Society then he would be, too.

FOURTEEN

The Planet Etu

Only I, and I alone, can look into the future, and see that which awaits.

—The Oracle of Mount Pama

Torches had been lit as the sun descended over the west-ern horizon and spaced along the trail so that those making their way down the mountain could find their way to the encampment below. But the torchlit areas were separated by pools of darkness that made it advisable to watch one's step. It was chilly, and Norr was grateful when Rebo draped his red leather jacket over her shoulders, and wrapped a protective arm around her waist.

Dozens of campfires could be seen on the plain below. They appeared to blink as people walked in front of them and sent gouts of sparks whirling up into the air whenever one of the pilgrims added a piece of wood. Just the sight of them made the sensitive warmer, or maybe it was the feel of the runner's body next to hers; but whatever the reason, she enjoyed the steep decent and was sorry when it was over.

Lee and Hoggles stood waiting at the foot of the trail. Other reunions were taking place all around them as the foursome came back together. "What was it like?" the boy wanted to know. "And where's Logos? You found him, didn't you?"

Conscious of the fact that there were people all around them, some of whom were well within earshot, Rebo herded his companions off to one side before inviting Norr to give her report. Hoggles shook his head in amazement once she finished. "Logos is a machine? That you can wear like a coat? It's hard to believe."

"Where is he?" Lee demanded excitedly. "I want to wear him!"

"We don't know," Rebo replied evenly. "He told us to camp at the bottom of the mountain . . . Which makes sense since it's dark. Maybe he'll show up, but we have a ship to catch, so be ready to leave first thing in the morning. Coat or no coat."

Norr understood the need to keep moving—but hoped it wouldn't be necessary to leave the AI behind. That was why the sensitive kept a sharp eye out for strangers as she and her companions laid claim to a vacant campsite, purchased a bundle of wood, and lit a fire. But none of the people who swirled around them showed the least bit of interest in the foursome, so the sensitive, the heavy, and the boy slid into their makeshift sleeping bags while Rebo kept watch.

Even though Norr was fully dressed, and sandwiched between a pair of wool blankets, she felt cold. But the sensitive was so tired that she fell asleep anyway. She dreamed of being warm, dreams that were so real that when Lee woke her four hours later, an act of will was required to crawl out of her toasty sleeping bag. And it was then, after the sensitive was up on her feet, that she turned back toward her bed and saw the quilt that had been laid on top of her sleeping bag. "Lee . . . Where did the quilt come from?"

The boy, who had just completed a two-hour watch, was looking forward to slipping between his own blankets. He turned to look at her sleeping bag. "Quilt? What quilt? That looks like a coat to me."

Norr looked down to discover that what *had* been a quilt had mysteriously transformed itself into a coat. And a rather disreputable-looking garment at that. The sensitive felt something cold trickle into the pit of her stomach as she knelt next to the mysterious object. "You had the watch, Lee . . . Who left it?"

The boy shrugged apologetically. "I don't know. I took a trip to one of the latrines about an hour ago . . . Maybe someone left it there while I was gone."

"You should have woken someone," the sensitive replied sternly. "You know the rules."

Lee hung his head. "Everyone was tired. I was back in a matter of minutes."

Norr ran her fingers over the coat before picking it up. The garment was warm to the touch and surprisingly light. "I know your intentions were good, they always are, but a trained assassin could slit our throats in a matter of seconds. Remember that."

"I will," Lee promised contritely. Then, after a short pause, his head came back up. "Wait a minute . . . Is that it? Is that Logos?"

The sensitive had slipped her arms into the generously proportioned sleeves by then—and allowed the coat to set-tle onto her shoulders. "Yes," the AI replied emphatically, "*it is*. I was reactivated the moment the sensitive put me on. Quickly now . . . It's time to leave! I sent my previous host home—and hundreds of people are waiting to see her. Once, the sun comes up it will be obvious that she's missing! Everyone will be suspect, including you. I strongly recommend that you get well clear of the area before the madness begins."

The voice seemed to issue from the vicinity of the coat's collar, and Norr found the AI's rather authoritarian personality to be somewhat reminiscent of Lysander's. That was when the sensitive realized that rather than deal with just *one* disembodied personality, she would have to cope with *two*, both of whom were somewhat obnoxious. But the AI was correct, or so it seemed to Norr, who hurried to wake her companions. It took five minutes to convince them that Logos was resident in what appeared to be a ratty overcoat, twenty minutes to pack their gear, and another five to melt into the night. Then, with Mount Pama at their backs, the group set out for the spaceport at Overa.

A stable hand rousted Pala an hour before dawn, gave her a bowl of the same slops that he fed to the farmer's angens, and offered the heavy a gunar in return for sex. One of his friends had been part of a group that had gang-raped a heavy and never stopped talking about how much fun it was.

Pala refused, the stable hand kicked the bowl out of her hands by way of punishment, and stomped out of the barn. Disgusting though the slops were the variant knew that she would need the food in order to survive and took the only action she could. The nearly hairless prots were slightly larger than the average dog and made grunting noises as the variant forced them to make room in front of the trough. Then, having knelt in front of the long narrow box, the heavy scooped double handfuls of warm semiliquid mush into her mouth. The taste didn't matter. The important thing was to eat her fill, because Pala knew that once Kane climbed up into the sling-saddle, she would need every ounce of strength she could muster just to get through the day.

Fifteen minutes later there was a stir as a door opened, voices were heard, and Kane entered the barn. His blond hair was damp from a shower, his clothes were as clean as the farmer's wife could make them, and his stomach was full of hearty food. Pala had finished eating by then and stood at something akin to attention as the operative circled her. He wrinkled his nose. "You stink," the norm observed critically, "but we'll be crossing some rivers later in the day, and that should be sufficient to wash some of the filth off you. Now, kneel, so I can saddle you."

Pala wanted to grab the norm and break him in half. But he wore two guns, both of which were easily accessible, and there was the farmer to consider. Even if she managed to kill Kane, the rest of the norms would fetch weapons and quickly put her down.

The heavy knelt, waited while the operative fastened half a dozen straps in place, and felt the additional pull as the saddle took the norm's weight. "All right," Kane said as the variant came to her feet. "Let's hit the road. I hope to reach Mount Pama by noon."

The heavy exited the barn, slogged through the mix of mud and manure that surrounded it, and started to walk. Then, with Kane's spurs already nipping at her hips, Pala began to jog. It wasn't long before the twosome passed the farmer. He offered a cheerful wave, but having no further need for the local or his hospitality, Kane saw no reason to respond. Based on anecdotal evidence accumulated along the way, it appeared that the sensitive and her companions had departed the highway that would have taken them to Overa for the less-traveled route that swung past Mount Pama. Not that it made much difference to the technologist so long as he caught up with them.

Time passed, the sun arced across the sky, and it was mid-afternoon by the time the exhausted heavy lumbered out onto the plain that surrounded the cone-shaped mountain. The first thing Kane noticed was the fact that hundreds of people were milling around the tent city at the bottom of the mountain. Some were locked into animated conversations, while others sobbed hysterically, as they clung to each for support. Meanwhile dozens of downcast couples had packed their belongings and were streaming away.

It took interviews with a number of people in order to sort out what had taken place. It seemed that an oracle inhabited the top of Mount Pama, or had until the night before, when she mysteriously disappeared. Prior to that the blind woman had been known far and wide for her ability to predict whether a prospective couple would produce healthy children.

Kane only half listened to the accounts at first, fearful that he might miss his quarry in the mass of people around him, but paid more attention when it became clear that the predictions issued by the missing oracle were considered to be infallible. A level of reliability that could only be ascribed to a machine. And once *that* thought crossed his mind, it wasn't long before the Techno Society operative remembered Lysander's interest in the AI called Logos and knew what had taken place. Either by choice or happenstance, the computer had washed up on the planet Etu hundreds of years before and established itself as an oracle. Lysander had somehow gotten wind of that, guided the sensitive to Mount Pama, and convinced her to steal the AI.

But, unlike the crowd that surrounded him, Kane knew, or thought he knew, where the thieves were headed. So, assuming that he could catch up with the fugitives, the operative could retrieve the gate seed *and* Logos. That would not only restore his reputation within the Techno Society—but might vault him onto the council as well.

Tired though the operative was, he felt reenergized as he steered Pala over to the stockade where two dozen slaves were waiting to be sold. It took less than twenty minutes to purchase a second heavy, switch the saddle to his broad back, and climb aboard. Then, with Pala on a twenty-foot lead, Kane spurred his new mount toward the southwest. By switching back and forth between the two slaves, and traveling fifteen out of every twenty hours a day, the operative thought he could catch up. Then, with Norr in his sights, the rest would be easy.

It had taken three days of hard walking to reach Overa. Rather than having been built, the city had been carved out of a two-hundred-foot-high cliff and looked out over a vast expanse of glittering water. The approaches to the city were guarded, but none of the lightly armored soldiers saw any reason to stop the man with the homely wife, young son, and heavily burdened slave.

So, having paid the so-called gate fee and been allowed to round the headland that gave access to the Bay of Overa, the travelers followed a heavily trafficked road up onto the strip of land that fronted the multitiered cliff dwellings and sloped down to the rocky beach below. It was littered with piles of cordage, fishing nets, and upturned boats.

Wings could be seen out beyond the surf, circling above multicolored boats before they dived down into the water and disappeared for up to three minutes at a time before bursting up out of the sea with fish wriggling on their barbed spears. The variants looked as if they were free, but when Rebo, Norr, Lee, and Hoggles paused to buy water from one of the beach stalls, they soon learned differently. Though not fettered by the sort of chains Hoggles wore, the airborne variants were far from free. Each wing knew that if he or she were to turn and fly away, a parent, sibling, or child would be put to death. A cruel but effective system of restraints that kept all but the most uncaring variants under control.

Farther out, almost invisible from shore, something else could be seen. It was huge, at least half a mile across, and clearly made of metal because nothing else would have been strong enough to withstand countless storms. Rebo thought he knew what the structure was for, and the vendor confirmed it. Assuming that the spaceship it served was still alive, and if weather conditions allowed, an atmosphere-scarred shuttle would land on the platform the following day. That was when those crazy enough, or desperate enough, could go aboard. Others, those who were content to remain on Etu, would watch from the beach. They would buy things, the beach vendors would enjoy a very profitable day, and life would subsequently return to normal.

Rebo took a sip of water and looked down along the beach. Most of the fishing boats were out at sea during that time of day, each served by one or more wings, but a few remained ashore. Most were painted primary colors and rested on the rollers that were used to launch and retrieve them. But a few had seen better days, and having been turned upside down, served as seats for fisherfolk who were too old or too crippled to go to sea. They lounged in the sun, as the seabirds wheeled above, and the tides came and went.

Rebo found the scene to be hauntingly familiar and was

reminded of his childhood on Thara. Was his mother alive? And how had the village fared? Suddenly, more than ever, the runner wanted to go home.

Kane was halfway across a river when the heavies at-tacked him. At the time, he was mounted on Bruno, who, having agreed to a plan conceived by Pala, pretended to trip. The water was only about three feet deep at that point, but the current was swift, and water boiled around a boulder to his left. He fell facedown, hands out to protect himself, and took the norm with him.

Because the bottom of the swiftly flowing tributary was treacherous, Kane took the situation at face value, until the second variant approached him from behind. She wrapped a steely arm around his throat and began to tighten her grip. Not only was it too late to go for one of the guns by that time, but both of the operative's hands were busy trying to break Pala's hold, even as his lungs fought for air. But the heavy was stronger than he was, a *lot* stronger, and the operative had already begun to lose consciousness when the river came to his rescue. Because even as the life-and-death struggle continued the combatants were swept downstream, and into a clutch of lichen-covered boulders. Bruno hit hard, cracked two of his ribs, and felt the sling-saddle come loose.

Pala saw the collision coming and was forced to release Kane in order to protect herself. She hit with her feet, realized that Bruno was in trouble, and made a grab for the other heavy's harness. Then, propelled by the current, both of the slaves were carried out into the main channel and downriver. Though sorry to let Kane escape, Bruno meant more to her, and Pala had plans for the future. A vast wilderness lay to the east, which, if the rumors could be believed, served as a sanctuary for escaped slaves. Perhaps the two of them could make a home there.

The heavy kicked with her feet, pulled her companion into an eddy, and towed him ashore. Then, lying on a sandy beach, she started to laugh. Bruno had never heard the female laugh before and liked the sound of it. The river chuckled, the variant laughed in spite of the pain that it caused him, and both of them were free.

Hewhosingstosuns *dropped hyper, "saw" the Etu system* wipe itself onto his electronic vision, and gave thanks. Not for himself, since his fate was certain, but for those who rode in his belly. A random collection of biologicals who knew the great ships were dying but gambled their lives and were about to win.

But what about the others? Those waiting on the surface of Etu? Should he take them aboard? Knowing full well that the next jump would probably be his last? Or enter hyperspace alone and find his fate out among the stars?

One aspect of the AI's programming urged him to go on, to serve the creators as long as he possibly could, while a countervailing imperative insisted that he *protect* human lives rather than put them at risk.

However, the very beings he was fretting over had given *Hewhosings* something akin to free will, which meant that while he was subject to the equivalent of desires and preferences, it was his responsibility to make the final decision. But what if his cognitive abilities were starting to fail? What if his electronic brain, like the rest of his body, could no longer be relied upon?

And so it was that even as the spaceship dropped into orbit around Etu, and sent part of itself down to the planet's surface, the intelligence that controlled it struggled to make the most difficult decision it had ever faced. Whether to serve—or take itself off-line.

The oars creaked as four heavies pulled on them, the bright red fishing boat surged forward, and spray flew as the bow broke a white-topped wave. The temperature dropped as the twenty-five-foot-long craft entered the shadow cast by the platform above. Rebo, Norr, Lee, and Hoggles were seated in the boat's stern, just forward of its owner, and aft of the heavily muscled slaves.

Rebo fought to keep his breakfast down as he scanned the steel above. None of the locals he had spoken with were sure why the spaceport had been constructed offshore, although some were of the opinion that the sea had risen over the last few hundred years, indicating that the construct might have been closer to land when it was built.

The structure remained mute as the fisherman steered his boat in toward the rusty seaweed-draped platform that hung a few feet above the surging water. There was an insistent booming sound as waves broke against one of the platform's hollow legs, and the fisherman shouted to make himself heard. "You're lucky! The tide is high! The last time the ship came in we had to throw grappling hooks up onto the landing stage so passengers could pull themselves up. Five of them wound up in the drink, and one drowned."

The runner nodded, felt his stomach heave along with the boat, and fingered the amulet that hung around his neck as the heavies pulled on their oars. Another brightly painted craft, this one loaded with incoming passengers fell away on a wave and surged toward the shore. "Pull!" the fisherman commanded sternly. "Put your backs into it! Or would you like a taste of the lash?"

The variants pulled, the boat slid into position, and Hoggles stood. With feet firmly planted, and seemingly indifferent to the movement of the boat, the heavy lifted Lee up over his head. The boy literally flew through the air, hit the metal grating with a *clang,* and scrambled to collect the packs that began to land all about him.

Norr was next, followed by Rebo, who almost fell but managed to make the transfer unassisted, and Hoggles, who made the whole thing look easy. The fisherman raised a hand as the boat drifted away, waited for an opportunity to turn, and told the oarsmen to "Pull!" as he put the tiller over. It had been a profitable morning—and the norm was happy.

Grateful to have solid metal under his feet, the runner looked up to where flight after flight of rusty stairs switchbacked up into the gloom. Rebo assumed there had been some sort of elevator once, but there was no evidence of any now. "Okay," he said, hoisting a pack onto his back and clutching two more. "Let's get going. The last one to the top gets to cook dinner."

"It won't be me!" Lee shouted joyously, and scampered upward.

"No," the runner said philosophically, as he began the long, torturous climb. "It won't be you."

Gravel flew away from the big angen's hooves as Kane jerked on the reins and brought the animal to a skidding halt. A single sweeping gaze was sufficient to take in the cliff dwellings, the cluttered beach, and the enormous platform that loomed offshore.

The operative swung his right leg up over the bloodstained saddle and jumped to the ground. The angen shook its head and snorted loudly as Kane led the animal over to the nearest food stand. "The ship," the technologist demanded. "When will it land?"

"It already has," the woman replied mildly. "But there's no reason to fret . . . Take a seat. I'll make you some tea, and you can watch it take off."

"You expect it to lift that soon?"

"Yes," the vendor answered cheerfully. "The last of the incoming passengers came ashore a couple of hours ago, and the outgoing passengers should be up on top of the platform by now."

Kane swore. He had no way of knowing if Norr and her companions were among those on the platform, and there was no way to find out. That meant he would have to gamble—even if it meant traveling to Thara for nothing. But the black hats believed the boy was headed for Thara, which meant the man with the guns was headed for Thara, which meant that the sensitive was headed there, too. "I need to get out there before the ship lifts," Kane said desperately. "Do you know anyone who could help?"

"My husband could take you," the woman said warily. "But it would be expensive."

Having been spared by the river, the operative had crawled up onto a rocky beach, only to discover that both of the slaves had escaped. It had been a bad moment, a very bad moment, but one Kane had overcome. A short hike put him back on the road. After that it was a simple matter to set an ambush, wait for a well-mounted rider to pass, and shoot him in the back. Then, having murdered the man's wife as well, the technologist took possession of both angens. The first had already dropped from exhaustion, but the second had proven to be more resilient and stood not five feet away. "Here," the operative said, thrusting the reins into the woman's hands. "The animal is worth at least ten times what your husband would charge. Run! Get him! And a pack filled with provisions as well."

It was a generous offer, so generous that the woman ran full out, with the newly acquired angen trotting along behind her. Kane stepped around to the other side of the counter, where he stuffed half of a meat pie into his mouth and shrugged the pack off his shoulders. Maybe the woman would bring him something decent to eat and maybe she wouldn't. All the operative could do was take everything that wasn't nailed down and hope for the best.

Hewhosingstosuns *was in a quandary. The shuttle was* loaded and ready to lift. And part of him *wanted* to lift, to function, to remain relevant. But another part of him had doubts, serious doubts about his ability to reach Thara, which was why the transport remained where it was.

The passengers meanwhile had nothing to do but strap their belongings to the deck, converse in low voices, and wait for the shuttle to take off. Those who had ridden the great ships before were the least concerned. They knew how arbitrary and uncommunicative the starfaring AIs could be and were relatively relaxed.

Not so the first-timers, however, some of whom felt claustrophobic, and had a tendency to fidget. One couple became *so* disturbed, in fact, that they left the ship. And, as luck would have it, Kane arrived just in time to see the couple exit the shuttle. Two of the fisherman's sons, both burdened with packs, were right behind him. The long, arduous climb had left all three of them out of breath, and their legs felt as if they were made out of lead.

But, just as the operative experienced a sense of jubilation and allowed his pace to slow, *Hewhosings* made the decision he'd been struggling with. Despite doubts regarding his cognitive process, and the multitudinous ailments that plagued his electromechanical body, the AI would make one final trip to Thara.

There was a high-pitched *whine* as both of the shuttle's engines started to spin up, followed by a loud *hiss* as jets of vapor stabbed the surface of the landing pad, and a worrisome *thumping* sound as the main hatch began to close. "Come on!" Kane yelled, as he waved the teenagers forward. "Throw the packs through the door!"

Neither one of the youngsters had ever been that close to a flying machine before and showed every sign of remaining right where they were, until the operative pulled one of his pistols and fired it into the air. "I said move!"

The teenagers ran forward, heaved the packs into the air lock, and were barely clear when Kane rolled in under the steadily descending hatch. The door should have detected the movement and paused, but that particular motion detector had burned out some forty-six standard years earlier and never been replaced. The hatch closed with a *thud*, the hull began to vibrate, and the shuttle's skids left the guano-stained platform a few moments later.

Rebo felt a sense of relief as the ship flew out over the bay, released his grip on the good luck amulet and took Norr's hand. "We made it. We're in the clear."

The sensitive wasn't so sure. Something had changed over the last few minutes, and not for the better. But Norr didn't know what it was, so she smiled and told the runner what he wanted to hear. "Yes, we're in the clear." But the variant didn't believe it—even though she didn't know why.

The trip into space went smoothly, as did the transfer to the larger vessel, and the runner, sensitive, red hat, and heavy wasted little time in claiming a corner of the ship's murky hold for themselves. And, thanks to the experience gained during previous trips, they had set up camp and were already lounging about a tiny fire while many of the other passengers were still getting oriented.

One of them, a man who wore a black bandanna over his hair, had been overjoyed to discover that Norr and her companions *were* on the ship, and, judging from their relaxed demeanor, completely unaware of his presence. So, conscious of the fact that his primary quarry had some very unusual capabilities, the operative went out of his way to ingratiate himself with a group of five merchants. The relationship enabled him to blend his aura with those around him. Then, having hidden himself in plain sight, Kane began the long, careful process of stalking his prey.

Meanwhile, oblivious to the life-and-death drama being played out deep within his body *Hewhosings* executed a stomach-flipping leap into hyperspace, felt the electro-mechanical equivalent of severe pain, and knew that something had gone horribly wrong. The ensuing investigation took less than a minute, was repeated by way of a check, and quickly confirmed. The good news was that the jump into hyperspace had been successful. The bad news was that the last of four redundant phase arrays had finally gone down. Now, without the ability to make repairs, both the ship *and* its passengers were trapped in hyperspace.

Hewhosings processed something akin to a sense of overwhelming shame. It had been wrong to grant himself one more trip, and now, thanks to his selfishness, his passengers were going to die. And that raised an important question . . . Should he tell them? Or remain silent? And let the never-ending journey speak for itself? The answer was obvious, to the AI at least, since *Hewhosings* knew that if he were a biological, he would want to know.

Most of the great ships were extremely taciturn, so no one was more surprised than Rebo when dozens of rarely used speakers came to sudden life. "Greetings. My name is *Hewhosingstosuns*. I have roamed the stars for hundreds of years. During that time it was my privilege to serve millions of beings such as yourselves. But now, having suffered a mechanical malfunction that will make it impossible to exit hyperspace, my years of service have come to an end. While functional, the shuttle lacks a hyperdrive, and is therefore useless. I apologize for the lapse in judgment that led to this shameful situation—and assure you that I will do everything in my power to make your final days as pleasant as possible."

The loud *click* served to punctuate the end of the last sentence and echoed between steel bulkheads. There was silence at first, as dozens of passengers stared at each other in consternation and struggled to absorb what they had just heard.

Rebo, Norr, Lee, and Hoggles were just as stunned as everyone else, and were still trying to deal with what amounted to a death sentence when the people around them uttered a wail of mutual sorrow. The joint declaration of misery was soon punctuated by screams, the sounds of crying, and all manner of commentary, questions, and prayers.

The man who wore the black bandanna over his hair reacted somewhat differently however. Much to the amazement of the merchants seated all around him Kane began to laugh. And not just laugh, but howl as he remembered all the sacrifices he had made, the risks he had taken, all to end up aboard a doomed ship lost in the never land of hyperspace. The situation was funny, stupid, and sad all at once.

Strangely, or perhaps not so strangely, Lee was the first to try and comfort those around him. "Ah well," the boy said philosophically, "all of us have died many deaths. "What's one more? Not that I'm in a hurry to return to the spirit planes, mind you."

"Nor am I," the sensitive replied thoughtfully. "And I'm not ready to give up yet. Hand me that pack . . . Let's see what, if anything, our new friend has to say."

The sensitive had worn Logos a great deal at first, but soon grew tired of the computer's self-centered personality and began to carry the device instead. That effectively silenced the AI, who resented the fact that Norr could turn him off. "Where the hell are we?" Logos demanded, as the variant slipped her arms into raggedy coat sleeves.

"We're aboard a spaceship bound for Thara," the sensitive answered briskly. "But there's a problem."

"Of course there is," Logos replied sarcastically. "I assume that's why you put me on. Or is it about to rain?"

"No," the variant responded patiently, "it isn't going to rain. But you have as much of a stake in the present situation as we do—so you might want to pay attention."

Logos listened as the sensitive outlined what the ship had said. Then, once she was finished, the AI spoke again. The voice originated from *behind* her—and Norr managed to resist the desire to turn and look. "I'm not sure that I understand the nature of your problem," the computer said pompously. "You have one of my gate seeds . . . So use it."

Norr frowned. "I never told you that."

"No," the AI agreed smugly, "you didn't."

"Then how did you know?"

"I knew the same way that you know about your fingers and toes. I can *feel* the gate seeds. All of them."

"Even in hyperspace?"

"Even then," the computer confirmed.

"Excuse me," Rebo interrupted caustically, "but so what?"

"But can you *activate* my gate seed?" the sensitive persisted, still addressing herself to the AI. "We don't know how."

"Yes, of course," the artificial voice replied. "Not only can I activate them, but coordinate them as well. Such is my purpose."

"See?" Norr demanded, as she turned toward Rebo. "Logos can activate the gate seed—and we can use it reach Thara."

"Why Thara?" Logos demanded. "I need to reach Socket."

"Because that's where we're going," Rebo said unsympathetically. "So get used to it."

"What about the others?" Lee inquired, gesturing toward the rest of the hold. "It would be a crime to leave them here."

"If you help them, the secret will be out," Hoggles warned. "Everyone will know about the star gates."

"So? Who cares?" Rebo replied lightly. "It beats the heck out of leaving them here."

"The Techno Society cares," Norr answered wearily, "and once we make use of the seed, they'll hear about it. But Lee is correct . . . Once the gate has been established we'll have to send all the passengers through."

"So, what about power?" the heavy demanded pragmatically.

"It's all around us," the AI responded. "A dedicated source would be best, but most of the ship's systems run off broadcast power, and the gate can feed on that."

"But what if the ship objects?" Lee wanted to know.

"We'll deal with that when and if it comes up," the computer responded irritably. "Go play with something. We'll call you when it's time to leave."

"Let's get organized," Rebo said briskly. "I'll provide security for Lanni and Logos while the two of you go out and spread the word. I suspect that most of our fellow passengers will be rather skeptical to say the least."

"If anyone can sweet-talk them it would be Lee," Hoggles rumbled. "I'll go along to keep him out of trouble."

"Good," the runner agreed. "But let's pack our stuff first. We're going to need it once we reach Thara."

The foursome was packed and ready to leave twenty minutes later. Norr removed the gate seed from her pack while the heavy and the red hat disappeared into the surrounding murk. "All right," the sensitive said, as she held the sphere between the palms of her hands. "What now?"

"You will find that the seed has two dimples," Logos answered. "One located on the top of the globe and one on the bottom. All you have to do is press them at the same time."

"I did that once before," Norr objected. "Nothing happened."

"That's because you were impatient," the AI replied critically. "Now do as you were told."

The variant made a face, pressed an index finger into each dimple, and waited. Nothing happened. "All you have to do is maintain an even pressure," Logos said reassuringly. "Humans tend to be extremely impatient. Once they push a button they expect instantaneous results. A long delay is sufficient to keep all but the most persistent of them at bay."

And sure enough, once sixty seconds had passed, the sensitive felt something give. "Now," the AI continued, "grab hold of both hemispheres and twist them in opposite directions."

Norr obeyed and felt both halves of the globe give. Rebo, who had been watching the process, saw a crack appear as beams of light shot out into the murk. "It's moving!" the sensitive exclaimed, as her hands shook in sympathy with the oscillating gate seed.

"Let go of it," Logos instructed sternly, "or it will hurt you."

Such was the sensation that the variant was happy to release her grip on the object. But, rather than fall to the ship's deck the way she expected it to, the sphere floated in front of her!

"Good," the computer said, as he continued to monitor the situation via dozens of sensors embedded in the front of Norr's coat. "This is where it gets tricky. I will need to relay some messages through Socket in order to establish the gate—and it will take some time to get all of the equipment aligned. Now stand back."

Both Rebo and Norr were quick to back away as the globe began to spin faster and faster. Then, after thirty seconds or so, it disappeared!

Meanwhile, out in the surrounding murk, Kane listened as two of the people he was determined to kill invited both him and his companions to step through a star gate and thereby escape the dying ship! Given all he had gone through to catch up with them, and the artifacts they possessed, the invitation struck the technologist as both ridiculous and sublime.

Once Lee had finished his speech, a chubby merchant shook his head angrily. "Get out of here, kid . . . And take the freak with you. Oh, and put some chains on him. You'll be sorry if you don't."

The response was similar to the one the pair had already received from more than a dozen other people. The whole notion of star gates was more than they could accept. Hoggles frowned, took a step forward, but stopped when Lee grabbed his arm. "Forget it, Bo . . . They made their choice."

The variant nodded reluctantly and took a step backward. Kane saw his opportunity and was quick to seize it. The operative stood and bent to retrieve his pack. "Wait for me! I not only believe you—I volunteer to go first. Anything is better than starving to death on this ship."

Lee stared at the man. He looked familiar, but why?

"Good for you," Hoggles rumbled sincerely. "You won't be sorry."

Lee continued to feel doubts about the man in the black bandanna, but having been unable to place him, kept those concerns to himself as they left the merchants behind. "Let's go back," Hoggles suggested. "It seems as if no one wants to listen, and the gate should be established by now."

Kane managed to carry out a surreptitious check of his weapons and felt a keen sense of anticipation, as he followed the odd-looking pair over to their fire. The boy had yet to recognize him, nor had the heavy, but the sensitive would. That meant he would have to act quickly. The key was to kill the man with the guns, the heavy, and the female in that order. The boy would be easy. Then, with both the gate seed *and* Logos in his possession, he could return to Anafa.

Norr "felt" the technologist's presence before she actually saw him, turned, and opened her mouth to shout a warning. But Kane had already drawn his weapons by then. Lee saw the pistols appear and acted without thinking. The boy hit the operative from behind, heard one of the handguns go off, and felt a moment of nausea as they fell through the star gate together.

Rebo saw the air shimmer as the twosome disappeared and heard Norr shout "No!" as he followed them through.

Kane landed hard, felt the pistol fly out of his right hand, and heard a metallic clatter as it slid away. He scuttled forward, wrapped his fingers around the gun butt, and realized that something had gone awry. Either the gate had been locked onto the wrong destination, or was badly out of phase, because everything about the environment was wrong. Thara had a reputation as a rather pleasant planet but this world had been ravaged by war.

As the operative rolled over onto his back what he saw were banks of darkly roiling clouds punctuated by occasional shafts of orange sunlight and the occasional bolt of lightning. Thunder rolled across the land as drops of blood-warm rain hit his face, and Kane's lungs struggled to process the painfully thin air. The technologist fought to rise, discovered that his body was at least 20 percent heavier than it had been on the ship, and barely made it to his feet. Farther out, in the jagged, bomb-ravaged ruins that surrounded him, a tornado could be seen. The twister wandered through what remained of the once-proud city as if searching for something to kill. The operative might have seen more, but that was the moment when the man with the guns appeared out of nowhere and landed a few feet away.

What happened next was more the result of impulse than planning. Kane grappled with the man, let go of a gun to free up a hand, and grabbed a fistful of jacket. Then, moving as if in slow motion, the operative brought the remaining pistol in from the side. It connected with his opponent's head and drew blood. Rebo staggered, started to black out, and fell.

Lee threw a rock at the blond man, saw it hit, and began to run. Or *tried* to run, since it felt as if his lungs were on fire, and his legs were made of lead. There was a loud *bang* as Kane fired but missed the boy. Lee staggered along a debris-strewn street, wound his way through a maze of passageways, and found himself within the embrace of a U-shaped wall. A hole beckoned, the boy fought his way over a pile of bricks, and went down onto his knees. Then, just as he started to enter the heating duct Lee felt a set of viselike fingers wrap themselves around his ankle. The youth's fingernails clawed at duracrete as Kane dragged him out into the wan sunlight.

For the first time since giving them up Lee wished he had his knives. But they were in his pack back on the ship. The boy sought to turn, and had just managed to do so, when Kane pressed the gun barrel against the center of his forehead. The operative produced what was supposed to be a smile, but looked more like a grimace, and ordered the pistol to fire.

The message had left Kane's brain, and was halfway to his trigger finger, when Rebo beat him to it. The Hogger boomed, the .30-caliber slug blew half of Kane's head away, and sprayed Lee with gore. The youngster screamed, looked at his blood-drenched arms, and started to cry.

Kane felt the bullet nudge the side of his head and tried to object as the physical plane fell away. That was when the operative saw his most recent life pass before his eyes, *felt* the pain he had caused, and tried to scream. But, many years had passed since a *previous* him had given the order to nuke the planet Poxor, so no one was present to witness his anguish.

Meanwhile, Rebo discovered that his head hurt even more now that he had a moment to think about it, returned the weapon to its holster, and trudged over to where Lee lay. It took repeated attempts to help the youngster to his feet, but the third was successful, and the runner took the boy's hand. Hopefully, if they were lucky, the gate was open. If so, they could step through, and return to the ship.

But that was the moment when the runner realized that all of the ruins looked the same, that he had no idea which way to go, and that he was hopelessly lost. Lee, who had started to recover, felt Rebo pause. The reason for the runner's hesitancy was obvious, and the boy had just experienced the first stirrings of panic, when he spotted what could be their salvation. "Look!" the boy said. "Blood! We can follow it back!"

Rebo looked, saw that droplets of blood from the gash on the side of his head led out into the ruins, and realized that Lee was correct. Quickly, lest one of the rain showers wash the red dots away, the runner followed the regularly spaced blobs back to the spot where the empty shell casing marked the point of arrival. The air shimmered where the space-time continuum had been disrupted. "You—first," the runner gasped, and pushed the boy forward.

Rebo experienced a profound sense of gratitude as the youngster disappeared. Then, having achieved his goal, the runner collapsed. He fell into a well of darkness, felt his body start to spin, and waited to die.

FIFTEEN

The Planet Thara

In spite of all the wisdom that has been spoken, or preserved in manuscripts, each soul must search for enlightenment. There is no single path, but rather a multiplicity of ways, some short and some long. Go forth and find your path, help others along the way, and enjoy the journey. For this is life.

—The ascended master Teon,
An admonition to my students

Death isn't so bad after all, *the runner thought to himself,* as he opened his eyes and looked up through lacy fronds into a pale blue sky. Paradise felt deliciously warm, a soft breeze stirred the thick foliage off to his right, and brightly colored insects darted through his vision.

There was a problem, however—and that had to do with the persistent pain associated with the left side of his head. Dead people don't experience pain, or so Rebo assumed, although there was a great deal about the spirit realms that he couldn't remember. But then, as if to assure the runner that he really was in heaven, an angel appeared. She had high cheekbones, a narrow face, and her eyes were filled with concern. "Jak? Can you hear me?"

"Yes," the runner croaked. "Are we dead?"

Norr looked relieved. "No, silly. We're on Thara."

Rebo blinked. "On Thara? But how?"

"You fell through the portal onto the ship. Logos reset the gate for Thara, Bo carried you through, and I put some stitches into your scalp. You'll have a scar—but your hair will cover it. What else would you like to know?"

Rebo pushed himself up onto one elbow. He had been laid out on top of his sleeping bag. Packs were stacked all about. "Where's Lee?"

"Right here," the boy said as he knelt next to the runner. "Thanks to you."

Rebo felt a profound sense of relief. "We made it then . . . How 'bout the rest of the passengers?"

The sensitive looked down at the ground. "Bo made one last attempt to round them up . . . But none were willing to listen."

The runner thought about what it would be like. The strongest passengers would kill weaker ones and take their food. Then, once that was gone, they would start to feed on each other. Not a pleasant way to die.

"So," Rebo said out loud, "the man who was following you is dead. The rest should be easy."

"*Should* be, but won't be," Hoggles said darkly, as he entered the clearing. "Look at this . . . ."

The heavy handed a flyer to Norr, who looked at it and frowned before turning the document around so that the others could see it. "It looks like me!" Lee said in astonishment.

Rebo glanced at the crudely printed sketch, then at the boy. "You look a lot like you did when we were on Ning," the runner observed. "What does the text say? I can't read it from here."

Norr turned the flyer around. "Be on the lookout for this boy . . . Though posing as the reincarnated spirit of Nom

Maa, the youth called Tra Lee is actually little more than an imposter, bent on stealing the throne of CaCanth. All sightings should be reported to the nearest black hat monastery to receive a material as well as spiritual blessing."

"Where did you get that?" the runner wanted to know, his eyes on Hoggles.

"It was tacked to a tree next to the main road," the variant replied.

Rebo shook his head disgustedly. "It looks like the other kid managed to reach Thara before we did, and his supporters are hard at work."

"Which makes sense," Norr added thoughtfully, "since nobody was chasing him."

"Where are we? Does anyone know?" the runner inquired, as he struggled to stand. His head hurt and he felt dizzy.

"I spoke with a farmer," Hoggles replied. "He was on his way to a town called Nomath."

Even though Rebo had left Thara when he was very young, he still remembered the names of the cities that he and Crowley had passed through, and Nomath was one of them. He had obtained a map from the runner's guild on Anafa and the time had come to take a look at it. The norm dispatched Lee to fetch the document while he took a seat on a flat-topped rock and probed his bandage. It hurt. The boy returned, spread the map out on the ground, and pointed at one of the symbols. "Here's Nomath," Lee said, "and look! There's CaCanth!"

The youngster was correct, and it was then, as Rebo eyed the road that connected the two places together, that the reality of the situation struck him. He was home! And there, located in a small bay about a hundred miles east of the holy city of CaCanth, was the village of Lorval. Was his mother still alive? Or buried next to the symbolic resting places that she had established for her dead husband and sons? There was no way to know.

Something of what the runner felt must have registered on his face, or been visible among the colors that shimmered around him, because Norr knelt next to Rebo and placed an arm around his shoulders. "We must be close to the village in which you were born. Very close."

"Yes," the runner agreed. "We are . . . But CaCanth comes first. It's obvious that the black hats are out looking for us, and it wasn't for the completely unexpected manner in which we arrived, would have located us by now. We're safe for the moment—but someone is bound to report us."

"That's true," Lee agreed as he brought a grubby digit down onto the surface of the map, "but *here's* the solution."

Rebo squinted at the map. Part of the symbol was hidden by Lee's grubby finger. It lay a little to the north, in the direction of CaCanth, but east of the main road. "Nocar Rebu? What does that mean?"

"It means the 'Temple Red,' or the 'Red Temple,' in Tilisi."

"It's a red hat monastery," Norr observed. "Perhaps they could help."

"I like it," Rebo replied thoughtfully, as he remembered the well-armed Dib Wa warriors they had encountered on Pooz. "And who knows? Maybe they would supply us with an escort."

And so it was agreed that rather than strike out for Ca-Canth directly—the foursome would head for the Red Temple instead. The problem was how to complete the three-day march without attracting the wrong sort of attention. Norr was the one who came up with the solution *and* the clothing necessary to make it work. "There," the sensitive said, as she tied one of her scarves under Lee's chin. "I had to wear a disguise on Etu. Now it's your turn."

"But I don't *want* to dress like a girl!" the boy objected as he looked down at the hem of his skirt. It was too long for him, but the sensitive solved that problem by rolling the excess fabric up around his waist. When covered by a jacket the bulge made the youth look as though he was significantly overweight. A plus insofar as the disguise was concerned.

"And I didn't enjoy wearing chains," Hoggles put in unsympathetically. "Get over it."

There was a moment of silence followed by an embarrassed smile. At that particular moment it was as if the boy was someone much older. "It seems that even now, after many lifetimes, it is still difficult to focus on that which is truly important. I apologize."

There was no slavery on Thara, which meant that Rebo and Norr could pretend to be husband and wife, while Lee posed as their daughter. Then, in an effort to break up what would otherwise amount to an easily identifiable group, it was agreed that Hoggles would follow a quarter mile behind, thereby creating the impression the variant was alone. That stratagem would still allow the heavy to rush forward should that prove necessary.

The way north proved to be exactly two carts wide, and alternated between stretches of fused rock the ancients had laid down, and sections of poorly maintained dirt road. That particular portion of Thara's surface was not only tropical but relatively flat, which meant that there weren't many hills to deal with. There was plenty of water, however. It fell out of the sky at approximately the same time each afternoon and served to fill not only the native lakes, rivers, and streams but a complex network of ponds, canals, and ditches. The natural result was a road that not only wandered back and forth across the landscape, but crossed innumerable bridges, some of which were quite a bit wider than the current path and suggested that the thoroughfare had been larger at some point.

Most of what the travelers saw came in shades of green, since the frothy-looking trees, spiky undergrowth, and carefully tended fields were all variations of the same color. The exceptions included the brightly colored spirit poles that served to support neatly thatched roofs, clothing hung out to dry, and prayer ribbons that reminded Rebo of his youthful journey to the spaceport.

That had been a long time before, of course, and much of what the younger him had witnessed had been eroded by the passage of time, but some things were as they had been, including the enormous waterwheel that continued to grind tas for the village of Kua, a metal tower so strong that generations of scavengers had been unable to bring it down, and a twenty-foot-tall likeness of Emperor Hios, which though badly dented, still stared out over the land that had once been his.

The younger Rebo had been scared during that first journey, afraid of what might await him, and now these many years later, the grown-up was frightened as well. Not of the physical dangers that might lie in wait, but of what he had or had not become. Because, other than the considerable sum of money on deposit with the guild, the runner had returned to his home planet with none of the things by which most men measured their success. No friends other than those at his side, no home other than the one in his pack, and no family other than a mother who might or might not be alive.

Or was he wrong? The runner examined Norr from the

corner of his eye, tried to imagine a future without her, and found that it was difficult to do. But what did *she* want? A life on Thara? No, that seemed unlikely . . . And what about Lysander, Logos, and the Techno Society? The man with the blond hair was dead—but the danger continued. That wasn't *his* problem, of course, or was it?

A two-wheeled cart rumbled past. A little girl rode the angen's broad back while her father dozed high on a wooden seat. A cloud of dust rose, and the runner held his breath while it settled. The road stretched ahead.

Had Norr been paying attention, she might have picked up on some of Rebo's emotions, but her thoughts were centered on her own problems. Even though the journey would come to an end soon, *her* difficulties wouldn't, not so long as she had the being called Logos stuffed into her pack. Would she proceed alone? Or would Rebo accompany her? And if he did, would that be good or bad? Gradually, without intending to do so, the sensitive had allowed the runner to pass beyond the barriers she had erected to keep other norms at bay. But was such a course wise? In spite of the fact that they had been forced to act like a married couple, and been physically intimate, they remained strangers on certain levels. Perhaps it would be best to go her own way before she became too entangled with Rebo and set herself up for a painful fall.

Prayer ribbons fluttered gaily as the travelers passed between a cluster of neatly kept homes, and Lee fought a battle with himself. Though long and arduous, the journey to Thara had been liberating after all of the years spent within the monastery on Anafa. Now, as each step carried the boy closer to CaCanth and the test that would determine his future, a weight rode the pit of his stomach. What if he took the test and failed? Or, and the second possibility would be worse in some ways, what if he passed the test? And was he thereby sentenced to a life of meditation, deliberation, and probity? But such thoughts were not only selfish, but unworthy of his higher self, which had returned to the physical plane to be of service.

The red hat's thoughts were interrupted as he and his companions rounded a curve and ran into a checkpoint. It consisted of a pole that blocked the road, a black-clad monk, and four equally drab Dib Wa warriors. They had just finished searching a four-wheeled freight wagon. The pole was raised and the conveyance rattled loudly as it got under way.

Rebo's first inclination was to turn and flee, but the runner knew that could be disastrous, so he produced a determined smile as the monk crossed the road to intercept them. The black hat had a broad forehead, a long nose, and a pair of bright, inquisitive eyes. When he spoke it was with a Tharian accent. "Good afternoon . . . And where might the three of you be headed?"

In spite of the fact that Rebo's accent had all but disappeared during the years he'd been gone, the runner could bring it back when he chose to do so. "To attend my nephew's wedding, holy one."

"I see," the monk replied noncommittally, as he circled the travelers. "And where will the blessed event take place?"

"In Lorval," the runner replied, giving the name of his native village.

"Ah," the black hat said having come full circle. "So your nephew is a farmer?"

"No, holy one," Rebo answered humbly. "The land around Lorval is far too rocky to farm. My nephew makes his living from the sea."

It was not only a *good* answer, but the *correct* answer, and the monk was about to let the family pass when the girl caught his eye. Her face looked familiar, but why? Curious, and with no other travelers to attend to at the moment, the black hat chose to approach her. Lee felt his stomach perform a somersault as the man reached out to tug at the scarf. The knot came loose and the fabric fell away. "Well," the monk said smugly. "What have we here? A girl? Or a boy? And not just *any* boy, but one who bears a strong resemblance to the red hat imposter."

The Hogger was in Rebo's pack, but the Crosser was available, and the runner went for it. The Dib Wa warriors were armed with long double-barreled flintlock pistols, but the weapons were difficult to draw, and the semiautomatic handgun barked twice. Two of the soldiers fell, but Rebo knew the others would have time to bring their weapons into play, or would have if it hadn't been for Norr. For rather than simply stand there, as the warriors had assumed that she would, the female produced a strange-looking blade. It made a sizzling sound as it passed through the air and sank into flesh. One of the surviving black hats screamed while the other had the good sense to drop his pistol and back away. The monk did likewise.

Rebo raised the Crosser as if to fire, but Lee grabbed his arm. "No! Let them go."

"They'll bring more black hats down on us."

"It would happen anyway," Lee said philosophically. "Besides, it's one thing to kill in self-defense, and another to shoot an unarmed man."

Rebo wasn't so sure, but knew it would be a waste of time to trade words with the boy and waggled the pistol instead. "You heard Nom Maa . . . This is your lucky day. Run while you still can."

The black hats turned and ran. Lee took a moment to

watch them go before turning to his protector. "My name continues to be Tra Lee until such time as I prove otherwise."

"Sure," the runner replied, as Hoggles arrived on the scene. "Whatever you say."

"Come on," Norr said, as she eyed the road ahead. "It will take at least twelve hours to reach the temple. More if we take back roads. We'd better get moving."

Norr's words made sense, but the group soon discovered that there *weren't* any back roads, just a tangle of footpaths that led from field to field, home to home, and village to village. And without a map, or signs to guide them, the travelers soon lost their way.

That was when Lee sauntered up to what he assured his companions was a red hat house, rang the ornamental bell that hung out front, and spoke with the wizened little woman who appeared in the cloth-hung doorway. Then, once the woman had agreed to help, a child was dispatched to fetch her grown son. He arrived about ten minutes later. His baggy trousers were still wet from his work in the family's tas paddy. A rapid-fire exchange of Tilisi ensued. Finally, his questions having been answered, the farmer bowed to Rebo, Norr, and Hoggles. The next words were in standard. "My name is Twi. Come . . . I will take you to the Nocar Rebu (Red Temple), but we must hurry, or the black hats will cut us off."

The local took off at a ground-eating jog, which left the off-worlders with little choice but to do likewise. Though he was in good shape after weeks of arduous travel, Rebo's head continued to hurt, and the pounding did nothing to lessen the pain. Still, there was some satisfaction to be found in the fact that Twi's knowledge of the countryside would not only cut hours off the journey, but help ensure their safety. Because, like so much of Thara's surface, the area they were traveling through had long been divided into a patch-work quilt of black-hat- and red-hat-dominated fiefdoms.

The locals lived in peace most of the time, but there had been an increasing amount of friction as the time of choosing drew near. Especially since word had filtered out of Ca-Canth that, while the black hat boy had arrived weeks earlier, and continued to prepare for his test, the red hat equivalent had yet to appear.

A miserable state of affairs from a red hat point of view, but one that the black hats took considerable pleasure in, especially since the lack of a qualified candidate would provide their sect with an effortless victory. That was why the farmer was careful to lead his charges *around* certain villages—and straight through those he knew to be friendly.

Finally, after only two short breaks, and with darkness settling all around them, the fugitives turned onto the path that led up a statue-flanked path to the Red Temple. Iron oxide had been mixed into the plaster that covered the structure's gently curved dome, and it appeared to glow as the last rays of the quickly setting sun caressed it.

But no sooner had the travelers spotted the temple than they were spotted in return. A Dib Wa officer appeared up ahead and shadowlike warriors detached themselves from the surrounding gloom. Twenty minutes later Lee was deep inside the Nocar Rebu standing before the local abbot. The whitewashed room was bare except for a bas-relief likeness of Teon that occupied most of one wall, the incense burner that crouched in one corner, and the mat on which the elderly monk sat. No less than three pretenders had arrived on Thara over the last seven months—so the holy man was somewhat skeptical at first. However, unlike those who had arrived before him, *this* boy knew every single one of the code phrases that had been received two years earlier.

Upon hearing the last of them it was the abbot who rose, came forward, and knelt even as tears of joy ran down his cheeks. "Welcome to Thara, Excellency. We are truly blessed."

Lee smiled and bent to assist the old man. "Yes, we are, because life provides us with the opportunity to grow. I need to reach CaCanth, and the black hats are determined to stop me. Will you help?"

When the sun rose the next morning and bathed the countryside in golden light, the abbot's answer was plain to see. A force of a hundred heavily armed Dib Wa warriors stood waiting as Lee and his companions arrived to inspect them. They were backed by thirty red hat monks equipped with wooden staves, and roughly the same number of farmers armed with shovels, hoes, and axes. It was a veritable army by local standards and Lee was grateful. He told the abbot as much, and when asked for a blessing, gave the same one that *any* other member of the order could have bestowed. "May the great Teon watch over and guide you to the truth within."

Then, with a vanguard of warriors leading the way, the entire force set out for CaCanth. Things went well at first, and the miles seemed to melt away as the column snaked through a succession of small villages. But not all of them were friendly, as evidenced by the hostile stares and obscene gestures directed at the travelers.

Of more concern, however, were the reports that civilian scouts brought back. The reports went straight to Lee who, in spite of his age, was assumed to be none other than the great Nom Maa. Eventually, after repeated efforts to realign the command structure had failed, the boy effected what amounted to a compromise by insisting that both the senior

Dib Wa *and* his traveling companions be included when the scouts came in.

The most recent report, which had been delivered by a long-legged girl with dark eyes, was especially worrisome. It seemed that before the red hat procession could start up the road that led to the holy city of CaCanth, it would first be necessary to cross the bridge at a place called Noko Ree, where a large group of black hats had begun to gather.

"Can we circumvent the bridge?" Lee inquired hopefully. "I would like to avoid bloodshed if possible."

"No, Excellency," the girl replied. "The ancients built the bridge so they could cross high above the Ree Ree River, which passes hundreds of feet below. It would take weeks to go around."

But Lee didn't *have* weeks, not if he wanted to arrive in time to take the test. "So," the boy said, as he turned to his advisors. "What do you think?"

Rebo was about to tell Lee that he should go for it but Norr spoke first. Except that it wasn't Norr, not really, since the voice clearly belonged to Lysander. "There's more," the discarnate proclaimed. "Something the girl didn't see."

The Dib Wa officer and the scout looked understandably surprised as a distinctly male voice issued from Norr's mouth. Rebo had heard the sound before, didn't want to hear it again, and shook his head in disgust. "Wonderful . . . Just what we needed. Citizen star gate."

"I don't remember you objecting to star gates when your life was at stake," Lysander observed tartly. "Now, where was I? Oh, yes, the simulacrum."

Hoggles frowned. "The simu what?"

"A simulacrum is an image of something," the scientist explained patiently. "In this case the image resembles the personage once known as Teon. Except that this particular likeness can move around."

"So it's a metal man," Lee put in. "Like the ones the Techno Society has."

"Yes, and no," Lysander replied. "Yes, in that the simulacrum is a machine, but no, because it lacks the ability to make decisions for itself."

"The black hats possess such a thing," the Dib Wa officer confirmed. "A machine that *looks* like Teon—but is worn like a suit of armor. They keep it in the temple of Wat. The monks believe that the ancients built the device for use in processionals and festivals. It doesn't work though—so who cares?"

"*You* do," the discarnate insisted, "or you should, because the black hats hired a sensitive. A person who, though ignorant of mechanical things himself, channeled a being who has the requisite knowledge."

"Perfect," Rebo said sarcastically. "Just what we need. Is this simulacrum armed?"

"No," the scientist answered. "Not to my knowledge. But it's *big,* larger than a heavy, and that's dangerous enough. That's why I came . . . There's no point in proceeding farther. I recommend that you turn back."

"Because of the danger?" the runner inquired cynically. "Or because you want Lanni to transport Logos to Socket?"

"Because of *both,*" the discarnate answered honestly. "If my daughter were to be injured or killed, who would reunite Logos with the equipment necessary to reestablish the gates?"

"I know *I* wouldn't," Rebo confirmed sourly. "But Lanni can decide for herself. So go back to wherever you stay when you aren't bothering us and do whatever you do."

There was a slight hesitation, as if Lysander was considering what had been said, followed by a distinct change in Norr's demeanor as her chin fell, her shoulders slumped, and her head came back up. The locals looked on in wonder as the sensitive's eyes blinked, and her normal voice was restored. "Logos can wait. We have a boy to deliver."

Rebo was surprised to discover that he had been holding his breath. Lee grinned, and Hoggles put an enormous hand on his shoulder. "The Divine Wind is not a boy," the Dib Wa officer observed mildly, "but we are in agreement . . . The processional will continue."

As the procession continued to wend its way through the verdant countryside, word of its purpose spread like wildfire. As that occurred the column started to grow. Some people came because they were red hats, others came in hopes of obtaining a special blessing from Nom Maa, and still others came because they didn't want to miss the clash when red encountered black at Noko Ree.

But whatever their intentions, hopes, and desires, come they did until what had begun as a short, military-style formation, had grown into a column that was at least a mile long. Finally, by the time Lee called a halt, Rebo estimated that the processional included at least two thousand people. The number was so large that the monks, who had originally been sent along to support the Dib Wa, were forced to fill in as both policeman and healers as their engorged flock proceeded to squabble over campsites, give birth to babies, and die of natural causes.

Lee was stunned by the size of the crowd and watched from the top of a rise as a gentle rain began to fall, and hundreds of fires served to punctuate the gloom. He wasn't aware of Norr's presence until she hung a coat over his shoulders and looked out over field. "You must be very proud."

"No," Lee replied somberly. "I'm very, very, frightened. They believe in me . . . What if they're wrong?"

"But they *aren't* wrong," Norr replied confidently. "The monks on Anafa were correct. You were born for this."

"Maybe," the boy allowed uncertainly. "What about you? What were *you* born for?"

Norr looked up toward the sky only to discover that clouds blocked the stars. "I don't know," the sensitive replied softly. "Perhaps time will tell."

The cold, gray light of dawn arrived slowly, as if reluctant to begin a new day. Lee stood on the same rise he had the night before as his followers added fuel to their campfires, made tea, and exchanged ritual greetings. The faithful were in high spirits, but he was nervous, *very* nervous, knowing that the abandoned village of Noko Ree and a large force of black hats lay only a few miles ahead. Efforts had been made to provoke them during the night but without success. The bridge across the Ree Ree River was a natural choke point, and the black hat officers knew it. After all, why come out and battle the enemy on the plain if they could force them to attack what amounted to a well-defended funnel?

The boy felt sick to his stomach as he imagined what was to come. Many people would be injured, maimed, and killed, all in the name of Teon—a man who taught nonviolence and peace. And yet, the same Teon had said, ". . . To witness evil, yet raise no hand against it, is to perpetrate an even greater crime." And Lee was convinced that much of the dark sect's leadership was intent on the acquisition of power rather than the furtherance of Teon's teachings.

But was his perception correct? Or was he about to become the unwitting tool of a hierarchy that had raised him to believe that *they* were superior?

"It's tough to be a leader," Rebo observed, as he arrived at the boy's side. "That's why I strive to avoid it. Here, Bo sent this over."

Steam rose from the mug of hot tea as Lee wrapped his fingers around it. "Thank you . . . And yes, it is."

There was a moment of silence during which Lee took a sip of the scalding liquid. "Jak . . ."

"Yes?"

"Thank you."

Rebo smiled. "You're welcome."

"And Jak . . ."

"Yes?"

"I'm going to need my knives."

The runner removed a small bundle from under his right arm. "Here they are."

Lee looked up at his protector. "So you knew what I would decide to do?"

Rebo nodded solemnly. "Yes. I knew."

Though not especially amazing by ancient standards, the steel-arch bridge over the Ree Ree River was not only regarded as one of the twelve wonders of Thara, but was critical to commerce, and therefore guarded both day and night lest the voracious metal scavengers attack and destroy it. But the relatively small group of guards had been easily swept aside by a force of three hundred black-clad Dib Wa warriors under the leadership of an up-and-coming officer named Bitu Neor.

Now, as the insistent sun acted to burn the early-morning mist away, the soldier stood atop the southern abutment and stared through the brass telescope that had been presented to him by his superiors in recognition of his success in battling local bandits. What Neor saw surprised him. Rather than the massed rabble the officer expected to confront it appeared as though the red hats knew what they were doing. The leading element of the column consisted of about a hundred Dib Wa warriors, backed by ranks of stave-wielding monks, and a large number of hardy-looking farmers. The rabble, which was to say the noncombatants, were farther back. But there were lots of them, and now that they were in motion, the mob would be hard to stop. They had passed through Noko Ree by that time—and were a quarter mile from the bridge.

Which brought Neor back to the purpose of the impending conflict, which was to deny the red hat pretender access to CaCanth and thereby ensure that the *real* Nom Maa could ascend the throne. Surprisingly, from the Dib Wa's perspective at least, it appeared that the pretender had chosen to lead his followers from the front. He was mounted on a brutish-looking heavy who was armed with a gigantic war hammer. The pair of them marched only five ranks back and were flanked by a norm and a female sensitive. Bodyguards perhaps? Well, it would make very little difference, since all of them were going to wind up in unmarked graves. A boon to the plants that would sink roots into their skulls and the worms which would consume their flesh. The thought pleased Neor, who smiled as he lowered himself down to the ground.

Lee felt his heart beat in time with each step that the heavy took. Because he was riding high on the variant's back his followers could see him. Of course that meant the enemy could see him, too, something that troubled Rebo, but couldn't be avoided. Because if Lee was going to precipitate a battle, then he felt obliged to participate in it and take the same chances that everyone else did.

The position high atop Hoggles's back meant that the

boy had an excellent view, one that allowed him to see not only the rust-encrusted bridge, but the rush of black-clad warriors and the mechanical monster that followed along behind. The simulacrum was at least two feet taller than the heavy and, like most images of the ascended being, had six fully articulated arms. Each arm terminated in a hand, and each hand clutched a weapon. Even though the youth had been expecting to see it, the reality of what confronted him was worse than he had imagined, and he wasn't the only person who felt that way.

Upon spotting the simulacrum, the front row of red hats paused, the next rank collided with them, and that was the moment when Bitu Neor ordered his forces to attack. And, had it not been for the fact that they were being pushed forward from behind, the very sight of the mechanical Teon might have been sufficient to turn the red warriors. Partly because the simulacrum was so imposing, but mostly because the machine's presence conveyed the impression that the ascended master had chosen to ally himself with the black hats and sought to destroy their opponents.

Lee saw their hesitancy, understood the moment for what it was, and stood in the homemade stirrups. The voice that had once been high and shrill was deeper now. "Follow me!" the boy shouted, and the very sight of the being they believed to be the reincarnation of Nom Maa put heart into the assembled red hats. A cheer went up as Hoggles charged the enemy. Up ahead, perhaps fifty yards away, the simulacrum could be seen, the sun rippling across its gold alloy skin as it lurched forward.

Metal flashed as swords came into play, wooden staves clattered as they met, and the variant's war hammer made a dull *thumping* sound as it made contact with enemy heads. People on both sides screamed as they went down, cheers went up as one sect or the other gained a few feet of hotly contested ground, and the steady *boom* of the drums made for a predictable counterpoint to the more erratic *pop, pop, pop* of gunfire and a throaty *boom!* as a homemade bomb went off and red hats were hurled in every direction.

Lee had become a prime target by then, as was Hoggles. A hailstorm of bullets, arrows, and rocks came their way. The variant swore as an arrow penetrated his left shoulder, and staggered under the impact of two musket balls, but kept on going. Rebo had assigned himself the task of covering the heavy's left flank, while Norr had responsibility for the right, and two burly monks were protecting the variant's back.

Having fought off half a dozen black-clad Dib Wa, the runner had just slammed a fresh magazine into the Crosser when a *new* threat emerged. The black-clad mob parted long enough to let a team of four men through. They carried what amounted to a twelve-foot-long battering ram and hoped to attack Hoggles with it.

Rebo shot the lead men. They fell, the others tripped on them, and went down as well. Both rose, and were attempting to draw their swords, when the heavy took two steps forward, The already bloodied hammer fell, then fell again, as the variant put them down.

Meanwhile, off to the right, Norr parried a blow from a pike before pulling the vibro blade from its wooden sheath and pushing the thumb switch. The weapon hummed as it sliced through a wooden staff and sank into the skull beyond. Lee saw the black hats fall back, waved his followers forward, and heard them cheer as they set foot on the bridge deck.

Seeing that, and realizing that the red hats had started to gain the upper hand, Bitu Neor sent his reserves forward. They were civilians mostly, armed with little more than farm implements but led by fanatical monks. The officer hoped that they would add weight to a counterattack and help turn the red tide.

Norr *felt* the newest assault rather than saw it and fought to block out at least some of the pain, fear, and hatred that swirled around her. That was when the simulacrum and the heavy collided. Lee was forced to duck as two of the machine's six hands swung swords at him, even as the rest grappled with Hoggles, and sought to get a grip on the giant. The machine was taller, and heavier, but slower than the variant was.

Lee took advantage of the Teon's clumsy movements to free himself from the saddle. He scrambled up over Hoggles's right shoulder, nearly lost his balance, and threw himself onto the simulacrum's head. The unintended but nonetheless beneficial result of the youth's attack was to blind the behemoth, which let go of both swords in an attempt to remove the boy.

A communal wail went up as the red hats saw the machine grab Tra Lee, lift the youth up, and prepare to throw him down. That was when all sorts of things began to happen. Steel flashed as Lee used one of his knives to stab at the monster's face, there was a loud report as Rebo fired the Hogger into the simulacrum's torso, and sparks flew as Norr cut into one of the machine's legs. Lee's assault left the Teon half-blind, while Rebo's bullet nicked the sensitive inside the machine, and Norr's blade severed two critical cables. The results were spectacular.

The machine was in the process of squeezing the life out of Lee's body when the simulacrum stumbled, and the boy was forced to hang on as the golden machine began to topple. Screams were heard, two of the black hat soldiers were crushed as the likeness collapsed on top of them, and the boy rolled free.

And then, as if to confirm the red hat victory, a breeze

came out of nowhere. The sky grew momentarily dark, rain began to fall, and the bridge deck ran red with diluted blood. "It's the Divine Wind!" a monk shouted, and the faithful surged forward.

Bitu Neor ordered his troops to hold, and they tried, but were literally trampled to death by the scarlet-clad mob. The road to CaCanth was clear.

Three days had passed since the battle at the bridge. Once across, and determined to complete their journey before black hat reinforcements could arrive, the red hats surged ahead. Those who could walk did so. Those who couldn't were carried. Fearing that they might encounter some sort of ambush, Lee urged his followers to form ranks, but it was difficult to convince them of the need, and his efforts came to naught.

But even though the strictures against sectarian violence were often ignored out in the countryside, they were scrupulously observed within the vicinity of CaCanth and had been for thousands of years. Because of that there were no further attempts to stop Lee, and there was little that the black hat hierarchy could do but stand on their various balconies and fume as the red hat candidate and his rabble passed between gates that hadn't been closed in centuries.

The holy city of CaCanth was huge. Though little more than a remote settlement some two thousand years before, it was widely believed to be the place where Teon's last incarnation had begun, a fact that made it symbolically significant. And, back during the machine ages, when people could travel to the civilized planets by ship or star gate, millions made the pilgrimage to Thara, and the city had been enlarged to accommodate them. And, since *both* sects had influenced construction, the result was a vast layering of domes, towers, gates, balconies, walls, halls, gardens, vaults, crypts, walkways, aqueducts, stables, and now-antiquated landing platforms.

The city had been described as both beautiful *and* ugly, depending on the eye of the beholder, but one thing was for sure: It was complex. In fact, it was said that many monks lived entire lifetimes within the sturdy walls without having the opportunity or reason to visit all of the city's many rooms, chambers, and halls. Which was why a guide was assigned to strangers like Lee, Rebo, Norr, and Hoggles. The nun led them from their quarters through a maze of busy passageways and into the Hall of Deliberation, which was an enormous room boasting a vaulted ceiling, walls that were hung with intricately woven tapestries, and marble floors so glossy it was possible to see one's reflection in them.

Lee had chosen to wear a green, rather than red robe, just as Nom Maa had hundreds of years before. Regardless of which side they were on, none of the monks could openly criticize such an obvious call for unity. But was the act sincere? Or a cynical attempt to influence the council? *That* was open to interpretation, and squabbles broke out all over the room.

There were fifty rows of low bench-style seats, which had it not been for the back support they provided, would have been little different from sitting on the floor. There were cushions, however, which Rebo welcomed, although many monks tossed them aside. Thanks to their official capacity as Lee's bodyguards, his companions had not only been allowed to keep their weapons but given seats in the very front row. The heavy, who was still recovering from multiple wounds, sat with one leg resting on a footstool.

And there, on the opposite side of the aisle, was the flesh-and-blood version of the black hat teenager pictured in the drawing that Lee had been shown in the temple on Ning. In fact, now that Lee could see what Yanak actually looked like, he felt a new sense of respect for the artist who had so ably captured the other youth's thick brows, brooding eyes, and slightly petulant mouth.

Meanwhile, others had noticed the extent to which the boys resembled each other and the buzz went up a notch as a variety of theories were advanced. Some believed that the boys were related by blood, others suggested some sort of spiritual connection, while a third group believed the similarity was little more than a coincidence.

Lee bowed, Yanak rose to do likewise, and the tension in the hall increased. There was a great deal at stake because if Yanak and his sect were to take power, the black hat emphasis on intellectual concerns would percolate down through the religion to color everything from the sermons that local monks gave to the way that altars were configured. And, if the spiritual approach favored by the red hats were to gain ascendancy, then that too would have a profound effect. Not just on the direction of the religion, but on careers and which projects would be funded.

The council, seven members in all, were seated in a semicircle on a platform at the front of the room. There was a prayer, followed by a description of the selection process and a request for both candidates to stand.

The first monk, an individual named Brother Caspas, had a broad forehead, sunken cheeks, and a wispy white beard. His red robe appeared to be at least three sizes too large for him and puddled around the cushion he sat on. Slightly rheumy eyes sought Yanak and held him. "As our Inwa you will have tremendous power—how will your decisions be made?"

It was a question that Yanak was not only prepared to answer but had hoped for. Norr noticed that his words had a singsong quality, as if they had been written for the adolescent and rehearsed many times. "I will seek to govern wisely, always considering that which will be best for the majority, before arriving at a final decision."

It was a good if not especially deep answer but one likely to satisfy most of those in attendance. The monk with the wispy beard inclined his head respectfully and directed his gaze to Lee. "And you? How would *your* decisions be made?"

Rebo noticed that Lee's eyes were focused on a point above the old man's head. His voice was calm. "I will drop a stone into a pond, observe how the ripples expand, and note the way they touch the opposite shore. Then, mindful of stone, water, and shore, I will decide."

Outside of the fact that it was cast in more mystical terms—Lee's answer wasn't that much different from the one that Yanak had given. Subtleties such as that were important, however, especially in light of the fact that some felt the black hats had strayed from Teon's path and had a dangerous tendency to emphasize mind over spirit. So, while interesting, neither answer was clearly superior to the other.

The second monk had a round face, slanted eyes, and ears so prominent that some of his peers referred to him as "Brother Jug" behind his back. He wore a black hat, an immaculate robe, and a gold ring on his right pinkie finger. Never one to squander words, or any other form of energy for that matter, his question was limited to three parsimonious words. "What is money?"

Yanak responded with confidence. "Money is a medium of exchange—or a measure of value." The teenager was aware of the fact that his responses were being evaluated on brevity, clarity, and content. Yanak was confident that his reply met or exceeded all three criteria and allowed himself a momentary smirk.

Lee waited for some sort of prompt, and when none was forthcoming, gave his answer. It was inspired by memories of Omar, the way the back of his wagon smelled, and the loaves of bread kept there. "Money symbolizes the energy required to harvest grain, process it, and turn it into bread. It is therefore spiritual rather than material in nature and should be used accordingly."

It was clearly a much deeper and more thoughtful response than the one that Yanak had put forward, and even the black hats recognized it. Hoggles heard the murmurs and smiled.

The third council member was a nun. She wore a blue robe to symbolize the fact that, while loyal to Nom Maa, her order had thus far refused to align itself with either of the major sects. She was beautiful, so much so that many of her male peers had spent hundreds of hours trying to cleanse themselves of the fantasies she unknowingly stimulated, many without success. Her voice was like music, and the words seemed to float through the air. "Teon said that attachment equals suffering. What did he mean?"

Yanak was well aware of the fact that Lee's last answer had been superior to his and had no intention of letting that happen again. His brows came together and formed a single line. "In order to achieve true enlightenment, and therefore happiness, we must let go of our attachments to ideas, things, and people."

It was almost an exact quote from the *Path,* and for those who were content to simply to follow Teon's recipe for enlightenment, completely satisfactory. But, while no expert at such things, Rebo couldn't help but notice that Yanak's answer didn't really address the question. The nun tried again. "Lee? Teon said that attachment equals suffering. What did he mean?"

Lee remembered Abbot Marth and the black hat temple

in the city of Zand. "Everything will eventually pass away, so to the extent that we remain attached to it, we must eventually suffer. For some, even Teon's teachings can become an attachment that clouds their minds and bars the path to enlightenment."

There was a sudden buzz of excited conversation as monks of all persuasions turned to each other in amazement and consternation. Some found the suggestion that the religion itself could constitute an attachment to be a true revelation, a thesis that would generate discussion for years to come, while others saw it as inherently threatening. They were the more vocal of the two groups and didn't hesitate to make themselves heard. "That's absurd!" "It's red hat nonsense!" "Who taught the boy?"

The fourth council member wore no hat on his clean shaven skull but was swathed in red. If he had eyebrows, they were so minimal as to be invisible from a distance, and his nose was both broad and flat. Though not the question that he had originally planned to ask—the one he gave voice to was appropriate to the moment. "All of us experience emotions . . . One of the most dangerous is anger. How should we deal with it?"

Confident that Lee's most recent reply had been met with general disapproval and that he knew the answer to the current question, Yanak produced a serene smile. "Anger constitutes a loss of control. Through skillful thinking, and relentless self-discipline, anger can be suppressed."

In spite of his allegiance to the red sect, the questioner happened to agree, and nodded in acknowledgment. "Thank you. Master Lee? What is your view?"

Lee remembered the village of Urunu, the terraced gardens that cascaded down its rocky slopes, and the carefully maintained aqueducts that served them. "It's my opinion that any effort to suppress anger via an act of will is doomed to failure. However, just as the force of a raging river can be diverted into an irrigation system, an act of skillful understanding can transmute anger into positive energy." The council remained impassive, but the audience was less so. Some heads nodded as others rotated from side to side.

The fifth member of the council had a long, thin face, narrow shoulders, and the manner of a schoolmaster. He wore a black skullcap, a matching top, and baggy trousers. His feet were bare and so callused from walking country roads that they looked like tree roots. His voice had a deep resonant quality. "Everyone seeks happiness . . . What is it?"

Yanak frowned. His opponent had demonstrated an uncanny knack for coming up with answers that while a little off center seemed to be well received by at least some of the council. He chose his words with care. "Happiness is freedom from want, which is to say attachment, and consists of a state of enlightenment."

It was a good answer, an excellent answer, and Yanak's mentors exchanged congratulatory looks. Rebo, who was curious as to how Lee would respond, watched with interest as the fifth monk gestured toward his charge. "Tell us, son, what is happiness?"

Lee considered all that he and his companions had been through since his departure from Anafa. The answer seemed obvious. "Happiness consists of resistance, because only through encountering resistance can we learn, and thereby attain enlightenment."

Someone applauded, was ordered to stop, and sat shamefaced as the next council member prepared to take his turn. Though not a monk, he was a highly respected layperson, and one of the individuals who was expected to vote independently. He was a farmer by trade and looked the part. "As the Inwa what will your greatest challenge be?"

To purge the hierarchy of red hats, Yanak thought to himself, but knew better than to say that out loud. His voice was grave. "There are many who don't understand the way, or feel threatened by it, and seek to control or destroy it. The greatest challenge will be to counter their efforts without violating the precepts by which we live."

Heads nodded, many of those present smiled, and the farmer bowed from the waist. "Thank you . . . Master Lee?"

Lee looked up from the tiled floor. "The greatest challenge lies within . . . For that is where the monster called ego stares into its mirror, listens for the sound of its name, and mouths the words that will serve it."

The seventh, and last council member, was a black hat abbot. And, because that meant that Yanak automatically had three votes, the audience was well aware of the fact the decision would fall to the two independents. And the abbot, who was cognizant of that as well, had every intention of trying to sway both the nun and the farmer. He stared over his glasses, which were perched on the very end of a long, thin nose. And, rather than address himself to Yanak as the others had, the abbot fastened Lee with a clearly hostile look. "Needless to say the Inwa must live his life in a manner that is above reproach. However, according to information provided to me by Brother Lar Thota on Pooz, there is considerable evidence to suggest that you murdered a black hat monk during the voyage from Anafa. Do you deny the charge?"

There was a sudden commotion as the audience erupted into conversation, and the burly master-at-arms rapped his staff on the floor to silence them. Yanak shook his head, as if disappointed to hear such a serious charge levied against his peer, and smiled sadly. Norr, who was determined to object, started to rise. Lee gestured for the sensitive to remain where she was. He looked the abbot in the eye. "No, I do not deny the charge. A black hat monk was sent against me, and I killed him in an act of self-defense. Nor is that all . . . During the journey to Thara there were times when I surrendered to fear, hatred, and vanity."

A sigh ran through the crowd, Yanak tried to conceal a smirk, and the abbot nodded gravely. "Though your spirit is flawed, I admire your honesty, and hope that others learn from your example."

Having heard from both candidates, the council retired to another room, and the waiting began. Everyone knew that such deliberations could last for quite a while. In fact there had been cases when it had taken days or even weeks for a final decision to be rendered, which was why most of the attendees had come prepared for a long stay and had already started to set up what amounted to small camps throughout the great hall.

The candidates were besieged by both admirers and detractors, all of whom wanted to set each other right and were eager for verbal combat. But as the hours rolled by, the discussions began to cool, and a meal was served. Then, once stomachs were full, many of the participants opted for naps. And that's where most of them were, asleep on the floor, when the council reemerged. There was a mad scramble as everyone sought to reoccupy their seats, and the inevitable face reading began. "Uh-oh," Norr heard one red hat say, "it looks like the blacks have it."

"No, look at Caspas," another replied. "He's smiling!"

"That's no smile," a third interjected. "It's a grimace. He has gout, you know."

And so it went as the members of the audience continued to speculate on which boy would ascend the throne. Finally, after weeks of inner turmoil, Lee was pleased to discover that he no longer cared. If it was he who had been chosen, then he would do his best, and if Yanak had been chosen, he would still do his best.

For his part Yanak was not so philosophical and with good reason. *His* fate, should the other youth win, would be ignominious at best. His heart beat like a silversmith's hammer and his forehead was shiny with perspiration by the time the master-at-arms thumped the floor with his intricately carved staff. "Silence! There will be order! Brother Caspas?"

It took a moment for the old man to rise, but when a younger monk moved as if to offer assistance, Caspas waved him off. Then, having gained his feet, his rheumy eyes surveyed the room. "Our deliberations are complete," the red hat said definitively. "Nom Maa has returned and sits before us!"

The entire audience held its collective breath as the old man shuffled forward and paused halfway between the boys. Then, after what seemed like an eternity, the elderly monk turned his back on Yanak and bowed to Lee. "Welcome, oh great one. The throne is yours."

Lee bowed in return, and Rebo frowned. "What throne?" he whispered. "Where is it?"

Norr smiled. "Lee told me that the throne is spiritual rather than physical. That means that it can be everywhere and nowhere, both at the same time."

Hoggles shook his head bemusedly as the acceptance chant began. "You walked right into that one."

"Yeah," Rebo reflected, "I guess I did."

SIXTEEN

The Planet Thara

Runners have no homes other than the pillows beneath their heads, the closest saloon, and whatever world they happen to be on when the last starship dies.

—Thomas Crowley, Runner

Thanks to its location on the coast, most of those who chose to visit the village of Lorval came and went by boat. Because of that, as well as the fact that there was very little reason for outsiders to go there, the lightly rutted road was only one cart wide. Rebo, who was seated next to the driver, was forced to hold on tight as the heavily laden four-wheeled coach followed a pair of sturdy angens up a steep incline. Then, as the conveyance rattled over the top of the rise, a panoramic view was revealed, and the runner ordered the driver to stop.

Once Rebo had jumped down to the ground, he found himself standing at what had once been the southernmost border of his boyhood universe, the point beyond which he and his brothers weren't to go without permission from their parents. From there the road went steeply down past the ancient boatyard, the drying sheds, and into Lorval itself. Rocky hillsides left very little space on which to build, which meant that the houses stood shoulder to shoulder across the street from weathered docks and sheds that were partly supported by tar-coated wooden piles, huge timbers that could withstand the winter storms that rolled in from the east. But there was no sign of that now, as seabirds circled an incoming fishing boat, and sunlight glittered on the surface of the bay.

Farther on, past the hotel where Rebo's mother had been employed, a terraced graveyard could be seen. It contained twice the number of markers as actual graves. That was because the sea rarely surrendered the bodies of those it had claimed, leaving their families to grieve over tiny symbolic caskets.

And there, perched high on the promontory to the north, was the Halgo mansion. The very people to whom Crowley had delivered a letter those many years before, and by doing so forever changed a little boy's life.

Now, having spent so much time with Lee, the runner was struck by the fact that the village lacked any sort of temple or other religious structure. Because it was so remote? Or because the flinty fisherfolk who lived there had a tendency to view the sea as their supreme being? It hardly mattered.

Norr had a way of not only appearing at his side—but knowing what to say when she did. "It's beautiful."

Rebo slipped an arm around her waist. During the weeks spent resting in CaCanth, Lysander had made himself known yet again and offered to hire the runner. The task was to deliver both the sensitive and Logos to a place called Socket. Wherever that might be. An arrangement that allowed the two of them to stay together without peering too far into the future. "Thank you," Rebo replied. "But it isn't as beautiful as you are."

Norr smiled knowingly. "You say the sweetest things when you want to sleep with me."

The runner raised his eyebrows. "So, you *can* read minds."

"Men *have* minds but tend to think with something else," the sensitive observed tartly. "Still, you might get lucky."

Rebo laughed as a deep resonant voice was heard from within the coach, where Hoggles sat with one leg propped up on pillows. "Hey! Why did we stop? It's time for lunch."

"Sorry, master," the runner replied, as he helped Norr back inside. "We will get under way immediately."

"See that you do," the variant responded airily. "This is most inconvenient."

Rebo offered the heavy what he thought was an appropriate gesture, returned to the front of the carriage, and climbed up next to driver. Hooves clattered on loose shale as the carriage jerked into motion, and the last mile of the journey began. Deep down, and without having consulted Norr, Rebo knew that his mother was dead. But her essence was there in the breeze that swept in off the bay, the sharp tang of the sea, and the warmth that caressed his face. A boy had left—and a man had returned.

AUTHOR'S NOTE

The book Runner *was inspired by a* Time *magazine article* that appeared in the May 2, 1994, issue. The piece, under David Van Biema's byline, but with additional reporting by Patrick E. Cole in Los Angles and Jefferson Pemberthy in New Delhi, ran under a subhead that read, "Two different boys claim to be the reincarnated master of a popular school of Buddhism."

That alone was sufficient to capture my attention, but the body of the article, which went on to detail the ongoing battles between two different factions of the Black Hat sect to control "assets worth $1.2 billion, and the reverence of up to a million followers," got me to thinking about the possibility of a novel.

But ten years were to pass between the moment of initial

inspiration and the actual writing of the book. Part of that was due to the fact that I had other projects to pursue—but part of the delay stemmed from the fact that I wasn't sure how to handle the concept. Finally, having married the intergalactic courier outline that I had developed years earlier to the Buddhist story, I came up with a science fiction novel that honors fantasy and reacts to religion.

I feel it's important to note that while the story was inspired by one aspect of Buddhism, and those familiar with the religion may see numerous similarities between "The Way" and Buddhism, it was not my intent to replicate the Eightfold path or any other religious tradition. In fact the religion laid out in the book includes concepts borrowed from many faiths, all of which have value, and my respect.

For more information about author William C. Dietz and his upcoming novels, visit his website at www.williamcdietz.com.